The Hastur Cycle

Chaosium fiction

KING OF SARTAR
CASTLE OF EYES
THE HASTUR CYCLE
ROBERT BLOCH'S MYSTERIES OF THE WORM

in preparation

CTHULHU'S HEIRS
THE SHUB-NIGGURATH CYCLE

CALL OF CTHULHU ® BOOKS

The Hastur Cycle

13 Tales That Created and Define Dread Hastur,
the King in Yellow, Nighted Yuggoth, and Dire Carcosa

Ambrose Bierce

Robert W. Chambers

Karl Edward Wagner

James Blish

Arthur Machen

H.P. Lovecraft

Richard A. Lupoff

Ramsey Campbell

James Wade

August Derleth

Lin Carter

Selected and Introduced by

Robert M. Price

Chapter Decorations by Dreyfus

A Chaosium Book

1993

Contents

The Mythology of Hastur

CARCOSA

I sense, on crystal winter evenings
When constellations gleam through black-branched trees,
A night-dark star no earthly gazer sees
To which some dread malevolently clings.
No star-chart shows it—no—yet slumber brings
Its vision from the clustered Hyades—
Black waters over which a leaden breeze
Wafts the sad song that dead Cassilda sings.

No darker vision greets the sleeper than
That lake, from which the coiling cloud-waves pour
To break upon the long basaltic shore
Beneath the rays of red Aldebaran—
The lake whence dreamers flee in nameless dread
As Hastur rises from his slimy bed.

— RICHARD L. TIERNEY

Had August W. Derleth, coiner of the famous term, "the Cthulhu Mythos," followed his first inspiration, we might be speaking today of "the Mythology of Hastur." This bit of nomenclature young Augie suggested to H.P. Lovecraft whose bemused response (Hastur hardly figured in any of the stories!) punctured the disciple's balloon. Derleth was at work on one of his earliest Lovecraftian pastiches, "The Return of Hastur," and we may suspect, having elevated Hastur to the status of a major player in the pantheon of the Old Ones, Derleth was trying to secure the centrality of his new favorite by naming the whole game after him.

Petty and self-serving and inappropriate it might thus seem to us, but in what follows I want to suggest that Derleth, as he often did, had glimpsed an insight into Lovecraft's work and its sources that later critics would take generations to see for themselves. Indeed it is not clear that Derleth himself saw the implications of his own momentary insight.

Derleth once remarked that Robert W. Chambers' *The King in Yellow*, "with the work of Poe and Bierce, shares the distinction of having contributed to the famed Cthulhu mythos of H.P. Lovecraft." Note Derleth's implicit assumptions. For him Lovecraft and his Mythos are central. Chambers, Poe, and Bierce are lucky to be able to take the modest roles of precursors, way-pavers, John the Baptists to the Mythos Messiah, Lovecraft. This, it seems safe to say, would have been no less true had Derleth persisted in calling the whole myth system the Mythology of Hastur.

But the discarded term "Mythology of Hastur" points with an implicit logic in another direction altogether. Lovecraft shot it down because Hastur had so little to do with the myth-pattern as it was developing in his own stories and those of Clark Ashton Smith, Robert E. Howard, Robert Bloch and others. Yet this is precisely the merit of the term. For I will contend, as Derleth seemed to see for one fading moment, that Lovecraft's stories make more sense, not as seen in the context of his own evolving Mythos, but as links in a larger chain forged by other writers, pre- and post-Lovecraftian.

The issue here is whether we make Lovecraft and his Mythos central or whether we place HPL in orbit about some other central sun. The present collection is an experiment which takes the later option as its working hypothesis. We are seeing Lovecraft's "The Whisperer in Darkness" as one link in a chain beginning with Bierce and Arthur Machen and continuing on through Derleth, James Blish, Lin Carter, Karl Edward Wagner, and other contemporary writers.

Let me put it this way. We have learned from Lovecraft and Derleth to view the tales of Cthulhu and Yog-Sothoth as parts of a cycle of myth. Lovecraft always explained to correspondents that he did not achieve perfect consistency in his various stories, say, in what each said about Cthulhu or the *Necronomicon*, for the very good reason that he wanted his shuddery allusions to these eldritch items to reflect the inconsistencies, duplications, and redundancies of actual ancient myth cycles, where, *e.g.*, we find two or three origin tales for the same goddess or shrine.

Another implication of the mythic character of the Mythos made clear by the recent studies of A. Lord and others is that it is meaningless to speak of an "original" of a given tale or myth or epic. When we find variant versions, abridged or composite epics, or whatever, there is no way to choose one and declare it the "true" original, the definitive version. Each tale is a link in a chain, part of an evolving cycle. Each performance of the myth is a new "original," so to speak.

In the same way, it seems to me highly misleading to take Lovecraft's stories and myth-concepts as the definitive version and to view Chambers and the others as leading up to it, Derleth and the others as representing a declension from it. Each has its own integrity, its own priority. Lovecraft has his moment upon the stage, but then he is replaced by a new teller of a new version.

The upshot of this way of looking at things is that we will most profitably judge Lovecraft's achievement, as well as understand him in new ways, if we will understand his text as a retelling of older literary myths, and if we will see the later tales of others as new originals with a genetic relation to HPL's: dependent, yes, but not necessarily derivative. Surely Lovecraft would not have ascribed to his own work the same centrality we have lent it.

The Hastur Cycle (like others in the new series of Chaosium anthologies which it inaugurates) may be seen as a literary genealogy, a family tree in which Lovecraft's "The Whisperer in Darkness" is a single branch, with other branches stemming from it and going in their own directions. The family tree begins with Ambrose Bierce, who is represented by two brief tales, "Haïta the Shepherd" and "An Inhabitant of Carcosa." Robert W. Chambers culled certain evocative names from these two stories and used them yet more effectively in his own tales in the collection *The King in Yellow.*

As Lovecraft put it in a letter to Clark Ashton Smith (June 24, 1927), "Chambers must have been impressed with *An Inhabitant of Carcosa & Haïta the Shepherd,* which were first published during his youth. But he even improves on Bierce in creating a shuddering background of horror—a vague, disquieting memory which makes one reluctant to use the faculty of recollection too vigorously." Two tales from that volume are included here, those which provide the most evocative glimpses of the Carcosa Mythos, if you will, the poisonous plant Chambers cultivated from the few seeds planted by Bierce.

That plant was not left to die when Chambers passed from the scene. We will see in a moment that Lovecraft plucked a blossom or two from it himself, but there were others eager to tend the plant. James Blish, in his fascinating "More Light," actually ventures to show us what all the fuss was about. He dares to supply the text of "The King in Yellow," that is, the play to which Chambers' characters often allude, but of which Chambers provided no more than occasional snippets. Granted, it is a challenge no one can meet to create a text like the *Necronomicon* or "The King in Yellow"—it cannot possibly survive the unveiling. Standing as a naked text before our scrutiny, it cannot be half so frightening as our fears of it were.

Blish apologizes for this sad fact in the story itself. And yet I find Blish's reconstruction of the play from the mixed hints of Chambers to be so effective, so compelling, so perfectly natural, that as I reread Chambers, I find myself again and again deceived into placing Chamber's allusions and quotations into the context Blish has provided for them. As far as I am concerned, Blish has given us the real thing. He is one of the few who could have.

Chambers tells us that the publication of the play was greeted by universal denunciation from both pulpit and press. Why? Did it supply incantations to call up Satan? Hardly; it did not need to stretch so far to find poison to destroy the souls of its readers. The play set forth the nullity of all human hopes, exposed much-vaunted Truth as a mere phantom, and revealed the Nihil so no one could anymore deny it. Except those who dared not read the play, secretly fearing its truth.

As the sophisticates and avante-garde read the book, they became infected with its jaded nihilism. It spread like a plague, Chambers tells us, among the intelligentsia. That contagion reached as far as Blish and did not stop there. Later, Karl Edward Wagner, master of horror and sword-&-sorcery fiction, succumbed to the miasmal spell of the wicked book. His story, "The River of Night's Dreaming," shows that.

It is really remarkable that both Blish and Wagner have (unlike some others) picked up the late nineteenth-century flavor of "The King in Yellow" as Chambers must have imagined it. The King is swathed in yellow for the same reason Oscar Wilde wrote for *The Yellow Book.* It was the banner of Decadence in the Yellow Nineties. Blish thus depicts the royalty of Hastur as sunk deep in jaded ennui, while Wagner uncovers the night side of

Victorian sexuality, what happened when the twin suns set, the sort of thing we read of in Steven Marcus's excellent study *The Other Victorians*.

Thus far I have traced the Bierce-Chambers trajectory along a fairly strait line. Another tale that must be mentioned at this point, though it is not included here, is Raymond Chandler's detective story "The King in Yellow." The hero, something of an early precursor of Chandler's famous Philip Marlowe, is a house dick attached to a fancy hotel. He has the misfortune to find murdered in his rented bed a famous jazz trumpeter, King Leopardi. This "king" is deposited inelegantly on his bed wearing his trademark yellow silk pajamas. The detective takes one look at him and mutters, "The king in yellow," noting that it reminded him of a book he once read. Which book do you suppose that was?

Of course Chandler may simply have meant that the hero had once read Chambers. But I wonder, on second thought, if this hardboiled detective story is meant to be set in the fictive universe in which "The King in Yellow" was a notorious play of decadent tendencies. Had it blasted the once-idealistic naiveté of Chandler's typically hard-boiled protagonist? The raw-nerved realism of Chandler's detectives seems to me an authentic twentieth-century version of the illusionless clarity imparted by a reading of the infamous play.

And, whether we are thinking about the book Chambers did write or the play he did not write, the mention of *The King in Yellow* in Chandler's story functions exactly like the allusions to the play in Chambers's own tales. They punctuate by precedent. The action and the characters attain their authenticity by conforming to the dramaturgical prototypes of *The King in Yellow*.

This brings us to H.P. Lovecraft. His references to the Bierce-Chambers mythos occur most overtly in "The Whisperer in Darkness." Lovecraft's narrator, Albert Wilmarth, upon reading the disturbing epistles of Henry Akeley, bemoans that "I found myself faced by names and terms that I had heard elsewhere in the most hideous of connections ... Hastur, Yian, Leng, the Lake of Hali, Bethmoora, the Yellow Sign ... "

Leng, though apparently based on an old Tibetan place name (c.f. the Tibetan epic, *The Superhuman Life of Gesar of Ling*), is Lovecraft's own fictional creation. But it owes an obvious debt to Yian, a mysterious Oriental city in another work of Chambers's, *The Maker of Moons*. Expanding it to "Yian-Ho," Lovecraft would mention it again in other tales.

We hear later in the story of Hastur and the Yellow Sign when Akeley (or some entity impersonating him) tries to calm Wilmarth's suspicions about the evil intentions of the Outer Ones:

> There is a whole secret cult of evil men (a man of your mystical erudition will understand me when I link them with Hastur and the Yellow Sign) devoted to the purpose of tracking them down and injuring them on behalf of monstrous powers from other dimensions.

I am quite certain that the prototype of this cult (whether Lovecraft means us to understand that there is such a thing for the purposes of the story or not—it may be nothing but a smoke screen by the Outer Ones to mask their own intentions) is the sorcerous international brotherhood of the Kuen-Yuin from *The Maker of Moons*. You can see as well that Lovecraft appropriated their name to christen the subterranean dwelling place of the Old Ones in "The Mound": K'n-yan, also mentioned here in "The Whisperer in Darkness."

Indeed the influence of Chambers on Lovecraft has never been adequately gauged. Compare a passage from *The Maker of Moons* to one of the *Fungi from Yuggoth* sonnets.

> ... *When the light of my eyes has faded forever, then, even then I shall not forget the city of Yian. Why, it is my home,—mine! The river and the thousand bridges, the white peak beyond, the sweet-scented gardens, the lilies, the pleasant noise of the summer wind laden with bee music and the music of bells,—all these are mine.*

XVIII. THE GARDENS OF YIN

Beyond that Wall, whose ancient masonry
Reached almost to the sky in moss-thick towers,
There would be terraced gardens, rich with flowers,
And flutter of bird and butterfly and bee.
There would be walks, and bridges arching over
Warm lotus-pools reflecting temple eaves,
And cherry-trees with delicate boughs and leaves
Against a pink sky where herons hover.

All would be there, for had not old dreams flung
Open the gate to that stone-lanterned maze
Where drowsy streams spin out their winding ways,
Trailed by green vines from bending branches hung?
I hurried—but when the wall rose, grim and great,
I found there was no longer any gate.

The Gardens of Yin are plainly the Gardens of Yian.

Another *Fungi* sonnet speaks of "The Thing" which "wears a silken mask / Of yellow, whose queer folds appear to hide / A face not of this earth, though none dares ask / Just what those features are, which bulge inside." This being, which Lovecraft elsewhere calls "the Tcho-Tcho Lama of Leng," appears also in *The Dream-Quest of Unknown Kadath*, where he is called "the Veiled King" and sits upon a throne. I believe this Dalai Lama of the Elder Ones is supposed to be the King in Yellow himself, adopted into the Lovecraftian pantheon just as surely as was Clark Ashton Smith's Tsathoggua. Unlike Blish, as you will see, Lovecraft simply took the Pallid Mask to be the adornment of the King himself. Pale yellow? Why not?

The Pallid Mask may also be that mask donned by Nyarlathotep in "The Whisperer in Darkness." In the litany of the crustaceans recorded by Akeley on his Edison cylinder we hear of the Mighty Messenger that "He shall put on the semblance of men, the waxen mask and the robe that hides, and come down from the world of the Seven Suns to mock." Is it he who sits opposite Wilmarth in the guise of Akeley and whispers? That is the conjecture of William Fulwiler, and I accept it. "He had on a loose dressing-gown and was swathed around the head and high around the neck with a vivid yellow scarf or hood." Here Nyarlathotep has become the King in Yellow.

And what of Yuggoth on the rim? "There are mighty cities on Yuggoth — great tiers of terraced towers built of black stone ... The sun shines there no brighter than a star ... The black rivers of pitch ... flow under those mysterious cyclopean bridges ... " Is not this Lovecraft's version of fabled Carcosa, the city that seems not to be part of this world, whose towers rise behind the moon—because the city itself lies beyond the moon?

So the Bierce-Chambers stream empties into the Miskatonic. But it is not the only source of "The Whisperer in Darkness." Even more important to this Lovecraftian tale is Arthur Machen's "The Novel of the Black Seal." That Lovecraft's tale owes some debt of inspiation is is plain from the overt acknowledge ment in the story itself: "Most of my foes...were merely romanticists who insisted ofn trying to transfer to real life the fantastic lore of lurking :Little People" made popular by the magnificent horrer-fiction of Arthur Machen." But there is more involved than this passage might suggest. In fact I would go so far as to make Lovecraft's tale essentially a rewriting, a new version of Machen's. Consider the parallels:

In both cases we have a professor, an antiquarian, following his avocational interests in what most would dismiss as superstition on a dangerous expedition into a strange region of ominous domed hills. He is lured by a curiously engraved black stone which seems a survival from an elder prehuman race now hidden in those mysterious hills. Here Lovecraft splits the role of Machen's Professor Gregg between Professor Wilmarth and the scholarly recluse Akeley. And it is Akeley, not the Professor, who eventually disappears into the clutches of the elder race. Wilmarth remains behind to tell the tale, like Machen's Miss Lally.

I think we can identify specific sentences in Machen and their descendants in Lovecraft. "I conjured images of strange shapes gathering fast amidst the reeds, beside the wash in the river" (Machen). "Shortly after the flood . . . there appeared certain odd stories of things found floating in some of the swollen rivers" (Lovecraft). "What if the obscure and horrible race of the hills still survived, still remained haunting wild places and barren hills...?" (Machen). "Briefly summarized, it hinted at a hidden race of monstrous beings which lurked somewhere among the remoter hills—in the deep woods of the highest peaks, and the dark valleys where streams trickle from unknown sources" (Lovecraft).

Machen mentions "certain histories of children, and of men and women who vanished strangely from the earth." Was this the inspiration for Lovecraft having Akeley and previous interlopers literally spirited (in their cannisters) off the face of the earth?

Why does Akeley have a bust of Milton in his study? Because Professor Gregg had one of Pitt in his. In Machen's tale, the mysterious moving of the bust from high atop a cabinet served as an ominous clue of the entry of a nonhuman presence. In Lovecraft's tale the bust is a similar signal, but only indirectly, in that it means to remind you of the bust of Pitt and what it signaled.

A glance at "The Dunwich Horror" will show that Lovecraft had Machen on his mind as he wrote, as he mentions "The Great God Pan" by name twice. But I think it scarcely less obvious that the central character of Wilbur Whateley was inspired by the poor cretin Jervase Craddock in "The Novel of the Black Seal" (and remember "Jervas Dudley" in "The Tomb"). Jervase is a pathetic hybrid tainted by inheritance of the bloodline of the hidden Little People of the hills. Like his twin Wilbur Whateley, he is the spawn of earthlings and Old Ones together, and he still speaks the tongue of the Elder Race. And finally he stands (or lies) revealed as being teratologically fabulous, tentacles adorning a vaguely human frame.

If we have traced the pervasive influence of Machen's tale on Lovecraft this far, let us not shrink back now. I believe that the intertextuality between "The Whisperer in Darkness" and "The Novel of the Black Seal" gives us a crucial clue to understanding the latter as well as the former. We are told that the only trace of the ill-fated Professor Gregg was a crude parchment bag, tied with gut, containing the man's personal effects. The parchment itself was imprinted with the mysterious characters of the Black Seal stone itself. The sight of this signals the narrator as to the awful fate of her late employer.

What happened to him? At the close of "The Whisperer in Darkness" we are told that the fleeing Wilmarth lingered long enough to behold the peeled face and severed hands of Henry Akeley resting in his chair. Lovecraft must have interpreted the parchment sack as the tanned hide of Professor Gregg himself, stamped with the very stone seal that led him to his doom. So he had pretty much the same thing happen to hapless Akeley. I believe he is right, and it is easier to understand Machen in light of Lovecraft's interpretation of him.

Just as two major streams flow into Lovecraft's tale, so do two flow out of it. On the one hand, some subsequent writers found most fascinating the concept of the Living Fungi from Yuggoth, the Outer Ones themselves. Lovecraft himself would bring them back on stage in *At the Mountains of Madness* as enemies of the Star-Headed Old Ones. The young Ramsey Campbell featured the beings (though he transformed them into "lizard crustaceans") in "The Mine on Yuggoth." Another member of what Lin Carter dubbed The New Lovecraft Circle, James Wade, contributed a short tale to the Yuggoth sub-mythos, "Planetfall on Yuggoth." Neither story has been widely seen for too long.

Wade's theme of space explorers making an ill-advised "close encounter" with the beings of Yuggoth was also the theme, independently, of Richard Lupoff's better known "The Discovery of the Ghooric Zone, 2037" which appears in the second edition of the Arkham House anthology *Tales of the Cthulhu Mythos*. But Lupoff's "Documents in the Case of Elizabeth Akeley" is no less important. It forms a direct sequel to "The Whisperer in Darkness."

The other stream flowing from Lovecraft's tale of Plutonians in the Vermont woods is the Hastur trajectory. Here August Derleth demonstrated to just what extent he saw Bierce and Chambers having "contributed to the Cthulhu Mythos of Lovecraft." In a passage already quoted, Lovecraft has Wilmarth string out a long list of eerie names. In this list "Hastur" appears sandwiched between Nyarlathotep and Azathoth on one side and Yian, Leng, the Lake of Hali, and Bethmoora on the other. The first two are personal names, the last several being place names. To which category does Hastur belong? Seeing that in Chambers Hastur is a city, the city of Cassilda and the rest, we might assume Lovecraft intended Hastur to be a place as well.

But, as I have more than once argued elsewhere, Derleth had a skill for what Harold Bloom calls "misprision," or creative misreading of Lovecraft's texts, finding graft points in the ambiguities of Lovecraft's tales where he might allow new interpretations to flourish. Here he has chosen to place the name Hastur with the first half of the list, making him a fellow of Azathoth and Nyarlathotep.

It seems that Derleth retreated back beyond Chambers to his source, Bierce's "Haïta the Shepherd," where Hastur is a deity, albeit a benign one. Derleth's own version of Hastur may seem a far cry equally from Chambers, Lovecraft, and Bierce, since Derleth makes Hastur one of the Great Old Ones (an aquatic monster in "The Gable Window," a winged harpy in most of the rest of his tales), half-brother to Great Cthulhu. Yet as we see in "The Return of Hastur" and most of the stories constituting Derleth's *The Trail of Cthulhu*, Derleth pictures Hastur as a deity leagued with the human race against the devilish minions of Cthulhu.

Oh, to be sure, Derleth was interested in those crustaceans from far Yuggoth, but he subordinated them to the regnant notion of Hastur as a god, derived from Bierce. He made the Yuggoth Mi-Go into a race of servitors to Hastur, no longer primarily an alien race of extraterrestrials fearsome in their own right. More like angels to a god.

Derleth may have gone back to the source, Bierce, but he was far from wanting to leave behind the evocative mythology of Chambers. In "The Return of Hastur," we read a catalogue of names reminiscent, by no coincidence, of those in "The Whisperer in Darkness":

> *Among my Uncle Amos's papers there are many fearsome names written in his crabbed script:* Great Cthulhu, the Lake of Hali, Tsathoggua, Yog-Sothoth, Nyarlathotep, Azathoth, Hastur the Unspeakable, Yuggoth, Aldones, Thale, Aldebaran, the Hyades, Carcosa, *and others ... Hastur was hurled into outer space, into that place where the black stars hang, which is indicated as Aldebaran of the Hyades, which is the place mentioned by Chambers, even as he repeats the Carcosa of Bierce.*

This passage, displaying Derleth's characteristic flaw of cramming too much mythos data into a story, making it substitute for action and atmosphere, becomes an allegory of reading for his own text: Paul Tuttle says he is quoting Amos Tuttle's notes, but in reality it is Derleth himself whose story notes have invaded his text, when they should have remained unobtrusively in the background.

Derleth simply added his version of the Lovecraft Mythos onto Bierce and Chambers, forcing them where they did not naturally fit. It was left for the ingenious Lin Carter to iron it all out, he who delighted in systematizing and harmonizing the discordant data of the Mythos into a coherent, if hardly seamless, fabric. I have included, under the title "Tatters of the King," a set of three brief fragments which treat of the Hastur Cycle in different ways, two of them attempting to synthesize Derleth with Bierce and with Chambers. It is fair to say Lin gave it a bit more attention that Derleth bothered to do. How successful his efforts were, you may be the judge. He had a difficult challenge to meet.

It is fitting to invoke the shade of Lin Carter in closing, because the conception of the present Chaosium series was in large measure inspired by Lin's Ballantine Adult Fantasy volume *The Spawn of Cthulhu*, which even contained many of the same stories which appear between these covers. It was Lin's idea to take each major Lovecraft story and reprint it along with all the major stories to which HPL had made allusions, as well as some inspired by it.

I have departed from Lin's central focus on Lovecraft, as well as the agenda of simply providing elucidation of otherwise cryptic references. I prefer the approach I have outlined: tracing out the whole trajectory in which Lovecraft's story forms merely an important moment. Admittedly, the difference is a subtle one, and the results overlap. And Lin deserves some credit for what some might even view as a second, revised edition of his *The Spawn of Cthulhu*.

— Robert M. Price

A mbrose Bierce (1842-1914?) vanished from human ken while away in Mexico covering the adventures of Pancho Villa. Perhaps he died, as he said he hoped he might, before a firing squad.

His work is unsurpassed both in its bitterness and in its humor. His cynicism is manifest in his famous Devil's Dictionary. The present tale is surprising in the gentleness of its disillusionment. It appears here because it is certainly the origin of the "Hastur" that would become so important to Robert W. Chambers and August Derleth.

The name "Hastur" is, as Marion Zimmer Bradley notes ("... And Strange Sounding Names," in L. Sprague de Camp and George H. Scithers (eds.), The Conan Swordbook {Baltimore: Mirage Press, 1969}), probably derived from the name of the Spanish province Asturias. We may speculate that Bierce chose it for his shepherds' deity because it recalls the word "pasture." Chambers would take it and made it the name of the city of Cassilda and Camilla, but he retained Hastur as a personal name, that of a provincial groundskeeper in his story "The Demoiselle d' Ys."

Haïta The Shepherd

by AMBROSE BIERCE

In the heart of Haïta the illusions of youth had not been supplanted by those of age and experience. His thoughts were pure and pleasant, for his life was simple and his soul devoid of ambition. He rose with the sun and went forth to pray at the shrine of Hastur, the god of shepherds, who heard and was pleased. After performance of this pious rite Haïta unbarred the gate of the fold and with a cheerful mind drove his flock afield, eating his morning meal of curds and oat cake as he went, occasionally pausing to add a few berries, cold with dew, or to drink of the waters that came away from the hills to join the stream in the middle of the valley and be borne along with it, he knew not whither.

During the long summer day, as his sheep cropped the good grass which the gods had made to grow for them, or lay with their forelegs doubled under their breasts and chewed the cud, Haïta, reclining in the shadow of a tree, or sitting upon a rock, played so sweet music upon his reed pipe that sometimes from the corner of his eye he got accidental glimpses of the minor sylvan deities, leaning forward out of the copse to hear; but if he look at them directly they vanished. From this—for he must be thinking if he would not turn into one of his own sheep—he drew the solemn inference that happiness may come if not sought, but if looked for will never be seen; for next to the favor of Hastur, who never disclosed himself, Haïta most valued the friendly interest of his neighbors, the shy immortals of the wood and stream. At nightfall he drove his flock back to the fold, saw that the gate was secure, and retired to his cave for refreshment and for dreams.

So passed his life, one day like another, save when the storms uttered the wrath of an offended god. Then Haïta cowered in his cave, his face hidden in his hands, and prayed that he alone might be punished for his sins and the world saved from destruction. Sometimes when there was a great rain, and the stream came out of its banks, compelling him to urge his terrified flock to the uplands, he interceded for the people in the cities which he had been told lay in the plain beyond the two blue hills forming the gateway of his valley.

"It is kind of thee, O Hastur," so he prayed, "to give me mountains so near my dwelling and my fold that I and my sheep can escape the angry torrents; but the rest of the world thou must thyself deliver in some way that I know not of, or I will no longer worship thee."

And Hastur, knowing that Haïta was a youth who kept his word, spared the cities and turned the waters into the sea.

So he had lived since he could remember. He could not rightly conceive any other mode of existence. The holy hermit who dwelt at the head of the valley, a full hour's journey away, from whom he had heard the tale of the great cities where dwelt people—poor souls!— who had no sheep, gave him no knowledge of that early time, when, so he reasoned, he must have been small and helpless like a lamb.

It was through thinking on these mysteries and marvels, and on that horrible change to silence and decay which he felt sure must sometime come to him, as he had seen it come to so many of his flock—as it came to all living things except the birds—that Haïta first became conscious how miserable and hopeless was his lot.

"It is necessary," he said, "that I know whence and how I came; for how can one perform his duties unless able to judge what they are by the way in which he was entrusted with them? And what contentment can I have when I know not how long it is going to last? Perhaps before another sun I may be changed, and then what will become of the sheep? What, indeed, will have become of me?"

Pondering these things Haïta became melancholy and morose. He no longer spoke cheerfully to his flock, nor ran with alacrity to the shrine of Hastur. In every breeze he heard whispers of malign deities whose existence he now first observed. Every cloud was a portent signifying disaster, and the darkness was full of terrors. His reed pipe when applied to his lips gave out no melody, but a dismal wail; the sylvan and riparian intelligences no longer thronged the thicketside to listen, but fled from the sound, as he knew by the stirred leaves and bent flowers. He relaxed his vigilance, and many of his sheep strayed away into the hills and were lost. Those that remained became lean and ill for lack of good pasturage, for he would seek it for them, but conducted them day after day to the same spot, through mere abstraction, while puzzling about life and death—of immortality he knew not.

One day while indulging in the gloomiest reflections he suddenly sprang from the rock upon which he sat, and with a determined gesture of the right hand exclaimed, "I will no longer be a suppliant for knowledge which the gods withhold. Let them look to it that they do me no wrong. I will do my duty as best I can and if I err upon their own heads be it!"

Suddenly, as he spoke, a great brightness fell about him, causing him to look upward, thinking the sun had burst through a rift in the clouds; but there were no clouds. No more than an arm's length away stood a beautiful maiden. So beautiful she was that the flowers about her feet folded their petals in despair and bent their heads in token of submission; so sweet her look that the hummingbirds thronged her eyes, thrusting their thirsty bills almost into them, and the wild bees were about her lips. And such was her brightness that the shadows of all objects lay divergent from her feet, turning as she moved.

Haïta was entranced. Rising, he knelt before her in adoration, and she laid her hand upon his head.

"Come," she said in a voice that had the music of all the bells of his flock, "come, thou art not to worship me, who am no goddess, but if thou art truthful and dutiful I will abide with thee."

Haïta seized her hand, and stammering his joy and gratitude arose, and hand in hand they stood and smiled into each other's eyes. He gazed on her with reverence and rapture. He said, "I pray thee, lovely maid, tell me thy name and whence and why thou comest."

At this she laid a warning finger on her lip and began to withdraw. Her beauty underwent a visible alteration that made him shudder, he knew not why, for still she was beautiful. The landscape was darkened by a giant shadow sweeping across the valley with the speed of a vulture. In the obscurity the maiden's figure grew dim and indistinct and her voice seemed to come from a distance, as she said, in a tone of sorrowful reproach, "Presumptuous and ungrateful youth! Must I then so soon leave thee? Would nothing do but thou must at once break the eternal compact?"

Inexpressibly grieved, Haïta fell upon his knees and implored her to remain—rose and sought her in the deepening darkness—ran in circles, calling to her aloud, but all in vain. She was no longer visible, but out of the gloom he heard her voice saying, "Nay, thou shalt not have me by seeking. Go to thy duty, faithless shepherd, or we shall never meet again."

Night had fallen; the wolves were howling in the hills and the terrified sheep crowding around Haïta's feet. In the demands of the hour he forgot his disappointment, drove his sheep to the fold, and repairing to the place of worship poured out his heart to Hastur for permitting him to save his flock, then retired to his cave and slept.

When Haïta awoke the sun was high and shone in at the cave, illuminating it with a great glory. And there, beside him, sat the maiden. She smiled upon him with a smile that seemed the visible music of his pipe of reeds. He dared not speak, fearing to offend her as before, for he knew not what he could venture to say.

"Because," she said, "thou didst thy duty by the flock, and didst not forget to thank Hastur for staying the wolves of the night, I am come to thee again. Wilt thou have me for a companion?"

"Who would not have thee forever?" replied Haïta. "Oh! never again leave me until—until I—change and become silent and motionless."

Haïta had no word for death.

"I wish, indeed," he continued, "that thou wert of my own sex, that we might wrestle and run races and so never tire of being together."

At these words the maiden arose and passed out of the cave, and Haïta, springing from his couch of fragrant boughs to overtake and detain her, observed to this astonishment that the rain was falling and the stream in the middle of the valley had come out of its banks. The sheep were bleating in terror, for the rising waters had invaded their fold. And there was danger for the unknown cities of the distant plain.

It was many days before Haïta saw the maiden again. One day he was returning from the head of the valley, where he had gone with ewe's milk and oat cake and berries for the holy hermit, who was too old and feeble to provide himself with food.

"Poor old man!" he said aloud, as he trudged along homeward. "I will return tomorrow and bear him on my back to my own dwelling, where I can care for him. Doubtless it is for this that Hastur has reared me all these many years, and gives me health and strength."

As he spoke, the maiden, clad in glittering garments, met him in the path with a smile that took away his breath.

"I am come again," she said, "to dwell with thee if thou wilt now have me, for none else will. Thou mayest have learned wisdom, and art willing to take me as I am, nor care to know."

Haïta threw himself at her feet. "Beautiful being," he cried, "if thou wilt but deign to accept all the devotion of my heart and soul—after Hastur be served—it is thine forever. But, alas! thou art capricious and wayward. Before tomorrow's sun I may lose thee again. Promise, I beseech thee, that however in my ignorance I may offend, thou wilt forgive and remain always with me."

Scarcely had he finished speaking when a troop of bears came out of the hills, racing toward him with crimson mouths and fiery eyes. The maiden again vanished, and he turned and fled for his life. Nor did he stop until he was in the cot of the holy hermit, whence he had set out.

Hastily barring the door against the bears he cast himself upon the ground and wept.

"My son," said the hermit from his couch of straw, freshly gathered that morning by Haïta's hands, "it is not like thee to weep for bears—tell me what sorrow hath befallen thee, that age may minister to the hurts of youth which such balms as it hath of its wisdom."

Haïta told him all: how thrice he had met the radiant maid, and thrice she had left him forlorn. He related minutely all that had passed between them, omitting no word of what had been said.

When he had ended, the holy hermit was a moment silent, then said, "My son, I have attended to thy story, and I know the maiden. I have myself seen her, as have many. Know, then, that her name, which she would not even permit thee to inquire, is Happiness. Thou saidst the truth to her, that she is capricious, for she imposeth conditions that man cannot fulfill, and delinquency is punished by desertion. She cometh only when unsought, and will not be questioned. One manifestation of curiosity, one sign of doubt, one expression of misgiving, and she is away! How long didst thou have her at any time before she fled?"

"Only a single instant," answered Haïta, blushing with shame at the confession. "Each time I drove away in one moment."

"Unfortunate youth!" said the holy hermit, "but for thine indiscretion thou mightst have had her for two."

This tale is an early example of the genre of ghost stories in which the narrator finally discovers that he is the ghost. Jack Sullivan invokes this story as a prime example of Bierce's theme of the dread of immortality. As Lovecraft would later put it, life is more hideous than death. Oblivion, the great Grail to be desired, is denied us.

Carcosa, the dead city in this brief tale (again according to Bradley) perhaps derives from the Spanish city Carcassone, familiar from Lord Dunsany, but quite real. Carscosa appears again in Robert W. Chambers's The King in Yellow, where it becomes a ghostly city already in its lifetime, sort of a New Jerusalem hung suspended forever between heaven and earth (or whatever planet it is that has two suns in its sky).

The name Hali, which Chambers appropriated for the Lake on the shores of which Cassilda's city of Hastur is built, was for Bierce the name of an ancient prophet whose sayings might be quoted on a wide range of antique and occult subjects. Another epigram from Hali heads up "The Death of Halpin Frayser." "Hali" seems to be an aspirated version of the name Ali, the nephew and adopted son of the Prophet Muhammad. He was the fourth Caliph of Islam and the fountainhead of the Shi'ite Imams. While not strictly speaking a prophet in his own right, Ali and his successors were considered inspired interpreters of the Koran. It is certainly from this religious matrix that Bierce's prophet Hali stems.

One wonders if Lovecraft's ominous Necronomicon passages were inspired by these paragraphs in Bierce. Alhazred was apparently his own version of Hali. This is made all the more probable by the fact that Lovecraft first simply mentions Alhazred by name, as Bierce reffered to Hali, with no reference to the Necronomicon ("The Nameless City"). And in one of the first tales to mention the Necronomicon as the source of Alhazared's sayings ("The Festival"), Love creaft also explicitly cites "Oled Morryster's wild Marvels of Science," a creation of Bierce appearing in "The Man and the Snake" as the source of an epigram like those of Hali. Thus we see that when he was thinking of Alhazared, he had Bierce on his mind.

Marion Zimmer Bradley notes that Hali is the Arabic name for the constellation Taurus, which contains the Hyades and Albebaran. Given the mysterious importance of these stars in Chambers's mythos, one must suppose Bradley has correctly pinpointed the meaning Chambers saw in the name, but the crucial astronomical associations are absent from Bierce.

An Inhabitant of Carcosa

by AMBROSE BIERCE

For *there be divers sorts of death—some wherein the body remaineth; and in some it vanisheth quite away with the spirit. This commonly occurreth only in solitude (such is God's will) and, none seeing the end, we say the man is lost, or gone on a long journey—which indeed he hath; but sometimes it hath happened in sight of many, as abundant testimony showeth. In one kind of death the spirit also dieth, and this it hath been known to do while yet the body was in vigor for many years. Sometimes, as is veritably attested, it dieth with the body, but after a season is raised up again in that place where the body did decay.*

Pondering these words of Hali (whom God rest) and questioning their full meaning, as one who, having an intimation, yet doubts if there be not something behind, other than that which he has discerned, I noted not whither I had strayed until a sudden chill wind striking my face revived in me a sense of my surroundings. I observed with astonishment that everything seemed unfamiliar. On every side of me stretched a bleak and desolate expanse of plain, covered with a tall overgrowth of sere grass, which rustled and whistled in the autumn wind with heaven knows what mysterious and disquieting suggestion. Protruded at long intervals above it, stood strangely shaped and somber-colored rocks, which seemed to have an understanding with one another and to exchange looks of uncomfortable significance, as if they had reared their heads to watch the issue of some foreseen event. A few blasted trees here and there appeared as leaders in this malevolent conspiracy of silent expectation.

The day, I thought, must be far advanced, though the sun was invisible; and although sensible that the air was raw and chill my consciousness of that fact was rather mental than physical—I had no feeling of discomfort. Over all the dismal landscape a canopy of low, lead-colored clouds hung like a visible curse. In all this there were a menace and a portent—a hint of evil, an intimation of doom. Bird, beast, or insect there was none. The wind sighed in the bare branches of the dead trees and the gray grass bent to whisper its dread secret to the earth; but no other sound nor motion broke the awful repose of that dismal place.

I observed in the herbage a number of weather-worn stones, evidently shaped with tools. They were broken, covered with moss and half sunken in the earth. Some lay prostrate, some leaned at various angles, none was vertical. They were obviously headstones of graves, though the graves themselves no longer existed as either mounds or depression; the years had leveled all. Scattered here and there, more massive blocks showed where some pompous tomb or ambitious monument had once flung its feeble defiance at oblivion. So old seemed these relics, these vestiges of vanity and memorials of affection and piety, so battered and worn and stained—so neglected, deserted, forgotten the place, that I could not help thinking myself the discoverer of the burial-ground of a prehistoric race of men whose very name was long extinct.

Filled with these reflections, I was for some time heedless of the sequence of my own experiences, but soon I thought, "How came I hither?" A moment's reflection seemed to make this all clear and explain at the same time, though in a disquieting way, the singular character with which my fancy had invented all that I saw or heard. I was ill. I remembered now that I had been prostrated by a sudden fever, and that my family had told me that in my periods of delirium I had constantly cried out for liberty and air, and had been held in bed to prevent my escape out-of-doors. Now I had eluded the vigilance of my attendants and had wandered hither to—to where? I could not conjecture. Clearly I was at a considerable distance from the city where I dwelt—the ancient and famous city of Carcosa.

No signs of human life were anywhere visible nor audible; no rising smoke, no watchdog's bark, no lowing of cattle, no shouts of children at play—nothing but that dismal burial-place with its air of mystery and dread, due to my own disordered brain. Was I not becoming again delirious, there beyond human aid? Was it not indeed *all* an illusion of my madness? I called aloud the names of my wives and sons, reached out my hands in search of theirs, even as I walked among the crumbling stones and in the withered grass.

A noise behind me caused me to turn about. A wild animal—a lynx—was approaching. The thought came to me: If I break down here in the desert—if the fever return and I fail, this beast will be at my throat. I sprang toward it, shouting. It trotted tranquilly by within a hand's breadth of me and disappeared behind a rock.

A moment later a man's head appeared to rise out of the ground a short distance away. He was ascending the farther slope of a low hill whose crest was hardly to be distinguished from the general level. His whole figure soon came into view against the background of gray cloud. He was half naked, half clad in skins. His hair was unkempt, his beard long and ragged. In one hand he carried a bow and arrow; the other held a blazing torch with a long trail of black smoke. He walked slowly and with caution, as if he feared falling into some open grave concealed by the tall grass. This strange apparition surprised but did not alarm, and taking such a course as to intercept him I met him almost face to face, accosting him with the familiar salutation, "God keep you."

He gave no heed, nor did he arrest his pace.

"Good stranger," I continued, "I am ill and lost. Direct me, I beseech you, to Carcosa."

The man broke into a barbarous chant in an unknown tongue, passing on and away.

An owl on the branch of a decayed tree hooted dismally and was answered by another in the distance. Looking upward, I saw through a sudden rift in the clouds Aldebaran and the Hyades! In all this there was a hint of night—the lynx, the man with the torch, the owl. Yet I saw—I saw even the stars in absence of the darkness. I saw, but was apparently not seen nor heard. Under what awful spell did I exist?

I seated myself at the root of a great tree, seriously to consider what it were best to do. That I was mad I could no longer doubt, yet recognized a ground of doubt in the conviction. Of fever I had no trace. I had, withal, a sense of exhilaration and vigor altogether unknown to me—a feeling of mental and physical exaltation. My senses seemed all alert; I could feel the air as a ponderous substance; I could hear the silence.

A great root of the giant tree against whose trunk I leaned as I sat held inclosed in its grasp a slab of stone, a part of which protruded into a recess formed by another root. The stone was thus partly protected from the weather, though greatly decomposed. Its edges were worn round, its corners eaten away, its surface deeply furrowed and scaled. Glittering particles of mica were visible in the earth about it—vestiges of its decomposition. This stone had apparently marked the grave out of which the tree had sprung ages ago. The tree's exacting roots had robbed the grave and made the stone a prisoner.

A sudden wind pushed some dry leaves and twigs from the upper-most face of the stone; I saw the low-relief letters of an inscription and bent to read it. God in Heaven! *my* name in full!—the date of *my* birth!—the date of *my* death!

A level shaft of light illuminated the whole side of the tree as I sprang to my feet in terror. The sun was rising in the rosy east. I stood between the tree and his broad red disk—no shadow darkened the trunk!

A chorus of howling wolves saluted the dawn. I saw them sitting on their haunches, singly and in groups, on the summits of irregular mounds and tumuli filling a half of my desert prospect and extending to the horizon. And then I knew that these were ruins of the ancient and famous city of Carcosa.

Such are the facts imparted to the medium Bayrolles by the spirit Hoseib Alar Robardin.

Along the shore the cloud waves break,
The twin suns sink behind the lake,
The shadows lengthen
                    In Carcosa.

Strange is the night where black stars rise,
And strange moons circle through the skies,
But stranger still is
                    Lost Carcosa.

Songs that the Hyades shall sing,
Where flap the tatters of the King,
Must die unheard in
                    Dim Carcosa.

Songs of my soul, my voice is dead,
Die though, unsung, as tears unshed
Shall dry and die in
                    Lost Carcosa.

— Cassilda's Song in *The King in Yellow*, Act I, Scene 2.

Robert W. Chambers (1865-1933) was an American illustrator and the author of at least 87 books. A small portion of these are supernatural horror, most of the rest being facile and forgettable romances. But the tiny canon of Chambers's horror stories are easily enough to place horror aficionados forever in his debt. Like gold, they are so precious because so rare.

As in Lovecraft's "The Shadow over Innsmouth," much of the power of this exceedingly strange and eerie tale comes from the narrator rather than the narrative. In the present tale we have an example of what critics call the "unreliable narrator"— he tells us enough to enable us to understand his situation better than he himself does, and in a diametrically opposite manner.

Another comparison to Lovecraft suggests itself: Especially in "The Repairer of Reputations" the narrative universe of "The King in Yellow" (the play) seems to function almost as a shared world of paranoid delusion among characters in the story, much as the Dream World of Lovecraft is shared by his characters (King Kuranes, Richard Pickman, Randolph Carter) once they descend the onyx staircase and pass through the Gates of Deeper Slumber. Indeed, the madness of Hildred Castaigne and Mr. Wilde would seem to lie precisely in the fact that they move about their common world of dream while they and those around them are in the waking world.

The Repairer of Reputations

by ROBERT W. CHAMBERS

I

Ne raillons pas les fous; leur folie dur plus longtemps que la notre ...
Voilà toute la différénce.

Toward the end of the year 1920 the Government of the United States had practically completed the programme, adopted during the last months of President Winthrop's administration. The country was apparently tranquil. Everybody knows how the Tariff and Labor questions were settled. The war with Germany, incident on that country's seizure of the Samoan Islands, had left no visible scars upon the republic, and the temporary occupation of Norfolk by the invading army had been forgotten in the joy over repeated naval victories and the subsequent ridiculous plight of General Von Gartenlaube's forces in the State of New Jersey. The Cuban and Hawaiian investments had paid one hundred per cent and the territory of Samoa was well worth its cost as a coaling station. The country was in a superb state of defence. Every coast city had been well supplied with land fortifications; the army under the parental eye of the General Staff, organized according to the Prussian system, had been increased to 300,000 men with a territorial reserve of a million; and six magnificent squadrons of cruisers and battleships patrolled the six stations of the navigable seas, leaving a steam reserve amply fitted to control home waters. The gentlemen from the West had at least been constrained to acknowledge that a college for the training of diplomats was as necessary as law schools are for the training of barristers; consequently we were no longer represented abroad by incompetent patriots. The nation was prosperous. Chicago, for a moment paralyzed after a second great fire, had risen from its ruins, white and imperial, and more beautiful that the white city which had been built for its plaything in 1893. Everywhere good architecture was replacing bad, and even in New York, a sudden craving for decency had swept away a great portion of the existing horrors. Streets had been widened, properly paved and lighted, trees had been planted, squares laid out, elevated structures demolished and underground roads built to replace them. The new government buildings and barracks were fine bits of architecture, and the long system of stone quays which completely surrounded the island had been turned into parks which proved a godsend to the population. The subsidizing of the state theatre and state opera brought its own reward. The United States National Academy of Design was much like European institutions of the same kind. Nobody envied the Secretary of Fine Arts, either his cabinet position or his portfolio. The Secretary of Forestry and Game Preservation had a much easier time, thanks to the new system of National Mounted Police. We had profited well by the latest treaties with France and England; the exclusion of foreign-born Jews as a measure of national self-preservation, the settlement of the new independent Negro state of Suanee, the checking of immigration, the new laws concerning naturalization, and the gradual centralization of power in the executive all contributed to national calm and prosperity. When the Government solved the Indian problem and squadrons of Indian cavalry scouts in native costume were substituted for the pitiable organizations tacked on to the tail of skeletonized regiments by a former Secretary of War, the nation drew a long sigh of relief. When, after the colossal Congress of Religions, bigotry and intolerance were laid in their graves and kindness and charity began to draw warring sects together, many thought the millennium had arrived, at least in the new world, which after all is a world by itself.

But self-preservation is the first law, and the United States had to look on in helpless sorrow as Germany, Italy, Spain and Belgium writhed in the throes of Anarchy, while Russia, watching from the Caucasus, stooped and bound them one by one.

In the city of New York the summer of 1899 was signalized by the dismantling of the Elevated Railroads. The summer of 1900 will live in the memories of New York people for many a cycle; the Dodge Statue was removed in that year. In the following winter began that agitation for the repeal of the laws prohibiting suicide which bore its final fruit in the month of April, 1920, when the first Government Lethal Chamber was opened on Washington Square.

I had walked down that day from Dr. Archer's house on Madison Avenue, where I had been as a mere formality. Ever since that fall from my horse, four years before, I had been troubled at times with pains in the back of my head and neck, but now for months they had been absent, and the doctor sent me away that day saying there was nothing more to be cured in me. It was hardly worth his fee to be told that; I knew it myself. Still I did not begrudge him the money. What I minded was the mistake which he made at first. When they picked me up from the pavement where I lay unconscious, and somebody had mercifully sent a bullet through my horse's head, I was carried to Doctor Archer, and he, pronouncing my brain affected, placed me in his private asylum where I was obliged to endure treatment for insanity. At last he decided that I was well, and I, knowing that my mind had always been as sound as his, if not sounder, "paid my tuition" as he jokingly called it, and left. I told him, smiling, that I would get even with him for his mistake, and he laughed heartily, and asked me to call once in a while. I did so, hoping for a chance to even up accounts, but he gave me none, and I told him I would wait.

The fall from my horse had fortunately left no evil results; on the contrary it had changed my whole character for the better. From a lazy young man about town, I had become active, energetic, temperate, and above all—oh, above all else—ambitious. There was only one thing which troubled me. I laughed at my own uneasiness, and yet it troubled me.

During my convalescence I had bought and read for the first time, "The King in Yellow". I remembered after finishing the first act that it occurred to me that I had better stop. I started up and flung the book into the fireplace; the volume struck the barred grate and fell open on the hearth in the firelight. If I had not caught a glimpse of the opening words in the second act I should never have finished it, but as I stooped to pick it up, my eyes became riveted to the open page, and with a cry of terror, or perhaps it was of joy so poignant that I suffered in every nerve, I snatched the thing out of the coals and crept to my bedroom, where I read it and reread it, and wept and laughed and trembled with a horror which at times assails me yet. This is the thing that troubles me, for I cannot forget Carcosa where black stars hang in the heavens; where the shadows of men's thoughts lengthen in the afternoon, when the twin suns sink into the Lake of Hali; and my mind will bear forever the memory of the Pallid Mask. I pray God will curse the writer, as the writer has cursed the world with this beautiful, stupendous creation, terrible in its simplicity, irresistible in its truth—a world which now trembles before the King in Yellow. When the French Government seized the translated copies which had just arrived in Paris, London, of course, became eager to read it. It is well known how the book spread like an infectious disease, from city to city, from continent to continent, barred out here, confiscated there, denounced by press and pulpit, censured even by the most advanced of literary anarchists. No definite principles had been violated in those wicked pages, no doctrine promulgated, no convictions outraged. It could not be judged by any known standard, yet, although it was acknowledged that the supreme note of art had been struck in "The King in Yellow," all felt that human nature could not bear the strain, nor thrive on words in which the essence of purest poison lurked. The very banality and innocence of the first act only allowed the blow to fall afterward with more awful effect.

It was, I remember the 13th day of April, 1920, that the first Government Lethal Chamber was established on the south side of Washington Square, between Wooster Street and South Fifth Avenue.

The block which had formerly consisted of a lot of shabby old buildings, used as cafés and restaurants for foreigners, had been acquired by
the Government in the winter of 1898. The French and Italian cafés
were torn down; the whole block was enclosed by a gilded iron railing,
and converted into a lovely garden with lawns, flowers and fountains.
In the centre of the garden stood a small, white building, severely
classical in architecture, and surrounded by thickets of flowers. Six
Ionic columns supported the roof, and the single door was of bronze.
A splendid marble group of "The Fates" stood before the door, the work
of a young American sculptor, Boris YvRain, who had died in Paris
when only twenty-three years old.

The inauguration ceremonies were in progress as I crossed University Place and entered the square. I threaded my way through the silent
throng of spectators, but was stopped at Fourth Street by a cordon of
police. A regiment of United States lancers were drawn up in a hollow
square around the Lethal Chamber. On a raised tribune facing Washington Park stood the Governor of New York, and behind him were
grouped the Mayor of New York and Brooklyn, the Inspector-General
of Police, the Commandant of the state troops, Colonel Livingston,
military aide to the President of the United States, General Blount,
commanding at Governor's Island, Major-General Hamilton, commanding the garrison of New York and Brooklyn, Admiral Buffby of
the fleet in the North River, Surgeon-General Lanceford, the staff of
the National Free Hospital, Senators Wyse and Franklin of New York,
and the Commissioner of Public Works. The tribune was surrounded
by a squadron of hussars of the National Guard.

The Governor was finishing his reply to the short speech of the
Surgeon-General. I heard him say: "The laws prohibiting suicide and
providing punishment for any attempt at self-destruction have been
repealed. The Government has seen fit to acknowledge the right of
man to end an existence which may have become intolerable to him,
through physical suffering or mental despair. It is believed that the
community will be benefited by the removal of such people from their
midst. Since the passage of this law, the number of suicides in the
United States has not increased. Now that the Government has
determined to establish a Lethal Chamber in every city, town and
village in the country, it remains to be seen whether or not that class
of human creatures from whose desponding ranks new victims of
self-destruction fall daily will accept the relief thus provided." He
paused and turned to the white Lethal Chamber. The silence in the
street was absolute. "There a painless death awaits him who can no
longer bear the sorrows of this life. If death is welcome let him seek it
there." Then quickly turning to the military aide of the President's

household, he said, "I declare the Lethal Chamber open," and again facing the vast crowd he cried in a clear voice: "Citizens of New York and of the United States of America, through me the Government declares the Lethal Chamber to be open."

The solemn hush was broken by a sharp cry of command, the squadron of hussars filed after the Governor's carriage, the lancers wheeled and formed along Fifth Avenue to wait for the commandant of the garrison, and the mounted police followed them. I left the crowd to gape and stare at the white marble Death Chamber, and, crossing South Fifth Avenue, walked along the western side of that thorough-fare to Bleecker Street. Then I turned to the right and stopped before a dingy shop which bore the sign:

HAWBERK, ARMORER

I glanced in at the doorway and Hawberk busy in his little shop at the end of the hall. He looked up, and catching sight of me cried in his deep, hearty voice, "Come in, Mr. Castaigne!" Constance, his daughter, rose to meet me as I crossed the threshold, and held out her pretty hand, but I saw the blush of disappointment on her cheeks, knew that it was another Castaigne she had expected, my Cousin Louis. I smiled at her confusion and complimented her on the banner which she was embroidering from a colored plate. Old Hawberk sat riveting the worn greaves of some ancient suit of armor, and the ting! ting! ting! of his little hammer sounded pleasantly in the quaint shop. Presently he dropped his hammer, and fussed about for a moment with a tiny wrench. The soft clash of the mail sent a thrill of pleasure through me. I loved to hear the music of steel brushing against steel, the mellow shock of the mallet on thigh pieces, and the jingle of chain armor. That was the only reason I went to see Hawberk. He had never interested me personally, nor did Constance except for the fact of her being in love with Louis. This did occupy my attention, and sometimes even kept me awake at night. But I knew in my heart that all would come right, and that I should arrange their future as I expected to arrange that of my kind doctor, John Archer. However, I should never have troubled myself about visiting them just then, had it not been, as I say, that the music of the tinkling hammer had for me this strong fascina-tion. I would sit for hours, listening listening, and when a stray sunbeam struck the inlaid steel, the sensation it gave me was almost too keen to endure. My eyes would become fixed, dilating with a pleasure that stretched every nerve almost to breaking, until some movement of the old armorer cut off the ray of sunlight, then, still thrilling secretly, I leaned back and listened again to the sound of the polishing rag, swish! swish! rubbing rust from the rivets.

Constance worked with the embroidery over her knees, now and then pausing to examine more closely the pattern in the colored plate from the Metropolitan Museum.

"Who is this for?" I asked.

Hawberk explained, that in addition to the treasures of armor in the Metropolitan Museum of which he had been appointed armorer, he also had charge of several collections belonging to rich amateurs. This was the missing greave of a famous suit which a client of his had traced to a little shop in Paris on the Quai d'Orsay. He, Hawberk, had negotiated for and secured the greave, and now the suit was complete. He laid down his hammer and read me the history of the suit, traced since 1450 from owner to owner until it was acquired by Thomas Stainbridge. When his superb collection was sold, this client of Hawberk's bought the suit, and since then the search for the missing greave had been pushed until it was, almost by accident, located in Paris.

"Did you continue the search so persistently without any certainty of the greave being still in existence?" I demanded.

"Of course," he replied coolly.

Then for the first time I took a personal interest in Hawberk.

"It was worth something to you," I ventured.

"No," he replied, laughing, "my pleasure in finding it was my reward."

"Have you no ambition to rich?" I asked smiling.

"My one ambition is to be the best armorer in the world," he answered gravely.

Constance asked me if I had seen the ceremonies at the Lethal Chamber. She herself had noticed cavalry passing up Broadway that morning, and had wished to see the inauguration, but her father wanted the banner finished, and she had stayed at his request.

"Did you see your cousin, Mr. Castaigne, there?" she asked with the slightest tremor of her soft eyelashes.

"No," I replied carelessly. "Louis' regiment is manoeuvering out in Westchester County." I rose and picked up my hat and cane.

"Are you going upstairs to see the lunatic again?" laughed old Hawberk. If Hawberk knew how I loathe that word "lunatic," he would never use it in my presence. It rouses certain feelings within me which I do not care to explain. However, I answered him quietly: "I think I shall drop in and see Mr. Wilde for a moment or two."

"Poor fellow," said Constance, with a shake of her head, "it must be hard to live alone year after year, poor, crippled and almost demented. It is very good of you, Mr. Castaigne, to visit him as often as you do."

"I think he is vicious," observed Hawberk, beginning again with his hammer. I listened to the golden tinkle on the greave plates; when he had finished I replied:

"No, he is not vicious, nor is he in the least demented. His mind is a wonder chamber, from which he can extract treasures that you and I would give years of our lives to acquire."

Hawberk laughed.

I continued a little impatiently: "He knows history as no one else could know it. Nothing, however trivial, escapes his search, and his memory is so absolute, so precise in details, that were it known in New York that such a man existed the people could not honor him enough."

"Nonsense," muttered Hawberk, searching on the floor for a fallen rivet.

"Is it nonsense," I asked, managing to suppress what I felt, "is it nonsense when he says that the tassets and cuissard of the enamelled suit of armor commonly known as the 'Prince's Emblazoned' can be found among a mass of rusty theatrical properties, broken stoves and ragpicker's refuse in a garret in Pell Street?"

Hawberk's hammer fell to the ground, but he picked it up and asked, with a great deal of calm, how I knew that the tassets and left cuissard were missing from the "Prince's Emblazoned."

"I did not know until Mr. Wilde mentioned it to me the other day. He said they were in the garret of 998 Pell Street."

"Nonsense," he cried, but I noticed his hand trembling under his leathern apron.

"Is this nonsense too?" I asked pleasantly. "Is it nonsense when Mr. Wilde continually speaks of you as the Marquis of Avonshire and of Miss Constance—"

I did not finish, for Constance had started to her feet with terror written on every feature. Hawberk looked at me and slowly smoothed his leathern apron. "That is impossible," he observed, "Mr. Wilde may know a great many things—"

"About armor, for instance, and the 'Prince's Emblazoned,'" I interposed, smiling.

"Yes," he continued," slowly, "about armor also—may be—but he is wrong in regard to the Marquis of Avonshire, who, as you know, killed his wife's traducer years ago, and went to Australia where he did not long survive his wife."

"Mr. Wilde is wrong," murmured Constance. Her lips were blanched but her voice was sweet and calm.

"Let us agree, if you please, that in this one circumstance Mr. Wilde is wrong," I said.

II

I climbed the three dilapidated flights of stairs, which I had so often climbed before, and knocked at a small door at the end of the corridor. Mr. Wilde opened the door and I walked in.

When he had double-locked the door and pushed a heavy chest against it, he came and sat down beside me, peering up into my face with his little light-colored eyes. Half a dozen new scratches covered his nose and cheeks, and the silver wires which supported his artificial ears had become displaced. I thought I had never seen him so hideously fascinating. He had no ears. The artificial ones, which now stood out at an angle from the fine wire, were his one weakness. They were made of wax and painted a shell pink, but the rest of his face was yellow. He might better have revelled in the luxury of some artificial fingers for his left hand, which was absolutely fingerless, but it seemed to cause him no inconvenience, and he was satisfied with his wax ears. He was very small, scarcely higher than a child of ten, but his arms were magnificently developed, and his thighs as thick as any athlete's. Still, the most remarkable thing about Mr. Wilde was that a man of his marvelous intelligence and knowledge should have such a head. It was flat and pointed, like the heads of many of those unfortunates whom people imprison in asylums for the weak-minded. Many called him insane but I knew him to be as sane as I was.

I do not deny that he was eccentric; the mania he had for keeping that cat and teasing her until she flew at his face like a demon, was certainly eccentric. I never could understand why he kept the creature, nor what pleasure he found in shutting himself up in his room with the surly, vicious beast. I remembered once, glancing up from the manuscript I was studying by the light of some tallow dips, and seeing Mr. Wilde squatting motionless on his high chair, his eyes fairly blazing with excitement, while the cat, which had risen from her place before the stove, came creeping across the floor right at him. Before I could move she flattened her belly to the ground, crouched, trembled, and sprang into his face. Howling and foaming they rolled over and over the floor, scratching and clawing, until the cat screamed and fled under the cabinet, and Mr. Wilde turned over on his back, his limbs contracting and curling up like the legs of a dying spider. He *was* eccentric.

Mr. Wilde had climbed into his high chair, and, after studying my face, picked up a dog's-eared ledger and opened it.

"Henry B. Matthews," he read, "bookkeeper with Whysot Whysot and Company, dealers in church ornaments. Called April 3d. Reputation damaged on the race-track. Known as a welcher. Reputation to be repaired by August 1st. **Retainer Five Dollars.**" He turned the page and ran his fingerless knuckles down the closely-written columns.

"P. Greene Dusenberry, Minister of the Gospel, Fairbeach, New Jersey. Reputation damaged in the Bowery. To be repaired as soon as possible. Retainer $100."

He coughed and added, "Called, April 6th."

"Then you are not in need of money, Mr. Wilde," I inquired.

"Listen," he coughed again.

"Mrs. C. Hamilton Chester, of Chester Park, New York City. Called April 7th. Reputation damaged at Dieppe, France. To be repaired by October 1st. Retainer $500.

"Note—C. Hamilton Chester, Captain, U.S.S. 'Avalanche' ordered home from South Sea Squadron October 1st."

"Well," I said, "the profession of a Repairer of Reputations is lucrative."

His colorless eyes sought mine. "I only wanted to demonstrate that I was correct. You said it was impossible to succeed as a Repairer of Reputations; that even if I did succeed in certain cases it would cost me more than I would gain by it. To-day I have five hundred men in my employ, who are poorly paid, but who pursue the work with an enthusiasm which possibly may be born of fear. These men enter every shade and grade of society; some even are pillars of the most exclusive social temples; others are the prop and pride of the financial world; still others, hold undisputed sway among the 'Fancy and the Talent.' I choose them at my leisure from those who reply to my advertisements. It is easy enough, they are all cowards. I could treble the number in twenty days if I wished. So you see, those who have in their keeping the reputations of their fellow-citizens, *I* have in my pay."

"They may turn on you," I suggested.

He rubbed his thumb over his cropped ears, and adjusted the wax substitutes. "I think not," he murmured thoughtfully, "I seldom have to apply the whip, and then only once. Besides they like their wages."

"How do you apply the whip?" I demanded.

His face for a moment was awful to look upon. His eyes dwindled to a pair of green sparks.

"I invite them to come and have a little chat with me," he said in a soft voice.

A knock at the door interrupted him, and his face resumed its amiable expression.

"Who is it?" he inquired.

"Mr. Steylette," was the answer.

"Come to-morrow," replied Mr. Wilde.

"Impossible," began the other, but was silenced by a sort of bark from Mr. Wilde.

"Come to-morrow," he repeated.

We heard somebody move away from the door and turn the corner by the stairway.

"Who is that?" I asked.

"Arnold Steylette, Owner and Editor in Chief of the great New York daily."

He drummed on the ledger with his fingerless hand adding: "I pay him very badly, but he thinks it a good bargain."

"Arnold Steylette!" I repeated amazed.

"Yes," said Mr. Wilde with a self-satisfied cough.

The cat, which had entered the room as he spoke hesitated, looked up at him and snarled. He climbed down from the chair and squatting on the floor, took the creature into his arms and caressed her. The cat ceased snarling and presently began a loud purring which seemed to increase in timbre as he stroked her.

"Where are the notes?" I asked. He pointed to the table, and for the hundredth time I picked up the bundle of manuscript entitled

"THE IMPERIAL DYNASTY OF AMERICA"

One by one I studied the well-worn pages, worn only by my own handling, and although I knew all by heart, from the beginning, "When from Carcosa, the Hyades, Hastur, and Aldebaran," to "Castaigne, Louis de Calvados, born December 19th, 1877," I read it with an eager rapt attention, pausing to repeat parts of it aloud, and dwelling especially on "Hildred de Calvados, only son of Hildred Castaigne and Edythe Landes Castaigne, first in success," etc., etc.

When I finished, Mr. Wilde nodded and coughed.

"Speaking of your legitimate ambition," he said, "how do Constance and Louis get along?"

"She loves him," I replied simply.

The cat on his knee suddenly turned and struck at his eyes, and he flung her off and climbed on to the chair opposite me.

"And Doctor Archer! But that's a matter you can settle any time you wish," he added.

"Yes," I replied, "Doctor Archer can wait, but it is time I saw my cousin Louis."

"It is time," he repeated. Then he took another ledger from the table and ran over the leaves rapidly.

"We are now in communication with ten thousand men," he muttered. "We can count on one hundred thousand within the first twenty-eight hours, and in forty-eight hours the state will rise *en masse.* The country follows the state, and the portion that will not, I mean California and the Northwest, might better never have been inhabited. I shall not send them the Yellow Sign."

The blood rushed to my head, but I only answered, "A new broom sweeps clean."

"The ambition of Caesar and of Napolean pales before that which could not rest until it had seized the minds of men and controlled even their unborn thoughts," said Mr. Wilde.

"You are speaking of the King in Yellow," I groaned with a shudder.

"He is a king whom Emperors have served."

"I am content to serve him," I replied.

Mr. Wilde sat rubbing his ears with his crippled hand. "Perhaps Constance does not love him," he suggested.

I started to reply, but a sudden burst of military music from the street below drowned out my voice. The twentieth dragoon regiment, formerly in garrison at Mount St. Vincent, was returning from the manoeuvers in Westchester County, to its new barracks on East Washington Square. It was my cousin's regiment. They were a fine lot of fellows, in their pale-blue, tight-fitting jackets, jaunty busbys and white riding breeches with the double yellow stripe, into which their limbs seemed molded. Every other squadron was armed with lances, from the metal points of which fluttered yellow and white pennons. The band passed, playing the regimental march, then came the colonel and staff, the horses crowding and trampling, while their heads bobbed in unison, and the pennons fluttered from their lance points. The troopers, who rode with the beautiful English seat, looked brown as berries from their bloodless campaign among the farms of Westchester, and the music of their sabres against the stirrups, and the jingle of spurs and carbines was delightful to me. I saw Louis riding with his squadron. He was as handsome an officer as I have ever seen. Mr. Wilde, who had mounted a chair by the window, saw him too, but said nothing. Louis turned and looked straight at Hawberk's shop as he passed, and I could see the flush on his brown cheeks. I think Constance must have been at the window. When the last troopers had clattered by, and the last pennons vanished into South 5th Avenue, Mr. Wilde dragged the chest away from the door.

"Yes," he said, "it is time that you saw your cousin Louis."

He unlocked the door and I picked up my hat and stick and stepped into the corridor. The stairs were dark. Groping about, I set my foot on something soft, which snarled and spit, and I aimed a murderous blow at the cat, but my cane shivered to splinters against the balustrade, and the beast scurried back into Mr. Wilde's room.

Passing Hawberk's door again I saw him still at work on the armor, but I did not stop, and stepping out into Bleecker Street, I followed it to Wooster, skirted the grounds of the Lethal Chamber, and crossing Washington Park went straight to my rooms in the Benedick. Here I lunched comfortably, read the *Herald* and the *Meteor,* and finally went to the steel safe in my bedroom and set the time combination. The three and three-quarter minutes which it is necessary to wait, while the time lock is opening, are to me golden moments. From the instant I set the combination to the moment when I grasp the knobs and swing back the solid steel doors, I live in an ecstasy of expectation. Those moments must be like the moments passed in Paradise. I know what I am to find at the end of the time limit. I know what the massive safe holds secure for me, for me alone, and the exquisite pleasure of waiting is hardly enhanced when the safe opens and I lift, from its velvet crown, a diadem of purest gold, blazing with diamonds. I do this every day, and yet the joy of waiting and at last touching the diadem, only seems to increase as the days pass. It is a diadem fit for a King among kings, and Emperor among emperors. The King in Yellow might scorn it, but it shall be worn by his royal servant.

I held it in my arms until the alarm on the safe rang harshly, and then tenderly, proudly, I replaced it and shut the steel doors. I walked slowly back into my study, which faces Washington Square, and leaned on the window-sill. The afternoon sun poured into my windows, and a gentle breeze stirred the branches of the elms and maples in the park, now covered with buds and tender foliage. A flock of pigeons circled about the tower of the Memorial Church; sometimes alighting on the purple tiled roof, sometimes wheeling downward to the lotos fountain in front of the marble arch. The gardeners were busy with the flower beds around the fountain, and the freshly-turned earth smelled sweet and spicy. A lawn mower, drawn by a fat white horse, clinked across the green sward, and watering carts poured showers of spray over the asphalt drives. Around the statue of Peter Stuyvesant, which in 1897 had replaced the monstrosity supposed to represent Garibaldi, children played in the spring sunshine, and nurse girls wheeled elaborate baby-carriages with a reckless disregard for the pasty-faced occupants, which could probably be explained by the presence of half a dozen trim dragoon troopers languidly lolling on the benches. Through the trees, the Washington Memorial Arch glistened like silver in the sunshine, and beyond, on the eastern extremity of the square the gray stone barracks of the dragoons, and the white granite artillery stables were alive with color and motion.

I looked at the Lethal Chamber on the corner of the square opposite. A few curious people still lingered about the gilded iron railing, but inside the grounds the paths were deserted. I watched the fountains ripple and sparkle; the sparrows had already found this new bathing nook, and the basins were crowded with the dusty-feathered little things. Two or three white peacocks picked their way across the lawns, and a drab-colored pigeon sat so motionless on the arm of one of the Fates, that it seemed to be a part of the sculptured stone.

As I was turning carelessly away, a slight commotion in the group of curious loiterers around the gates attracted my attention. A young man had entered, and was advancing with nervous strides along the gravel path which leads to the bronze doors of the Lethal Chamber. He paused a moment before the Fates, and as he raised his head to those three mysterious faces, the pigeon rose from its sculptured perch, circled about for a moment and wheeled to the east. The young man pressed his hands to his face, and then with an undefinable gesture sprang up the marble steps, the bronze doors closed behind him, and half an hour later the loiterers slouched away, and the frightened pigeon returned to its perch in the arms of Fate.

I put on my hat and went out into the park for a little walk before dinner. As I crossed the central driveway a group of officers passed, and one of them called out, "Hello, Hildred," and came back to shake hands with me. It was my Cousin Louis, who stood smiling and tapping his spurred heels with his riding-whip.

"Just back from Westchester," he said; "been doing the bucolic; milk and curds, you know, dairy-maids in sunbonnets, who say 'haeow' and 'I don't think' when you tell them they are pretty. I'm nearly dead for a square meal at Delmonico's. What's the news?"

"There is none," I replied pleasantly. "I saw your regiment coming in this morning."

"Did you? I didn't see you. Where were you?"

"In Mr. Wilde's window."

"Oh hell!" he began impatiently, "that man is stark mad! I don't understand why you——"

He saw how annoyed I felt by this outburst, and begged my pardon.

"Really, old chap," he said, "I don't mean to run down a man you like, but for the life of me I can't see what the deuce you find in common with Mr. Wilde. He's not well-bred, to put it generously; he's hideously deformed; his head is the head of a criminally insane person. You know yourself he's been in an asylum—"

"So have I," I interrupted calmly.

Louis looked startled and confused for a moment, but recovered and slapped me heartily on the shoulder.

"You were completely cured," he began, but I stopped him again.

"I suppose you mean that I was simply acknowledged never to have been insane."

"Of course that—that's what I meant," he laughed.

I disliked his laugh because I knew it was forced, but I nodded gaily and asked him where he was going. Louis looked after his brother officers who had now almost reached Broadway.

"We had intended to sample a Brunswick cocktail, but to tell you the truth I was anxious for an excuse to go and see Hawberk instead. Come along, I'll make you my excuse."

We found old Hawberk, neatly attired in a fresh spring suit, standing at the door of his shop and sniffing the air.

"I had just decided to take Constance for a little stroll before dinner," he replied to the impetuous volley of questions from Louis. "We thought of walking on the park terrace along the North River."

At that moment Constance appeared and grew pale and rosy by turns as Louis bent over her small gloved fingers. I tried to excuse myself, alleging an engagement up-town, but Louis and Constance would not listen, and I saw I was expected to remain and engage old Hawberk's attention. After all it would be just as well if I kept my eye on Louis, I though, and when they hailed a Spring Street horsecar, I got in after them and took my seat beside the armorer.

The beautiful line of parks and granite terraces overlooking the wharves along the North River, which were built in 1910 and finished in the autumn of 1917, had become one of the most popular promenades in the metropolis. They extended from the battery to 190th Street, overlooking the noble river and affording a fine view of the Jersey shore and the Highlands opposite. Cafés and restaurants were scattered here and there among the trees, and twice a week military bands from the garrison played in the kiosques on the parapets.

We sat down in the sunshine on the bench at the foot of the equestrian statue of General Sheridan. Constance tipped her sunshade to shield her eyes, and she and Louis began a murmuring conversation which was impossible to catch. Old Hawberk, leaning on his ivory-headed cane, lighted an excellent cigar, the mate to which I politely refused, and smiled at vacancy. The sun hung low above the Staten

Island woods, and the bay was dyed with golden hues reflected from the sunwarmed sails of the shipping in the harbor.

Brigs, schooners, yachts, clumsy ferry-boats, their decks swarming with people, railroad transports carrying lines of brown, blue and white freight cars, stately sound steamers, *declassé* tramp steamers, coasters, dredgers, scows, and everywhere pervading the entire bay impudent little tugs puffing and whistling officiously;—these were the crafts which churned the sunlit waters as far as the eye could reach. In calm contrast to the hurry of sailing vessel and steamer a silent fleet of white warships lay motionless in mid-stream.

Constance's merry laugh aroused me from my reverie.

"What *are* you staring at?" she inquired.

"Nothing—the fleet," I smiled.

Then Louis told us what the vessels were, pointing out each by its relative position to the old Red Fort on Governor's Island.

"That little cigar-shaped thing is a torpedo boat," he explained; "there are four more lying close together. They are the 'Tarpon,' the 'Falcon,' the 'Sea Fox' and the 'Octopus.' The gun-boats just above are the 'Princeton,' the 'Champlain,' the 'Still water' and the 'Erie.' Next to them lie the cruisers 'Farragut' and 'Los Angeles,' and above them the battleships 'California' and 'Dakota,' and the 'Washington' which is the flagship. Those two squatty-looking chunks of metal which are anchored there off Castle William are the double-turreted monitors 'Terrible' and 'Magnificent'; behind them lies the ram, 'Osceola.'"

Constance looked at him with deep approval in her beautiful eyes. "What loads of things you know for a soldier," she said, and we all joined in the laugh which followed.

Presently Louis rose with a nod to us and offered his arm to Constance, and they strolled away along the river wall. Hawberk watched for a moment and then turned to me.

"Mr. Wilde was right," he said. "I have found the missing tassets and left cuissard of the 'Prince's Emblazoned,' in a vile old junk garret in Pell Street."

"998?" I inquired, with a smile.

"Yes."

"Mr. Wilde is a very intelligent man," I observed.

"I want to give him the credit of this most important discovery," continued Hawberk. "And I intend it shall be known that he is entitled to the fame of it."

"He won't thank you for that," I answered sharply; "please say nothing about it."

"Do you know what it is worth?" said Hawberk.

"No, fifty dollars, perhaps."

"It is valued at five hundred, but the owner of the 'Prince's Emblazoned' will give two thousand dollars to the person who completes his
suit; that reward also belongs to Mr. Wilde."

"He doesn't want it! He refuses!" I answered angrily. "What do you
know about Mr. Wilde? He doesn't need the money. He is rich—or
will be—richer than any living man except myself. What will we care
for money then—what will we care, he and I, when—when—"

"When what?" demanded Hawberk, astonished.

"You will see," I replied, on my guard again.

He looked at me narrowly, much as Doctor Archer used to, and I
knew he thought I was mentally unsound. Perhaps it was fortunate for
him that he did not use the word lunatic just then.

"No," I replied to his unspoken thought, "I am not mentally weak;
my mind is as healthy as Mr. Wilde's. I do not care to explain just yet
what I have on hand, but it is an investment which will pay more than
mere gold, silver and precious stones. It will secure the happiness and
prosperity of a continent—yes, a hemisphere!"

"Oh," said Hawberk.

"And eventually," I continued more quietly, "it will secure the
happiness of the whole world."

"And incidentally your own happiness and prosperity as well as Mr.
Wilde's?"

"Exactly," I smiled. But I could have throttled him for taking that
tone.

He looked at me in silence for a while and then said very gently,
"Why don't you give up your books and studies, Mr. Castaigne, and
take a tramp among the mountains somewhere or other? You used to
be fond of fishing. Take a cast or two at the trout in the Rangeleys."

"I don't care for fishing any more," I answered, without a shade of
annoyance in my voice.

"You used to be fond of everything," he continued, "athletics,
yachting, shooting, riding—"

"I have never cared to ride since my fall," I said quietly.

"Ah, yes, your fall," he repeated looking away from me.

I thought this nonsense had gone far enough, so I turned the
conversation back to Mr. Wilde; but he was scanning my face again in
a manner highly offensive to me.

"Mr. Wilde," he repeated, "do you know what he did this afternoon?
He came down stairs and nailed a sign over the hall door next to mine;
it read:

MR. WILDE
REPAIRER OF REPUTATIONS
3d Bell

Do you know what a Repairer of Reputations can be?"

"I do," I replied, suppressing the rage within.

"Oh," he said again.

Louis and Constance came strolling by and stopped to ask if we would join them. Hawberk looked at his watch. At the same moment a puff of smoke shot from the casements of Castle William, and the boom of the sunset gun rolled across the water and was reechoed from the Highlands opposite. The flag came running down from the flag-pole, the bugles sounded on the white decks of the warships, and the first electric light sparkled out from the Jersey shore.

As I turned into the city with Hawberk I heard Constance murmur something to Louis which I did not understand; but Louis whispered "My darling," in reply; and again, walking ahead with Hawberk through the square I heard a murmur of "sweetheart," and "my own Constance," and I knew the time had nearly arrived when I should speak of important matters with my Cousin Louis.

III

One morning early in May I stood before the steel safe in my bedroom, trying on the golden jewelled crown. The diamonds flashed fire as I turned to the mirror, and the heavy beaten gold burned like a halo about my head. I remembered Camilla's agonized scream and the awful words echoing through the streets of Carcosa. They were the last lines in the first act, and I dared not think of what followed—dared not, even in the spring sunshine, there in my own room, surrounded with familiar objects, reassured by the bustle from the street and the voices of the servants in the hallway outside. For those poisoned words had dropped slowly into my heart, as death-sweat drops upon a bed-sheet and is absorbed. Trembling, I put the diadem from my head and wiped my forehead. But I thought of Hastur and of my own rightful ambition, and I remembered Mr. Wilde as I had last left him, his face all torn and bloody from the claws of that devil's creature, and what he said—ah, what he said! The alarm bell in the safe began to whirr harshly, and I knew my time was up; but I would not heed it, and replacing the flashing circlet upon my head I turned defiantly to the mirror. I stood for a long time absorbed in the changing expression of my own eyes. The mirror reflected a face which was like my own, but whiter, and so thin that I hardly recognized it. And all the time I kept repeating between my clenched teeth, "The day has come! the day has come!" while the alarm in the safe whirred and clamored, and the diamonds sparked and flamed above my brow. I heard a door open but did not heed it. It was only when I saw two faces in the mirror;—it was only when another face rose over my shoulder, and two other eyes met mine. I wheeled like a flash and seized a long knife from the dressing-table, and my cousin sprang back very pale, crying: "Hildred! for God's sake!" then as my hand fell, he said: "It is I, Louis, don't you know me?" I stood silent. I could not have spoken for my life. He walked up to me and took the knife from my hand.

"What is all this?" he inquired, in a gentle voice. "Are you ill?"

"No," I replied. But I doubt if he heard me.

"Come, come, old fellow," he cried, "take off that brass crown and toddle into the study. Are you going to a masquerade? What's all this theatrical tinsel anyway?"

I was glad he thought the crown was made of brass and paste, yet I didn't like him any the better for thinking so. I let him take it from my hand, knowing it was best to humor him. He tossed the splendid diadem in the air, and catching it, turned to me smiling.

"It's dear at fifty cents," he said. "What's it for?"

I did not answer, but took the circlet from his hands, and placing it in the safe shut the massive steel door. The alarm ceased its infernal din at once. He watched me curiously, but did not seem to notice the sudden ceasing of the alarm. He did, however, speak of the safe as a biscuit box. Fearing lest he might examine the combination I led the way into the study. Louis threw himself on the sofa and flicked at flies with his eternal riding-whip. He wore his fatigue uniform with the braided jacket and jaunty cap, and I noticed that his riding-boots were all splashed with red mud.

"Where have you been," I inquired.

"Jumping mud creeks in Jersey," he said. "I haven't had time to change yet; I was rather in a hurry to see you. Haven't you got a glass of something? I'm dead tired; been in the saddle twenty-four hours."

I gave him some brandy from my medicinal store, which he drank with a grimace.

"Damned bad stuff," he observed. "I'll give you an address where they sell brandy that is brandy."

"It's good enough for my needs," I said indifferently. "I used it to rub my chest with." He stared and flicked at another fly.

"See here, old fellow," he began, "I've got something to suggest to you. It's four years now that you've shut yourself up in here like an owl, never going anywhere, never taking any healthy exercise, never doing a damned thing but poring over those books up there on the mantel-piece."

He glanced along the row of shelves. "Napoleon, Napoleon, Napoleon!" he read. "For heaven sake, have you nothing but Napoleons there?"

"I wish they were bound in gold," I said. "But wait, yes, there is another book, 'The King in Yellow.'" I looked him steadily in the eye.

"Have you never read it?" I asked.

"I? No, thank God! I don't want to be driven crazy."

I saw he regretted his speech as soon as he had uttered it. There is only one word which I loathe more than I do lunatic and that word is crazy. But I controlled myself and asked him why he thought "The King in Yellow" dangerous.

"Oh, I don't know," he said, hastily. "I only remember the excitement it created and the denunciations from pulpit and press. I believe the author shot himself after bringing forth this monstrosity, didn't he?"

"I understand he is still alive," I answered.

"That's probably true," he muttered; "bullets couldn't kill a fiend like that."

"It is a book of great truths," I said.

"Yes," he replied, "Of 'truths' which send men frantic and blast their lives. I don't care if the thing is, as they say, the very supreme essence of art. It's a crime to have written it, and I for one shall never open its pages."

"Is that what you have come to tell me?" I asked.

"No," he said, "I came to tell you that I am going to be married."

I believe for a moment my heart ceased to beat, but kept my eyes on his face.

"Yes," he continued, smiling happily, "married to the sweetest girl on earth."

"Constance Hawberk," I said mechanically.

"How did you know?" he cried, astonished. "I didn't know it myself until that evening last April when we strolled down to the embankment before dinner."

"When is it to be?" I asked.

"It was to have been next September, but an hour ago a dispatch came ordering our regiment to the Presidio, San Francisco. We leave at noon to-morrow. To-morrow," he repeated. "Just think, Hildred, to-morrow I shall be the happiest fellow that ever drew breath in this jolly world, for Constance will go with me."

I offered him my hand in congratulation, and he seized and shook it like the good-natured fool he was—or pretended to be.

"I am going to get my squadron as a wedding present," he rattled on. "Captain and Mrs. Louis Castaigne, eh, Hildred?"

Then he told me where it was to be and who were to be there, and made me promise to come and be best man. I set my teeth and listened to his boyish chatter without showing what I felt, but—

I was getting to the limit of my endurance, and when he jumped up, and, switching his spurs until they jingled, said he must go, I did not detain him.

"There's one thing I want to ask of you," I said quietly.

"Out with it, it's promised," he laughed.

"I want you to meet me for a quarter of an hour's talk tonight."

"Of course, if you wish," he said, somewhat puzzled. "Where?"

"Anywhere, in the park there."

"What time, Hildred?"

"Midnight."

"What in the name of—" he began, but checked himself and laughingly assented. I watched him go down the stairs and hurry away, his sabre banging at every stride. He turned into Bleecker Street, and I knew he was going to see Constance. I gave him ten minutes to disappear and then followed in his footsteps, taking with me the jewelled crown and the silken robe embroidered with the Yellow Sign. When I turned into Bleecker Street, and entered the doorway which bore the sign

MR. WILDE
REPAIRER OF REPUTATIONS
3d Bell

I saw old Hawberk moving about in his shop, and imagined I heard Constance's voice in the parlor; but I avoided them both and hurried up the trembling stairways to Mr. Wilde's apartment. I knocked, and entered without ceremony. Mr. Wilde lay groaning on the floor, his face covered with blood, his clothes torn to shreds. Drops of blood were scattered about over the carpet, which had also been ripped and frayed in the evidently recent struggle.

"It's that cursed cat," he said, ceasing his groans, and turning his colorless eyes to me; "she attacked me while I was asleep. I believe she will kill me yet."

This was too much, so I went into the kitchen and seizing a hatchet from the pantry, started to find the infernal beast and settle her then and there. My search was fruitless, and after a while I gave it up and came back to find Mr. Wilde squatting on his high chair by the table.

He had washed his face and changed his clothes. The great furrows which the cat's claws had ploughed up in his face he had filled with collodion, and a rag hid the wound in his throat. I told him I should kill the cat when I came across her, but he only shook his head and turned to the open ledger before him. He read name after name of the people who had come to him in regard to their reputation, and the sums he had amassed were startling.

"I put the screws on now and then," he explained.

"One day or other some of these people will assassinate you," I insisted.

"Do you think so?" He said, rubbing his mutilated ears.

It was useless to argue with him, so I took down the manuscript entitled Imperial Dynasty of America, for the last time I should ever take it down in Mr. Wilde's study. I read it through, thrilling and trembling with pleasure. When I had finished Mr. Wilde took the manuscript and, turning to the dark passage which leads from his study to his bed-chamber, called out in a loud voice, "Vance." Then for the first time, I noticed a man crouching there in the shadow. How I had overlooked him during my search for the cat, I cannot imagine.

"Vance, come in," cried Mr. Wilde.

The figure rose and crept toward us, and I shall never forget the face that he raised to mine, as the light from the window illuminated.

"Vance, this is Mr. Castaigne," said Mr. Wilde. Before he had finished speaking, the man threw himself on the ground before the table, crying and gasping, "Oh, God! Oh, my God! Forgive me—Oh, Mr. Castaigne, keep that man away. You cannot, you cannot mean it! You are different—save me! I am broken down—I was in a madhouse and now—when all was coming right—when I had forgotten the King—the King in Yellow and—but I shall go mad again—I shall go mad—"

His voice died into a choking rattle, for Mr. Wilde had leapt on him and his right hand encircled the man's throat. When Vance fell in a heap on the floor, Mr. Wilde clambered nimbly into his chair again, and rubbing his mangled ears with the stump of his hand, turned to me and asked me for the ledger. I reached it down from the shelf and he opened it. After a moment's searching among the beautifully written pages, he coughed complacently, and pointed to the name Vance.

"Vance," he read aloud, "Osgood Oswald Vance." At the sound of his name, the man on the floor raised his head and turned a convulsed face to Mr. Wilde. His eyes were injected with blood, his lips tumefied. "Called April 28th," continued Mr. Wilde. "Occupation, cashier in the Seaforth National Bank, has served a term of forgery at Sing Sing, from whence he was transferred to the Asylum for the Criminal Insane. Pardoned by the Governor of New York, and discharged from the Asylum, January 19, 1918. Reputation damaged at Sheepshead Bay. Rumors that he lives beyond his income. Reputation to be repaired at once. Retainer $1,500.

"Note—Has embezzled sums amounting to $20,000 since March 20th, 1919, excellent family, and secured present position through uncle's influence. Father President of Seaforth Bank."

I looked at the man on the floor.

"Get up, Vance," said Mr. Wilde in a gentle voice. Vance rose as if hypnotized. "He will do as we suggest now," observed Mr. Wilde, and opening the manuscript, he read the entire history of the Imperial Dynasty of America. Then in a kind and soothing murmur he ran over the important points with Vance, who stood like one stunned. His eyes were so blank and vacant that I imagined he had become half-witted, and remarked it to Mr. Wilde who replied that it was of no consequence anyway. Very patiently we pointed out to Vance what his share in the affair would be, and he seemed to understand after a while. Mr. Wilde explained the manuscript, using several volumes on Heraldry, to substantiate the result of his researches. He mentioned the establishment of the Dynasty in Carcosa, the lake which connected Hastur, Aldebaran and the mystery of the Hyades. He spoke of Cassilda and Camilla, and sounded the cloudy depths of Demhe, and the lake of Hali. "The scalloped tatters of the King in Yellow must hide Yhtill forever," he muttered, but I do not believe Vance heard him. Then by degrees he led Vance along the ramifications of the Imperial family, to Uoht and Thale, from Naotalba and Phantom of Truth, to Aldones, and then tossing aside his manuscript and notes, he began the wonderful story of the Last King. Fascinated and thrilled I watched him. He threw up his head, his long arms were stretched out in a magnificent gesture of pride and power, and his eyes blazed deep in their sockets like two emeralds. Vance listened stupefied. As for me, when at last Mr. Wilde had finished, and pointing to me, cried. "The cousin of the King!" my head swam with excitement.

Controlling myself with a superhuman effort, I explained to Vance why I alone was worthy of the crown and why my cousin must be exiled or die. I made him understand that my cousin must never marry, even after renouncing all his claims, and how that least of all he should marry the daughter of the Marquis of Avonshire and bring England into the question. I showed him a list of thousands of names which Mr. Wilde had drawn up; every man whose name was there had received the Yellow Sign which no living human being dared disregard. The city, the state, the whole land, were ready to rise and tremble before the Pallid Mask.

The time had come, the people should know the son of Hastur, and the whole world bow to the Black Stars which hang in the sky over Carcosa.

Vance leaned on the table, his head buried in his hands. Mr. Wilde drew a rough sketch on the margin of yesterday's *Herald* with a bit of lead pencil. It was a plan of Hawberk's rooms. Then he wrote out the order and affixed the seal, and shaking like a palsied man I signed my first writ of execution with my name Hildred-Rex.

Mr. Wilde clambered to the floor and unlocking the cabinet, took a long square box from the first shelf. This he brought to the table and opened. A new knife lay in the tissue paper inside and I picked it up and handed it to Vance, along with the order and the plan of Hawberk's apartment. Then Mr. Wilde told Vance he could go; and he went, shambling like an outcast of the slums.

I sat for a while watching the daylight fade behind the square tower of the Judson Memorial Church, and finally, gathering up the manuscript and notes, took my hat and started for the door.

Mr. Wilde watched me in silence. When I had stepped into the hall I looked back. Mr. Wilde's small eyes were still fixed on me. Behind him, the shadows gathered in the fading light. Then I closed the door behind me and went out into the darkening streets.

I had eaten nothing since breakfast, but I was not hungry. A wretched half-starved creature, who stood looking across the street at the Lethal Chamber, noticed me and came up to tell me a tale of misery. I gave him money, I don't know why, and he went away without thanking me. An hour later another outcast approached and whined his story. I had a blank bit of paper in my pocket, on which was traced the Yellow Sign and I handed it to him. He looked at it stupidly for a moment and then with an uncertain glance at me, folded it with what seemed to me exaggerated care and placed it in his bosom.

The electric lights were sparkling among the trees, and the new moon shone in the sky above the Lethal Chamber. It was tiresome waiting in the square; I wandered from the Marble Arch to the artillery stables, and back again to the lotos fountain. The flowers and grass exhaled a fragrance which troubled me. The jet of the fountain played in the moonlight, and the musical clash of falling drops reminded me of the tinkle of chained mail in Hawberk's shop. But it was not so fascinating, and the dull sparkle of the moonlight on the water brought no such sensations of exquisite pleasure, as when the sunshine played over the polished steel of a corselet on Hawberk's knee. I watched the bats darting and turning above the water plants in the fountain basin, but their rapid, jerky flight set my nerves on edge, and I went away again to walk aimlessly to and fro among the trees.

The artillery stables were dark, but in the cavalry barracks the officer's windows were brilliantly lighted, and the sallyport was constantly filled with troopers in fatigue, carrying straw and harness and baskets filled with tin dishes.

Twice the mounted sentry at the gates was changed, while I wandered up and down the asphalt walk. I looked at my watch. It was nearly time. The lights in the barracks went out one by one, the barred gate was closed, and every minute or two an officer passed in through the side wicket, leaving a rattle of accoutrements and a jingle of spurs on the night air. The square had become very silent. The last homeless loiterer had been driven away by the gray-coated park policemen, the car tracks along Wooster Street were deserted, and the only sound which broke the stillness was the stamping of the sentry's horse and the ring of his sabre against the saddle pommel. In the barracks, the officer's quarters were still lighted, and military servants passed and repassed before the bay windows. Twelve o'clock sounded from the new spire of St. Francis Xavier, and at the last stroke of the sadtoned bell a figure passed through the wicket beside the portcullis, returned the salute of the sentry, and crossing the street entered the square and advanced toward the Benedick apartment house.

"Louis," I called.

The man pivoted on his spurred heels and came straight toward me.

"Is that you, Hildred?"

"Yes, you are on time."

I took his offered hand, and we strolled toward the Lethal Chamber.

He rattled on about his wedding and the graces of Constance, and their future prospects, calling my attention to his captain's shoulder straps, and the triple gold arabesque on his sleeve and fatigue cap. I believe I listened as much to the music of his spurs and sabre as I did to his boyish babble, and at last we stood under the elms on the Fourth Street corner of the square opposite the Lethal Chamber. Then he laughed and asked me what I wanted with him. I motioned him to a seat on a bench under the electric light, and sat down beside him. He looked at me curiously, with that same searching glance which I hate and fear so in doctors. I felt the insult of his look, but he did not know it, and I carefully concealed my feelings.

"Well, old chap," he enquired, "what can I do for you?"

I drew from my pocket the manuscript and notes of the Imperial Dynasty of America, and looking him in the eye said:

"I will tell you. On your word as a soldier, promise me to read this manuscript from beginning to end, without asking me a question. Promise me to read these notes in the same way, and promise me to listen to what I have to tell later."

"I promise, if you wish it," he said pleasantly, "Give me the paper, Hildred."

He began to read, raising his eyebrows with a puzzled whimsical air, which made me tremble with suppressed anger. As he advanced, his eyebrows contracted, and his lips seemed to form the word, "rubbish."

Then he looked slightly bored, but apparently for my sake read, with an attempt at interest, which presently ceased to be an effort. He started when in the closely-written pages he came to his own name, and when he came to mine he lowered the paper, and looked sharply at me for a moment. But he kept his word, and resumed his reading, and I let the half-formed question die on his lips unanswered. When he came to the end and read the signature of Mr. Wilde, he folded the paper carefully and returned it to me. I handed him the notes, and he settled back, pushing his fatigue cap up to his forehead, with a boyish gesture, which I remembered so well in school. I watched his face as he read, and when he finished I took the notes with the manuscript, and placed them in my pocket. Then I unfolded a scroll marked with the Yellow Sign. He saw the sign, but he did not seem to recognize it, and I called his attention to it somewhat sharply.

"It is the Yellow Sign," I said angrily.

"Oh, that's it, is it?" said Louis, in that flattering voice Doctor Archer used to employ with me, and would probably have employed again, had I not settled his affair for him.

I kept my rage down and answered as steadily as possible, "Listen, you have engaged your word?"

"I am listening, old chap," he replied soothingly.

I began to speak very calmly.

"Dr. Archer, having by some means become possessed of the secret of the Imperial Succession, attempted to deprive me of my right, alleging that because of a fall from my horse four years ago, I had become mentally deficient. He presumed to place me under restraint in his own house in hopes of either driving me insane or poisoning me. I have not forgotten it. I visited him last night and the interview was final."

Louis turned quite pale, but did not move. I resumed triumphantly, "There are yet three people to be interviewed in the interests of Mr. Wilde and myself. They are my cousin Louis, Mr. Hawberk, and his daughter Constance."

Louis sprang to his feet and I arose also, and flung the paper marked with the Yellow Sign to the ground.

"Oh, I don't need that to tell you what I have to say," I cried with a laugh of triumph. "You must renounce the crown to me, do you hear, to *me*."

Louis looked at me with a startled air, but recovering himself said kindly, "Of course I renounce the—what is it I must renounce?"

"The crown," I said angrily.

"Of course," he answered. "I renounce it. Come, old chap, I'll walk back to your rooms with you."

"Don't try any of your doctor's tricks on me," I cried trembling with fury. "Don't act as if you think I am insane."

"What nonsense," he replied. "Come, it's getting late, Hildred."

"No," I shouted, "you must listen. You cannot marry, I forbid it. Do you hear? I forbid it. You shall renounce the crown, and in reward I grant you exile, but if you refuse you shall die."

He tried to calm me but I was roused at last, and drawing my long knife barred his way.

Then I told him how they would find Dr. Archer in the cellar with his throat open, and I laughed in his face when I thought of Vance and his knife, and the order signed by me.

"Ah, you are the King," I cried, "but I shall be King. Who are you to keep me from Empire over all the habitable earth! I was born the cousin of a king, but I shall be King!"

Louis stood white and rigid before me. Suddenly a man came running up Fourth Street, entered the gate of the Lethal Temple, traversed the path to the bronze doors at full speed, and plunged into the death chamber with the cry of one demented, and I laughed until I wept tears, for I had recognized Vance, and knew that Hawberk and his daughter were no longer in my way.

"Go," I cried to Louis, "you have ceased to be a menace. You will never marry Constance now, and if you marry anyone else in your exile, I will visit you as I did my doctor last night. Mr. Wilde takes charge of you to-morrow." Then I turned and darted into South Fifth Avenue, and with a cry of terror Louis dropped his belt and sabre and followed me like the wind. I heard him close behind me at the corner of Bleecker Street, and I dashed into the doorway under Hawberk's sign. He cried, "Halt, or I fire!" but when he saw that I flew up the stairs leaving Hawberk's shop below, he left me and I heard him hammering and shouting at their door as though it was possible to rouse the dead.

Mr. Wilde's door was open, and I entered crying, "It is done, it is done! Let the nations rise and look upon their King!" but I could not find Mr. Wilde, so I went to the cabinet and took the splendid diadem from its case. Then I drew on the white silk robe, embroidered with the Yellow Sign, and placed the crown upon my head. At last I was King, King by my right in Hastur. King because I knew the mystery of the Hyades, and my mind had sounded the depths of the Lake of Hali. I was King! The first grey pencillings of dawn would raise a tempest which would shake two hemispheres. Then as I stood, my every nerve pitched to the highest tension, faint with the joy and splendor of my thoughts, without, in the dark passage, a man groaned.

I seized the tallow dip and sprang to the door. The cat passed me like a demon, and the tallow dip went out, but my long knife flew swifter than she, and I heard her screech, and I knew that my knife had found her. For a moment I listened to her tumbling and thumping about in the darkness, and then when her frenzy ceased, I lighted a lamp and raised it over my head. Mr. Wilde lay on the floor with his throat torn open. At first I thought he was dead, but as I looked, a green sparkle came into his sunken eyes, his mutilated hand trembled, and then a spasm stretched his mouth from ear to ear. For a moment my terror and despair gave place to hope, but as I bent over him his eyeballs rolled clean around in his head, and he died. Then while I stood, transfixed with rage and despair, seeing my crown, my empire, every hope and every ambition, my very life, lying prostrate there with the dead master, *they* came, seized me from behind, and bound me until my veins stood out like cords, and my voice failed with paroxysms of my frenzied screams. But I still raged, bleeding and infuriated among them, and more than one policeman felt my sharp teeth. Then when I could no longer move they came nearer; I saw old Hawberk, and behind him my cousin Louis' ghastly face, and farther away, in the corner, a woman, Constance, weeping softly.

"Ah! I see it now!" I shrieked. "You have seized the throne and the empire. Woe! woe to you who are crowned with the crown of the King in Yellow!"

[EDITOR'S NOTE.—Mr. Castaigne died yesterday in the Asylum for the Criminal Insane.]

*C*hambers lived in Paris from 1886 to 1893, studying painting. These experiences led him to write In the Quarter. That period of his life also provides the raw material for "The Yellow Sign."

In this story the mythology of "The King in Yellow," which has functioned more in the nature of symbolic commentary on the real-world action of the previous stories, comes off the page and invades the world in which the story's characters live. They do not merely read the decadent classic "The King in Yellow;" they are actually pressed into service as characters in a continuation of its events.

A word must be said about the symbolism of lost innocence in "The Yellow Sign." It is no accident that the sexual encounter between the artist and his model coincides with the reading of the infernal drama, and that this is followed by the advent of the hearse-driver. As in the Eden myth, innocence is shattered by carnal knowledge, and death is the result.

The Yellow Sign

by ROBERT W. CHAMBERS

I

Let the red dawn surmise
What we shall do,
When this blue starlight dies
And all is through.

There are so many things which are impossible to explain! Why should certain chords in music make me think of the brown and golden tints of autumn foliage? Why should the Mass of Sainte Cécile send my thoughts wandering among caverns whose walls blaze with ragged masses of virgin silver? What was it in the roar and turmoil of Broadway at six o'clock that flashed before my eyes the picture of a still Breton forest where sunlight filtered through spring foliage and Sylvia bent, half curiously, half tenderly, over a small green lizard, murmuring: "To think that this also is a little ward of God!"

When I first saw the watchman his back was toward me. I looked at him indifferently until he went into the church. I paid no more attention to him than I had to any other man who lounged through Washington Square that morning, and when I shut my window and turned back into my studio I had forgotten him. Late in the afternoon, the day being warm, I raised the window again and leaned out to get a sniff of air. A man was standing in the courtyard of the church, and I noticed him again with as little interest as I had that morning. I looked across the square to where the fountain was playing and then, with my mind filled with vague impressions of trees, asphalt drives, and the moving groups of nursemaids and holiday-makers, I started to walk back to my easel. As I turned, my listless glance included the man below in the churchyard. His face was toward me now, and with a perfectly involuntary movement I bent to see it. At the same moment he raised his head and looked at me. Instantly I thought of a coffin-worm. Whatever it was about the man that repelled me I did not know, but the impression of a plump white grave-worm was so intense and nauseating that I must have shown it in my expression, for he turned his puffy face away with a movement which made me think of a disturbed grub in a chestnut.

I went back to my easel and motioned the model to resume her pose. After working awhile I was satisfied that I was spoiling what I had done as rapidly as possible, and I took up a palette knife and scraped the color out again. The flesh tones were sallow and unhealthy, and I did not understand how I could have painted such sickly color into a study which before that had glowed with healthy tones.

I looked at Tessie. She had not changed, and the clear flush of health dyed her neck and cheeks as I frowned.

"Is it something I've done?" she said.

"No,—I've made a mess of this arm, and for the life of me I can't see how I came to paint such mud as that into the canvas," I replied.

"Don't I pose well?" she insisted.

"Of course, perfectly."

"Then it's not my fault?"

"No, it's my own."

"I'm very sorry," she said.

I told her she could rest while I applied rag and turpentine to the plague spot on my canvas, and she went off to smoke a cigarette and look over the illustrations in the *Courier Français.*

I did not know whether it was something in the turpentine or a defect in the canvas, but the more I scrubbed the more that gangrene seemed to spread. I worked like a beaver to get it out, and yet the disease appeared to creep from limb to limb of the study before me. Alarmed I strove to arrest it, but now the color on the breast changed and the whole figure seemed to absorb the infection as a sponge soaks up water. Vigorously I plied palette knife, turpentine, and scraper, thinking all the time what a séance I should hold with Duval who had sold me the canvas; but soon I noticed it was not the canvas which was defective, nor yet the colors of Edward. "It must be the turpentine," I thought angrily, "or else my eyes have become so blurred and confused by the afternoon light that I can't see straight." I called Tessie, the model. She came and leaned over my chair blowing rings of smoke into the air.

"What *have* you been doing to it?" she exclaimed.

"Nothing," I growled, "it must be this turpentine!"

"What a horrible color it is now," she continued. "Do you think my flesh resembles green cheese?"

"No, I don't," I said angrily. "Did you ever know me to paint like that before?"

"No, indeed!"

"Well, then!"

"It must be the turpentine, or something," she admitted.

She slipped on a Japanese robe and walked to the window. I scraped and rubbed until I was tired and finally picked up my brushes and hurled them through the canvas with a forcible expression, the tone alone of which reached Tessie's ears.

Nevertheless she promptly began: "That's it! Swear and act silly and ruin your brushes. You've been three weeks on that study, and now look! What's the good of ripping the canvas? What creatures artists are!"

I felt about as much ashamed as I usually did after such an outbreak, and I turned the ruined canvas to the wall. Tessie helped me clean my brushes, and then danced away to dress. From the screen she regaled me with bits of advice concerning whole or partial loss of temper, until, thinking, perhaps, I had been tormented sufficiently, she came out to implore me to button her waist where she could not reach it on the shoulder.

"Everything went wrong from the time you came back from the window and talked about that horrid-looking man you saw in the churchyard," she announced.

"Yes, he probably bewitched the picture," I said yawning. I looked at my watch.

"It's after six, I know," said Tessie, adjusting her hat before the mirror.

"Yes," I replied, "I didn't mean to keep you so long." I leaned out of the window but recoiled with disgust, for the young man with the pasty face stood below in the churchyard. Tessie saw my gesture of disapproval and leaned from the window.

"Is that the man you don't like?" she whispered.

I nodded.

"I can't see his face, but he does look fat and soft. Someway or other," she continued, turning to look at me, "he reminds me of a dream,—an awful dream I once had. Or," she mused, looking down at her shapely shoes, "was it a dream after all?"

"How should I know?" I smiled.

Tessie smiled in reply.

"You were in it," she said, "so perhaps you might know something about it."

"Tessie! Tessie!" I protested, "don't you dare flatter by saying that you dream about me!"

"But I did," she insisted; "shall I tell you about it?"

Tessie leaned back on the open window-sill and began very seriously.

"One night last winter I was lying in bed thinking about nothing at all in particular. I had been posing for you and I was tired out, yet it seemed impossible for me to sleep. I heard the bells in the city ring, ten, eleven, and midnight. I must have fallen asleep about midnight because I don't remember hearing the bells after that. It seemed to me that I had scarcely closed my eyes when I dreamed that something impelled me to go to the window. I rose, and raising the sash leaned out. Twenty-fifth Street was deserted as far as I could see. I began to be afraid; everything outside seemed so—so black and uncomfortable. Then the sound of wheels in the distance came to my ears, and it seemed to me as though that was what I must wait for. Very slowly the wheels approached, and, finally, I could make out a vehicle moving along the street. It came nearer and nearer, and when it passed beneath my window I saw it was a hearse. Then, as I trembled with fear, the driver turned and looked straight at me. When I awoke I was standing by the open window shivering with cold, but the black-plumed hearse and the driver were gone. I dreamed this dream again in March last, and again awoke beside the open window. Last night the dream came again. You remember how it was raining; when I awoke, standing at the open window, my night-dress was soaked."

"But where did I come into the dream?" I asked.

"You—you were in the coffin; but you were not dead."

"In the coffin?"

"Yes."

"How did you know? Could you see me?"

"No; I only knew you were there."

"Had you been eating Welsh rarebits, or lobster salad?" I began laughing, but the girl interrupted me with a frightened cry.

"Hello! What's up?" I said, as she shrank into the embrasure by the window.

"The—the man below in the churchyard;—he drove the hearse."

"Nonsense," I said, but Tessie's eyes were wide with terror. I went to the window and looked out. The man was gone. "Come, Tessie," I urged, "don't be foolish. You have posed too long; you are nervous."

"Do you think I could forget that face?" she murmured. "Three times I saw the hearse pass below my window, and every time the driver turned and looked up at me. Oh, his face was so white and—and soft? It looked dead—it looked as if it had been dead a long time."

I induced the girl to sit down and swallow a glass of Marsala. Then I sat down beside her, and tried to give some advice.

"Look here, Tessie," I said, "you go to the country for a week or two, and you'll have no more dreams about hearses. You pose all day, and when night comes your nerves are upset. You can't keep this up. Then again, instead of going to bed when your day's work is done, you run off to picnics at Sulzer's Park, or go to the Eldorado or Coney Island, and when you come down here next morning you are fagged out. There was no real hearse. That was a soft-shell crab dream."

She smiled faintly.

"What about the man in the churchyard?"

"Oh, he's only an ordinary unhealthy, everyday creature."

"As true as my name is Tessie Reardon, I swear to you, Mr. Scott, that the face of the man below in the churchyard is the face of the man who drove the hearse!"

"What of it?" I said. "It's an honest trade."

"Then you think I *did* see the hearse?"

"Oh," I said diplomatically, "if you really did, it might not be unlikely that the man below drove it. There is nothing in that."

Tessie rose, unrolled her scented handkerchief and taking a bit of gum from a knot in the hem, placed it in her mouth. Then drawing on her gloves she offered me her hand, with a frank, "Good-night, Mr. Scott," and walked out.

II

The next morning, Thomas, the bellboy, brought me the *Herald* and a bit of news. The church next door had been sold. I thanked Heaven for it, not that it being a Catholic I had any repugnance for the congregation next door, but because my nerves were shattered by a blatant exhorter, whose every word echoes through the aisle of the church as if it had been my own rooms, and who insisted on his r's with a nasal persistence which revolted my every instinct. Then, too, there was a fiend in human shape, an organist, who reeled off some of the grand old hymns with an interpretation of his own, and I longed for the blood of a creature who could play the doxology with an amendment of minor chords which one hears only in a quartet of very young undergraduates. I believe the minister was a good man, but when he bellowed: "And the Lorrrd said unto Moses, the Lorrrd is a man of war; the Lorrrd is his name. My wrath shall wax hot and I will kill you with the sworrrd!" I wondered how many centuries of purgatory it would take to atone for such a sin.

"Who bought the property?" I asked Thomas. "Nobody that I knows, sir. They do say the gent wot owns this 'ere 'Amilton flats was lookin' at it, 'E might be a bildin' more studios."

I walked to the window. The young man with the unhealthy face stood by the churchyard gate, and at the mere sight of him the same overwhelming repugnance took possession of me.

"By the way, Thomas," I said, "who is that fellow down there?"

Thomas sniffed. "That there worm, sir? 'E's night-watchman of the church, sir. 'E maikes me tired-a-sittin' out all night on them steps and lookin' at you insultin' like. I'd a punched 'is 'ed, sir—beg pardon, sir—"

"Go on, Thomas."

"One night a comin' 'ome with 'Arry, the other English boy, I sees 'im a sittin' there on them steps. We 'ad Molly and Jen with us, sir, the two girls on the tray service, and 'e looks so insultin' at us that I up and sez: 'Wat you lookin hat, you fat slug?—beg pardon, sir, but that's 'ow I sez, sir. Then 'e don't say nothin' and I sez: 'Come out and I'll punch that puddin' 'ed.' Then I hopens the gate and goes in, but 'e don't say nothin', only looks insultin' like. Then I 'its 'im one, but ugh! 'is 'ed was that cold and mushy it ud sicken you to touch 'im."

"What did he do then?" I asked, curiously.

"Im? Nawthin'."

"And you, Thomas?"

The young fellow flushed with embarrassment and smiled uneasily.

"Mr. Scott, sir, I ain't no coward an' I can't make it out at all why I run. I was in the 5th Lawncers, sir, bugler at Tel-el-Kebir, an' was shot by the wells."

"You don't mean to say you ran away?"

"Yes, sir; I run."

"Why?"

"That's just what I want to know, sir. I grabbed Molly an' run, an' the rest was as frightened as I."

"But what were they frightened at?"

Thomas refused to answer for a while, but now my curiosity was aroused about the repulsive young man below and I pressed him. Three years' sojourn in America had not only modified Thomas' cockney dialect but had given him the American's fear of ridicule.

"You won't believe me, Mr. Scott, sir?"

"Yes, I will."

"You will lawf at me, sir?"

"Nonsense!"

He hesitated. "Well, sir, it's Gawd's truth that when I 'it 'im 'e grabbed me wrists, sir, and when I twisted 'is soft, mushy fist one of 'is fingers come off in me 'and."

The utter loathing and horror of Thomas' face must have been reflected in my own for he added:

"It's orful, an' now when I see 'im I just go away. 'E maikes me hill."

When Thomas had gone I went to the window. The man stood beside the church-railing with both hands on the gate, but I hastily retreated to my easel again, sickened and horrified, for I saw that the middle finger of his right hand was missing.

At nine o'clock Tessie appeared and vanished behind the screen with a merry "Good morning, Mr. Scott." When she had reappeared and taken her pose upon the model-stand I started a new canvas much to her delight. She remained silent as long as I was on the drawing, but as soon as the scrape of the charcoal ceased and I took up my fixative she began to chatter.

"Oh, I had such a lovely time last night. We went to Tony Pastor's."

"Who are 'we'?" I demanded.

"Oh, Maggie, you know, Mr. Whyte's model, and Pinkie McCormack—we call her Pinkie because she's got that beautiful red hair you artists like so much—and Lizzie Burke."

I sent a shower of spray from the fixative over the canvas, and said: "Well, go on."

"We saw Kelly and Baby Barnes the skirt-dancer and—and all the rest. I made a mash."

"Then you have gone back on me, Tessie?"

She laughed and shook her head.

"He's Lizzie Burke's brother, Ed. He's a perfect gen'l'man."

I felt constrained to give her some parental advice concerning mashing, which she took with a bright smile.

"Oh, I can take care of a strange mash," she said, examining her chewing gum, "but Ed is different. Lizzie is my best friend."

Then she related how Ed had come back from the stocking mill in Lowell, Massachusetts, to find her and Lizzie grown up, and what an accomplished young man he was, and how he thought nothing of squandering half a dollar for ice-cream and oysters to celebrate his entry as a clerk into the woollen department of Macy's. Before she finished I began to paint, and she resumed the pose, smiling and chattering like a sparrow. By noon I had the study fairly well rubbed in and Tessie came to look at it.

"That's better," she said.

I thought so too, and ate my lunch with a satisfied feeling that all was going well. Tessie spread her lunch on a drawing table opposite me and we drank our claret from the same bottle and lighted our cigarettes from the same match. I was very much attached to Tessie. I had watched her shoot up into a slender but exquisitely formed woman from a frail, awkward child. She had posed for me during the last three years, and among all my models she was my favorite. It would have troubled me very much indeed had she become "tough" or "fly," as the phrase goes, but I never noticed any deterioration of her manner, and felt at heart that she was all right. She and I never discussed morals at all, and I had no intention of doing so, partly because I had none myself, and partly because I knew she would do what she liked in spite of me. Still I did hope she would steer clear of complications, because I wished her well, and then also I had a selfish desire to retain the best model I had. I knew that mashing, as she termed it, had no significance with girls like Tessie, and that such things in America did not resemble in the least the same things in Paris. Yet having lived with my eyes open, I also knew that somebody would take Tessie away some day, in one manner or another, and though I professed to myself that marriage was nonsense, I sincerely hoped that, in this case, there would be a priest at the end of the vista. I am a Catholic. When I listen to high mass, when I sign myself, I feel that everything, including myself, is more cheerful, and when I confess, it does me good. A man who lives as much alone as I do, must confess to somebody. Then, again, Sylvia was Catholic, and it was reason enough for me. But I was speaking of Tessie, which is very different. Tessie also was Catholic and much more devout than I, so, taking it all in all, I had little fear for my pretty model until she should fall in love. But *then* I knew that fate alone would decide her future for her, and I prayed inwardly that fate would keep her away from men like me and throw into her path nothing but Ed Burkes and Jimmy McCormacks, bless her sweet face!

Tessie sat blowing rings of smoke up to the ceiling and tinkling the ice in her tumbler.

"Do you know that I also had a dream last night?" I observed.

"Not about that man," she laughed.

"Exactly. A dream similar to yours, only much worse."

It was foolish and thoughtless of me to say this, but you know how little tact the average painter has.

"I must have fallen asleep about 10 o'clock," I continued, "and after awhile I dreamt that I awoke. So plainly did I hear the midnight bells, the wind in the tree branches, and the whistle of steamers from the bay, that even now I can scarcely believe I was not awake. I seemed to be lying in a box which had a glass cover. Dimly I saw the street lamps as I passed, for I must tell you, Tessie, the box in which I reclined appeared to lie in a cushioned wagon which jolted me over a stony pavement. After a while I became impatient and tried to move but the box was too narrow. My hands were crossed on my breast so I could not raise them to help myself. I listened and then tried to call. My voice was gone. I could hear the trample of the horses attached to the wagon and even the breathing of the driver. Then another sound broke upon my ears like the raising of a window sash. I managed to turn my head a little, and found I could look, not only through the glass cover of my box, but also through the glass panes in the side of the covered vehicle. I saw houses, empty and silent, with neither light nor life about any of them excepting one. In that house a window was open on the first floor and a figure all in white stood looking down into the street. It was you."

Tessie had turned her face away from me and leaned on the table with her elbow.

"I could see your face," I resumed, "and it seemed to me to be very sorrowful. Then we passed on and turned into a narrow black lane. Presently the horses stopped. I waited and waited, closing my eyes with fear and impatience, but all was as silent as the grave. After what seemed to me hours, I began to feel uncomfortable. A sense that somebody was close to me made me unclose my eyes. Then I saw the white face of the hearse-driver looking at me through the coffin-lid—"

A sob from Tessie interrupted me. She was trembling like a leaf. I saw I had made an ass of myself and attempted to repair the damage.

"Why, Tess," I said, "I only told you this to show you what influence your story might have on another person's dreams. You don't suppose I really lay in a coffin, do you? What are you trembling for? Don't you see that your dream and my unreasonable dislike for that inoffensive watchman of the church simply set my brain working as soon as I fell asleep?"

She laid her head between her arms and sobbed as if her heart would break. What a precious triple donkey I had made of myself! But I was about to break my record. I went over and put my arm about her.

"Tessie, dear, forgive me," I said; "I had no business to frighten you with such nonsense. You are too sensible a girl, too good a Catholic to believe in dreams."

Her hand tightened on mine and her head fell back upon my shoulder, but she still trembled and I petted and comforted her.

"Come, Tess, open your eyes and smile."

Her eyes opened with a slow languid movement and met mine, but their expression was so queer that I hastened to reassure her again.

"It's all humbug, Tessie, you surely are not afraid that any harm will come to you because of that."

"No," she said, but her scarlet lips quivered.

"Then what's the matter? Are you afraid?"

"Yes. Not for myself."

"For me, then?" I demanded gaily.

"For you," she murmured in a voice almost inaudible, "I—I care for you."

At first I started to laugh but when I understood her, a shock passed through me and I sat like one turned to stone. This was the crowning bit of idiocy I had committed. During the moment which elapsed between her reply and my answer I thought of a thousand responses to the innocent confession. I could pass it by with a laugh, I could misunderstand her and reassure her as to my health, I could simply point out that it was impossible she could love me. But my reply was quicker than my thoughts, and I might think and think now when it was too late, for I had kissed her on the mouth.

That evening I took my usual walk in Washington Park, pondering over the occurrences of the day. I was thoroughly committed. There was no back out now, and I stared the future straight in the face. I was not good, not even scrupulous, but I had no idea of deceiving either myself or Tessie. The one passion of my life lay buried in the sunlit forests of Brittany. Was it buried there forever? Hope cried "No!" For three years I had been listening to the voice of Hope, and for three years I had waited for a footstep on my threshold. Had Sylvia forgotten? "No!" cried Hope.

I said that I was not good. That is true, but still I was not exactly a comic opera villain. I had led an easy-going reckless life, taking what invited me of pleasure, deploring and sometimes bitterly regretting consequences. In one thing alone, except my painting, was I serious, and that was something which lay hidden if not lost in the Breton forests.

It was too late now for me to regret what had occurred during the day. Whatever it had been, pity, a sudden tenderness for sorrow, or the more brutal instinct of gratified vanity, it was all the same now, and unless I wished to bruise an innocent heart my path lay marked before me. The fire and strength, the depth of passion of a love which I had never even suspected, with all my imagined experience in the world, left me no alternative but to respond or send her away. Whether because I am so cowardly about giving pain to others, or whether it was that I have little of gloomy Puritan in me, I do not know, but I shrank from disclaiming responsibility for that thoughtless kiss, and in fact had no time to do so before the gates of her heart opened and the flood poured forth. Others who habitually do their duty and find a sullen satisfaction in making themselves and everybody else unhappy, might have withstood it. I did not. I dared not. After the storm had abated I did tell her that she might better have loved Ed Burke and worn a plain gold ring, but she would not hear of it, and I thought perhaps that as long as she had decided to love somebody she could not marry, it had better be me. I, at least could treat her with an intelligent affection, and whenever she became tired of her infatuation she could go none the worse for it. For I was decided on that point although I knew how hard it would be. I remember the usual termination of Platonic liaisons and thought how disgusted I had been whenever I heard of one. I knew I was undertaking a great deal for unscrupulous a man as I was, and I dreaded the future, but never for one moment did I doubt that she was safe with me. Had it been anybody but Tessie I should not have bothered my head about scruples. For it did not occur to me to sacrifice Tessie as I would have sacrificed a woman of the world. I looked the future squarely in the face and saw the several probable endings to the affair. She would either tire of the whole thing, or become so unhappy that I should have either to marry her or go away. If I married her we would be unhappy. I with a wife unsuited to me, and she with a husband unsuitable for any woman. For my past life could scarcely entitle me to marry. If I went away she might either fall ill, recover, and marry some Eddie Burke, or she might recklessly or deliberately go and do something foolish. On the other hand if she tired of me, then her whole life would be before her with beautiful vistas of Eddie Burkes and marriage rings and twins and Harlem flats and Heaven knows what. As I strolled along through the trees by the Washington Arch, I decided that she should find a substantial friend in me anyway and the future could take care of itself. Then I went into the house and put on my evening dress for the little faintly perfumed note on my dresser said, "Have a cab at the stage door at eleven," and the note was signed "Edith Carmichel, Metropolitan Theater."

I took supper that night, or rather we took supper, Miss Carmichel and I, at Solari's and the dawn was just beginning to gild the cross on the Memorial Church as I entered Washington Square after leaving Edith at the Brunswick. There was not a soul in the park as I passed among the trees and took the walk which leads from the Garibaldi statue to the Hamilton Apartment House, but as I passed the church-yard I saw a figure sitting on the stone steps. In spite of myself a chill crept over me at the sight of the white puffy face, and I hastened to pass. Then he said something which might have been addressed to me or might merely have been a mutter to himself, but a sudden furious anger flamed up within me that such a creature should address me. For an instant I felt like wheeling about and smashing my stick over his head, but I walked on, and entering the Hamilton went to my apartment. For some time I tossed about the bed trying to get the sound of his voice out of my ears, but could not. If filled my head, that muttering sound, like thick oily smoke from a fat-rendering vat or an odor of noisome decay. And as I lay and tossed about, the voice in my ears seemed more distinct, and I began to understand the words he had muttered. They came to me slowly as if I had forgotten them, and at last I could make some sense out of the sounds. It was this:

"Have you found the Yellow Sign?"

"Have you found the Yellow Sign?"

"Have you found the Yellow Sign?"

I was furious. What did he mean by that? Then with a curse upon him and his I rolled over and went to sleep, but when I awoke later I looked pale and haggard, for I had dreamed the dream of the night before and it troubled me more than I cared to think.

I dressed and went down into my studio. Tessie sat by the window, but as I came in she rose and put both arms around my neck for an innocent kiss. She looked so sweet and dainty that I kissed her again and then sat down before the easel.

"Hello! Where's the study I began yesterday?" I asked.

Tessie looked conscious, but did not answer. I began to hunt among the piles of canvases, saying, "Hurry up, Tess, and get ready; we must take advantage of the morning light."

When at last I gave up the search among the other canvases and turned to look around the room for the missing study I noticed Tessie standing by the screen with her clothes still on.

"What's the matter," I asked, "don't you feel well?"

"Yes."

"Then hurry."

"Do you want me to pose as—as I have always posed?"

Then I understood. Here was a new complication. I had lost, of course, the best nude model I had ever seen. I looked at Tessie. Her face was scarlet. Alas! Alas! We had eaten of the tree of knowledge, and Eden and native innocence were dreams of the past—I mean for her.

I suppose she noticed the disappointment on my face, for she said: "I will pose if you wish. The study is behind the screen here where I put it."

"No," I said, "we will begin something new;" and I went into my wardrobe and picked out a Moorish costume which fairly blazed with tinsel. It was a genuine costume, and Tessie retired to the screen with it enchanted. When she came forth again I was astonished. Her long black hair was bound above her forehead with a circlet of turquoises, and the ends curled about her glittering girdle. Her feet were encased in the embroidered pointed slippers and the skirt of her costume, curiously wrought with arabesques in silver, fell to her ankles. The deep metallic blue vest embroidered with silver and the short Mauresque jacket spangled and sewn with turquoises became her wonderfully. She came up to me and held up her face smiling. I slipped my hand into my pocket and drawing out a gold chain with a cross attached, dropped it over her head.

"It's yours, Tessie."

"Mine?" she faltered.

"Yours. Now go and pose." then with a radiant smile she ran behind the screen and presently reappeared with a little box on which was written my name.

"I had intended to give it to you when I went home tonight," she said, "but I can't wait now."

I opened the box. On the pink cotton inside lay a clasp of black onyx, on which was inlaid a curious symbol or letter in gold. It was neither Arabic nor Chinese, nor as I found afterwards did it belong to any human script.

"It's all I had to give you for a keepsake," she said, timidly.

I was annoyed, but I told her how much I should prize it, and promised to wear it always. She fastened it on my coat beneath the lapel.

"How foolish, Tess, to go and buy me such a beautiful thing as this," I said.

"I did not buy it," she laughed.

Then she told me how she had found it one day while coming from the Aquarium in the Battery, how she had advertised it and watched the papers, but at last gave up all hopes of finding the owner.

"That was last winter," she said, "the very day I had the first horrid dream about the hearse."

I remembered my dream of the previous night but said nothing, and presently my charcoal was flying over a new canvas, and Tessie stood motionless on the model stand.

III

The day following was a disastrous one for me. While moving a framed canvas from one easel to another my foot slipped on the polished floor and I fell heavily on both wrists. There were so badly sprained that it was useless to attempt to hold a brush, and I was obliged to wander about the studio, glaring at unfinished drawings and sketches until despair seized me and I sat down to smoke and twiddle my thumbs with rage. The rain blew against the windows and rattled on the roof of the church, driving me into a nervous fit with its interminable patter. Tessie sat sewing by the window, and every now and then raised her head and looked at me with such innocent compassion that I began to feel ashamed of my irritation and looked about for something to occupy me. I had read all the papers and all the books in the library, but for the sake of something to do I went to the bookcases and shoved them open with my elbow. I knew every volume by its color and examined them all, passing slowly around the library and whistling to keep up my spirits. I was turning to go into the dining-room when my eye fell upon a book bound in serpent skin, standing in a corner of the top shelf of the last bookcase. I did not remember it and from the floor could not decipher the pale lettering on the back, so I went to the smoking-room and called Tessie. She came in from the studio and climbed up to reach the book.

"What is it?" I asked.

" 'The King in Yellow.'"

I was dumfounded. Who had placed it there? How came it in my rooms? I had long ago decided that I should never open that book, and nothing on earth could have persuaded me to buy it. Fearful lest curiosity might tempt me to open it, I had never even looked at it in book-stores. If I ever had had any curiosity to read it, the awful tragedy of young Castaigne, who I knew, prevented me from exploring its wicked pages. I had always refused to listen to any description of it, and indeed, nobody ever ventured to discuss the second part aloud, so I had absolutely no knowledge of what those leaves might reveal. I stared at the poisonous mottled binding as I would at a snake.

"Don't touch it, Tessie," I said; "come down."

Of course my admonition was enough to arouse her curiosity, and before I could prevent it she took the book and, laughing, danced off into the studio with it. I called to her but she slipped away with a tormenting smile at my helpless hands, and I followed her with some impatience.

"Tessie!" I cried, entering the library, "listen, I am serious. Put that book away. I do not wish you to open it." The library was empty. I went into both drawing-rooms, then into the bedrooms, laundry, kitchen, and finally returned to the library and began a systematic search. She had hidden herself so well that it was half an hour later when I discovered her crouching white and silent by the latticed window in the store-room above. At first glance I saw she had been punished for her foolishness. "The King in Yellow" lay at her feet, but the book was open at the second part. I looked at Tessie and saw it was too late. She had opened "The King in Yellow." Then I took her by the hand and led her into the studio. She seemed dazed, and when I told her to lie down on the sofa she obeyed me without a word. After a while she closed her eyes and her breathing came regular and deep, but I could not determine whether or not she slept. For a long while I sat silently beside her, but she neither stirred nor spoke, and at last I rose and entering the unused store-room took the book in my least injured hand. It seemed heavy as lead, but I carried it into the studio again; and sitting down on the rug beside the sofa, opened it and read it through from beginning to end.

When, faint with the excess of my emotions, I dropped the volume and leaned wearily back against the sofa, Tessie opened her eyes and looked at me.

We had been speaking for some time in a dull monotonous strain before I realized that we were discussing "The King in Yellow." Oh the sin of writing such words,—words which are clear as crystal, limpid and musical as bubbling springs, words which sparkle and glow like the poisoned diamonds of the Medicis! Oh the wickedness, the hopeless damnation of a soul who could fascinate and paralyze human creatures with such words,—words understood by the ignorant and wise alike, words which are more precious than jewels, more soothing than music, more awful than death!

We talked on, unmindful of the gathering shadows, and she was begging me to throw away the clasp of black onyx quaintly inlaid with what we now knew to be the Yellow Sign. I never shall know why I refused, though even at this hour, here in my bedroom as I write this confession, I should be glad to know *what* it was that prevented me from tearing the Yellow Sign from my breast and casting it into the fire. I am sure I wished to do so, and yet Tessie pleaded with me in vain. Night fell and hours dragged on, but still we murmured to each other of the King and the Pallid

Mask, and midnight sounded from the misty spires in the fog-wrapped city. We spoke of Hastur and of Cassilda, while outside the fog rolled against the blank window-panes as the cloud waves roll and break on the shores of Hali.

The house was very silent now and not a sound came up from the misty streets. Tessie lay among the cushions, her face a gray blot in the gloom, but her hands were clasped in mine and I knew that she knew and read my thoughts as I read hers, for we had understood the mystery of the Hyades and the Phantom of Truth was laid. Then as we answered each other, swiftly, silently, thought on thought, the shadows stirred in the gloom about us, and far in the distant streets we heard a sound. Nearer and nearer it came, the dull crunching wheels, nearer and yet nearer, and now, outside before the door it ceased, and I dragged myself to the window and saw a black-plumed hearse. The gate below opened and shut, and I crept shaking to my door and bolted it, but I knew no bolts, no locks, could keep that creature out who was coming for the Yellow Sign. And now I heard him moving very softly along the hall. Now he was at the door, and the bolts rotted at his touch. Now he had entered. With eyes starting from my head I peered into the darkness, but when he came into the room I did not see him. It was only when I felt him envelope me in his cold soft grasp that I cried out and struggled with deadly fury, but my hands were useless and he tore the onyx clasp from my coat and struck me full in the face. Then, as I fell, I heard Tessie's soft cry and her spirit fled: and while falling I longed to follow her, for I knew that the King in Yellow had opened his tattered mantle and there was only God to cry to now.

I would tell more, but I cannot see what help it will be to the world. As for me I am past human help or hope. As I lie here, writing, careless even whether or not I die before I finish, I can see the doctor gathering up his powders and phials with a vague gesture to the good priest beside me, which I understand.

They will be very curious to know the tragedy—they of the outside world who write books and print millions of newspapers, but I shall write no more, and the father confessor will seal my last words with the seal of sanctity when his holy office is done. They of the outside world may send their creatures into wrecked homes and death-smitten firesides, and their newspapers will batten on blood and tears, but with me their spies must halt before the confessional. They know that Tessie is dead and that I am dying. They know how the people in the house, aroused by an infernal scream, rushed into my room and found one living and two dead, but they do not know what I shall tell them now; they do not know that the doctor said as he pointed to a horrible decomposed heap on the floor—the livid corpse of the watchman from the church: "I have no theory, no explanation. That man must have been dead for months!"

I think I am dying. I wish the priest would—

Again, as in Chambers's own tales, here the play "The King in Yellow" serves as a script for madness for those who read it and are driven mad by it. Its pages become their delusions. But more than this, Wagner's story highlights an insight from Michel Foucault already evident in Chambers, namely that sanity itself may be seen as simply one more comforting delusion, albeit one shared, like the Lovecraftian Dream World, between many dreamers. Sanity, it seems, is the visible tip of a vast submerged iceberg called madness. One's present, like Cassilda's in the story, is illumined by the "recollection" of pasts that have never been present experiences.

One sees, too, in "The River of Night's Dreaming," the doctrine of Jacques Derrida that the meaning of a term is dependent for its meaning precisely on its polar opposite, with the result that all terms bear the trace, are the empty track, of their opposites. It becomes clear that the seeming propriety and prudery of Cassilda's Victorian hosts is not so much given the lie by their secret nocturnal revels, as it is rather the necessary backdrop against which their secret sexuality must be defined. To taste so sweet this forbidden fruit must be forbidden by the very people who rejoice to savor it! They forbid it just so they can delight in violating their own prohibition.

And speaking of Derrida, one also sees in Wagner's tale, as well as in all of Chambers's stories of "The King in Yellow," a prime example of the literary technique of Mise-en-Abyme, or infinite regress, whereby the text is seen to contain a microcosm of the experience of the reading of the text itself. We read of those who read a text called "The King in Yellow" and are swept away to decadent ennui and dangerous visions. But Chambers and Wagner provide only the merest glimpses of this text. We feel frustrated, but then we do not need to know more than the plain fact that it is we who are the enrapt and endangered readers of a text (though a set of stories, not a play) called The King in Yellow. It is as if we are viewing ourselves through the wrong end of the telescope. "The King in Yellow" turns out, then, to be just like the towers of Carcosa which seemingly should appear in front of the moon but in fact lie behind it.

The River of Night's Dreaming

by KARL EDWARD WAGNER

Everywhere: greyness and rain.

The activities bus with its uniformed occupants. The wet pavement that crawled along the crest of the high bluff. The storm-fretted waters of the bay far below. The night itself, gauzy with grey mist and traceries of rain, feebly probed by the wan headlights of the bus.

Greyness and rain merged in a slither of skidding rubber and a protesting bawl of brakes and tearing metal.

For an instant the activities bus paused upon the broken guard rail, hung half-swallowed by the greyness and rain upon the edge of the precipice. Then, with thirty voices swelling a chorus to the screams of rubber and steel, the bus plunged over the edge.

Halfway down it struck glancingly against the limestone face, shearing off wheels amidst a shower of glass and bits of metal, its plunge unchecked. Another carom, and the bus began to break apart, tearing open before its final impact onto the wave-frothed jumble of boulders far below. Water and sound surged upward into the night, as metal crumpled and split open, scattering bits of humanity like seeds flung from a bursting melon.

Briefly those trapped within the submerging bus made despairing noises—in the night they were no more than the cries of kittens, tied in a sack and thrown into the river. Then the waters closed over the tangle of wreckage, and greyness and rain silenced the torrent of sound.

She struggled to the surface and dragged air into her lungs in a shuddering spasm. Treading water, she stared about her—her actions still automatic, for the crushing impact into the dark waters had all but knocked her unconscious. Perhaps for a moment she *had* lost consciousness; she was too dazed to remember anything very clearly. Anything.

Fragments of memory returned. The rain and the night, the activities bus carrying them back to their prison. Then the plunge into darkness, the terror of her companions, metal bursting apart. Alone in another instant, flung helplessly into the night, and the stunning embrace of the waves.

Her thoughts were clearing now. She worked her feet out of her tennis shoes and tugged damp hair away from her face, trying to see where she was. The body of the bus had torn open, she vaguely realized, and she had been thrown out of the wreckage and into the bay. She could see the darker bulk of the cliff looming out of the greyness not far from her, and dimly came the moans and cries of other survivors. She could not see them, but she could imagine their presence, huddled upon the rocks between the water and the vertical bluff.

Soon the failure of the activities bus to return would cause alarm. The gap in the guard rail would be noticed. Rescuers would come, with lights and ropes and stretchers, to pluck them off the rocks and hurry them away in ambulances to the prison's medical ward.

She stopped herself. Without thought, she had begun to swim toward the other survivors. But why? She took stock of her situation. As well as she could judge, she had escaped injury. She could easily join the others where they clung to the rocks, await rescue—and once the doctors were satisfied she was whole and hearty, she would be back on her locked ward again. A prisoner, perhaps until the end of her days.

Far across the bay, she could barely make out the phantom glimmering of the lights of the city. The distance was great—in miles, two? three? more?—for the prison was a long drive beyond the outskirts of the city and around the sparsely settled shore of the bay. But she was athletically trim and a strong swimmer—she exercised regularly to help pass the long days. How many days, she could not remember. She only knew she would not let them take her back to that place.

The rescue workers would soon be here. Once they'd taken care of those who clung to the shoreline, they'd send divers to raise the bus—and when they didn't find her body among those in the wreckage, they'd assume she was drowned, her body washed away. There would surely be others who were missing, others whose bodies even now drifted beneath the bay. Divers and boatmen with drag hooks would search for them. Some they might never find.

Her they would never find.

She turned her back to the cliff and began to swim out into the bay. Slow, patient strokes—she must conserve her strength. This was a dangerous act, she knew, but then they would be all the slower to suspect when they discovered she was missing. The rashness of her decision only meant that the chances of escape were all the better. Certainly, they would search along the shoreline close by the wreck—perhaps use dogs to hunt down any who might have tried to escape along the desolate stretch of high cliffs. But they would not believe that one of their prisoners would attempt to swim across to the distant city—and once she reached the city, no bloodhounds could seek her out there.

The black rise of rock vanished into the grey rain behind her, and with it dwindled the sobbing wails of her fellow prisoners. No longer her fellows. She had turned her back on that existence. Beyond, where lights smeared the distant greyness, she would find a new existence for herself.

For a while she swam a breast stroke, switching to a back stroke whenever she began to tire. The rain fell heavily onto her upturned face; choppy waves spilled into her mouth, forcing her to abandon the back stroke each time before she was fully rested. Just take it slow, take your time, she told herself. Only the distant lights gave any direction to the greyness now. If she tried to turn back, she might swim aimlessly through the darkness, until . . .

Her dress, a drab prison smock, was weighting her down. She hesitated a moment—she would need clothing when she reached the shore, but so encumbered she would never reach the city. She could not waste strength agonizing over her dilemma. There was no choice. She tugged at the buttons. A quick struggle, and she was able to wrench the wet dress over her head and pull it free. She flung the shapeless garment away from her, and it sank into the night. Another struggle, and her socks followed.

She struck out again for the faraway lights. Her bra and panties were no more drag than a swimsuit, and she moved through the water cleanly—berating herself for not having done this earlier. In the rain and the darkness it was impossible to judge how far she had swum. At least halfway, she fervently hoped. The adrenalin that had coursed through her earlier with its glib assurances of strength was beginning to fade, and she became increasingly aware of bruises and wrenched muscles suffered in the wreck.

The lights never appeared to come any closer, and by now she had lost track of time, as well. She wondered whether the flow of the current might not be carrying her away from her destination whenever she rested, and that fear sent new power into her strokes. The brassiere straps chafed her shoulders, but this irritation was scarcely noticed against the gnawing ache of fatigue. She fought down her growing panic, concentrating her entire being upon the phantom lights in the distance.

The lights seemed no closer than the stars might have been—only the stars were already lost in the greyness and rain. At times the city lights vanished as well, blotted out as she labored through a swell. She was cut off from everything in those moments, cut off from space and from time and from reality. There was only the greyness and the rain, pressing her deeper against the dark water. Memories of her past faded—she had always heard that a drowning victim's life flashes before her, but she could scarcely remember any fragment of her life before they had shut her away. Perhaps that memory would return when at last her straining muscles failed, and the water closed over her face in an unrelinquished kiss.

But then the lights *were* closer—she was certain of it this time. True, the lights were fewer than she had remembered, but she knew it must be far into the night after her seemingly endless swim. Hope sped renewed energy into limbs that had moved like a mechanical toy, slowly winding down. There was a current here, she sensed, seeking to drive her away from the lights and back into the limitless expanse she had struggled to escape.

As she fought against the current, she found she could at last make out the shoreline before her. Now she felt a new rush of fear. Sheer walls of stone awaited her. The city had been built along a bluff. She might reach the shore, but she could never climb its rock face.

She had fought too hard to surrender to despair now. Grimly she attacked the current, working her way along the shoreline. It was all but impossible to see anything—only the looming wall of blackness that cruelly barred her from the city invisible upon its heights. Then, beyond her in the night, the blackness seemed to recede somewhat. Scarcely daring to hope, she swam toward this break in the wall. The current steadily increased. Her muscles stabbed with fatigue, but now she had to swim all the harder to keep from being swept away.

The bluff was indeed lower here, but as a defense against the floods, they had built a wall where the natural barrier fell away. She clutched at the mossy stones in desperation—her clawing fingers finding no purchase. The current dragged her back, denying her a moment's respite.

She sobbed a curse. The heavy rains had driven the water to highest levels, leaving no rim of shoreline beneath cliff or dike. But since there was no escape for her along the direction she had come, she forced her aching limbs to fight on against the current. The line of the dike seemed to be curving inward, and she thought surely she could see a break in the barrier of blackness not far ahead.

She made painful progress against the increasing current, and at length was able to understand where she was. The seawall rose above a river that flowed through the city and into the bay. The city's storm sewers swelling its stream, the river rushed in full flood against the man-made bulwark. Its force was almost more than she could swim against now. Again and again she clutched at the slippery face of the wall, striving to gain a hold. Each time the current dragged her back again.

Storm sewers, some of them submerged now, poured into the river from the wall—their cross currents creating whirling eddies that shielded her one moment, tore at her the next, but allowed her to make desperate headway against the river itself. Bits of debris, caught up by the flood, struck at her invisibly. Rats, swimming frenziedly from the flooded sewers, struggled past her, sought to crawl onto her shoulders and face. She hit out at them, heedless of their bites, too intent on fighting the current herself to feel new horror.

A sudden eddy spun her against a recess in the sea wall, and in the next instant her legs bruised against a submerged ledge. She half swam, half-crawled forward, her fingers clawing slime-carpeted steps. Her breath sobbing in relief, she dragged herself out of the water and onto a flight of stone steps set out from the face of the wall.

For a long while she was content to press herself against the wet stone, her aching limbs no longer straining to keep her afloat, her chest hammering in exhaustion. The flood washed against her feet, its level still rising, and a sodden rat clawed onto her leg—finding refuge as she had done. She crawled higher onto the steps, becoming aware of her surroundings once more.

So. She had made it. She smiled shakily and looked back toward the direction she had come. Rain and darkness and distance made an impenetrable barrier, but she imagined the rescue workers must be checking off the names of those they had found. There would be no checkmark beside her name.

She hugged her bare ribs. The night was chill, and she had no protection from the rain. She remembered now that she was almost naked. What would anyone think who saw her like this? Perhaps in the darkness her panties and bra would pass for a bikini—but what would a bather be doing out at this hour and in this place? She might explain that she had been sunbathing, had fallen asleep, taken refuge from the storm, and had then been forced to flee from the rising waters. But when news of the bus wreck spread, anyone who saw her would remember.

She must find shelter and clothing—somewhere. Her chance to escape had been born of the moment; she had not had time yet to think matters through. She only knew she could not let them recapture her now. Whatever the odds against her, she would face them.

She stood up, leaning against the face of the wall until she felt her legs would hold her upright. The flight of steps ran diagonally down from the top of the seawall. There was no railing on the outward face, and the stone was treacherous with slime and streaming water. Painfully, she edged her way upward, trying not to think about the rushing waters below her. If she slipped, there was no way she could check her fall; she would tumble down into the black torrent, and this time there would be no escape.

The climb seemed as difficult as had her long swim, and her aching muscles seemed to rebel against the task of bearing her up the slippery steps, but at length she gained the upper landing and stumbled onto the storm-washed pavement atop the sea wall. She blinked her eyes uncertainly, drawing a long breath. The rain pressed her black hair to her neck and shoulders, sluiced away the muck and filth from her skin.

There were no lights to be seen along here. A balustrade guarded the edge of the seawall, with a gap to give access to the stairs. A street, barren of any traffic at this hour, ran along the top of the wall, and, across the empty street, rows of brick buildings made a second barrier. Evidently she had come upon a district of warehouses and such—and, from all appearances, this section was considerably run-down. There were no streetlights here, but even in the darkness she could sense the disused aspect of the row of buildings with their boarded-over windows and filthy fronts, the brick street with its humped and broken paving.

She shivered. It was doubly fortunate that none were here to mark her sudden appearance. In a section like this, and dressed as she was, it was unlikely that anyone she might encounter would be of Good Samaritan inclinations.

Clothing. She had to find clothing. Any sort of clothing. She darted across the uneven paving and into the deeper shadow of the building fronts. Her best bet would be to find a shop: perhaps some sordid second-hand place such as this street might well harbor, a place without elaborate burglar alarms, if possible. She could break in, or at worse find a window display and try her luck at smash and grab. Just a simple raincoat would make her feel far less vulnerable. Eventually she would need money, shelter and food, until she could leave the city for someplace faraway.

As she crept along the deserted street, she found herself wondering whether she could find anything at all here. Doorways were padlocked and boarded over; behind rusted gratings, windows showed rotting planks and dirty shards of glass. The waterfront street seemed to be completely abandoned—a deserted row of ancient buildings enclosing forgotten wares, cheaper to let rot than to haul away, even as it was cheaper to let these brick hulks stand than to pull them down. Even the expected winos and derelicts seemed to have deserted this section of the city. She began to wish she might encounter at least a passing car.

The street had not been deserted by the rats. Probably they had been driven into the night by the rising waters. Once she began to notice them, she realized there were more and more of them—creeping boldly along the street. Huge, knowing brutes; some of them as large as cats. They didn't seem to be afraid of her, and at times she thought they might be gathering in a pack to follow her. She had heard of rats attacking children and invalids, but surely . . . She wished she were out of this district.

The street plunged on atop the riverside, and still there were no lights or signs of human activity. The rain continued to pour down from the drowned night skies. She began to think about crawling into one of the dark warehouses to wait for morning, then thought of being alone in a dark, abandoned building with a closing pack of rats. She walked faster.

Some of the empty buildings showed signs of former grandeur, and she hoped she was coming toward a better section of the river-front. Elaborate entranceways of fluted columns and marble steps gave onto the street. Grotesque Victorian facades and misshapen statuary presented imposing fronts to buildings filled with the same musty decay as the brick warehouses. She must be reaching the old merchants' district of the city, although these structures as well appeared long abandoned, waiting only for the wrecking ball of urban renewal. She wished she could escape this street, for there seemed to be more rats in the darkness behind her than she could safely ignore.

Perhaps she might find an alleyway between buildings that would let her flee this waterfront section and enter some inhabited neighborhood—for it became increasingly evident that this street had long been derelict. She peered closely at each building, but never could she find a gap between them. Without a light, she dared not enter blindly and try to find her way through some ramshackle building.

She paused for a moment and listened. For some while she had heard a scramble of wet claws and fretful squealings from the darkness behind her. Now she heard only the rain. Were the rats silently closing in on her?

She stood before a columned portico—a bank or church?—and gazed into the darker shadow, wondering whether she might seek shelter. A statue—she supposed it was of an angel or some symbolic figure—stood before one of the marble columns. She could discern little of its features, only that it must have been malformed—presumably by vandalism—for it was hunched over and appeared to be supported against the column by thick cables or ropes. She could not see its face.

Not liking the silence, she hurried on again. Once past the portico, she turned quickly and looked back—to see if the rats were creeping after her. She saw no rats. She could see the row of columns. The misshapen figure was no longer there.

She began to run then. Blindly, not thinking where her panic drove her.

To her right, there was only the balustrade, marking the edge of the wall, and the rushing waters below. To her left, the unbroken row of derelict buildings. Behind her, the night and the rain, and something whose presence had driven away the pursuing rats. And ahead of her—she was close enough to see it now—the street made a dead end against a rock wall.

Stumbling toward it, for she dared not turn back the way she had run, she saw that the wall was not unbroken—that a stairway climbed steeply to a terrace up above. Here the bluff rose high against the river once again, so that the seawall ended against the rising stone. There were buildings crowded against the height, fronted upon the terrace a level above. In one of the windows, a light shone through the rain.

Her breath shook in ragged gasps and her legs were rubbery, but she forced herself to half run, half clamber up the rain-slick steps to the terrace above. Here, again a level of brick paving and a balustrade to guard the edge. Boarded windows and desolate facades greeted her from a row of decrepit houses, shouldered together on the rise. The light had been to her right, out above the river.

She could see it clearly now. It beckoned from the last house on the terrace—a looming Victorian pile built over the bluff. A casement window, level with the far end of the terrace, opened out onto a neglected garden. She climbed over the low wall that separated the house from the terrace, and crouched outside the curtained window.

Inside, a comfortable-looking sitting room with old-fashioned appointments. An older woman was crocheting, while in a chair beside her a young woman, dressed in a maid's costume, was reading aloud from a book. Across the corner room, another casement window looked out over the black water far below.

Had her fear and exhaustion been less consuming, she might have taken a less reckless course, might have paused to consider what effect her appearance would make. But she remembered a certain shuffling sound she had heard as she scrambled up onto the terrace, and the way the darkness had seemed to gather upon the top of the stairway when she glanced back a moment gone. With no thought but to escape the night, she tapped her knuckles sharply against the casement window.

At the tapping at the window, the older woman looked up from her work, the maid let the yellow bound volume drop onto her white apron. They stared at the casement, not so much frightened as if uncertain of what they had heard. The curtain inside veiled her presence from them.

Please! she prayed, without a voice to cry out. She tapped more insistently, pressing herself against the glass. They would see that she was only a girl, see her distress.

They were standing now, the older woman speaking too quickly for her to catch the words. The maid darted to the window, fumbled with its latch. Another second, and the casement swung open, and she tumbled into the room.

She knelt in a huddle on the floor, too exhausted to move any farther. Her body shook and water dripped from her bare flesh. She felt like some half-drowned kitten, plucked from the storm to shelter. Vaguely, she could hear their startled queries, the protective clash as the casement latch closed out the rain and the curtain swept across the night.

The maid had brought a coverlet and was furiously towelling her dry. Her attentions reminded her that she must offer some sort of account of herself—before her benefactors summoned the police, whose investigation would put a quick end to her freedom.

"I'm all right now," she told them shakily. "Just let me get my breath back, get warm."

"What's your name, child?" the older woman inquired solicitously. "Camilla, bring some hot tea."

She groped for a name to tell them. "Cassilda." The maid's name had put this in mind, and it was suited to her surroundings. "Cassilda Archer." Dr. Archer would indeed be interested in *that* appropriation.

"You poor child! How did you come here? Were you . . . attacked?"

Her thoughts worked quickly. Satisfy their curiosity, but don't make them suspicious. Justify your predicament, but don't alarm them.

"I was hitchhiking." She spoke in uncertain bursts. "A man picked me up. He took me to a deserted section near the river. He made me take off my clothes. He was going to . . . " She didn't have to feign her shudder.

"Here's the tea, Mrs. Castaigne. I've added a touch of brandy."

"Thank you, Camilla. Drink some of this, dear."

She used the interruption to collect her thoughts. The two women were alone here, or else any others would have been summoned.

"When he started to pull down his trousers . . . I hurt him. Then I jumped out and ran as hard as I could. I don't think he came after me, but then I was wandering, lost in the rain. I couldn't find anyone to help me. I didn't have anything with me except my underwear. I think a tramp was following me. Then I saw your light and ran toward it.

"Please don't call the police!" She forestalled their obvious next move. "I'm not hurt. I know I couldn't face the shame of a rape investigation. Besides, they'd never be able to catch that man by now."

"But surely you must want me to contact someone for you."

"There's no one who would care. I'm on my own. That man has my pack and the few bucks in my handbag. If you could please let me stay here for the rest of the night, lend me some clothes just for tomorrow, and in the morning I'll phone a friend who can wire me some money."

Mrs. Castaigne hugged her protectively. "You poor child! What you've been through! Of course you'll stay with us for the night—and don't fret about having to relive your terrible ordeal for a lot of leering policemen! Tomorrow there'll be plenty of time for you to decide what you'd like to do.

"Camilla, draw a nice hot bath for Cassilda. She's to sleep in Constance's room, so see that there's a warm comforter, and lay out a gown for her. And you, Cassilda, must drink another cup of this tea. As badly chilled as you are, child, you'll be fortunate indeed to escape your death of pneumonia!"

Over the rim of her cup, the girl examined the room and its occupants more closely. The sitting room was distinctly old-fashioned—furnished like a parlor in an old photograph, or like a set from some movie that was supposed to be taking place at the turn of the century. Even the lights were either gas or kerosene. Probably this house hadn't changed much since years ago, before the neighborhood had begun to decay. Anyone would have to be a little eccentric to keep staying on here, although probably this place was all Mrs. Castaigne had, and Mr. Castaigne wasn't in evidence. The house and property couldn't be worth much in this neighborhood, although the furnishings might fetch a little money as antiques—she was no judge of that, but everything looked to be carefully preserved.

Mrs. Castaigne seemed well fitted to this room and its furnishings. Hers was a face that might belong to a woman of forty or sixty—well featured, but too stern for a younger woman, yet without the lines and age marks of an elderly lady. Her figure was still very good, and she wore a tight-waisted, ankle-length dress that seemed to belong to the period of the house. The hands that stroked her bare shoulders were strong and white and unblemished, and the hair she wore piled atop her head was as black as the girl's own.

It occurred to her that Mrs. Castaigne must surely be too young for this house. Probably she was a daughter, or, more likely, a granddaughter of its original owners—a widow who lived alone with her young maid. And who might Constance be, whose room she was to sleep in?

"Your bath is ready now, Miss Archer." Camilla reappeared. Wrapped in the coverlet, the girl followed her. Mrs. Castaigne helped support her, for her legs had barely strength to stand, and she felt ready to pass out from fatigue.

The bathroom was spacious—steamy from the vast, claw-footed tub, and smelling of bath salts. Its plumbing and fixtures were no more modern than the rest of the house. Camilla entered with her, and to her surprise, helped her remove her scant clothing and assisted her into the tub. She was too tired to feel ill at ease at this unaccustomed show of attention, and when the maid began to rub her back with scented soap, she sighed at the luxury.

"Who else lives here?" she asked casually.

"Only Mrs. Castaigne and myself, Miss Archer."

"Mrs. Castaigne mentioned someone—Constance?—whose room I am to have."

"Miss Castaigne is no longer with us, Miss Archer."

"Please call me Cassilda. I don't like to be so formal."

"If that's what you wish to be called, of course . . . Cassilda."

Camilla couldn't be very far from her own age, she guessed. Despite the old-fashioned maid's outfit—black dress and stockings with frilled white apron and cap—the other girl was probably no more than in her early twenties. The maid wore her long blonde hair in an upswept topknot like her mistress, and she supposed she only followed Mrs. Castaigne's preferences. Camilla's figure was full—much more buxom than her own boyish slenderness—and her cinch-waised costume accented this. Her eyes were a bright blue, shining above a straight nose and wide-mouthed face.

"You've hurt yourself." Camilla ran her fingers tenderly along the bruises that marred her ribs and legs.

"There was a struggle. And I fell in the darkness—I don't know how many times."

"And you've cut yourself." Camilla lifted the other girl's black hair away from her neck. "Here on your shoulders and throat. But I don't believe it's anything to worry about." Her fingers carefully touched the livid scrapes. "Are you certain there isn't someone whom we should let know of your safe whereabouts?"

"There is no one who would care. I am alone."

"Poor Cassilda."

"All I want is to sleep," she murmured. The warm bath was easing the ache from her flesh, leaving her deliciously sleepy.

Camilla left her, to return with large towels. The maid helped her from the tub, wrapping her in one towel as she dried her with another. She felt faint with drowsiness, allowed herself to relax against the blonde girl. Camilla was very strong, supporting her easily as she towelled her small breasts. Camilla's fingers found the parting of her thighs, lingered, then returned again in a less than casual touch.

Her dark eyes were wide as she stared into Camilla's luminous blue gaze, but she felt too pleasurably relaxed to object when the maid's touch became more intimate. Her breath caught, and held.

"You're very warm, Cassilda."

"Hurry, Camilla." Mrs. Castaigne spoke from the doorway. "The poor child is about to drop. Help her into her nightdress."

Past wondering, she lifted her arms to let Camilla drape the beribboned lawn nightdress over her head and to her ankles. In another moment she was being ushered into a bedroom, furnished in the fashion of the rest of the house, and to an ornate brass bed whose mattress swallowed her up like a wave of foam. She felt the quilts drawn over her, sensed their presence hovering over her, and then she slipped into a deep sleep of utter exhaustion.

"Is there no one?"

"Nothing at all."

"Of course. How else could she be here? She is ours."

Her dreams were troubled by formless fears—deeply disturbing as experienced, yet their substance was already forgotten when she awoke at length on the echo of her outcry. She stared about her anxiously, uncertain where she was. Her disorientation was the same as when she awakened after receiving shock, only this place wasn't a ward, and the woman who entered the room wasn't one of her wardens.

"Good morning, Cassilda," The maid drew back the curtains to let long shadows streak across the room. "I should say, good evening, as it's almost that time. You've slept throughout the day, poor dear."

Cassilda? Yes, that was she. Memory came tumbling back in a confused jumble. She raised herself from her pillows and looked about the bedchamber she had been too tired to examine before. It was distinctly a woman's room—a young woman's—and she remembered that it had been Mrs. Castaigne's daughter's room. It scarcely seemed to have been unused for very long: the brass bed was brightly polished, the walnut of the wardrobe, the chests of drawers and the dressing table made a rich glow, and the gay pastels of the curtains and wallpaper offset the gravity of the high, tinned ceiling and parquetry floor. Small oriental rugs and pillows upon the chairs and chaise lounge made bright points of color. Again she thought of a movie set, for the room was altogether lacking in anything modern. She knew very little about antiques, but she guessed that the style of furnishings must go back before the First World War.

Camilla was arranging a single red rose in a crystal bud vase upon the dressing table. She caught her gaze in the mirror. "Did you sleep well, Cassilda? I thought I heard you cry out, just as I knocked."

"A bad dream, I suppose. But I slept well. I don't usually." They had made her take pills to sleep.

"Are you awake, Cassilda? I thought I heard your voices." Mrs. Castaigne smiled from the doorway and crossed to her bed. She was dressed much the same as the night before.

"I didn't mean to sleep so long," she apologized.

"Poor child! I shouldn't wonder that you slept so, after your dreadful ordeal. Do you feel strong enough to take a little soup?"

"I really must be going. I can't impose any further."

"I won't hear anymore of that, my dear. Of course you'll be staying with us until you're feeling stronger." Mrs. Castaigne sat beside her on the bed, placed a cold hand against her brow. "Why, Cassilda, your face is simply aglow. I do hope you haven't taken a fever. Look, your hands are positively trembling!"

"I feel all right." In fact, she did not. She did feel as though she were running a fever, and her muscles were so sore that she wasn't sure she could walk. The trembling didn't concern her: the injections they gave her every two weeks made her shake, so they gave her little pills to stop the shaking. Now she didn't have those pills, but since it was time again for another shot, the injection and its side effects would soon wear off.

"I'm going to bring you some tonic, dear. And Camilla will bring you some good nourishing soup, which you must try to take. Poor Cassilda, if we don't nurse you carefully, I'm afraid you may fall dangerously ill."

"But I can't be such a nuisance to you," she protested, as a matter of form. "I really must be going."

"Where to, dear child?" Mrs. Castaigne held her hands gravely. "Have you someplace else to go? Is there someone you wish to inform of your safety?"

"No," she admitted, trying to make everything sound right. "I've no place to go; there's no one who matters. I was on my way down the coast, hoping to find a job during the resort season. I know one or two old girlfriends who could put me up until I get settled."

"See there. Then there's no earthly reason why you can't just stay here until you're feeling strong again. Why, perhaps I might find a position for you myself. But we shall discuss these things later, when you're feeling well. For the moment, just settle back on your pillow and let us help you get well."

Mrs. Castaigne bent over her, kissed her on the forehead. Her lips were cool. "How lovely you are, Cassilda," she smiled, patting her hand.

She smiled back, and returned the other woman's firm grip. She'd seen no sign of a television or radio here, and an old eccentric like Mrs. Castaigne probably didn't even read the newspapers. Even if Mrs. Castaigne had heard about the bus wreck, she plainly was too overjoyed at having a visitor to break her lonely routine to concern herself with a possible escapee—assuming they hadn't just listed her as drowned. She couldn't have hoped for a better place to hide out until things cooled off.

The tonic had a bitter licorice taste and made her drowsy, so that she fell asleep not long after Camilla carried away her tray. Despite her long sleep throughout the day, fever and exhaustion drew her back down again—although her previous sleep robbed this one of restful oblivion. Again came troubled dreams, this time cutting more harshly into her consciousness.

She dreamed of Dr. Archer—her stern face and mannish shoulders craning over her bed. Her wrists and ankles were fixed to each corner of the bed by padded leather cuffs. Dr. Archer was speaking to her in a scolding tone, while her wardens were pulling up her skirt, dragging down her panties. A syringe gleamed in Dr. Archer's hand, and there was a sharp stinging in her buttock.

She was struggling again, but to no avail. Dr. Archer was shouting at her, and a stout nurse was tightening the last few buckles of the straitjacket that bound her arms to her chest in a loveless hug. The straps were so tight she could hardly draw breath, and while she could not understand what Dr. Archer was saying, she recognized the spurting needle that Dr. Archer thrust into her.

She was strapped tightly to the narrow bed, her eyes staring at the gray ceiling as they wheeled her through the corridors to Dr. Archer's special room. Then they stopped; they were there, and Dr. Archer was bending over her again. Then came the sting in her arm as they penetrated her veins, the helpless headlong rush of the drug—*and Dr. Archer smiles and turns to her machine, and the current blasts into her tightly strapped skull and her body arches and strains against the restraints and her scream strangles against the rubber gag clenched in her teeth.*

But the face that looks into hers now is not Dr. Archer's, and the hands that shake her are not cruel.

"Cassilda! Cassilda! Wake up! It's only a nightmare!"

Camilla's blonde-and-blue face finally focused into her awakening vision.

"Only a nightmare," Camilla reassured her. "Poor darling." The hands that held her shoulders lifted to smooth her black hair from her eyes, to cup her face. Camilla bent over her, kissed her gently on her dry lips.

"What is it?" Mrs. Castaigne, wearing her nightdress and carrying a candle, came anxiously into the room.

"Poor Cassilda has had bad dreams," Camilla told her. "And her face feels ever so warm."

"Dear child!" Mrs. Castaigne set down her candlestick. "She must take some more tonic at once. Perhaps you should sit with her, Camilla, to see that her sleep is untroubled."

"Certainly, madame. I'll just fetch the tonic."

"Please, don't bother . . . " But the room became a vertiginous blur as she tried to sit up. She slumped back and closed her eyes tightly for a moment. Her body *did* feel feverish, her mouth dry, and the trembling when she moved her hand to take the medicine glass was so obvious that Camilla shook her head and held the glass to her lips herself. She swallowed dutifully, wondering how much of this was a reaction to the Prolixin still in her flesh. The injection would soon be wearing off, she knew, for when she smiled back at her nurses, the sharp edges of color were beginning to show once again through the haze the medication drew over her perception.

"I'll be all right soon," she promised them.

"Then do try to sleep, darling." Mrs. Castaigne patted her arm. "You must regain your strength. Camilla will be here to watch over you."

"Be certain that the curtains are drawn against any night vapors," she directed her maid. "Call me, if necessary."

"Of course, madame. I'll not leave her side."

She was dreaming again—or dreaming still.

Darkness surrounded her like a black leather mask, and her body shook with uncontrollable spasms. Her naked flesh was slick with chill sweat, although her mouth was burning dry. She moaned and tossed— striving to awaken order from out of the damp blackness, but the blackness only embraced her with smothering tenacity.

Cold lips were crushing her own, thrusting a cold tongue into her feverish mouth, bruising the skin of her throat. Fingers, slender and strong, caressed her breasts, held her nipples to hungry lips. Her hands thrashed about, touched smooth flesh. It came to her that her eyes were indeed wide open, that the darkness was so profound she could no more than sense the presence of other shapes close beside her.

Her own movements were languid, dreamlike. Through the spasms that racked her flesh, she became aware of a perverse thrill of ecstasy. Her fingers brushed somnolently against the cool flesh that crouched over her, with no more purpose or strength than the drifting limbs of a drowning victim.

A compelling lassitude bound her, even as the blackness blinded her. She seemed to be drifting away, apart from her body, apart from her dream, into deeper, even deeper darkness. The sensual arousal that lashed her lost reality against the lethargy and fever that held her physically, and rising out of the eroticism of her delirium shrilled whispers of underlying revulsion and terror.

One pair of lips imprisoned her mouth and throat now, sucking at her breath, while other lips crept down across her breasts, hovered upon her navel, then pounced upon the opening of her thighs. Her breath caught in a shudder, was sucked away by the lips that held her mouth, as the coldness began to creep into her burning flesh.

She felt herself smothering, unable to draw breath, so that her body arched in panic, her limbs thrashed aimlessly. Her efforts to break away were as ineffectual as was her struggle to awaken. The lips that stole her breath released her, but only for a moment. In the darkness, she felt other flesh pinion her tossing body, move against her with cool strength. Chill fire tormented her loins, and as she opened her mouth to cry out, or to sigh, smooth thighs pressed down onto her cheeks, and coldness gripped her breath. Mutely, she obeyed the needs that commanded her, that overwhelmed her, and through the darkness blindly flowed her silent scream of ecstasy and of horror.

Cassilda awoke.

Sunlight spiked into her room—the colored panes creating a false prism effect. Camilla, who had been adjusting the curtains, turned and smiled at the sound of her movement.

"Good morning, Cassilda. Are you feeling better this morning?"

"A great deal better." Cassilda returned her smile. "I feel as if I'd slept for days." She frowned slightly, suddenly uncertain.

Camilla touched her forehead. "Your fever has left you; Mrs. Castaigne will be delighted to learn that. You've slept away most of yesterday and all through last night. Shall I bring your breakfast tray now?"

"Please—I'm famished. But I really think I should be getting up."

"After breakfast, if you wish. And now I'll inform madame that you're feeling much better."

Mrs. Castaigne appeared as the maid was clearing away the breakfast things. "How very much better you look today, Cassilda. Camilla tells me you feel well enough to sit up."

"I really can't play the invalid and continue to impose upon your hospitality any longer. Would it be possible that you might lend me some clothing? My own garments . . . " Cassilda frowned, trying to remember why she had burst in on her benefactress virtually naked.

"Certainly, my dear." Mrs. Castaigne squeezed her shoulder. "You must see if some of my daughter's garments won't fit you. You cannot be very different in size from Constance, I'm certain. Camilla will assist you."

She was lightheaded when first she tried to stand, but Cassilda clung to the brass bedposts until her legs felt strong enough to hold her. The maid was busying herself at the chest of drawers, removing items of clothing from beneath neat coverings of tissue paper. A faint odor of dried rose petals drifted from a sachet beneath the folded garments.

"I do hope you'll overlook it if these are not of the latest mode, "Mrs. Castaigne was saying. "It has been some time since Constance was with us here."

"Your daughter is . . . ?"

"Away."

Cassilda declined to intrude further. There was a dressing screen behind which she retired, while Mrs. Castaigne waited upon the chaise lounge. Trailing a scent of dried roses from the garments she carried, Camilla joined her behind the screen and helped her out of the nightdress.

There were undergarments of fine silk, airy lace and gauzy pastels. Cassilda found herself puzzled, both from their unfamiliarity and at the same time their familiarity, and while her thoughts struggled with the mystery, her hands seemed to dress her body with practiced movements. First the chemise, knee-length and trimmed with tight lace and ribbons. Seated upon a chair, she drew on pale stockings of patterned silk, held at mid-thigh by beribboned garters. Then silk knickers, open front and back and tied at the waist, trimmed with lace and ruching where they flared below her stocking tops. A frilled petticoat fell almost to her ankles.

"I won't need that," Cassilda protested. Camilla had presented her with a boned corset of white-and-sky broché.

"Nonsense, my dear," Mrs. Castaigne directed, coming around the dressing screen to oversee. "You may think of me as old-fashioned, but I insist that you not ruin your figure."

Cassilda submitted, suddenly wondering why she had thought anything out of the ordinary about it. She hooked the straight busk together in front, while Camilla gathered the laces at the back. The maid tugged sharply at the laces, squeezing out her breath. Cassilda bent forward and steadied herself against the back of the chair, as Camilla braced a knee against the small of her back, pulling the laces as tight as possible before tying them. Once her corset was secured, she drew over it a camisole of white cotton lace trimmed with ribbon, matching her petticoat. Somewhat dizzy, Cassilda sat stiffly before the dressing table, while the maid brushed out her long, black hair and gathered it in a loose knot atop her head, pinning it in place with tortoise-shell combs. Opening the wardrobe, Camilla found her a pair of shoes with high heels that mushroomed outward at the bottom, which fit her easily.

"How lovely, Cassilda!" Mrs. Castaigne approved. "One would scarcely recognize you as the poor drowned thing that came out of the night!"

Cassilda stood up and examined herself in the full-length dressing mirror. It was as if she looked upon a stranger, and yet she knew she looked upon herself. The corset constricted her waist and forced her slight figure into an "S" curve—hips back, bust forward—imparting an unexpected opulence, further enhanced by the gauzy profusion of lace and silk. Her face, dark-eyed and finely boned, returned her gaze watchfully from behind a lustrous pile of black hair. She touched herself, almost in wonder, almost believing that the reflection in the mirror was a photograph of someone else.

Camilla selected for her a long-sleeved linen shirtwaist, buttoned at the cuffs and all the way to her throat, then helped her into a skirt of some darker material that fell away from her cinched waist to her ankles. Cassilda studied herself in the mirror, while the maid fussed about her.

I look like someone in an old illustration—a Gibson girl, she thought, then puzzled at her thought.

Through the open window she could hear the vague noises of the city, and for the first time she realized that intermingled with these familiar sounds was the clatter of horses' hooves upon the brick pavement.

"You simply must not say anything more about leaving us, Cassilda," Mrs. Castaigne insisted, laying a hand upon the girl's knee as she leaned toward her confidentially.

Beside her on the settee, Cassilda felt the pressure of her touch through the rustling layers of petticoat. It haunted her, this flowing whisper of sound that came with her every movement, for it seemed at once strange and again familiar—a shivery sigh of silk against silk, like the whisk of dry snow sliding across stone. She smiled, holding her teacup with automatic poise, and wondered that such little, commonplace sensations should seem at all out of the ordinary to her. Even the rigid embrace of her corset seemed quite familiar to her now, so that she sat gracefully at ease, listening to her benefactress, while a part of her thoughts stirred in uneasy wonder.

"You have said yourself that you have no immediate prospects," Mrs. Castaigne continued. "I shouldn't have to remind you of the dangers the city holds for unattached young women. You were extremely fortunate in your escape from those white slavers who had abducted you. Without family or friends to question your disappearance—well, I shan't suggest what horrible fate awaited you."

Cassilda shivered at the memory of her escape—a memory as formless and uncertain, beyond her *need* to escape, as that of her life prior to her abduction. She had made only vague replies to Mrs. Castaigne's gentle questioning, nor was she at all certain which fragments of her story were half-truths, or lies.

Of one thing she was certain beyond all doubt: the danger from which she had fled awaited her beyond the shelter of this house.

"It has been so lonely here since Constance went away," Mrs. Castaigne was saying. "Camilla is a great comfort to me, but nonetheless she has her household duties to occupy her, and I have often considered engaging a companion. I should be only too happy if you would consent to remain with us in this position—at least for the present time."

"You're much too kind! Of course I'll stay."

"I promise you that your duties shall be no more onerous than to provide amusements for a rather old-fashioned lady of retiring disposition. I hope it won't prove too dull for you, my dear."

"It suits my temperament perfectly," Cassilda assured her. "I am thoroughly content to follow quiet pursuits within doors."

"Wonderful!" Mrs. Castaigne took her hands. "Then it's settled. I know Camilla will be delighted to have another young spirit about the place. And you may relieve her of some of her tasks."

"What shall I do?" Cassilda begged her, overjoyed at her good fortune.

"Would you read to me, please, my dear? I find it so relaxing to the body and so stimulating to the mind. I've taken up far too much of Camilla's time from her chores, having her read to me for hours on end."

"Of course." Cassilda returned Camilla's smile as she entered the sitting room to collect the tea things. From her delight, it was evident that the maid had been listening from the hallway. "What would you like me to read to you?"

"That book over there beneath the lamp." Mrs. Castaigne indicated a volume bound in yellow cloth. "It is a recent drama—and a most curious work, as you shall quickly see. Camilla was reading it to me on the night you came to us."

Taking up the book, Cassilda again experienced a strange sense of unaccountable *déjà vu*, and she wondered where she might previously have read *The King in Yellow*, if indeed she ever had.

"I believe we are ready to begin the second act," Mrs. Castaigne told her.

Cassilda was reading in bed when Camilla knocked tentatively at her door. She set aside her book with an almost furtive movement. *"Entrez vous."*

"I was afraid you might already be asleep," the maid explained, "but then I saw light beneath your door. I'd forgotten to bring you your tonic before retiring."

Camilla, *en déshabillé*, carried in the medicine glass on a silver tray. Her fluttering lace and pastels seemed a pretty contrast to the black maid's uniform she ordinarily wore.

"I wasn't able to go to sleep just yet," Cassilda confessed, sitting up in bed. "I was reading."

Camilla handed her the tonic. "Let me see. Ah, yes. What a thoroughly wicked book to be reading in bed!"

"Have you read *The King in Yellow?*"

"I have read it through aloud to madame, and more than once. It is a favorite of hers."

"It is sinful and more than sinful to imbue such decadence with so compelling a fascination. I cannot imagine that anyone could have allowed it to be published. The author must have been mad to pen such thoughts."

"And yet, you read it."

Cassilda made a place for her at the edge of the bed. "Its fascination is too great a temptation to resist. I wanted to read further after Mrs. Castaigne bade me good night."

"It was Constance's book." Camilla huddled close beside her against the pillows. "Perhaps that is why madame cherishes it so."

Cassilda opened the yellow-bound volume to the page she had been reading. Camilla craned her blonde head over her shoulder to read with her. She had removed her corset, and her ample figure swelled against her beribboned chemise. Cassilda in her nightdress felt almost scrawny as she compared her own small bosom to the other girl's.

"Is it not strange?" she remarked. "Here in this decadent drama we read of Cassilda and Camilla."

"I wonder if we two are very much like them," Camilla laughed.

"They are such very dear friends."

"And so are we, are we not?"

"I do so want us to be."

"But you haven't read beyond the second act, dear Cassilda. How can you know what may their fate be?"

"Oh, Camilla!" Cassilda leaned her face back against Camilla's perfumed breasts. "Don't tease me so!"

The blonde girl hugged her fiercely, stroking her back. "Poor, lost Cassilda."

Cassilda nestled against her, listening to the heartbeat beneath her cheek. She was feeling warm and sleepy, for all that the book had disturbed her. The tonic always carried her to dreamy oblivion, and it was pleasant to drift to sleep in Camilla's soft embrace.

"Were you and Constance friends?" she wondered.

"We were the very dearest of friends."

"You must miss her very much."

"No longer."

Cassilda sat at the escritoire in her room, writing in the journal she had found there. Her petticoats crowded against the legs of the writing table as she leaned forward to reach the inkwell. From time to time she paused to stare pensively past the open curtains of her window, upon the deepening blue of the evening sky as it met the angled rooftops of the buildings along the waterfront below.

"I think I should feel content here," she wrote. "Mrs. Castaigne is strict in her demands, but I am certain she takes a sincere interest in my own well-being, and that she has only the kindliest regard for me. My duties during the day are of the lightest nature and consist primarily of reading to Mrs. Castaigne or of singing at the piano while she occupies herself with her needlework, and in all other ways making myself companionable to her in our simple amusements.

"I have offered to assist Camilla at her chores, but Mrs. Castaigne will not have it that I perform other than the lightest household tasks. Camilla is a very dear friend to me, and her sweet attentions easily distract me from what might otherwise become a tedium of sitting about the house day to day. Nonetheless, I have no desire to leave my situation here, nor to adventure into the streets outside the house. We are not in an especially attractive section of the city here, being at some remove from the shops and in a district given over to waterfront warehouses and commercial establishments. We receive no visitors, other than the tradesmen who supply our needs, nor is Mrs. Castaigne of a disposition to wish to seek out the society of others.

"Withal, my instincts suggest that Mrs. Castaigne has sought the existence of a recluse out of some very great emotional distress which has robbed life of its interests for her. It is evident from the attention and instruction she has bestowed upon me that she sees in me a reflection of her daughter, and I am convinced that it is in the loss of Constance where lies the dark secret of her self-imposed withdrawal from the world. I am sensible of the pain Mrs. Castaigne harbors within her breast, for the subject of her daughter's absence is never brought into our conversations, and for this reason I have felt loath to question her, although I am certain that this is the key to the mystery that holds us in this house."

Cassilda concluded her entry with the date: June 7th, 189—

She frowned in an instant's consternation. What *was* the date? How silly. She referred to a previous day's entry, then completed the date. For a moment she turned idly back through her journal, smiling faintly at the many pages of entries that filled the diary, each progressively dated, each penned in the same neat hand as the entry she had just completed.

Cassilda sat at her dressing table in her room. It was night, and she had removed her outer clothing preparatory to retiring. She gazed at her reflection—the gauzy paleness of her chemise, stockings and knickers was framed against Camilla's black maid's uniform as the blonde girl stood behind her, brushing out her dark hair.

Upon the dressing table she had spread out the contents of a tin box she had found in one of the drawers, and she and Camilla had been looking over them as she prepared for bed. There were paper dolls, valentines and greeting cards, illustrations clipped from magazines, a lovely cutout of a swan. She also found a crystal ball that rested upon an ebony cradle. Within the crystal sphere was a tiny house, covered with snow, with trees and a frozen lake and a young girl playing. When Cassilda picked it up, the snow stirred faintly in the transparent fluid that filled the globe. She turned the crystal sphere upside down for a moment, then quickly righted it, and a snowstorm drifted down about the tiny house.

"How wonderful it would be to dwell forever in a crystal fairyland just like the people in this little house," Cassilda remarked, peering into the crystal ball.

Something else seemed to stir within the swirling snowflakes, she thought, but when the snow had settled once more, the tableau was unchanged. No: there was a small mound, there beside the child at play, that she was certain she had not seen before. Cassilda overturned the crystal globe once again, and peered more closely. There it was. Another tiny figure spinning amidst the snowflakes. A second girl. She must have broken loose from the tableau. The tiny figure drifted to rest upon the frozen lake, and the snowflakes once more covered her from view.

"Where is Constance Castaigne?" Cassilda asked.

"Constance . . . became quite ill," Camilla told her carefully. "She was always subject to nervous attacks. One night she suffered one of her fits, and she . . . "

"Camilla!" Mrs. Castaigne's voice from the doorway was stern. "You know how I despise gossip—especially idle gossip concerning another's misfortunes."

The maid's face was downcast. "I'm very sorry, madame. I meant no mischief."

The other woman scowled as she crossed the room. Cassilda wondered if she meant to strike the maid. "Being sorry does not pardon the offense of a wagging tongue. Perhaps a lesson in behavior will improve your manners in the future. Go at once to your room."

"Please, madame . . . "

"Your insolence begins to annoy me, Camilla."

"Please, don't be harsh with her!" Cassilda begged, as the maid hurried from the room. "She was only answering my question."

Standing behind the seated girl, Mrs. Castaigne placed her hands upon her shoulders and smiled down at her. "An innocent question, my dear. However, the subject is extremely painful to me, and Camilla well knows the distress it causes me to hear it brought up. I shall tell you this now, and that shall end the matter. My daughter suffered a severe attack of brain fever. She is confined in a mental sanatorium."

Cassilda crossed her arms over her breasts to place her hands upon the older woman's wrists. "I'm terribly sorry."

"I'm certain you can appreciate how sorely this subject distresses me." Mrs. Castaigne smiled, meeting her eyes in the mirror.

"I shan't mention it again."

"Of course not. And now, my dear, you must hurry and make yourself ready for bed. Too much exertion so soon after your illness will certainly bring about a relapse. Hurry along now, while I fetch your tonic."

"I'm sure I don't need any more medicine. Sometimes I think it must bring on evil dreams."

"Now don't argue, Cassilda dear." The fingers on her shoulders tightened their grip. "You must do as you're told. You can't very well perform your duties as companion if you lie about ill all day, now can you? And you *do* want to stay."

"Certainly!" Cassilda thought this last had not been voiced as a question. "I want to do whatever you ask."

"I know you do, Cassilda. And I only want to make you into a perfect young lady. Now let me help you into your night things."

Cassilda opened her eyes into complete darkness that swirled about her in an invisible current. She sat upright in her bed, fighting back the vertigo that she had decided must come from the tonic they gave her nightly. Something had wakened her. Another bad dream? She knew she often suffered them, even though the next morning she was unable to recall them. Was she about to be sick? She was certain that the tonic made her feel drugged.

Her wide eyes stared sleeplessly at the darkness. She knew sleep would not return easily, for she feared to lapse again into the wicked dreams that disturbed her rest and left her lethargic throughout the next day. She could not even be certain that this, now, might not be another of those dreams.

In the absolute silence of the house, she could hear her heart pulse, her breath stir anxiously.

There was another sound, more distant, and of almost the same monotonous regularity. She thought she heard a woman's muffled sobbing.

Mrs. Castaigne, she thought. The talk of her daughter had upset her terribly. Underscoring the sobbing came a sharp, rhythmic crack, as if a rocker sounded against a loose board.

Cassilda felt upon the nightstand beside her bed. Her fingers found matches. Striking one, she lit the candle that was there—her actions entirely automatic. Stepping down out of her bed, she caught up the candlestick and moved cautiously out of her room.

In the hallway, she listened for the direction of the sound. Her candle forced a small nimbus of light against the enveloping darkness of the old house. Cassilda shivered and drew her nightdress closer about her throat; its gauzy lace and ribbons were no barrier to the cold darkness that swirled about her island of candlelight.

The sobbing seemed no louder as she crept down the hallway toward Mrs. Castaigne's bedroom. There, the bedroom door was open, and within was only silent darkness.

"Mrs. Castaigne?" Cassilda called softly, without answer.

The sound of muffled sobbing continued, and now seemed to come from overhead. Cassilda followed its sound to the end of the hallway, where a flight of stairs led to the maid's quarters in the attic. Cassilda paused fearfully at the foot of the stairway, thrusting her candle without effect against the darkness above. She could still hear the sobbing, but the other sharp sound had ceased. Her head seemed to float in the darkness as she listened, but, despite her dreamlike lethargy, she knew her thoughts raced too wildly now for sleep. Catching up the hem of her nightdress, Cassilda cautiously ascended the stairs.

Once she gained the landing above, she could see the blade of yellow light that shone beneath the door to Camilla's room, and from within came the sounds that had summoned her. Quickly Cassilda crossed to the maid's room and knocked softly upon the door.

"Camilla? It's Cassilda. Are you all right?"

Again no answer, although she sensed movement within. The muffled sobs continued.

Cassilda tried the doorknob, found it was not locked. She pushed the door open and stepped inside, dazzled a moment by the bright glare of the oil lamp.

Camilla, dressed only in her corset and undergarments, stood bent over the foot of her bed. Her ankles were lashed to the base of either post, her wrists tied together and stretched forward by a rope fixed to the headboard. Exposed by the open-style knickers, her buttocks were crisscrossed with red welts. She turned her head to look at Cassilda, and the other girl saw that Camilla's cries were gagged by a complicated leather bridle strapped about her head.

"Come in, Cassilda, since you wish to join us," said Mrs. Castaigne from behind her. Cassilda heard her close the door and lock it, before the girl had courage enough to turn around. Mrs. Castaigne wore no more clothing than did Camilla, and she switched her riding crop anticipatorily. Looking from mistress to maid, Cassilda saw that both pairs of eyes glowed alike with the lusts of unholy pleasure.

For a long interval Cassilda resisted awakening, hovering in a languor of unformed dreaming despite the rising awareness that she still slept. When she opened her eyes at last, she stared at the candlestick on her nightstand, observing without comprehension that the candle had burned down to a misshapen nub of cold wax. Confused memories came to her, slipping away again as her mind sought to grasp them. She had dreamed . . .

Her mouth seemed bruised and sour with a chemical taste that was not the usual anisette aftertaste of the tonic, and her limbs ached as if sore from too strenuous exercise the day before. Cassilda hoped she was not going to have a relapse of the fever that had stricken her after she had fled the convent that stormy night so many weeks ago.

She struggled for a moment with that memory. The sisters in black robes and white aprons had intended to wall her up alive in her cell because she had yielded to the temptation of certain unspeakable desires ... The memory clouded and eluded her, like the fragment of some incompletely remembered book.

There were too many elusive memories, memories that died unheard ... Had she not read that? *The King in Yellow* lay open upon her nightstand. Had she been reading, then fallen asleep to such dreams of depravity? But dreams, like memories, faded miragelike whenever she touched them, leaving only tempting images to beguile her.

Forcing her cramped muscles to obey her, Cassilda climbed from her bed. Camilla was late with her tray this morning, and she might as well get dressed to make herself forget the dreams. As she slipped out of her nightdress, she looked at her reflection in the full length dressing mirror.

The marks were beginning to fade now, but the still painful welts made red streaks across the white flesh of her shoulders, back and thighs. Fragments of repressed nightmare returned as she stared in growing fear. She reached out her hands, touching the reflection in wonder. There were bruises on her wrists, and unbidden came a memory of her weight straining against the cords that bound her wrists to a hook from an attic rafter.

Behind her, in the mirror, Mrs. Castaigne ran the tip of her tongue along her smiling lips.

"Up and about already, Cassilda? I hope you've made up your mind to be a better young lady today. You were most unruly last night."

Her brain reeling under the onrush of memories, Cassilda stared mutely. Camilla, obsequious in her maid's costume, her smile a cynical sneer, entered carrying a complex leather harness of many straps and buckles.

"I think we must do something to improve your posture, Cassilda," Mrs. Castaigne purred. "You may think me a bit old-fashioned, but I insist that a young lady's figure must be properly trained if she is to look her best."

"What are you doing to me?" Cassilda wondered, feeling panic.

"Only giving you the instruction a young lady must have if she is to serve as my companion. And you *do* want to be a proper young lady, don't you, Cassilda?"

"I'm leaving this house. Right now."

"We both know why you can't. Besides, you don't really want to go. You quite enjoy our cozy little *menage à trois*."

"You're deranged."

"And you're one to talk, dear Cassilda." Mrs. Castaigne's smile was far more menacing than any threatened blow. "I think, Camilla, the scold's bridle will teach this silly girl to mind that wicked tongue."

A crash of thunder broke her out of her stupor. Out of reflex, she tried to dislodge the hard rubber ball that filled her mouth, choked on saliva when she failed. Half strangled by the gag strapped over her face, she strained in panic to sit up. Her wrists and ankles were held fast, and, as her eyes dilated in unreasoning fear, a flash of lightning beyond the window rippled down upon her spread-eagled body, held to the brass bedposts by padded leather cuffs.

Images, too chaotic and incomprehensive to form coherent memory, exploded in bright shards from her shattered mind.

She was being forced into a straitjacket, flung into a padded cell, and they were bricking up the door ... no, it was some bizarre corset device, forcing her neck back, crushing her abdomen, arms laced painfully into a single glove at her back ... Camilla was helping her into a gown of satin and velvet and lace, and then into a hood of padded leather that they buckled over her head as they led her to the gallows ... and the nurses held her down while Dr. Archer penetrated her with a grotesque syringe of vile poison, and Mrs. Castaigne forced the yellow tonic down her throat as she pinned her face between her thighs ... and Camilla's lips dripped blood as she rose from her kiss, and her fangs were hypodermic needles, injecting poison, sucking life ... they were wheeling her into the torture chamber, where Dr. Archer awaited her ("It's only a frontal lobotomy, just to relieve the pressure on these two diseased lobes.") and plunges the bloody scalpel deep between her thighs ... and they were strapping her into the metal chair in the death cell, shoving the rubber gag between her teeth and blinding her with the leather hood, and Dr. Archer grasps the thick black handle of the switch and pulls it down and sends the current ripping through her nerves ... she stands naked in shackles before the black-masked judges, and Dr. Archer gloatingly exposes the giant needle ("Just an injection of my elixir, and she's quite safe for two more weeks.") ... and the nurses in rubber aprons hold her writhing upon the altar, while Dr. Archer adjusts the hangman's mask and thrusts the electrodes into her breast ... ("Just a shot of my prolixir, and she's quite sane for two more weeks.") ... then the judge in wig and mask and black robe smacks down the braided whip and screams "She must be locked away forever!" ... she tears away the mask and Mrs. Castaigne screams "She must be locked away forever!" ... she tears away the mask and her own face screams "She must be locked in you forever!" ... then Camilla and Mrs. Castaigne lead her back into her cell, and they strap her to her bed and force the rubber gag between her teeth, and Mrs. Castaigne adjusts her surgeon's mask while Camilla clamps the electrodes to her nipples, and the current rips into her and her brain screams and screams unheard ... "I think she no longer needs to be drugged." Mrs. Castaigne smiled, and her lips are bright with blood. "She's one of us now. She always has been one with us" ... and they leave her alone in darkness on the promise "We'll begin again tomorrow" and the echo "She'll be good for two more weeks."

She moaned and writhed upon the soiled sheets, struggling to escape the images that spurted like foetid purulence from her tortured brain. With the next explosive burst of lightning, her naked body lifted in a convulsive arc from the mattress, and her scream against the gag was like the first agonized outcry of the newborn.

The spasm passed. She dropped back limply onto the sodden mattress. Slippery with sweat and blood, her relaxed hand slid the rest of the way out of the padded cuff. Quietly, in the darkness, she considered her free hand—suddenly calm, for she knew she had slipped wrist restraints any number of times before this.

Beneath the press of the storm, the huge house lay in darkness and silence. With her free hand she unbuckled the other wrist cuff, then the straps that held the gag in place, and the restraints that pinned her ankles. Her tread no louder than a phantom's, she glided from bed and crossed the room. A flicker of lightning revealed shabby furnishings and a disordered array of fetishist garments and paraphernalia, but she threw open the window and looked down upon the black waters of the lake and saw the cloud waves breaking upon the base of the cliff, and when she turned away from that vision her eyes knew what they beheld and her smile was that of a lamia.

Wraithlike she drifted through the dark house, passing along the silent rooms and hallways and stairs, and when she reached the kitchen she found what she knew was the key to unlock the dark mystery that bound her here. She closed her hand upon it, and her fingers remembered its feel.

Camilla's face was tight with sudden fear as she awakened at the clasp of fingers closed upon her lips, but she made no struggle as she stared at the carving knife that almost touched her eyes.

"What happened to Constance?" The fingers relaxed to let her whisper, but the knife did not waver.

"She had a secret lover. One night she crept through the sitting room window and ran away with him. Mrs. Castaigne showed her no mercy."

"Sleep now," she told Camilla, and kissed her tenderly as she freed her with a swift motion that her hand remembered.

In the darkness of Mrs. Castaigne's room she paused beside the motionless figure on the bed.

"Mother?"

"Yes, Constance?"

"I've come home."

"You're dead."

"I remembered the way back."

And she showed her the key and opened the way.

It only remained for her to go. She could no longer find shelter in this house. She must leave as she had entered.

She left the knife. That key had served its purpose. Through the hallways she returned, in the darkness her bare feet sometimes treading upon rich carpets, sometimes dust and fallen plaster. Her naked flesh tingled with the blood that had freed her soul.

She reached the sitting room and looked upon the storm that lashed the night beyond. For one gleam of lightning the room seemed festooned with torn wallpaper; empty wine bottles littered the floor and dingy furnishings. The flickering mirage passed, and she saw that the room was exactly as she remembered. She must leave by the window.

There was a tapping at the window.

She started, then recoiled in horror as another repressed memory escaped into consciousness.

The figure that had pursued her through the darkness on that night she had sought refuge here. It waited for her now at the window. Half-glimpsed before, she saw it now fully revealed in the glare of the lightning.

Moisture glistened darkly upon its rippling and exaggerated musculature. Its uncouth head and shoulders hunched forward bullishly; its face was distorted with insensate lust and drooling madness. A grotesque phallus swung between its misshapen legs—serpentine, possessed of its own life and volition. Like an obscene worm, it stretched blindly toward her, blood oozing from its toothless maw.

She raised her hands to ward it off, and the monstrosity pawed at the window, mocking her every terrified movement as it waited there on the other side of the rain-slick glass.

The horror was beyond enduring. There was another casement window to the corner sitting room, the one that overlooked the waters of the river. She spun about and lunged toward it—noticing from the corner of her eye that the creature outside also whirled about, sensing her intent, flung itself toward the far window to forestall her.

The glass of the casement shattered, even as its blubbery hands stretched out toward her. There was no pain in that release, only dreamlike vertigo as she plunged into the greyness and the rain. Then the water and the darkness received her falling body, and she set out again into the night, letting the current carry her, she knew not where.

* * *

"A few personal effects remain to be officially disposed of, Dr. Archer—since there's no one to claim them. It's been long enough now since the bus accident, and we'd like to be able to close the files on this catastrophe."

"Let's have a look." The psychiatrist opened the box of personal belongings. There wasn't much; there never was in such cases, and had there been anything worth stealing, it was already unofficially disposed of.

"They still haven't found a body," the ward superintendent wondered. "Do you suppose . . . ?"

"Callous as it sounds, I rather hope not," Dr. Archer confided. "This patient was a paranoid schizophrenic—and dangerous."

"Seemed quiet enough on the ward."

"Thanks to a lot of ECT—and to depot phenothiazines. Without regular therapy, the delusional system would quickly regain control, and the patient would become frankly murderous."

There were a few toiletry items and some articles of clothing, a brassiere and pantyhose. "I guess send this over to Social Servuces. These shouldn't be allowed on a locked ward—" the psychiatrist pointed to the nylons "—nor these smut magazines."

"They always find some way to smuggle the stuff in," the ward superintendent sighed, "and I've been working here at Coastal State since back before the War. What about these other books?"

Dr. Archer considered the stack of dog-eared gothic romace novels. "Just return these to the Patients' Library. What's this one?"

Beneath the paperbacks lay a small hardcover volume, bound in yellow cloth, somewhat soiled from age.

"Out of the Patients' Library too, I suppose. People have donated all sorts of books over the years, and if the patients don't tear them up, they just stay on the shelves forever."

"*The King in Yellow*," Dr. Archer read from the spine, opening the book. On the flyleaf a name was penned in a graceful script: *Constance Castaigne.*

"Perhaps the name of a patient who left it here," the superintendent suggested. "Around the turn of the century this was a private sanitorium. Somehow, though, the name seems to ring a distant bell."

"Let's just be sure this isn't vintage porno."

"I can't be sure—maybe something the old-timers talked about when I first started here. I seem to remember there was some famous scandal involving one of the wealthy families in the city. A murderess, was it? And something about a suicide, or was it an escape? I can't recall . . . . "

"Harmless nineteenth-century romantic nonsense," Dr. Archer concluded. "Send it on back to the library."

The psychiatrist glanced at a last few lines before closing the book:

> CASSILDA   I tell you, I am lost! Utterly lost!
> CAMILLA *(terrified herself)*: You have seen the King . . . ?
> CASSILDA   And he has taken from me the power to direct
>   or to escape my dreams.

Most of what you will read in the following about author Blish having been a youthful correspondent of H.P. Lovecraft is quite true. And the letter quoted at length in the story is real—mostly. At least it is closely based on a real one from HPL to Blish and William Miller, Jr. (June 3, 1936). The relevant portion of the real thing reads as follows:

"As for bringing the *Necronomicon* into objective existence—I wish indeed that I had the time and imagination to assist in such a project ... but I'm afraid it's a rather large order—especially since the dreaded volume is supposed to run to something like a thousand pages! I have "quoted" from pages as high as 770 or thereabouts. Moreover, one can never *produce* anything even a tenth as terrible and impressive as one can awesomely *hint* about. If anyone were to try to *write* the *Necronomicon*, it would disappoint all those who have shuddered at cryptic references to it. The most one could do—and I may try that some time—is to "translate" isolated chapters of the mad Arab's monstrous tome ...the less terrible chapters, which ordinary human beings may read without danger of laying themselves open to siege by the Shapes from the Abyss of Azathoth ... *A collected series of such extracts might later be offered as an "abridged and expunged* Necronomicon ...."

More Light

by JAMES BLISH

I

I have never trusted Bill Atheling. Like me, he has a mean streak in him (and I don't say so just because he once tore a story of mine to shreds in a review; that's what critics are for). But perhaps for the same reason, I also rather like him. Hence when I first saw him again in New York—after I'd spent two years in exile, lobbying before Senate committees—I was shocked. My instant impression was that he was dying.

I thought at first that it was only the effect of a new beard, which was then just two weeks old and would have made any man look scruffy. And in part it was, for surprisingly, the beard was coming out white, though Bill is only forty-seven and is gray only at the temples.

But there was more to it than that. He had lost some twenty or thirty pounds, which he could ill afford, since he never weighed more than 150 at his best, and stood 5'10" or so. His skin was gray, his neck crepy, his hands trembling, his eyes bleached, his cough tubercular; he stared constantly over my shoulder while we talked, and his voice kept fading out in the middle of sentences. If he was not seriously ill, then he had taken even more seriously to the bottle, which wasn't a pleasant thought either.

This was hardly the shape in which I had expected to find a man with a new young wife (the artist Samantha Brock) and a fine new house in Brooklyn Heights (it had once been a Gay Nineties house of ill fame, and Samantha had decorated it in that style: red plush, beaded curtains, crystal light fixtures, gold spray on the capitals of Corinthian wooden pillars, an ancient Victrola with a horn in the parlor—all *very* high camp). But I made as light of it as I could manage.

"You look terrible," I told him over the brandy. "What in God's name have you been doing to yourself? Reading the *Complete Works* of Sam Moskowitz? Or have you taken up LSD?"

He came back with his usual maddening indirection; at least *that* hadn't changed. "What do you know about Robert W. Chambers?" he said, looking off to the left.

"Damn little, I'm glad to say. I read some of his stuff when I was in college. As I recall, I liked his stories about his art-student days in Paris better than the fantasies. But that isn't saying much."

"Then you remember *The King in Yellow*."

"Vaguely. It was one of the first semi-hoaxes, wasn't it? An imaginary book? People who read it were supposed to go mad, or be visited by monsters, or things like that. Like the *Nekronomikon*."

"As a matter of fact, it was supposed to have been a play," Atheling said. "But go on."

"You're a pedant to the last. But there's nothing to go on about. Nobody can believe any more that a book could drive anybody mad. Real life's become too horrible; not even William Burroughs can top Dachau." Suddenly, I was overcome with suspicion, and something very like disgust. "Sour Bill Atheling, are you about to tell me you've found the play in your cellar, and that you've been haunted ever since? And then pony up a concocted manuscript to prove it? If that's the case, I'll just throw up my dinner and go home. You know damn well it'll never sell, anyhow."

"It was you who asked me what was wrong with me," he said, reasonably enough. "Simmer down. If you don't want to credit my explanation, then the burden of concocting another one falls on you."

"Concocting—!"

"If you can't stop squeaking, you might as well go home."

"All right. Observe me; I am breathing evenly. Now, is this honestly the explanation you're about to offer me?"

"Yes," Atheling said. "I do in fact have the play."

I sat back, completely at a loss. Nobody peddles such nonsense any more. At last I said: "I think the decor around here has gone to your head. Well, go on, I'll listen. Just don't expect me to be taken in. Who wrote this Dreadful Work—as if I didn't know?"

"You don't know, and neither do I, but I'm pretty sure it was Chambers himself. It's interesting that you mentioned the *Nekronomikon* without any prompting, because it was through Lovecraft that I got the play in the first place—which also explains why I hadn't read it until last year. But I'd better give you the story in sequence. Come upstairs with me."

He got up and I followed him, not failing to pick up the Grand Marnier bottle as I passed it. Atheling's office was as always almost pathologically neat—another trait that, in a writer, automatically inspires mistrust in me—but it had been recently painted a brilliant chrome yellow with a faint, bilious trace of green in it, a scheme which would have driven me out of my mind in short order, with no help needed from any imaginary play. There was a Vermeer reproduction on one wall which, against all that flat yellow paint, looked almost exactly like a window, except that it had in it a window of its own which looked even realer. I was surprised; in this atmosphere I would have expected a Parrish, or maybe even a Bok.

Atheling pointed me to a straight and inhospitable-looking chair, and then produced from a four-drawer file cabinet a fairly thick folder which he brought back to his desk. From this, in turn, he extracted two small sheets of blue paper closely covered with tiny handwriting in dark blue pen.

"Is that it?" I said. "Or are those just the commercials?"

"No, that's not it," he said in a rather dangerously flat tone of voice. "Just shut up for ten seconds and listen, Jim, will you? If you keep on nattering, I may run out of guts. I'm none too sure as it is that I ought to be talking to you."

"Then why do you bother? You know damn well I won't believe a word you say."

"Because you're just slightly less stupid than anybody else I know, and once upon a time knew something about magic. Now are you going to listen?"

"Fire at will," I said, with spurious resignation. I really could not imagine how even Atheling could make a good story out of such a stock opening, but I was thoroughly interested in hearing him try it—as of course he knew as well as I did.

"All right. I was a Lovecraft fan when I was a kid, as you probably know; so were you. And I believed devoutly in all those spurious books that he and the other members of the Cthulhu circle concocted to make their tales sound more plausible. I was completely taken in. I wrote to the Widener Library to try to borrow a copy of the *Nekronomikon*; I looked for it in secondhand bookstores; I tried to buy it in a plain sealed wrapper from Panurge Press. Nothing worked, so finally—this was when I was fifteen years old—I wrote to Lovecraft himself for help.

"Well, you can guess what happened. He politely told me that he had invented the book. But at fifteen I wasn't easily dashed. Instead I proposed that, since the book didn't exist, he should write it, and I would publish it. In installments, of course, in some sort of amateur magazine."

I laughed. "He must have gotten twoscore letters like that."

"I don't doubt it. In any event, he declined, very politely, of course. He said he had already quoted the *Nekronomikon* from pages well beyond nine hundred or a thousand, and he didn't really think he

wanted to undertake writing a volume of that size. Well, I more or less
took the hint. But I couldn't prevent myself from adding that I hoped
he'd get around to writing at least a few chapters some day, and if he
did, well Willy Atheling hoped he would remember who stood ready
to publish it. I was a terrible little snot in those days. Please don't add
any footnotes, because here is one of my own."

He handed me one of the sheets of blue notepaper. I have seen
Lovecraft holographs before; this one, with its tiny, utterly legible
handwriting which looked as though it had been constructed along a
straightedge, was either the real thing or it had been made by a master
forger, a talent I was pretty sure Atheling lacked. Atheling pointed to
one long paragraph, which read as follows:

> Yr persistence is flattering indeed, but really I do
> think that for me to write more than a few sentences of the
> *Nekronomikon* here and there, would be folly. Were I to do
> so, I would most seriously risk spoiling the effectiveness of
> the stories I have based upon it. I have seen at least one
> writer of genius so stumble, namely Robt. Chambers, who
> actually sat down to write his infamous and horrible *King
> in Yellow* (I refer, naturally, to the play, not the existing
> book), whereas, he might much better have left it afloat in
> the imagination of the reader. The play is a fine work, but
> it could not possibly have been either as fine or as frighten-
> ing as his stories adumbrated. It is his good fortune, and
> ours, that it has never been published, so that we are free
> to continue to dream of it fearfully and never know what it
> says or means.

I once exchanged a few letters with Lovecraft myself, as you may see
in his volume of collected letters; I knew not only the handwriting and
the letter paper, but also the epistolary style. This was authentic. I said,
"I begin to see where this is going."

"Of course you do. But bear in mind that back in those days—you
see the date, 1937—I had never heard of Chambers. I hunted down
the short-story collection. Then nothing would prevent me from seeing
the play. Conscienceless teen-ager that I was, I *demanded* that HPL send
me a copy. And here's the reply."

Another sheet of blue notepaper was passed to me. It said:

> I do not really know what disposal to make of the
> *King in Yellow*, for Chambers and I were never intimate and
> I was staggered that he sent me the play upon my own
> very tentative inquiry—so much like yours, and others',
> about the *Nekron.* etc. The MS. now in my hands is I think

> quite superb; yet, as I have already told you, I would be
> hesitant to see it used to destroy the effective hints of it in
> his stories. On the other side, it *is* an object lesson, in
> when *not* to follow up such hints; and contains much
> beauty, as well as much terror, that should not remain hid-
> den. What therefore I have done is to have a typescript
> made by a young lady who has been trading me secretarial
> work for some small editing services of my own; and I send
> you herewith the carbon copy, with the injunction that *no*
> right of publication inheres in its transmission.

This too was an authentic letter, I was convinced. "All right," I said.
"That was thirty years ago. And yet you didn't read the play then, if
in fact you did get it. You say you hadn't read it until just a little while
ago. Why not?"

"I was outgrowing Lovecraft and all that crowd. Also, I was ashamed
to have been taken in by the *Nekronomikon*, and didn't want to be taken
in again. I was having a fight with a fat boy down the block over an
even fatter redhead. And a lot of other things intervened. In short, I
put off reading it for a couple of weeks, and during those couple of
weeks, Lovecraft died, before I had even the courtesy to thank him for
having sent me the play. After that, I was also embarrassed for my own
thoughtlessness, and I put the play away, and soon after, Jim, I
managed to forget all about it. No earthquake could have buried it
more thoroughly than my own sense of guilt, plus my own contempt
at myself for ever having been a fantasy fan at all. If you don't
understand how that could have happened, then I will abort the rest
of the story right here."

"No, I understand it well enough. I'm not sure I credit it, but I do
understand it. Go on."

"I didn't think of it again until 1967, when Ace republished the
short-story collection. Then of course I was reminded that, if indeed there
had ever been such a play, I was the only one in the world who had a copy.
At least, no such thing ever turned up in Chambers' own papers—he died
in 1933—and Lovecraft's top typed copy and the manuscript must have
been lost."

"What makes you think so?"

"Lovecraft's literary executors have been publishing every scrap of
HPL they could find, including his laundry list. If they had found *The
King in Yellow*, the world would know it by now. If my copy is real, it
is the last one and the only one. So, I got it out of my safe-deposit box
and read it."

"What does Samantha make of all this?"

"Oh," he said, "she knows most of what I've told you, but she just thinks I'm being more than usually neurotic—'You know how writers are.' These City College types have pat explanations out of Karen Horney and Erich Fromm for everything; it saves them the trouble of thinking. And I'm not about to change her mind, either. I certainly haven't shown her the play."

"Female common sense would blow the whole thing sky-high in a minute," I agreed. "And you're now about to tell me that you won't show it to me either."

"On the contrary," he said, a malicious grin splitting his beard and mustache apart. "It's really not so terrible; I'm sure it can't hurt you a bit. As you said downstairs, life is more horrible than any possible book."

"Then what *is* the matter with you, Bill? You're a good deal more hard-nosed than I am; you're the *last* person I'd expect to be scared by Oscar Wilde or Lovecraft or Arthur Machen or any of the rest of that crowd. I can't imagine your trying to scare me, either; you know I know better."

"That's not the point," Atheling said. "As I've said, the play isn't very frightening. But I say that with reservations, because I have not read all of it, not even yet."

"I don't follow you."

"I have not been able to finish reading it," Atheling said, with a kind of sad patience. "There is a point in the play at which I have to quit. It varies, from reading to reading, by a line or so to one side or the other, but I do know the place that I haven't yet been able to get beyond.

"Now, I know from another Lovecraft letter, which I'll show you *after* you've read the play, that he also found this to be the case for him—but that he had to quit several whole pages before I did. I find this curious and I have no explanation for it at all. I want to know when *you* have to stop—if you do."

"May I suggest a very simple expedient?"

"Oh God, sure. Turn to the last page. I've done that. I know how it ends. I know every line of it. I could set it to music if I had to. That's not my point. I'm talking only about the cumulative *effect*, not the state of the text. I want to know how far you get, the first time through."

"I'll finish it," I said. "Have you messed with the typescript at all, Bill?"

"No. There were notes at the back that evidently were intended to be put into a later draft, and I've prepared a version into which I've incorporated them—or those I could understand. But this in the folder is the original."

He handed the folder to me. Well, I was hooked—or, anyhow, prepared to be amused, and, if possible, admiring of Sour Bill's ingenuity. "Okay. Where do I sleep?"

"You can have our room. Samantha's with her mother for the whole week to come—some psychiatric casework sort of chore—so you can rattle around at will. I'll use the guest room. Take the bottle, I don't need it—but don't tell me in the morning that you had to quit reading because you got fried. I want a complete report."

"You'll get it." I opened the folder. Inside it was what would have been the most brittle sheaf of yellow, brown-edged second sheets in the world, had they not each been carefully cased in plastic. I bore them off.

II

The bed was a magnificent old four-poster, quite in keeping with the house, and it had a small, projector-style reading lamp fastened to the headboard. I washed up and settled down. Just as I did so, either Atheling's furnace or his refrigerator went on and all the lights in the house dimmed momentarily—evidently his wiring needed tending to, which wasn't unusual in these old brownstones either. It was a nice coincidence and I relished it. Then I poured myself a sizable slug of the brandy and began to read.

And this is what I read:

ACT ONE

(A balcony of the palace in Hastur, overlooking the Lake of Hali, which stretches to the horizon, blank, motionless and covered with a thin haze. The two suns sink toward the rippleless surface.

(The fittings of the balcony are opulent; but dingy with time. Several stones have fallen from the masonry, and lie unheeded.

(CASSILDA, a Queen, lies on a couch overlooking the Lake, turning in her lap a golden diadem set with jewels. A servant enters and offers her a tray, but it is nearly empty: some bread, a jug. She looks at it hopelessly and waves it away. The servant goes out.

(Enter PRINCE UOHT, a portly man in his early millions.)

UOHT:	Good day, mother.
CASSILDA:	Good-bye , day.
UOHT:	You have been looking at Carcosa again.

CASSILDA: No. . . . Nobody can see Carcosa
before the Hyades rise. I was only looking at the
Lake of Hali. It swallows so many suns.

UOHT: And you will see it swallow so many more.
These mists are bad for you; they seep
into everything. Come inside.

CASSILDA: No, not now.
I am not afraid of a little mist; nor,
of a little time. I have seen quite a lot
of both.

UOHT: This interminable siege!
Would that the Lake would swallow Alar for once,
Instead of the suns.

CASSILDA: Not even Hali
can do that, since Alar sits upon Dehme,
which is quite another lake.

UOHT: One lake
is like another: water and fog, fog and water.
If Hastur and Alar changed sites between moons,
nobody would notice. They are
the two worst situated cities in the world.

CASSILDA: Necessarily,
since they are the only ones.

UOHT: Except Carcosa
. . . Well?

CASSILDA: I am not sure, my Prince,
that Carcosa is in the world. In any event,
it is certainly fruitless to talk about the matter
(CAMILLA, *a Princess, enters, then hesitates.*)

CAMILLA: Oh. I—

CASSILDA: Come ahead, Camilla, hear us.
There are no secrets any longer. Everything
has been worn thin, and Time has stopped.
(*Enter* THALE, *the younger Prince.*)

THALE: Nonsense again, mother?

CASSILDA: If it pleases you
to call it that, Prince Thale. As for me,
I am only a Queen; I can be mocked at will.

THALE: But no, I didn't mean—

UOHT: Mockery or no,
Prince Thale is right. Time does not stop.
It is a contradiction in terms.

CASSILDA: Time stops,
my Uoht, when you have heard every possible banality
every possible number of times. Whenever
has anything happened in Hastur,please?

Any new word, or any new event? The siege,
as you very justly and repeatedly observe,
is right flat-out interminable, and that's that.
Neither Hastur nor Alar will ever prevail.
We shall both just wear down into dust—
or boredom, whichever arrives first. Ah,
I am sorry for you Uoht, but I'm afraid
you only remind me now that there's no future
in being human. Even as a baby,
you were a little dull.

UOHT: You may say
what you please of me, too, for royalty
of course has its privileges. All the same,
not all time is in the past, Cassilda.
It lies in your power to change things,
were you not so weary of us—and of yourself.

CASSILDA: Oh, are we to talk of the Succession again?
Nothing is duller than dynasties.

THALE Mother, must the Dynasty die only because you
are bored?
Only a word from you, and the Black Stars
would rise again. Whatever your soothsaying,
Alar could not stand against them; you know
that. It would be—it would be an act of mercy,
to the people.

CASSILDA: The people! Who are they?
You care as little for the people as Uoht does.
Thale, I know your heart, and his as well.
All the diadem means to either of you is your sister.
There's no other reward now, for being a king
in Hastur. As for black stars, enough!
They radiate nothing but the night.

THALE Camilla loves me.

UOHT: Liar!

CASSILDA: Camilla?

UOHT: Ask her, if you dare.

THALE Who would dare,
without the diadem? You're not so bold, Uoht.
Have *you* found the Yellow Sign?

UOHT: Stop your mouth!

CASSILDA: And stop your bickering,
you two frogs! . . . *I* will ask her.

CAMILLA I am not ready to be asked, mother.

CASSILDA: No? Camilla, *you* could have the diadem.
Then you could take your pick of your brothers,
and we'd have an end to all our problems.

	See how I tempt you. The Dynasty would go on,
	and you'd be free of all this conniving.
	Perhaps, even, the siege would end ...
	Well, Camilla, speak!
CAMILLA	No, no. Please.
	You cannot give the diadem to me.
	I will not have it.
CASSILDA	And why not?
CAMILLA	Then *I* would be sent the Yellow Sign.
CASSILDA	Possibly, if one can believe the runes.
	But would that be so very terrible?
	Tell us, Camilla, what, after all, does happen
	when one receives the Yellow Sign?
CAMILLA (*whispering*):	It . . . It is come for.
CASSILDA	So they say.
	I have never seen it happen. But suppose
	it does. Who comes for it?
CAMILLA	The Phantom of Truth.
CASSILDA	And what is that?
CAMILLA	Please, I do not know.
CASSILDA	No more do I. But suppose, Camilla,
	whatever it is, that perhaps it's real.
	What then? Does it frighten you?
CAMILLA	Yes, mother.
CASSILDA	All right. If that's the case,
	then I shall give the diadem to one of your brothers,
	and end this steamy botheration in some other way.
	You have only to choose between them, as they ask.
	I would be delighted to give you a marriage
	in the utmost of state. At the very least,
	it would be a novelty, in a small and noisy way.
UOHT	A wise decision.
THALE	And not a small one, mother.
CAMILLA	But mother, there *is* something new;
	we do not need a stately wedding yet.
	That's what I came to tell you, just before
	the old quarrel started up again.
CASSILDA	And what is that?
CAMILLA	Mother, there's a stranger in the city.
CASSILDA	A stranger! Now living god, hear that.
	You all have the mists of Hali in your brains.
	I know every face in Hastur, and in Alar, too.
	Camilla, how many people do you think there are
	in the living world? A spate of handfuls,
	and I've seen them all.

CAMILLA: This one is new in Hastur.

CASSILDA: Nobody, nobody these days goes about Hastur
but the hearse-driver. Sensible people hide
their faces even from themselves.

CAMILLA: But that's it.
You can't see his face. He's walking masked.

CASSILDA: Oh, covered with a veil? Or is he hooded?

CAMILLA: Neither, mother. He wears another face.
A white mask—whiter than the mists.
The eyes are blank, and it has no expression.

CASSILDA: Hmm...In all conscience, strange enough.
How does he explain it?

CAMILLA: He speaks to no one.

CASSILDA: I will see him. He will speak to me.
Everyone does; and then he'll be unmasked.

UOHT: But mother, this is only a conceit.
It is of no moment in the tree of time.
If Camilla will but choose—

THALE: And bring back the Succession—

CASSILDA   *(placing the diadem upon her head)*:
                                We will talk of that some other time.
Send me now Noatalba, and the man
in the pallid mask. Camilla does not wish
to choose now, and no more do I.

UOHT: Time is running out. There has been no king
in Hastur since the last Aldones—

CASSILDA: Do not tell me again the story of the Last King!
Oh, I am so sick, so sick of you all!
I tell you now, do you goad me further,
there will be no other king in Hastur till the King in
     Yellow!

*(There is a long, shocked silence. CAMILLA, UOHT and THALE go out,
stunned and submissive. CASSILDA lies back, exhausted and brooding.*

*(Enter A CHILD, with jeweled fingers, wearing a small duplicate of the
diadem.)*

CHILD: Tell me a story.

CASSILDA: Not now.

CHILD: Please, tell me a story. Please.

CASSILDA: I do not feel like telling you a story now.

CHILD *(menacingly)*: Grandmother?

        (CASSILDA sits up resignedly. She does not look at the CHILD.)

CASSILDA: Once upon a time . . .

CHILD: That's better.

CASSILDA:
    ... There were two lakes in the heart of Gondwanaland, called Dehme
and Hali. For millions of years they lay there with no-one to see them,
while strange fishes bit their surfaces. Then, there appeared a city by
the Lake of Hali—

*(During the course of this scene, the suns set. Across the water, the Hyades
come out, slightly blurred by the mists.)*

CHILD: That's not a story, that's only history.

CASSILDA: It is the only story that there is.
                Besides, if you'll be quiet, I shall tell you
                the rest that's in the runes. Is that agreed?

CHILD: Oh good! I'm not supposed to know what's in the runes.

CASSILDA: That doesn't matter now. But to go on:
This city had four singularities. The first singularity was that it
appeared overnight. The second singularity was that one could not
tell whether the city sat upon the waters, or beyond them on the
invisible other shore. The third singularity was that when the moon
rose, the towers of the city appeared to be behind it, not in front of
it. Shall I go on?

CHILD: Of course, I know all the rest.

CASSILDA: Misfortunate prince.
    Well then, the fourth singularity was that as soon as one looked upon
the city, one knew what its name was.

CHILD: Carcosa.

CASSILDA: Even as today. And after a long time, men came to the lakes
and built mud huts. The huts grew into the city of Hastur and soon a
man arose who proclaimed himself king in Hastur.

CHILD: Aldones. My grandfather.

CASSILDA: Yes, some ages back.
    And he decreed that all the kings in Hastur thereafter should bear
his name. He promised that if his Dynasty be maintained, then
someday Hastur would be as great as Carcosa across the waters.

CHILD: Thank you. That's enough.

CASSILDA: No, it is not enough.
    That night some one heard him. You have asked, and must hear the
end.

CHILD: I have to leave now. I forgot something.

CASSILDA *(her eyes closed)*:   And that same night,
                he found the Yellow Sign.

*(The CHILD runs out. CASSILDA opens her eyes and resumes watching across
the Lake. A page enters with a torch, fixes it in a sconce, and goes out again.
CASSILDA does not stir.)*

(In the near-darkness, NOATALBA, a priest, enters.)

NOATALBA: My Queen.

CASSILDA: My priest.

NOATALBA	You forgot the fifth singularity.
CASSILDA	And you are an incurable eavesdropper. I am not surprised. In any event, one does not mention the Mystery of the Hyades to a child.
NOATALBA	No. But you think of it.
CASSILDA	No. Everyone today imputes philosophy to me. I'm not so thoughtful. It is only that the shadows of men's thoughts lengthen commonly in the afternoon. Dusk is dusk.
NOATALBA	Long thoughts cast long shadows at any time of day.
CASSILDA	And no news is good news. Noatalba, must you wash me clean with banalities too? Next, you will be speaking of the Succession.
NOATALBA	As a matter of fact, nothing was farther from my mind.
CASSILDA	A good place for nothing.
NOATALBA	I am pleased to hear you jesting. Nonetheless, I have something else to tell you.
CASSILDA	The man in the pallid mask?
NOATALBA	You have heard. Good. Then I will be brief.
CASSILDA	Good.
NOATALBA	I think you should not see him.
CASSILDA	What! Nothing will prevent me! Do you think I will refuse the only novelty in human history, such as it is? You know me little.
NOATALBA	I know you better than you know yourself.
CASSILDA	And nothing is certain but death and . . . Oh living God!
NOATALBA	You spoke?
CASSILDA	Ignore me. Why should I not see this man?
NOATALBA	It is by no means certain that he is a man. And if he is, at best, he is a spy from Alar.

(There is a very long silence, as if something had interrupted the action; both CASSILDA and NOATALBA remain absolutely immobile throughout it. Then their dialogue resumes, as if both were quite unaware of the break.)

CASSILDA	A poor spy then, to be so conspicuous. And in any event, poor priest, what is there that Alar does not know about us? That is why we are in this impasse in the war: We know everything. Were one stone to fall in Alar that I did not hear about, the war would be over; and Aldones, poor man, is in the same whale.

But he knows me, and I know him, and that's
the end of the matter. We shall die
of this glut of familiarity, he and I,
lying in the same tomb, measuring away
at each other's hair and fingernails
in the hope of some advantage even in death.
Why would he send a spy? He is the father
of my tiresome children, and the architect
of my miserable city. Oh, Noatalba, how
I wish I could tell him something he does not know!
He would die of joy, and Alar would sink
into the Lakes—Hastur thereafter!

NOATALBA   Perhaps. You think more highly of novelty than
I do; it is a weakness in you. But I myself
do not think this creature in the pallid mask
to be a spy. You are surprised? But no;
I only said of that possibility:"At best."

CASSILDA (*with a short chopping gesture*): All right, I yield you that.
The worst, then?

NOATALBA   This thing may be the Phantom of Truth.
Only ghosts go about in white.

CASSILDA (*slowly*):   Oh. Oh.
Is that moment come? I see. Then I was wise
to abort the Dynasty, after all. I am not
often wise. But perhaps any end is a good
end ... if it is truly an end. But ... Noatalba—

NOATALBA   Speak.

CASSILDA   I have not found the Sign.

NOATALBA (*indulgently*):   Of course not, or you would
have told me. But we cannot be sure that the
Sign is always sent. The sender—

(*He falls silent.* CASSILDA, *perceiving that she has the upper hand again,
grins mercilessly.*)

CASSILDA   —is the King in Yellow.

NOATALBA: Well ... yes. The King ...warns ...as he warned
the first Aldones. We know nothing about him
but that. And should not know.

CASSILDA   Why not?
Perhaps he is dead.

(NOATALBA *abruptly hides his face.*)
Or too busy in Carcosa, so that he has forgotten
to send the Sign. Why not? We are well taught
that with the King in Yellow, all things
are possible.

NOATALBA   (*unmasking his face slowly*): I have not heard you.
You did not speak.

CASSILDA   I only spoke to your point, my priest ...

that this man in the pallid mask may indeed
be the Phantom of Truth, though I
have not found the Sign, no more than you.
That was what you were saying, was it not?
Be silent if you wish. Well, I'll chance it.

NOATALBA   Blasphemy!

CASSILDA   Is the King a god? I think not.
In the meantime, Noatalba, I would dearly love
to see the face of Truth. It must be curious.
I have laid every other ghost in the world;
send me this man or phantom!*

(Exit NOATALBA).

(The STRANGER enters. He is wearing a silken robe on which the Yellow
Sign is embroidered: a single character in no human script, in gold against
a circular black ground. The QUEEN turns to look at him, and then with
a quick and violent motion, plucks the torch from the sconce and hurls it
from the balcony into the Lake. Now there is only starlight.)

CASSILDA   I have not seen you! I have not seen you!

STRANGER   You echo your priest. You are all blind and deaf—
obviously by choice.

CASSILDA   I . . . suppose it is too late
to be afraid. Well then; I am not.

STRANGER   Well spoken, Queen. There is in fact
nothing to be afraid of.

CASSILDA   Please,
phantom, no nonsense. You wear the Sign.

STRANGER   How do you know that? You have never seen
the Yellow Sign.

CASSILDA   Oh, I know. The Sign
is in the blood. That is why
I aborted the Dynasty. No blood should have to carry
such knowledge through a human heart;
no children's teeth so set on edge.

STRANGER   You face facts. That is a good beginning.
Very well; then, yes, in fact this is the Sign.
Nevertheless, Cassilda—

CASSILDA   Your Majesty—

STRANGER   —Cassilda, there is nothing to fear.

---

* Here indeed I did have to stop for a moment—not because I was in the least frightened, but
because my eyes were tiring after so many pages of dim-rubbed, time-browned carbon copy, and
just at this instant, the *Queen Mary* or whatever it was Atheling kept in his basement got under
way again and dimmed the lights, too, to the point where the letters swam in front of my eyes.
Then the light came up again. I took another pull at the brandy and went on.

	You see how I wear it with impunity.
	Be reassured; it has no power left.
CASSILDA:	Is that...a truth?
STRANGER:	It is the shadow
	cast by a truth. Nothing else
	is ever vouchsafed us, Queen Cassilda.
	That is why I am white: in order to survive
	such colored shadows. And the Pallid Mask
	protects me—as it will protect you.
CASSILDA	How?
STRANGER	It deceives. That is the function of a mask.
	What else?
CASSILDA:	You are not very full of straight answers.
STRANGER	There are no straight answers. But I tell you this:
	Anyone who wears the Pallid Mask need never fear
	the Yellow Sign. You tremble. All the same,
	my Queen, that era is over. Whatever else
	could you need to know? Now your Dynasty
	can start again; again there can be a king
	in Hastur; and again, Cassilda, the Black Stars
	can mount the sky once more against the Hyades.
	The siege can be lifted. Humankind
	can have its future back.
CASSILDA	So many dreams!
STRANGER	Only wear the Mask, and these are given.
	There's no other thing required of us.
CASSILDA	Who tells me this?
STRANGER	I am called Yhtill.
CASSILDA	That is only Alaran for "stranger."
STRANGER	And Aldones
	is only Hasturic for "father." What of that?
CASSILDA	Your facts are bitterer than your mysteries.
	And what will happen to you, Yhtill,
	you with the Yellow Sign on your bosom,
	when the Sign is sent for?
STRANGER	Nothing at all.
	What has Carcosa ever had to do
	with the human world, since you all lived in mud huts?
	The King in Yellow has other concerns, as is only
	supernatural.
	Once you don the Pallid Mask, he cannot even see you.
	Do you doubt me? You have only to look again for yourself
	across the Lake. Carcosa does not sit upon the Earth.
	It is, perhaps, not even real; or not so real
	as you and I. Certainly, the Living God does
	not believe in it. Then why should you?
CASSILDA	You are plausible, you in your ghost face. You talk

as if you know the Living God. Do you also hear
the Hyades sing in the evening of the world?

STRANGER (*shortly*):   No. That is strictly the King's business.
It is of no earthly interest to me.

CASSILDA (*once more recovering a little of her aplomb*):
I daresay. How can I trust any of these answers?
Do we indeed have to do nothing more
to be saved than don white masks? It sounds to me
like a suspiciously easy answer.

STRANGER   Test it then.

CASSILDA   And die. Thank you very much.

STRANGER   Not so fast.
I would not kill you, or myself. I propose a masque,
if you will pardon me the word-play. All will wear
exactly what they choose, except that all will also wear
the Pallid Mask. I myself shall wear the Yellow Sign,
just as I do now. When you are all convinced, the masks
will be doffed; and then you may announce
the Succession, all in perfect safety.

CASSILDA   Oh, indeed.
And then the King descends.

STRANGER   And if the King
should then descend, we are all lost, and I have lost my bet.
I have nothing to lose but my life. You have more.
And if the King does not descend, what then?
Think! The Yellow Sign denatured, human life
suddenly charged with meaning, hope flowering
    everywhere,
the Phantom of Truth laid forever, and the Dynasty
free of all fear of Carcosa and whatever monsters live there,
free of all fear of the King in Yellow and his tattered,
    smothering, inhuman robes!

CASSILDA   Oh Living God!
How would I dare to believe you?

STRANGER   You do not dare not to ...

(*During this conversation, the moon has been rising slowly, contrary to
the direction of sunset, and the stars fade, though they do not quite
disappear. Long waves of clouds begin to pass over the surface of the Lake
of Hali, which begins to sigh and heave. Spray rises. The* STRANGER *and*
CASSILDA *stare at each other in a dawn and sunset of complicity and
hatred.*)

CASSILDA   Why would I not dare?
I who am Cassilda, I, I who am I?

STRANGER   Because, Cassilda, risk nothing, and you risk
it all. That is the first law of rulership.

	And, too, because, Cassilda, in your ancient

And, too, because, Cassilda, in your ancient
heart you love your children.

CASSILDA   Oh, you are a demon!
You have found me out.

STRANGER   That is what I came for.
Very well. I shall see you tomorrow, after sunset.
Wear the Mask, and all eyes will be opened,
all ears unstopped. Good night, my Queen.

CASSILDA   If you are human, you'll regret this.

STRANGER   Utterly.
And so, good night.

(The STRANGER goes out. CASSILDA puts her hand to her head and finds that she is no longer wearing the diadem. She gropes for it, and finally locates it among the cushions. She starts to put it on, and then instead stands at the balcony rail, turning the crown in her hands. The lights go down into semidarkness.

The fog rises in the moonlight: the stars disappear. On the horizon, seemingly afloat upon the Lake of Hali, appear the towers of Carcosa, tall and lightless. The center of the city is behind the rising moon, which seems to be dripping white blood into the lake.

Enter NOATALBA.)

NOATALBA   And so, good night, my Queen.
You saw him?

CASSILDA   I . . . think so.

NOATALBA   And—?

CASSILDA: He says . . . he says the King in Yellow
can be blinded.

NOATALBA   And you heard him out.
Now, very surely, we are indeed all mad.

(Curtain)

Right while I was in the middle of that last long stage direction, the damned lights flickered again, and this time they did not come all the way back to full brightness. Sour Bill really ought to have that wiring checked, or someday soon his fine old Victorian bagnio was going to burn down.

However, this was a natural place to pause and ponder. The text thus far at least settled one suspicion that I had not mentioned to Atheling: that if Atheling himself hadn't written it, perhaps Lovecraft had. Having already invented a number of imaginary literary works, HPL was in theory quite likely to have concocted still another one.

In theory; but Lovecraft never wrote more than a few fragments of his own imaginary reference works; why should he attempt to create the whole of one imagined by another author? Moreover, a play in blank verse was not a likely sort of production for Lovecraft, whose poetic gifts were feeble at best; whereas Chambers, I seemed to recall, had not only published several volumes of verse, but several plays and even an opera libretto. Also, the text thus far already showed a few flashes of humor, a trait not at all characteristic of Lovecraft.

Of course, none of this ruled out Atheling as the probable author, despite the aged paper, but I was pretty sure it did rule out the Spook of Innsmouth.

What about the play proper, then? Horrifying it was not; it was not even as evil as a seventeenth-century "tragedy of blood." Also it was pretty derivative, chiefly of Wilde and of Poe's "The Silence" and "The Mask of the Red Death." And it was terribly dated. I suppose no man living today is in a position to understand why so many of the writers of the 1890's thought that yellow was an especially ominous color.

Grumbling about the light, I brought the smudged pages closer, wondering why I was bothering at all. By this time, I was tired as well as impatient, and, I am afraid, in fact a little drunk, despite Atheling's warning.

Then I discovered that the next page was a misplaced one. Instead of the first page of the second act, it was the "Dramatis Personae" page, which should have been all the way at the front. With one exception, it was nothing but a list of the names—including Aldones, who so far hadn't appeared at all. But the exception was this notation:

"*N.B.* Except for the Stranger and the King, everyone who appears in the play is black."

Nota bene, indeed. It would be hard to imagine another single instruction which could so completely change the whole apparent thrust and effect of what I had read so far. Or did it? Perhaps I was only projecting our current racial troubles into the direction; Chambers may merely have meant to suggest (if he had been that much of an anthropologist) that after all, all our remote prehistoric ancestors had been black. But then I remembered, too, that in the very first story about *The King in Yellow*, Chambers had proposed banishing all Negroes to a "new free state of Suanee."

Now both wider awake and a great deal more disoriented, I put the misplaced page aside and plunged on:

ACT TWO

(The CHILD *appears before the curtain.)*

THE CHILD: I am not the Prologue, nor the Afterword;

call me the Prototaph. My role is this:
to tell you it is now too late to close the book
or quit the theatre. You already thought
you should have done so earlier, but you stayed.
How harmless it all is! No definite
principles are involved, no doctrines
promulgated in these pristine pages,
no convictions outraged...but the blow has fallen,
and now it is too late. And shall I tell you
where the sin lies? It is yours.
You listened to us; and all the same you stay
to see the Sign. Now you are ours, or, since the runes
also run backwards, we are yours . . . forever.

(The stage is in darkness when the curtains part. After a pause, there are a few soft spare chords of music, and the voice of CASSILDA *is heard singing.)*

CASSILDA   Along the shore the cloud waves break,
The twin suns sink behind the lake,
The shadows lengthen
               in Carcosa.
Strange is the night where black stars rise,
And strange moons circle through the skies,
But stranger still is
               Lost Carcosa.
Songs that the Hyades shall sing
Where flap the tatters of the King,
Must die unheard in
               Dim Carcosa.
Song of my soul, my voice is dead,
Die thou unsung, as tears unshed
Shall dry and die in
               Lost Carcosa. [*]

(A murmur of voices and music rises under the last verse. The lights go up to reveal that the front of the stage has become a crowded ballroom, with the balcony at its back. The STRANGER *and all the Hasturites are present; all the latter wear white masks with the visage of the* STRANGER, *to which individual taste has added grotesque variations. The result is that each mask looks like a famous person. The costumes are also various and fantastic. The* STRANGER *still wears the silken robe with the Yellow Sign, and* CASSILDA, *though masked, still wears the diadem, as does the* CHILD. *Many are dancing to a formal measure, something like a sarabande, something like stalking.*

CAMILLA *is talking to the* STRANGER, *front left.* CASSILDA *watches the masque from the balcony, Carcosa and the Hyades behind her; the moon has vanished.)*

STRANGER   There, Princess, you see that there has been
no sending, and there will be none.

---

[*] If this is the correct text of this song, all the others are corrupt in the last verse.

The Pallid Mask is the perfect disguise.
CAMILLA How would we know a sending if it came?

(CASSILDA *descends and joins them.*)

STRANGER The messenger of the King drives a hearse.
CASSILDA Oho, half the population of Hastur does that.
It is the city's most popular occupation,
since the siege began. All that is talk.

STRANGER I have heard what the Talkers were talking— the talk
of the beginning and the end;
but I do not talk of the beginning or the end.
CAMILLA But—the sending? Let us hear.
STRANGER Also,
the messenger of the King is a soft man.
Should you greet him by the hand, one of his fingers
would come off to join yours.

(CAMILLA *recoils in delicate disgust.* NOATALBA, *who has been circling
closer and closer to the group, now joins it.*)

NOATALBA A pretty story.
You seem to know everything. I think perhaps
you could even tell us, given gold,
the mystery of the Hyades.

STRANGER He is King there.
NOATALBA As everywhere. Everyone knows that.
STRANGER He is not King in Aldebaran. That is why
Carcosa was built. It is a city in exile.
These two mighty stars are deep in war,
like Hastur and Alar.

NOATALBA Oh, indeed.
Who then lives in Carcosa?

STRANGER Nothing human.
More than that, I cannot tell you.

NOATALBA Your springs of invention run dry
with suspicious quickness.

CASSILDA Be silent.
Stranger, how did you come by all this?
STRANGER My sigil is Aldebaran. I hate the King.
NOATALBA And his is the Yellow Sign, which you mock him
by flaunting before the world. I tell you this:
he will not be mocked. He is a King
whom Emperors have served; and that is why
he scorns a crown. All this is in the runes.

STRANGER There are great truths in the runes.
Nevertheless, my priest, Aldebaran
is his evil star. Thence comes the Pallid Mask.

NOATALBA Belike, belike. But I would rather be
deep in the cloudy depths of Dehme

than to wear what you wear on your bosom.
When the King opens his mantle—

(Somewhere in the palace, a deep-toned gong begins to strike.)

CASSILDA: Have done ...
Now is the time I never thought to see:
I must go, and announce the Succession.
Perhaps...perhaps the world itself
is indeed about to begin again. How strange!

(As the gong continues to strike, everyone begins to unmask. There are murmurs and gestures of surprise, real or polite, as identities are recognized or revealed. Then there is a wave of laughter. The music becomes louder and increases in tempo.)

CAMILLA   You, sir, should unmask.

STRANGER   Indeed?

CAMILLA   Indeed, it's time. We have all laid aside
disguise but you.

STRANGER   I wear no mask.

CAMILLA   No mask? *(To* CASSILDA*):* No mask!

STRANGER   *I*
am the Pallid Mask itself. I, I, I
am the Phantom of Truth. I came from Alar.
My star is Aldebaran. Truth is our invention,
it is our weapon of war. And see—
By this sign we have conquered, and the siege
of good and evil is ended . . . .

(On the horizon, the towers of Carcosa begin to glow.)

NOATALBA*(pointing):* Look, look! Carcosa—Carcosa is on fire!

(The STRANGER *laughs and seizes* CAMILLA *by the wrists.)*

CAMILLA *(in agony):* His hands! *His hands!*

(At her cry the music dies discordantly. Then a tremendous, inhuman voice rolls from Carcosa across the Lake of Hali.)

THE KING: Yhtill!
Yhtill!
Yhtill!

(The STRANGER *releases* CAMILLA, *who screams wordlessly and falls.)**

THE KING: Have you found the Yellow Sign?
Have you found the Yellow Sign?
Have you found the Yellow Sign?

---

* The light faded further with a distant mechanical rumble. My eyes ached abominably, and I realized that I should have had a bath; I felt itchy. The carbon by this time was so weak that the letters looked as though they had been typed in ashes; there were whole lines I simply could not read; and I was developing a clamorous headache. God damn Atheling and his hypnotic tricks!

STRANGER(*shouting*):   I am the Phantom of Truth!
                    Tremble, O King in tatters!
THE KING: The Phantom of Truth shall be laid.
                    The scalloped tatters of the King must hide
                    Yhtill forever. As for thee, Hastur—
ALL: No! No, no!
THE KING: And as for thee,
                    we tell thee this; it is a fearful thing
                    to fall into the hands of the living god.

(*The* STRANGER *falls, and everyone else sinks slowly to the ground after him.*

THE KING *can now be seen, although only faintly. He stands in state upon the balcony. He has no face, and is twice as tall as a man. He wears pointed shoes under his tattered, fantastically colored robes, and a streamer of silk appears to fall from the pointed tip of his hood. Behind his back he holds inverted a torch with a turned and jeweled shaft, which emits smoke, but no light. At times he appears to be winged; at others, haloed. These details are for the costumer; at no time should* THE KING *be sufficiently visible to make them all out.*

Behind him, Carcosa and the Lake of Hali have vanished. Instead, there appears at his back a huge sculptured shield, in shape suggesting a labrys, of onyx, upon which the Yellow Sign is chased in gold.

The rest of the stage darkens gradually, until, at the end, it is lit only by the decomposed body of the STRANGER, *phosphorescing bluely.*)

THE KING: I have enfolded Yhtill, and the Phantom of Truth
                    is laid. (*More quietly*): Henceforth,
                    the ancient lies will rule as always . . . Now. Cassilda!

(CASSILDA *rises mutely to her knees.*)

THE KING: Thou wert promised a Dynasty by Truth,
                    and in truth shalt thou have a dynasty.
                    The Kingdom of Hastur was first in all the world,
                    and would have ruled the world, except for this;
                    Carcosa did not want it. Hence, thereafter,
                    Hastur and Alar divided; but those in Alar
                    sent you from Aldebaran the Phantom of Truth
                    and all was lost; together, you forgot
                    the Covenant of the Sign. Now there is much
                    which needs to be undone.

NOATALBA(*faintly*):   How, King, how?
THE KING: Henceforth, Hastur and Alar will be
                    divided forever. Forever shalt thou contend
                    for mastery, and strive in bitter blood
                    to claim which shall be uppermost;
                    flesh or phantom, black or white. In due
                    course of starwheels, this strife will come to issue;
                    but not now; oh, no, not now.

CASSILDA *(whispering):*   And—until then?

THE KING: Until then,
Carcosa will vanish; but my rule, I tell you now,
you now, is permanent, despite Aldebaran. Be warned.
Also be promised: He who triumphs in this war
shall be my ...can I be honest? ...inheritor,
and so shall have the Dynasty back. But think:
Already you own the world. The great query is,
Can you rule it? The query is the gift.
The King in Yellow gives it into your hands,
to hold . . . or to let loose. Choose, terrible children.

NOATALBA *(faintly):*   You are King, and are most gracious.
We thank you.

THE KING: *You* thank *me?* I am the living god!
Bethink thyself, priest. There is a price,
I have not as yet stated the half of it.

(Everyone waits, petrified.)

THE KING: The price is: the fixing of the Mask.

(Silence.)

THE KING: You do not understand me. I will explain
it once and then no more. Hastur, you
acceded to, and wore the Pallid Mask.
That is the price. Henceforth, all in Hastur
shall wear the Mask, and by this sign be known.
And war between the masked men and the naked
shall be perpetual and bloody, until I come
again...or fail to come.

(NOATALBA starts to his knees.)

NOATALBA   Unfair, unfair!
It was Alar invented the Pallid Mask!
Aldones—

THE KING: Why should I be fair? I am
the living god. As for Aldones, he
is the father of you all. That is the price:
the fixing of the Mask.

ALL: Oh!

CASSILDA *(bitterly):* Not upon us, oh King; not upon us!

ALL: No! Mercy! Not upon us!

THE KING: Yhtill!
Yhtill!
Yhtill!

*(THE KING vanishes, and with him his throne. The Hyades and Carcosa
are once more visible over the balcony rail. The mass of corruption that had
been the STRANGER rises slowly and uncertainly. The CHILD runs out from
the crowd, and seizing the STRANGER by one mushy hand, leads him*

shambling out across the balcony in the wake of THE KING. *There is a
low, composite moan as they exit.)*
CASSILDA *(standing and throwing her arms wide)*: Not upon us!
      Not upon us!
THE KING *(offstage, remote, diminishing)*: What!
      Did you think to be human still?
NOATALBA   And if we now ...

The light faded out entirely ... and high time to ... I was so exhausted I was outright sick. Odd noises rang through my pounding
head; sometimes I thought I could hear lines from the play being
spoken, as if in an echo chamber, or, sometimes, even being sung.
Occasionally, too, there was a spitting howl which seemed to come
from behind the house; I remembered that the Athelings kept cats,
though I had not seen any during this visit. And the rumbling below
ground was now continuous, like stones being slowly and mindlessly
crushed to powder.

Atheling had won . . . whether by suggestion or by alcohol I could
not tell, but I could not finish *The King in Yellow* . . . and worse, much
worse, was that I felt so dirty that I could hardly bear to touch myself;
I was a blackened man lying in a pool of soot; my rings were cutting
off my fingers, there were maggots feeding in my ears, and deaf, dumb,
blind, anosmic, numb and convicted, I came apart into a universe of
slimy saffron rags.

III

I awoke in a blast of painful yellow sunlight, with that lowering
feeling of being about to be Found Out which is for me the most
intolerable symptom of a hangover. There were neither curtains nor
shades on the windows, which made it worse; no matter how recently
I had moved into a new place, curtaining the master bedroom would
have been the first thing I'd have done.

Then I realized that Atheling was standing over me, in that holier-
than-thou pose he assumes when he thinks he's about to lose an
argument, looking absurdly knobby in a short red flannel nightshirt
and a tasseled red nightcap, and holding out to me a tall red drink.

"Bloody Mary," he said tersely. "Breakfast below in a while. Where
did you stop?"

I looked around confusedly. The pages in their plastic sheaths turned
out to be all over the floor on the window side of the bed. Getting up,
I risked dizziness to pick them up and align them on the bedside table,
wincing a little at the sharp *cracks* the plastic edges made against the
wood.

"Never mind that, I'll do it later," he said. "*Where did you stop?*"

"Uh . . . let me think a minute, will you? I hate people who expect me to be awake before noon. I stopped at—at Noatalba's speech, just after The King's."

"Which speech of The King's?"

"The off-stage one, where he asks, 'Did you think to be human still?'"

"Damn you," Atheling said. "That's farther than I ever got. You were almost, almost at the end."

"What does happen at the end?"

"Nothing. The Child comes back on stage and draws the curtain."

"That's all?"

"That's all. I can't understand it. You were so close. Only one line short. There must be *somebody* who can get to the end by first intention. What stopped you?"

"The simplest thing in the world, Bill: your damned wiring. The lights kept fading on me. Eventually my eyes wore out and I fell asleep. No mystery. Just eyestrain." I added honestly, "Probably the brandy helped."

"Oh," he said. And then again, "Oh. No more than that. Evidently it doesn't matter who reads it, after all. . . . Leave the play on the nightstand. I'll put it in my wall safe and forget about it. Samantha won't have any trouble forgetting about it, she thinks it's all psycho-somatic anyhow. And you might as well forget about it too."

"It's not the most memorable thing I ever read, that's for sure."

"No." He stood silent for a moment. Then he said: "But I'll tell you something irrelevant now."

But he didn't. He just stood there.

"Well?"

"When I first bought this place," he went on in a remote voice, "I planned to have air conditioning installed—mainly to keep the soot out of Samantha's studio. And off the windowsills. You know how filthy this town is."

This seemed irrelevant indeed; but knowing Atheling, I waited.

"So," he said, "I had the house converted to two hundred and twenty volts. Top to bottom. All in BX cables. We had to rip out half the walls to do it. It cost a fortune, but I could run a machine-shop in here now if I had to."

"Then—" I swallowed and started again. "Then what the hell is that grumbling in the cellar? That couldn't have been only eyestrain."

"You've been out of town too long," he said. "The Seventh Avenue IRT goes by only two blocks from here. I don't own any heavy machinery, and there is nothing wrong with the wiring. Nothing."

He continued to hold out the drink to me over the bed, but I was no longer in the bed—hadn't been for at least five minutes. The raw sunlight beat upon the blind and pallid mask of his face through the naked, dirty windows. He went on looking over my shoulder, or where my shoulder would have been, had I been where he thought I was.

I left the house as quickly as I decently could. I hear lately that the Athelings have given it up and moved to England. I should worry about them, I suppose, and I would if I had not just broken my fourth pair of new glasses, right in the middle of a long novel project.

I do sometimes wonder what he did with the play, but not often. The old adage is sadly true: Out of sight, out of mind.

Arthur Machen (1863-1947), a mystically inclined Welshman, wrote a number of the most highly regarded tales of supernatural horror and ancient survivals. In three of these, "The Novel of the Black Seal," "The Shining Pyramid," and "The Red Hand," Machen takes as his premise the possibility that the elfin Little People of Celtic legend were mythic reflections of a pre-Celtic race of squat and malevolent savages who, driven into hiding, linger still in remote places, snatching the unwary to sacrifice them in their ancient unhallowed rites. "The Novel of the Black Seal" first formed part of a longer book, The Three Impostors, in which various long tales were traded among the characters one night.

It is important to note that Machen's conception of the Little People, along with Margaret Alice Murray's speculations upon the subject (The Witch Cult in Western Europe, 1921), was a major influence on Lovecraft's myth of the Old Ones who survive from ancient times. Though we usually picture Lovecraft's Old Ones as transcendent superhuman forces like that which figures in Blackwood's "The Willows" (Lovecraft's favorite among all weird fiction), reading him in light of Machen helps us recognize that often for him the Old Ones are simply hidden, though monstrously alien, races of beings analogous to ourselves. This is more obvious in "The Whisperer in Darkness," less so but equally true in "The Dunwich Horror." Robert E. Howard, too, embraced Machen's idea of the Little People, borrowing it wholesale for his Bran Mak Morn tales, as well as in stories like "Children of the Night" and "The Little People."

The Novel of the Black Seal

by ARTHUR MACHEN

"I see you are a determined rationalist," she said. "Did you not hear me say that I have had experiences even more terrible? I too was once a sceptic, but after what I have known I can no longer doubt."

"Madam," replied Mr. Phillipps, "no one shall make me deny my faith. I will never believe, nor will I pretend to believe that two and two make five, nor will I on any pretences admit the existence of two-sided triangles."

"You are a little hasty," rejoined the lady. "But may I ask you if you ever heard the name of Professor Gregg, the authority on ethnology and kindred subjects?"

"I have done much more than merely hear of Professor Gregg," said Phillipps. "I always regarded him as one of our most acute and clear-headed observers; and his last publication, the 'Textbook of Ethnology,' struck me as being admirable in its kind. Indeed, the book had but come into my hands when I heard of the terrible accident which cut short Gregg's career. He had, I think, taken a country house in the West of England for the summer, and is supposed to have fallen into a river. So far as I remember, his body was never recovered."

"Sir, I am sure that you are discreet. Your conversation seems to declare as much, and the very title of that little work of yours which you mentioned assures me that you are no empty trifler. In a word, I feel that I may depend on you. You appear to be under the impression that Professor Gregg is dead; I have no reason to believe that is the case."

"What?" cried Phillipps, astonished and perturbed. "you do not hint that there was anything disgraceful? I cannot believe it. Gregg was a man of the clearest character; his private life was one of great benevolence; and though I myself am free from delusions, I believe him to have been a sincere and devout Christian. Surely you cannot mean to insinuate that some disreputable history forced him to flee the country?"

"Again you are in a hurry," replied the lady. "I said nothing of all this. Briefly, then, I must tell you that Professor Gregg left his house one morning in full health both of mind and body. He never returned, but his watch and chain, a purse containing three sovereigns in gold, and some loose silver, with a ring that he wore habitually, were found three days later on a wild and savage hillside, many miles from the river. These articles were placed beside a limestone rock of fantastic form; they had been wrapped into a parcel with a kind of rough parchment which was secured with gut. The parcel was opened, and the inner side of the parchment bore an inscription done with some red substance; the characters were undecipherable, but seemed to be a corrupt cuneiform."

"You interest me intensely," said Phillipps. "Would you mind continuing your story? The circumstance you have mentioned seems to me of the most inexplicable character, and I thirst for elucidation."

The young lady seemed to meditate for a moment, and she then proceeded to relate the

Novel of the Black Seal

I must now give you some fuller particulars of my history. I am the daughter of a civil engineer, Steven Lally by name, who was so unfortunate as to die suddenly at the outset of his career, and before he had accumulated sufficient means to support his wife and her two children.

My mother contrived to keep the small household going on resources which must have been incredibly small; we lived in a remote country village, because most of the necessaries of life were cheaper than in a town, but even so we were brought up with the severest economy. My father was a clever and well-read man, and left behind him a small but select collection of books, containing the best Greek, Latin, and English classics, and these books were the only amusement we possessed. My brother, I remember, learnt Latin out of Descartes' "Meditationes," and I, in place of the little tales which children are usually told to read, had nothing more charming than a translation of the "Gesta Romanorum." We grew up thus, quiet, and studious children, and in course of time my brother provided for himself in the manner I have mentioned. I continued to live at home; my poor mother had become an invalid, and demanded my continual care, and about two years ago she died after many months of painful illness. My situation was a terrible one; the shabby furniture barely sufficed to pay the debts I had been forced to contract, and the books I dispatched to my brother, knowing how he would value them. I was absolutely alone; I was aware how poorly my brother was paid; and though I came up to London in the hope of finding employment, with the understanding that he would defray my expenses, I swore it should only be for a month, and that if I could not in that time find some work, I would starve rather than deprive him of the few miserable pounds he had laid by for his day of trouble. I took a little room in a distant suburb, the cheapest that I could find; I lived on bread and tea, and I spent my time in vain answering of advertisements, and vainer walks to addresses I had noted. Day followed on day, and week on week, and still I was unsuccessful, till at last the term I had appointed drew to a close, and I saw before me the grim prospect of slowly dying of starvation. My landlady was good-natured in her way; she knew the slenderness of my means, and I am sure that she would not have turned me out of doors; it remained for me then to go away, and to try to die in some quiet place. It was winter then and a thick white fog gathered in the early part of the afternoon, becoming more dense as the day wore on; it was a Sunday, I remember, and the people of the house were at chapel. At about three o'clock I crept out and walked away as quickly as I could, for I was weak from abstinence. The white mist wrapped all the streets in silence, a hard frost had gathered thick upon the bare branches of the trees, and frost crystals glittered on the wooden fences, and on the cold, cruel ground beneath my feet. I walked on, turning to right and left in utter haphazard, without caring to look up at the names of the streets, and all that I remember of my walk on that Sunday afternoon seems but the broken fragments of an evil dream. In a confused vision I stumbled on, through roads half town and half country, grey fields melting into the cloudy world of mist on one side of me, and on the other comfortable villas with a glow of firelight flickering on the walls, but all unreal; red brick walls and lighted windows, vague trees, and glimmering country, gas-lamps beginning to star the white shadows, the vanishing perspectives of the railway line beneath high embankments, the green and red of the signal lamps,—all these were but momentary pictures flashed on my tired brain and senses numbed by hunger. Now and then I would hear a quick step ringing on the iron road, and men would pass me well wrapped up, walking fast for the sake of warmth, and no doubt eagerly foretasting the pleasures of a glowing hearth, with curtains tightly drawn about the frosted panes, and the welcomes of their friends; but as the early evening darkened and night approached, foot-passengers got fewer and fewer, and I passed through street after street alone. In the white silence I stumbled on, as desolate as if I trod the streets of a buried city; and as I grew more weak and exhausted, something of the horror of death was folding thickly round my heart. Suddenly, as I turned a corner, some one accosted me courteously beneath the lamp-post, and I heard a voice asking if I could kindly point the way to Avon Road. At the sudden shock of human accents I was prostrated, and my strength gave way; I fell all huddled on the sidewalk, and wept and sobbed and laughed in violent hysteria. I had gone out prepared to die, and as I stepped across the threshold that had sheltered me, I consciously bade adieu to all hopes and all remembrances; the door clanged behind me with the noise of thunder, and I felt that an iron curtain had fallen on the brief passages of my life, that henceforth I was to walk a little way in a world of gloom and shadow; I entered on the stage of the first act of death. Then came my wandering in the mist, the whiteness wrapping all things, the void streets, and muffled silence, till when that voice spoke to me it was as if I had died and life returned to me. In a few minutes I was able to compose my feelings, and as I rose I saw that I was confronted by a middle-aged gentleman of pleasing appearance, neatly and correctly dressed. He looked at me with an expression of great pity, but before I could stammer out my ignorance of the neighbourhood, for indeed I had not the slightest notion of where I had wandered, he spoke.

"My dear madam;" he said, "you seem in some terrible distress. You cannot think how you alarmed me. But may I inquire the nature of your trouble? I assure you that you can safely confide in me."

"You are very kind," I replied, "but I fear there is nothing to be done. My condition seems a hopeless one."

"Oh, nonsense, nonsense! You are too young to talk like that. Come, let us walk down here, and you must tell me your difficulty. Perhaps I may be able to help you."

There was something very soothing and persuasive in his manner, and as we walked together I gave him an outline of my story, and told of the despair that had oppressed me almost to death.

"You were wrong to give in so completely," he said, when I was silent. "A month is too short a time in which to feel one's way in London. London, let me tell you, Miss Lally, does not lie open and undefended; it is a fortified place, fossed and double-moated with curious intricacies. As must always happen in large towns, the conditions of life have become hugely artificial; no mere simple palisade is run up to oppose the man or woman who would take the place by storm, but serried lines of subtle contrivances, mines, and pitfalls which it needs a strange skill to overcome. You, in your simplicity, fancied you had only to shout for these walls to sink into nothingness, but the time is gone for such startling victories as these. Take courage; you will learn the secret of success before long."

"Alas! sir," I replied, "I have no doubt your conclusions are correct, but at the present moment I seem to be in a fair way to die of starvation. You spoke of a secret; for heaven's sake tell it me, if you have any pity for my distress."

He laughed genially. "There lies the strangeness of it all. Those who know the secret cannot tell it if they would; it is positively as ineffable as the central doctrine of Freemasonry. But I may say this, that you

yourself have penetrated at least the outer husk of the mystery," and
he laughed again.

"Pray do not jest with me," I said. "What have I done, *que sçais-je?*
I am not so far ignorant that I have not the slightest idea of how my
next meal is to be provided."

"Excuse me. You ask what have you done. You have met me. Come,
we will fence no longer. I see you have self-education, the only education
which is not infinitely pernicious, and I am in want of a governess for my
two children. I have been a widower for some years; my name is Gregg.
I offer you the post I have named, and shall we say a salary of a hundred
a year?"

I could only stutter out my thanks, and slipping a card with his address,
and a banknote by way of earnest into my hand, Mr. Gregg bade me
good-bye, asking me to call in a day or two.

Such was my introduction to Professor Gregg, and can you wonder that
the remembrance of despair and the cold blast that had blown from the
gates of death upon me made me regard him as a second father? Before
the close of the week I was installed in my new duties. The professor had
leased an old brick manor-house in a western suburb of London, and here,
surrounded by pleasant lawns and orchards, and soothed with the murmur
of ancient elms that rocked their boughs above the roof, the new chapter
of my life began. Knowing as you do the nature of the professor's
occupations, you will not be surprised to hear that the house teemed with
books, and cabinets full of strange, and even hideous objects filled every
available nook in the vast low rooms. Gregg was a man whose one thought
was for knowledge, and I too before long caught something of his
enthusiasm, and strove to enter into his passion for research. In a few
months I was perhaps more his secretary than the governess of the two
children, and many a night I have sat at the desk in the glow of the shaded
lamp while he, pacing up and down in the rich gloom of the firelight,
dictated to me the substance of his "Textbook of Ethnology." But amidst
these more sober and accurate studies I always detected a something
hidden, a longing and desire for some object to which he did not allude;
and now and then he would break short in what he was saying and lapse
into reverie, entranced, as it seemed to me, by some distant prospect of
adventurous discovery. The textbook was at last finished, and we began
to receive proofs from the printers, which were entrusted to me for a first
reading, and then underwent the final revision of the professor. All the
while his weariness of the actual business he was engaged on increased,
and it was with the joyous laugh of a schoolboy when term is over that he
one day handed me a copy of the book. "There," he said, "I have kept my
word; I promised to write it, and it is done with. Now I shall be free to

live for stranger things; I confess it, Miss Lally, I covet the renown of
Columbus; you will, I hope, see me play the part of an explorer."

"Surely," I said, "there is little left to explore. You have been born a few
hundred years too late for that."

"I think you are wrong," he replied; "there are still, depend upon it,
quaint, undiscovered countries and continents of strange extent. Ah, Miss
Lally! believe me, we stand amidst sacraments and mysteries full of awe,
and it doth not yet appear what we shall be. Life, believe me, is no simple
thing, no mass of grey matter and congeries of veins and muscles to be
laid naked by the surgeon's knife; man is the secret which I am about to
explore, and before I can discover him I must cross over weltering seas
indeed, and oceans and the mists of many thousand years. You know the
myth of the lost Atlantis; what if it be true, and I am destined to be called
the discoverer of that wonderful land?"

I could see the excitement boiling beneath his words, and in his face
was the heat of the hunter; before me stood a man who believed himself
summoned to tourney with the unknown. A pang of joy possessed me
when I reflected that I was to be in a way associated with him in the
adventure, and I too burned with the lust of the chase, not pausing to
consider that I knew not what we were to unshadow.

The next morning Professor Gregg took me into his inner study, where,
ranged against the wall, stood a nest of pigeon-holes, every drawer neatly
labelled, and the results of years of toil classified in a few feet of space.

"Here," he said, "is my life; here are all the facts which I have gathered
together with so much pains, and yet it is all nothing. No, nothing to
what I am about to attempt. Look at this"; and he took me to an old
bureau, a piece fantastic and faded, which stood in a corner of the room.
He unlocked the front and opened one of the drawers.

"A few scraps of paper," he went on, pointing to the drawer, "and a
lump of black stone, rudely annotated with queer marks and scratches—
that is all that drawer holds. Here you see an old envelope with the dark
red stamp of twenty years ago, but I have pencilled a few lines at the back;
here is a sheet of manuscript and here some cuttings from obscure local
journals. And if you ask me the subject-matter of the collection, it will
not seem extraordinary—a servant-girl at a farm-house, who disappeared
from her place and has never been heard of, a child supposed to have
slipped down some old working on the mountains, some queer scribbling
on a limestone rock, a man murdered with a blow from a strange weapon;
such is the scent I have to go upon. Yes, as you say, there is a ready
explanation for all this; the girl may have run away to London, or
Liverpool, or New York; the child may be at the bottom of the disused
shaft; and the letters on the rock may be the idle whims of some vagrant.

Yes, Yes, I admit all that; but I know I hold the true key. Look!" and he held out a slip of yellow paper.

Characters found inscribed on a limestone rock on the Grey Hills, I read, and then there was a word erased, presumably the name of a county, and a date some fifteen years back. Beneath was traced a number of uncouth characters, shaped somewhat like wedges or daggers, as strange and outlandish as the Hebrew alphabet.

"Now the seal," said Professor Gregg, and he handed me the black stone, a thing like an old-fashioned tobacco-stopper, much enlarged.

I held it up to the light, and saw to my surprise the characters on the paper repeated on the seal.

"Yes," said the professor, "they are the same. And the marks on the limestone rock were made fifteen years ago, with some red substance. And the characters on the seal are four thousand years old at least. Perhaps much more."

"Is it a hoax?" I said.

"No, I anticipated that. I was not to be led to give my life to a practical joke. I have tested the matter very carefully. Only one person besides myself knows of the mere existence of that black seal. Besides, there are other reasons which I cannot enter into now."

"But what does it all mean?" I said. "I cannot understand to what conclusion this all leads."

"My dear Miss Lally, that is a question I would rather leave unanswered for some little time. Perhaps I shall never be able to say what secrets are held here in solution; a few vague hints, the outlines of village tragedies, a few marks done with red earth upon a rock, and an ancient seal. A queer set of data to go upon? Half a dozen pieces of evidence, and twenty years before even so much could be got together; and who knows what mirage or *terra incognita* may be beyond all this? I look across deep waters, Miss Lally, and the land beyond may be but a haze after all. But still I believe it is not so, and a few months will show whether I am right or wrong."

He left me, and alone I endeavoured to fathom the mystery, wondering to what goal such eccentric odds and ends of evidence could lead. I myself am not wholly devoid of imagination, and I had reason to respect the professor's solidity of intellect; yet I saw in the contents of the drawer but the materials of a fantasy, and vainly tried to conceive what theory could be founded on the fragments that had been placed before me. Indeed, I could discover in what I had heard and seen but the fist chapter of an extravagant romance; and yet deep in my heart I burned with curiosity, and day after day I looked eagerly in Professor Gregg's face for some hint of what was to happen.

It was one evening after dinner that the word came.

"I hope you can make your preparations without much trouble," he said suddenly to me. "We shall be leaving here in a week's time."

"Really!" I said in astonishment. "Where are we going?"

"I have taken a country house in the west of England, not far from Caermaen, a quiet little town, once a city, and the headquarters of a Roman legion. It is very dull there, but the country is pretty, and the air is wholesome."

I detected a glint in his eyes, and guessed that this sudden move had some relation to our conversation of a few days before.

"I shall just take a few books with me," said Professor Gregg, "that is all. Everything else will remain here for our return. I have got a holiday," he went on, smiling at me, "and I shan't be sorry to be quit for a time of my old bones and stones and rubbish. Do you know," he went on, "I have been grinding away at facts for thirty years; it is time for fancies."

The days passed quickly; I could see that the professor was all quivering with suppressed excitement, and I could scarce credit the eager appetence of his glance as we left the old manor-house behind us and began our journey. We set out at midday, and it was in the dusk of the evening that we arrived at a little country station. I was tired and excited, and the drive through the lanes seems all a dream. First the deserted streets of a forgotten village, while I heard Professor Gregg's voice talking of the Augustan Legion and the clash of arms, and all the tremendous pomp that followed the eagles; then the broad river swimming to full tide with the last afterglow glimmering duskily in the yellow water, the wide meadows, the cornfields whitening, and the deep lane winding on the slope between the hills and the water. At last we began to ascend, and the air grew rarer. I looked down and saw the pure white mist tracking the outline of the river like a shroud, and a vague and shadowy country; imaginations and fantasy of swelling hills and hanging woods, and half-shaped outlines of hills beyond, and in the distance the glare of the furnace fire on the mountain, growing by turns a pillar of shining flame and fading to a dull point of red. We were slowly mounting a carriage drive, and then there came to me the cool breath and the secret of the great wood that was above us; I seemed to wander in its deepest depths, and there was the sound of trickling water, the scent of the gren leaves, and the breath of the summer night. The carriage stopped at last, and I could scarcely distinguish the form of the house as I waited a moment at the pillared porch. The rest of the evening seemed a dream of strange things bounded by the great silence of the wood and the valley and the river.

The next morning, when I awoke and looked out of the bow window of the big, old-fashioned bedroom, I saw under a grey sky a country that was still all mystery. The long, lovely valley, with the river winding in and out below, crossed in mid-vision by a mediæval bridge of vaulted and buttressed stone, the clear presence of the rising ground beyond, and the woods that I had only seen in shadow the night before, seemed tinged with enchantment, and the soft breath of air that sighed in at the opened pane was like no other wind. I looked across the valley, and beyond, hill followed on hill as wave on wave, and here a faint blue pillar of smoke rose still in the morning air from the chimney of an ancient grey farmhouse, there was a rugged height crowned with dark firs, and in the distance I saw the white streak of a road that climbed and vanished into some unimagined country. But the boundary of all was a great wall of mountain, vast in the west, and ending like a fortress with a steep ascent and a domed tumulus clear against the sky.

I saw Professor Gregg walking up and down the terrace path below the windows, and it was evident that he was revelling in the sense of liberty, and the thought that he had for a while bidden good-bye to task-work. When I joined him there was exultation in his voice as he pointed out the sweep of valley and the river that wound beneath the lovely hills.

"Yes," he said, "it is a strangely beautiful country; and to me, at least, it seems full of mystery. You have not forgotten the drawer I showed you, Miss Lally? No; and you guessed that I have come here not merely for the sake of the children and the fresh air?"

"I think I have guessed as much as that," I replied; "but you must remember I do not know the mere nature of your investigations; and as for the connection between the search and this wonderful valley, it is past my guessing."

He smiled queerly at me. "You must not think I am making a mystery for the sake of a mystery," he said. "I do not speak out because, so far, there is nothing to be spoken, nothing definite, I mean, nothing that can be set down in hard black and white, as dull and sure and irreproachable as any blue-book. And then I have another reason: Many years ago a chance paragraph in a newspaper caught my attention, and focussed in an instant the vagrant thoughts and half-formed fancies of many idle and speculative hours into a certain hypothesis. I saw at once that I was treading on a thin crust; my theory was wild and fantastic in the extreme, and I would not for any consideration have written a hint of it for publication. But I thought that in the company of scientific men like myself, men who knew the course of discovery, and were aware that the gas that blazes and flares in the gin-palace was once a wild hypothesis—I thought that with such men as these I might hazard my dream—let us say Atlantis, or the philosopher's stone, or what you like—without danger of ridicule. I found I was grossly mistaken; my friends looked blankly at me and at one another, and I could see something of pity, and something also of insolent contempt, in the glances they exchanged. One of them called on me the next day, and hinted that I must be suffering from overwork and brain exhaustion. 'In plain terms,' I said, 'you think I am going mad. I think not'; and I showed him out with some little appearance of heat. Since that day I vowed that I would never whisper the nature of my theory to any living soul; to no one but yourself have I ever shown the contents of that drawer. After all, I may be following a rainbow; I may have been misled by the play of coincidence; but as I stand here in this mystic hush and silence amidst the woods and the wild hills, I am more than ever sure that I am hot on the scent. Come, it is time we went in."

To me in all this there was something both of wonder and excitement; I knew how in his ordinary work Professor Gregg moved step by step, testing every inch of the way, and never venturing on assertion without proof that it was impregnable. Yet I divined more from his glance and the vehemence of his tone than from the spoken word, that he had in his every thought the vision of the almost incredible continually with him; and I, who was with some share of imagination no little of a sceptic, offended at a hint of the marvellous, could not help asking myself whether he were cherishing a monomania, and barring out from this one subject all the scientific method of his other life.

Yet, with this image of mystery haunting my thoughts, I surrendered wholly to the charm of the country. Above the faded house on the hillside began the great forest—a long, dark line seen from the opposing hills, stretching above the river for many a mile from north to south, and yielding in the north to even wilder country, barren and savage hills, and ragged common-land, a territory all strange and unvisited, and more unknown to Englishmen than the very heart of Africa. The space of a couple of steep fields alone separated the house from the wood, and the children were delighted to follow me up the long alleys of undergrowth, between smooth pleached walls of shining beech, to the highest point in the wood, whence one looked on one side across the river and the rise and fall of the country to the great western mountain wall, and on the other over the surge and dip of the myriad trees of the forest, over level meadows and the shining yellow sea to the faint coast beyond. I used to sit at this point on the warm sunlit turf which marked the track of the Roman Road, while the two children raced about hunting for the whinberries that grew here and there on the banks. Here beneath the deep blue sky and the great clouds rolling, like olden galleons with sails full-bellied, from the sea to the hills, as I listened to the whispered charm of the great and ancient wood, I lived solely for delight, and only remembered strange things when we would return to the house and find Professor Gregg either shut up in the little room he had made his study, or else pacing the terrace with the look, patient and enthusiastic, of the determined seeker.

One morning, some eight or nine days after our arrival, I looked out of my window and saw the whole landscape transmuted before me. The clouds had dipped low and hidden the mountain in the west; a southern wind was driving the rain in shifting pillars up the valley, and the little brooklet that burst the hill below the house now raged, a red torrent, down the river. We were perforce obliged to keep snug within-doors; and when I had attended to my pupils, I sat down in the morning-room where the ruins of a library still encumbered an old-fashioned bookcase. I had inspected the shelves once or twice, but their contents had failed to attract me; volumes of eighteenth-century sermons, an old book on farriery, a collection of *Poems* by "persons of quality," Prideaux's *Connection*, and an odd volume of Pope, were the boundaries of the library, and there seemed little doubt that everything of interest or value had been removed. Now however, in desperation, I began to re-examine the musty sheepskin and calf bindings, and found, much to my delight, a fine old quarto printed by the Stephani, containing the three books of Pomponius Mela, *De Situ Orbis*, and other of the ancient geographers. I knew enough of Latin to steer my way through an ordinary sentence, and I soon became absorbed in the odd mixture of fact and fancy—light shining on a little space of the world, and beyond, mist and shadow and awful forms. Glancing over the clear-printed pages, my attention was caught by the heading of a chapter in Solinus, and I read the words:—

"MIRA DE INTIMIS GENTIBUS LIBYAE, DE LAPIDE

HEXECONTALITHO,"

—"The wonders of the people that inhabit the inner parts of Libya, and of the stone called Sixtystone."

The odd title attracted me, and I read on:— "Gens ista avia et secreta habitat, in montibus horrendis fœda mysteria celebrat. De hominibus nihil aliud illi praeferunt quam figuram, ab humano ritu prorsus exulant, oderunt deum lucis. Stridunt potius quam loquuntur; vox absona nec sine horrore auditur. Lapide quodam gloriantur, quem Hexecontalithon vocant; dicunt enim hunc lapidem sexaginta notas ostendere. Cujus lapidis nomen secretum ineffabile colunt: quod Ixaxar."

"This folk," I translated to myself, "dwells in remote and secret places, and celebrates foul mysteries on savage hills. Nothing have they in common with men save the face, and the customs of humanity are wholly strange to them; and they hate the sun. They hiss rather than speak; their voices are harsh, and not to be heard without fear. They boast of a certain stone, which they call Sixtystone; for they say that it displays sixty characters. And this stone has a secret unspeakable name; which is Ixaxar."

I laughed at the queer inconsequence of all this, and thought it fit for "Sinbad the Sailor," or other of the supplementary Nights. When I saw Professor Gregg in the course of the day, I told him of my find in the bookcase, and the fantastic rubbish I had been reading. To my surprise he looked up at me with an expression of great interest.

"That is really very curious," he said. "I have never thought it worth while to look into the old geographers, and I dare say I have missed a good deal. Ah, that is the passage, is it? It seems a shame to rob you of your entertainment, but I really think I must carry off the book."

The next day the professor called me to come to the study. I found him sitting at a table in the full light of the window, scrutinizing something very attentively with a magnifying glass.

"Ah, Miss Lally," he began, "I want to use your eyes. This glass is pretty good, but not like my old one that I left in town. Would you mind examining the thing yourself, and telling me how many characters are cut on it?"

He handed me the object in his hand. I saw that it was the black seal he had shown me in London, and my heart began to beat with the thought that I was presently to know something. I took the seal, and, holding it up to the light, checked off the grotesque dagger-shaped characters one by one.

"I make sixty-two," I said at last.

"Sixty-two? Nonsense; it's impossible. Ah, I see what you have done, you have counted that and that," and he pointed to two marks which I had certainly taken as letters with the rest.

"Yes, yes," Professor Gregg went on, "but those are obvious scratches, done accidentally; I saw that at once. Yes, then that's quite right. Thank you very much, Miss Lally."

I was going away, rather disappointed at my having been called in merely to count the number of marks on the black seal, when suddenly there flashed into my mind what I had read in the morning.

"But, Professor Gregg," I cried, breathless, "the seal, the seal. Why, it is the stone Hexecontalithos that Solinus writes of; it is Ixaxar."

"Yes," he said, "I suppose it is. Or it may be a mere coincidence. It never does to be too sure, you know, in these matters. Coincidence killed the professor."

I went away puzzled at what I had heard, and as much as ever at a loss to find the ruling clue in this maze of strange evidence. For three days the bad weather lasted, changing from driving rain to a dense mist, fine and dripping, and we seemed to be shut up in a white cloud that veiled all the world away from us. All the while Professor Gregg was darkling in his room, unwilling, it appeared, to dispense confidences or talk of any kind, and I heard him walking to and fro with a quick, impatient step, as if he were in some way wearied of inaction. The fourth morning was fine, and at breakfast, the professor said briskly—

"We want some extra help around the house; a boy of fifteen or sixteen, you know. There are a lot of little odd jobs that take up the maids' time which a boy could do much better."

"The girls have not complained to me in any way," I replied. "Indeed, Anne said there was much less work than in London, owing to there being so little dust."

"Ah, yes, they are very good girls. But I think we shall do much better with a boy. In fact, that is what has been bothering me for the last two days."

"Bothering you?" I said in astonishment, for as a matter of fact the professor never took the slightest interest in the affairs of the house.

"Yes," he said, "the weather, you know. I really couldn't go out in that Scotch mist; I don't know the country very well, and I should have lost my way. But I am going to get the boy this morning."

"But how do you know there is such a boy as you want anywhere about?"

"Oh, I have no doubt as to that. I may have to walk a mile or two at the most, but I am sure to find just the boy I require."

I thought the professor was joking, but though his tone was airy enough there was something grim and set about his features that puzzled me. He got his stick, and stood at the door looking meditatively before him, and as I passed through the hall he called to me.

"By the way, Miss Lally, there was one thing I wanted to say to you. I dare say you may have heard that some of these country lads are not ever bright; idiotic would be a harsh word to use, and they are usually called 'naturals,' or something of the kind. I hope you won't mind if the boy I am after should turn out not too keen-witted; he will be perfectly harmless, of course, and blacking boots doesn't need much mental effort."

With that he was gone, striding up the road that led to the wood, and I remained stupefied; and then for the first time my astonishment was mingled with a sudden note of terror, arising I knew not whence, and all unexplained even to myself, and yet I felt about my heart for an instant something of the chill of death, and that shapeless, formless dread of the unknown that is worse than death itself. I tried to find courage in the sweet air that blew up from the sea, and in the sunlight after rain, but the mystic woods seemed to darken around me; and the vision of the river coiling between the reeds, and the silver grey of the ancient bridge, fashioned in my mind symbols of vague dread, as the mind of a child fashions terror from things harmless and familiar.

Two hours later Professor Gregg returned. I met him as he came down the road, and asked quietly if he had been able to find a boy.

"Oh, yes," he answered; "I found one easily enough. His name is Jervase Cradock, and I expect he will make himself very useful. His father has been dead for many years, and the mother, whom I saw, seemed very glad at the prospect of a few shillings extra coming in on Saturday nights. As I expected, he is not too sharp, has fits at times, the mother said; but as he will not be trusted with the china, that doesn't much matter, does it? And he is not in any way dangerous, you know, merely a little weak."

"When is he coming?"

"To-morrow morning at eight o'clock. Anne will show him what he has to do, and how to do it. At first he will go home every night, but perhaps it may ultimately turn out more convenient for him to sleep here, and only go home for Sundays."

I found nothing to say to all this; Professor Gregg spoke in a quiet tone of matter-of-fact, as indeed was warranted by the circumstance; and yet I could not quell my sensation of astonishment at the whole affair. I knew that in reality no assistance was wanted in the housework, and the professor's prediction that the boy he was to engage might prove a little 'simple,' followed by so exact a fulfillment, struck me as bizarre in the extreme. The next morning I heard from the house-maid that the boy Cradock had come at eight, and that she had been trying to make him useful. "He doesn't seem quite all there, I don't think, miss," was her comment, and later in the day I saw him helping the old man who worked in the garden. He was a youth of about fourteen, with black hair and black eyes and an olive skin, and I saw at once from the curious vacancy of his expression that he was mentally weak. He touched his forehead awkwardly as I went by, and I heard him answering the gardener in a queer, harsh voice that caught my attention; it gave me the impression of some one speaking deep below under the earth, and there was a strange sibilance, like the hissing of a phonograph as the pointer travels over the cylinder. I heard that he seemed anxious to do what he could, and was quite docile and obedient, and Morgan the gardener, who knew his mother, assured me he was perfectly harmless. "He's always been a bit queer," he said, "and no wonder, after what his mother went through before he was born. I did know his father, Thomas Cradock, well, and a very fine workman he was too, indeed. He got something wrong with his lungs owing to working in the wet woods, and never got over it, and went off quite sudden like. And they do say as how Mrs. Cradock was quite off her head; anyhow, she was found by Mr. Hillyer, Ty Coch, all crouched up on the Grey Hills, over there, crying and weeping like a lost soul. And Jervase, he was born about eight months afterwards, and as I was saying, he was a bit queer always; and they do say when he could scarcely walk he would frighten the other children into fits with the noises he would make."

A word in the story had stirred up some remembrance within me, and, vaguely curious, I asked the old man where the Grey Hills were.

"Up there," he said, with the same gesture he had used before; "you go past the 'Fox and Hounds,' and through the forest, by the old ruins. It's a good five mile from here, and a strange sort of a place. The poorest soil between this and Monmouth, they do say, though it's good feed for sheep. Yes, it was a sad thing for poor Mrs. Cradock."

The old man turned to his work, and I strolled on down the path between the espaliers, gnarled and gouty with age, thinking of the story I had heard, and groping for the point in it that had some key to my memory. In an instant it came before me; I had seen the phrase "Grey Hills" on the slip of yellowed paper that Professor Gregg had taken from the drawer in his cabinet. Again I was seized with pangs of mild curiosity and fear; I remembered the strange characters copied from the limestone rock, and then again their identity with the inscriptions on the age-old seal, and the fantastic fables of the Latin geographer. I saw beyond doubt that, unless coincidence had set all the scene and disposed all these bizarre events with curious art, I was to be a spectator of things far removed from the usual and customary traffic and jostle of life. Professor Gregg I noted day by day; he was hot on his trail, growing lean with eagerness; and in the evenings, when the sun was swimming on the verge of the mountain, he would pace the terrace to and fro with his eyes on the ground, while the mist grew white in the valley, and the stillness of the evening brought far voices near, and the blue smoke rose a straight column from the diamond-shaped chimney of the grey farm-house, just as I had seen it on the first morning. I have told you I was of sceptical habit; but though I understood little or nothing, I began to dread, vainly proposing to myself the iterated dogmas of science that all life is material, and that in the system of things there is no undiscovered land, even beyond the remotest stars, where the supernatural can find a footing. Yet there struck in on this the thought that matter is as really awful and unknown as spirit, that science itself but dallies on the threshold, scarcely gaining more than a glimpse of the wonders of the inner place.

There is one day that stands up from amidst the others as a grim red beacon, betokening evil to come. I was sitting on a bench in the garden, watching the boy Cradock weeding, when I was suddenly alarmed by a harsh and choking sound, like the cry of a wild beast in anguish, and I was unspeakably shocked to see the unfortunate lad standing in full view before me, his whole body quivering and shaking at short intervals as though shocks of electricity were passing through him, his teeth grinding, foam gathering on his lips, and his face all swollen and blackened to a hideous mask of humanity. I shrieked with terror, and Professor Gregg came running; and as I pointed to Cradock, the boy with one convulsive shudder fell face forward, and lay on the wet earth, his body writhing like a wounded blind worm, and an inconceivable babble of sounds bursting and rattling and hissing from his lips. He seemed to pour forth an infamous jargon, with words, or what seemed words, that might have belonged to a tongue dead since untold ages, and buried deep beneath Nilotic mud, or in the inmost reaches of the Mexican forest. For a moment the thought passed through my mind, as my ears were still revolted with that infernal clamour, "Surely this is the very speech of hell," and then I cried out again and again, and ran away shuddering to my inmost soul. I had seen Professor Gregg's face as he stooped over the wretched boy and raised him, and I was appalled by the glow of exultation that shone on every lineament and feature. As I sat in my room with drawn blinds, and my eyes hidden in my hands, I heard heavy steps beneath, and I was told afterwards that Professor Gregg had carried Cradock to his study, and had locked the door. I heard voices murmur indistinctly, and I trembled to think of what might be passing within a few feet of where I sat; I longed to escape to the woods and sunshine, and yet I dreaded the sights that might confront me on the way; and at last, as I held the handle of the door nervously, I heard Professor Gregg's voice calling to me with a cheerful ring. "It's all right now, Miss Lally," he said. "The poor fellow has got over it, and I have been arranging for him to sleep here after to-morrow. Perhaps I may be able to do something for him."

"Yes," he said later, "it was a very painful sight, and I don't wonder you were alarmed. We may hope that good food will build him up a little, but I am afraid he will never really be cured," and he affected the dismal and conventional air with which one speaks of hopeless illness; and yet beneath it I detected the delight that leapt up rampant within him, and fought and struggled to find utterance. It was as if one glanced down on the even surface of the sea, clear and immobile, and saw beneath raging depths and a storm of contending billows. It was indeed to me a torturing and offensive problem that this man, who had so bounteously rescued me from the sharpness of death, and showed himself in all the relations of life full of benevolence, and pity, and kindly forethought, should so manifestly be for once on the side of the demons, and take a ghastly pleasure in the torments of an afflicted fellow-creature. Apart, I struggled with the horned difficulty, and strove to find the solution; but without the hint of a clue, beset by mystery and contradiction. I saw nothing that might help me, and began to wonder whether, after all, I had not escaped from the white mist of the suburb at too dear a rate. I hinted something of my thought to the professor; I said enough to let him know that I was in the most acute perplexity, but the moment after regretted what I had done when I saw his face contort with a spasm of pain.

"My dear Miss Lally," he said, "you surely do not wish to leave us? No, no, you would not do it. You do not know how I rely on you; how confidently I go forward, assured that you are here to watch over my children. You, Miss Lally, are my rearguard; for let me tell you the business in which I am engaged is not wholly devoid of peril. You have not forgotten what I said the first morning here; my lips are shut by an old and firm resolve till they can open to utter no ingenious hypothesis or vague surmise but irrefragable fact, as certain as a demonstration in mathematics. Think it over, Miss Lally: not for a moment would I endeavour to keep you here against your own instincts, and yet I tell you frankly that I am persuaded it is here, here amidst the woods, that your duty lies."

I was touched by the eloquence of his tone, and by the remembrance that the man, after all, had been my salvation, and I gave him my hand on a promise to serve him loyally and without question. A few days later the rector of our church—a little church, grey and severe and quaint, that hovered on the very banks of the river and watched the tides swim and return—came to see us, and Professor Gregg easily persuaded him to stay and share our dinner. Mr. Meyrick was a member of an antique family of squires, whose old manor-house stood amongst the hills some seven miles away, and thus rooted in the soil, the rector was a living store of all the old fading customs and lore of the country. His manner, genial, with a deal of retired oddity, won on Professor Gregg; and towards the cheese, when a curious Burgundy had begun its incantations, the two men glowed like the wine, and talked of philology with the enthusiasm of a burgess over the peerage. The parson was expounding the pronunciation of the Welsh *ll*, and producing sounds like the gurgle of his native brooks, when Professor Gregg struck in.

"By the way," he said, "that was a very odd word I met the other day. You know my boy, poor Jervase Cradock? Well, he has got the bad habit of talking to himself, and the day before yesterday I was walking in the garden here and heard him; he was evidently quite unconscious of my presence. A lot of what he said I couldn't make out, but one word struck me distinctly. It was such an odd sound, half sibilant, half guttural, and as quaint as those double *ls* you have been demonstrating. I do not know whether I can give you an idea of the sound; 'Ishakshar' is perhaps as near as I can get. But the *k* ought to be a Greek *chi* or a Spanish *j*. Now what does it mean in Welsh?"

"In Welsh?" said the parson. "There is no such word in Welsh, nor any word remotely resembling it. I know the book-Welsh, as they call it, and the colloquial dialects as well as any man, but there's no word like that from Anglesea to Usk. Besides, none of the Cradocks speaks a word of Welsh; it's dying out around here."

"Really. You interest me extremely, Mr. Meyrick. I confess the word didn't strike me as having the Welsh ring. But I thought it might be some local corruption."

"No, I have never heard such a word, or anything like it. Indeed," he added, smiling whimsically, "if it belongs to any language, I should say it must be that of the fairies—the Tylwydd Têg, as we call them."

The talk went on to the discovery of a Roman villa in the neighbourhood; and soon after I left the room, and sat down apart to wonder at the drawing together of such strange clues of evidence. As the professor had spoken of the curious word, I had caught the glint of his eye upon me; and though the pronunciation he gave was grotesque in the extreme, I recognized the name of the stone of sixty characters mentioned by Solinus, the black seal shut up in some secret drawer of the study, stamped for ever by a vanished race with signs no man could read, signs that might, for all I knew, be the veils of awful things done long ago, and forgotten before the hills were moulded into form.

When the next morning I came down, I found Professor Gregg pacing the terrace in his eternal walk.

"Look at that bridge," he said, when he saw me; "observe the quaint and Gothic design, the angles between the arches, and the silvery grey of the stone in the awe of the morning light. I confess it seems to me symbolic; it should illustrate a mystical allegory of the passage from one world to another."

"Professor Gregg," I said quietly, "it is time that I knew something of what has happened, and of what is to happen."

For the moment he put me off, but I returned again with the same question in the evening, and then Professor Gregg flamed with excitement. "Don't you understand yet?" he cried. "But I have told you a good deal; yes, and shown you a good deal; you have heard pretty nearly all that I have heard, and seen what I have seen; or at least," and his voice chilled as he spoke, "enough to make a good deal clear as noonday. The servants told you, I have no doubt, that the wretched boy Cradock had another seizure the night before last; he awoke me with cries in that voice you heard in the garden, and I went to him, and God forbid you should see what I saw that night. But all this is useless; my time here is drawing to a close; I must be back in town in three weeks, as I have a course of lectures to prepare, and need all my books about me. In a very few days it will all be over, and I shall no longer hint, and no longer be liable to ridicule as a madman and a quack. No, I shall speak plainly, and I shall be heard with such emotions as perhaps no other man has ever drawn from the breasts of his fellows."

He paused, and seemed to grow radiant with the joy of great and wonderful discovery.

"But all that is for the future, the near future certainly, but still the future," he went on at length. "There is something to be done yet; you will remember my telling you that my researches were not altogether devoid of peril? Yes, there is a certain amount of danger to be faced; I did not know how much when I spoke on the subject before, and to a certain extent I am still in the dark. But it will be a strange adventure, the last of all, the last demonstration in the chain."

He was walking up and down the room as he spoke, and I could hear in his voice the contending tones of exultation and despondence, or perhaps I should say awe, the awe of a man who goes forth on unknown waters, and I thought of his allusion to Columbus on the night he had laid his book before me. The evening was a little chilly, and a fire of logs had been lighted in the study where we were; the remittent flame and the glow on the walls reminded me of the old days. I was sitting silent in an arm-chair by the fire, wondering over all I had heard, and still vainly speculating as to the secret springs concealed from me under all the phantasmagoria I had witnessed, when I became suddenly aware of a sensation that change of some sort had been at work in the room, and that there was something unfamiliar in its aspect. For some time I looked about me, trying in vain to localize the alteration that I knew had been made; the table by the window, the chairs, the faded settee were all as I had known them. Suddenly, as a sought-for recollection flashes into mind, I knew what was amiss. I was facing the professor's desk, which stood on the other side of the fire, and above the desk was a grimy-looking bust of Pitt, that I had never seen there before. And then I remembered the true position of this work of art; in the furthest corner by the door was an old cupboard, projecting into the room, and on the top of the cupboard, fifteen feet from the floor, the bust had been, and there, no doubt, it had delayed, accumulating dirt, since the early years of the century.

I was utterly amazed, and sat silent still, in a confusion of thought. There was, so far as I knew, no such thing as a step-ladder in the house, for I had asked for one to make some alterations on the curtains of my room, and a tall man standing on a chair would have found it impossible to take down the bust. It had been placed, not on the edge of the cupboard, but far back against the wall; and Professor Gregg was, if anything, under the average height.

"How on earth did you manage to get down Pitt?" I said at last.

The professor looked curiously at me, and seemed to hesitate a little.

"They must have found you a step-ladder, or perhaps the gardener brought in a short ladder from outside?"

"No, I have had no ladder of any kind. Now, Miss Lally," he went on with an awkward simulation of jest, "there is a little puzzle for you; a problem in the manner of the inimitable Holmes; there are the facts, plain and patent; summon your acuteness to the solution of the puzzle. For Heaven's sake," he cried with a breaking voice, "say no more about it! I tell you, I never touched the thing," and he went out of the room with horror manifest on his face, and his hand shook and jarred the door behind him.

I looked around the room in vague surprise, not at all realizing what had happened, making vain and idle surmises by way of explanation, and wondering at the stirring of black waters by an idle word and the trivial change of an ornament. "This is some petty business, some whim on which I have jarred," I reflected; "the professor is perhaps scrupulous and superstitious over trifles, and my question may have outraged unacknowledged fears, as though one killed a spider or spilled the salt before the eyes of a practical Scotchwoman." I was immersed in these fond suspicions, and began to plume myself a little on my immunity from such empty fears, when the truth fell heavily as lead upon my heart, and I recognized with cold terror that some awful influence had been at work. The bust was simply inaccessible; without a ladder no one could have touched it.

I went out to the kitchen and spoke as quietly as I could to the housemaid.

"Who moved that bust from the top of the cupboard, Anne?" I said to her. "Professor Gregg says he has not touched it. Did you find an old step-ladder in one of the outhouses?"

The girl looked at me blankly.

"I never touched it," she said. "I found it where it is now the other morning when I dusted the room. I remember now, it was Wednesday morning, because it was the morning after Cradock was taken bad in the night. My room is next to his, you know, miss," the girl went on piteously, "and it was awful to hear how he cried out and called out names that I couldn't understand. It made me feel all afraid; and then master came, and I heard him speak, and he took down Cradock to the study and gave him something."

"And you found that bust moved the next morning?"

"Yes, miss. There was a queer sort of smell in the study when I came down and opened the windows; a bad smell it was, and I wondered what it could be. Do you know, miss, I went a long time ago to the Zoo in London with my cousin Thomas Barker, one afternoon that I had off, when I was at Mrs. Prince's in Stanhope Gate, and we went into the snake-house to see the snakes, and it was just the same sort of smell; very sick it made me feel, I remember, and I got Barker to take me out. And it was just the same kind of a smell in the study, as I was saying, and I was wondering what it could be from, when I see that bust with Pitt cut in it, standing on the master's desk, and I thought to myself, Now who has done that, and how have they done it? And when I came to dust the things, I looked at the bust, and I saw a great mark on it where the dust was gone, for I don't think it can have been touched with a duster for years and years, and it wasn't like finger-marks, but a large patch like, broad and spread out. So I passed my hand over it, without thinking what I was doing, and where that patch was it was all sticky and slimy, as if a snail had crawled over it. Very strange, isn't it, miss? and I wonder who can have done it, and how that mess was made."

The well-meant gabble of the servant touched me to the quick; I lay down upon my bed, and bit my lip that I should not cry out loud in the sharp anguish of my terror and bewilderment. Indeed, I was almost mad with dread; I believe that if it had been daylight I should have fled hot foot, forgetting all courage and all the debt of gratitude that was due to Professor Gregg, not caring whether my fate were that I must starve slowly, so long as I might escape from the net of blind and panic fear that every day seemed to draw a little closer round me. If I knew, I thought, if I knew what there were to dread, I could guard against it; but here, in this lonely house, shut in on all sides by the olden woods and the vaulted hills, terror seems to spring inconsequent from every covert, and the flesh is aghast at the half-heard murmurs of horrible things. All in vain I strove to summon scepticism to my aid, and endeavoured by cool common sense to buttress my belief in a world of natural order, for the air that blew in at the open window was a mystic breath, and in the darkness I felt the silence go heavy and sorrowful as a mass of requiem, and I conjured images of strange shapes gathering fast amidst the reeds, beside the wash of the river.

In the morning from the moment that I set foot in the breakfast-room, I felt that the unknown plot was drawing to a crisis; the professor's face was firm and set, and he seemed hardly to hear our voices when we spoke.

"I am going out for a rather long walk," he said when the meal was over. "You mustn't be expecting me, now, or thinking anything has happened if I don't turn up to dinner. I have been getting stupid lately, and I dare say a miniature walking tour will do me good. Perhaps I may even spend the night in some little inn, if I find any place that looks clean and comfortable."

I heard this and knew by my experience of Professor Gregg's manner that it was no ordinary business or pleasure that impelled him. I knew not, nor even remotely guessed, where he was bound, nor had I the vaguest notion of his errand, but all the fear of the night before returned; and as he stood, smiling, on the terrace, ready to set out, I implored him to stay, and to forget all his dreams of the undiscovered continent.

"No, no, Miss Lally," he replied still smiling, "it's too late now. *Vestigia nulla retrorsum,* you know is the device of all true explorers, though I hope it won't be literally true in my case. But, indeed, you are wrong to alarm yourself so; I look upon my little expedition as quite commonplace; no more exciting than a day with the geological hammers. There is a risk, of course, but so there is on the commonest excursion. I can afford to be jaunty; I am doing nothing so hazardous as 'Arry does a hundred times over in the course of every Bank Holiday. Well, then, you must look more cheerfully; and so good-bye till to-morrow at latest."

He walked briskly up the road, and I saw him open the gate that marks the entrance of the wood, and then he vanished in the gloom of the trees.

All the day passed heavily with a strange darkness in the air, and again I felt as if imprisoned amidst the ancient woods, shut in an olden land of mystery and dread, and as if all was long ago and forgotten by the living outside. I hoped and dreaded; and when the dinner-hour

came I waited, expecting to hear the professor's step in the hall, and
his voice exulting at I knew not what triumph. I composed my face to
welcome him gladly, but the night descended dark, and he did not
come.

In the morning, when the maid knocked at my door, I called out to
her, and asked if her master had returned; and when she replied that
his bedroom stood open and empty, I felt the cold clasp of despair. Still,
I fancied he might have discovered genial company, and would return
for luncheon, or perhaps in the afternoon, and I took the children for
a walk in the forest, and tried my best to play and laugh with them,
and to shut out the thoughts of mystery and veiled terror. Hour after
hour I waited, and my thoughts grew darker; again the night came
and found me watching, and at last, as I was making much ado to finish
my dinner, I heard steps outside and the sound of a man's voice.

The maid came in and looked oddly at me. "Please, miss," she began,
"Mr. Morgan the gardener wants to speak to you for a minute, if you
didn't mind."

"Show him in, please," I answered, and set my lips tight.

The old man came slowly into the room, and the servant shut the
door behind him.

"Sit down, Mr. Morgan," I said; "what is it that you want to say to
me?"

"Well, miss, Mr. Gregg he gave me something for you yesterday
morning, just before he went off; and he told me particular not to hand
it up before eight o'clock this evening exactly, if so be as he wasn't back
home again before, and if he should come home before I was just to
return it to him in his own hands. So, you see, as Mr. Gregg isn't here
yet, I suppose I'd better give you the parcel directly."

He pulled something from his pocket, and gave it to me, half rising.
I took it silently, and seeing that Morgan seemed doubtful as to what
he was to do next, I thanked him and bade him good-night, and he
went out. I was left alone in the room with the parcel in my hand—a
paper parcel neatly sealed and directed to me, with the instructions
Morgan had quoted, all written in the professor's large loose hand. I
broke the seals with a choking at my heart, and found an envelope
inside, addressed also, but open, and took the letter out.

"MY DEAR MISS LALLY," it began,—"To quote the old logic manual,
the case of your reading this note is a case of my having made a blunder
of some sort, and, I am afraid, a blunder that turns these lines into a
farewell. It is practically certain that neither you nor any one else will
ever see me again. I have made my will with provision for this
eventuality, and I hope you will consent to accept the small remem-

brance addressed to you, and my sincere thanks for the way in which you joined your fortunes to mine. The fate which has come upon me is desperate and terrible beyond the remotest dreams of man; but this fate you have a right to know—if you please. If you look in the left-hand drawer of my dressing-table, you will find the key of the escritoire, properly labelled. In the well of the escritoire is a large envelope sealed and addressed to your name. I advise you to throw it forthwith into the fire; you will sleep better of nights if you do so. But if you must know the history of what has happened, it is all written down for you to read."

The signature was firmly written below, and again I turned the page and read out the words one by one, aghast and white to the lips, my hands cold as ice, and sickness choking me. The dead silence of the room, and the thought of the dark woods and hills closing me in on every side, oppressed me, helpless and without capacity, and not knowing where to turn for counsel. At last I resolved that though knowledge should haunt my whole life and all the days to come, I must know the meaning of the strange terrors that had so long tormented me, rising grey, dim, and awful, like the shadows in the wood at dusk. I carefully carried out Professor Gregg's directions, and not without reluctance broke the seal of the envelope, and spread out his manuscript before me. That manuscript I always carry with me, and I see that I cannot deny your unspoken request to read it. This, then, was what I read that night, sitting at the desk, with a shaded lamp beside me.

The young lady who called herself Miss Lally then proceeded to recite

The Statement of William Gregg, F.R.S., etc.

It is many years since the first glimmer of the theory which is now almost, if not quite, reduced to fact dawned on my mind. A somewhat extensive course of miscellaneous and obsolete reading had done a good deal to prepare the way, and, later, when I became somewhat of a specialist, and immersed myself in the studies known as ethnological, I was now and then startled by facts that would not square with orthodox scientific opinion, and by discoveries that seemed to hint at something still hidden for all our research. More particularly I became convinced that much of the folk-lore of the world is but an exaggerated account of events that really happened, and I was especially drawn to consider the stories of the fairies, the good folk of the Celtic races. Here I thought I could detect the fringe of embroidery and exaggeration, the fantastic guise, the little people dressed in green and gold sporting in the flowers, and I thought I saw a distinct analogy between the name

given to this race (supposed to be imaginary) and the description of
their appearance and manners. Just as our remote ancestors called the
dreadful beings "fair" and "good" precisely because they dreaded them,
so they had dressed them up in charming forms, knowing the truth to
be the very reverse. Literature, too, had gone early to work, and had
lent a powerful hand in the transformation, so that the playful elves of
Shakespeare are already far removed from the true original, and the
real horror is disguised in a form of prankish mischief. But in the older
tales, the stories that used to make men cross themselves as they sat
round the burning logs, we tread a different stage; I saw a widely
opposed spirit in certain histories of children and of men and women
who vanished strangely from the earth. They would be seen by a
peasant in the fields walking toward some green and rounded hillock,
and seen no more on earth; and there are stories of mothers who have
left a child quietly sleeping, with the cottage door rudely barred with
a piece of wood, and have returned, not to find the plump and rosy
little Saxon, but a thin and wizened creature, with sallow skin and
black, piercing eyes, the child of another race. Then, again, there were
myths darker still; the dread of witch and wizard, the lurid evil of the
Sabbath, and the hint of demons who mingled with the daughters of
men. And just as we have turned the terrible "fair folk" into a company
of benignant, if freakish, elves, so we have hidden from us the black
foulness of the witch and her companions under a popular *diablerie* of
old women and broomsticks and a comic cat with tail on end. So the
Greeks called the hideous furies benevolent ladies, and thus the
northern nations have followed their example. I pursued my investigations, stealing odd hours from other and more imperative labours,
and I asked myself the question: Supposing these traditions to be true,
who were the demons who are reported to have attended the Sabbaths?
I need not say that I laid aside what I may call the supernatural
hypothesis of the Middle Ages, and came to the conclusion that fairies
and devils were of one and the same race and origin; invention, no
doubt, and the Gothic fancy of old days, had done much in the way of
exaggeration and distortion; yet I firmly believe that beneath all this
imagery there was a black background of truth. As for some of the
alleged wonders, I hesitated. While I should be very loath to receive
any one specific instance of modern spiritualism as containing even a
grain of the genuine, yet I was not wholly prepared to deny that human
flesh may now and then, once perhaps in ten million cases, be the veil
of powers which seem magical to us—powers which, so far from
proceeding from the heights and leading men thither, are in reality
survivals from the depth of being. The amoeba and the snail have
powers which we do not possess; and I thought it possible that the

theory of reversion might explain many things which seem wholly
inexplicable. Thus stood my position; I saw good reason to believe that
much of the tradition, a vast deal of the earliest and uncorrupted
tradition of the so-called fairies, represented solid fact, and I thought
that the purely supernatural element in these traditions was to be
accounted for on the hypothesis that a race which had fallen out of the
grand march of evolution might have retained, as a survival, certain
powers which would be to us wholly miraculous. Such was my theory
as it stood conceived in my mind; and working with this in view, I
seemed to gather confirmation from every side, from the spoils of a
tumulus or a barrow, from a local paper reporting an antiquarian
meeting in the country, and from general literature of all kinds.
Amongst other instances, I remember being struck by the phrase
"articulate-speaking men" in Homer, as if the writer knew or had heard
of men whose speech was so rude that it could hardly be termed
articulate; and on my hypothesis of a race who had lagged far behind
the rest, I could easily conceive that such a folk would speak a jargon
but little removed from the inarticulate noises of brute beasts.

Thus I stood, satisfied that my conjecture was at all events not far
removed from fact, when a chance paragraph in a small country print
one day arrested my attention. It was a short account of what was to
all appearance the usual sordid tragedy of the village—a young girl
unaccountably missing, and evil rumour blatant and busy with her
reputation. Yet, I could read between the lines that all this scandal was
purely hypocritical, and in all probability invented to account for what
was in any other manner unaccountable. A flight to London or
Liverpool, or an undiscovered body lying with a weight about its neck
in the foul depths of a woodland pool, or perhaps murder—such were
the theories of the wretched girl's neighbours. But as I idly scanned
the paragraph, a flash of thought passed through me with the violence
of an electric shock: what if the obscure and horrible race of the hills
still survived, still remained haunting the wild places and barren hills,
and now and then repeating the evil of Gothic legend, unchanged and
unchangeable as the Turanian Shelta, or the Basques of Spain? I have
said that the thought came with violence; and indeed I drew in my
breath sharply, and clung with both hands to my elbow-chair, in a
strange confusion of horror and elation. It was as if one of my *confrères*
of physical science, roaming in a quiet English wood, had been suddenly stricken aghast by the presence of the slimy and loathsome terror
of the ichthyosaurus, the original of the stories of the awful worms
killed by valorous knights, or had seen the sun darkened by the
pterodactyl, the dragon of tradition. Yet as a resolute explorer of
knowledge, the thought of such a discovery threw me into a passion

of joy, and I cut out the slip from the paper and put it in a drawer in my old bureau, resolved that it should be but the first piece in a collection of the strangest significance. I sat long that evening dreaming of the conclusions I should establish, nor did cooler reflection at first dash my confidence. Yet as I began to put the case fairly, I saw that I might be building on an unstable foundation; the facts might possibly be in accordance with local opinion, and I regarded the affair with a mood of some reserve. Yet I resolved to remain perched on the look-out, and I hugged to myself the thought that I alone was watching and wakeful, while the great crowd of thinkers and searchers stood heedless and indifferent, perhaps letting the most prerogative facts pass by unnoticed.

Several years elapsed before I was enabled to add to the contents of the drawer; and the second find was in reality not a valuable one, for it was a mere repetition of the first, with only the variation of another and distant locality. Yet I gained something; for in the second case, as in the first, the tragedy took place in a desolate and lonely country, and so far my theory seemed justified. But the third piece was to me far more decisive. Again, amongst outland hills, far even from a main road of traffic, an old man was found done to death, and the instrument of execution was left beside him. Here, indeed, there were rumour and conjecture, for the deadly tool was a primitive stone axe, bound by gut to the wooden handle, and surmises the most extravagant and improbable were indulged in. Yet, as I thought with a kind of glee, the wildest conjectures went far astray; and I took the pains to enter into correspondence with the local doctor, who was called at the inquest. He, a man of some acuteness, was dumb-foundered. "It will not do to speak of these things in country places," he wrote to me; "but frankly, there is some hideous mystery here. I have obtained possession of the stone axe, and have been so curious as to test its powers. I took it into the back-garden of my house one Sunday afternoon when my family and servants were all out, and there, sheltered by the poplar hedges, I made my experiments. I found the thing utterly unmanageable; whether there is some peculiar balance, some nice adjustment of weights, which require incessant practice, or whether an effectual blow can be struck only by a certain trick of the muscles, I do not know; but I can assure you that I went into the house with but a sorry opinion of my athletic capacities. It was like an inexperienced man trying 'putting the hammer'; the force exerted seemed to return on oneself, and I found myself hurled backwards with violence, while the axe fell harmless to the ground. On another occasion I tried the experiment with a clever woodman of the place; but this man, who had handled his axe for forty years, could do nothing with the stone implement, and missed every stroke most ludicrously. In short, if it were not so supremely absurd, I should say that for four thousand years no one on earth could have struck an effective blow with the tool that undoubtedly was used to murder the old man." This, as may be imagined, was to me rare news; and afterwards, when I heard the whole story, and learned that the unfortunate old man had babbled tales of what might be seen at night on a certain wild hillside, hinting at unheard-of wonders, and that he had been found cold one morning on the very hill in question, my exultation was extreme, for I felt I was leaving conjecture far behind me. But the next step was of still greater importance. I had possessed for many years an extraordinary stone seal—a piece of dull black stone, two inches long from the handle to the stamp, and the stamping end a rough hexagon an inch and a quarter in diameter. Altogether, it presented the appearance of an enlarged tobacco stopper of an old-fashioned make. It had been sent to me by an agent in the East, who informed me that it had been found near the site of the ancient Babylon. But the characters engraved on the seal were to me an intolerable puzzle. Somewhat of the cuneiform pattern, there were yet striking differences, which I detected at the first glance, and all efforts to read the inscription on the hypothesis that the rules for deciphering the arrow-headed writing would apply proved futile. A riddle such as this stung my pride, and at odd moments I would take the Black Seal out of the cabinet, and scrutinize it with so much idle perseverance that every letter was familiar to my mind, and I could have drawn the inscription from memory without the slightest error. Judge, then, of my surprise when I one day received from a correspondent in the west of England a letter and an enclosure that positively left me thunderstruck. I saw carefully traced on a large piece of paper the very characters of the Black Seal, without alteration of any kind, and above the inscription my friend had written: *Inscription found on a limestone rock on the Grey Hills, Monmouthshire. Done in some red earth, and quite recent.* I turned to the letter. My friend wrote: "I sent you the enclosed inscription with all due reserve. A shepherd who passed by the stone a week ago swears that there was then no mark of any kind. The characters, as I have noted, are formed by drawing some red earth over the stone, and are of an average height of one inch. They look to me like a kind of cuneiform character, a good deal altered, but this, of course, is impossible. It may be either a hoax, or more probably some scribble of the gipsies, who are plentiful enough in this wild country. They have, as you are aware, many hieroglyphics which they use in communicating with one another. I happened to visit the stone in question two days ago in connection with a rather painful incident which has occurred here."

As may be supposed, I wrote immediately to my friend, thanking him for the copy of the inscription, and asking him in a casual manner the history of the incident he mentioned. To be brief, I heard that a woman named Cradock, who had lost her husband a day before, had set out to communicate the sad news to a cousin who lived some five miles away. She took a short cut which led by the Grey Hills. Mrs. Cradock, who was then quite a young woman, never arrived at her relative's house. Late that night a farmer who had lost a couple of sheep, supposed to have wandered from the flock, was walking over the Grey Hills, with a lantern and his dog. His attention was attracted by a noise, which he described as a kind of wailing, mournful and pitiable to hear; and, guided by the sound, he found the unfortunate Mrs. Cradock crouched on the ground by the limestone rock, swaying her body to and fro, and lamenting and crying in so heartrending a manner that the farmer was, as he says, at first obliged to stop his ears, or he would have run away. The woman allowed herself to be taken home, and a neighbour came to see to her necessities. All the night she never ceased her crying, mixing her lament with words of some unintelligible jargon, and when the doctor arrived he pronounced her insane. She lay on her bed for a week, now wailing, as people said, like one lost and damned for eternity, and now sunk in a heavy coma; it was thought that grief at the loss of her husband had unsettled her mind, and the medical man did not at one time expect her to live. I need not say that I was deeply interested in this story, and I made my friend write to me at intervals with all the particulars of the case. I heard then that in the course of six weeks the woman gradually recovered the use of her faculties, and some months later she gave birth to a son, christened Jervase, who unhappily proved to be of weak intellect. Such were the facts known to the village; but to me, while I whitened at the suggested thought of the hideous enormities that had doubtless been committed, all this was nothing short of conviction, and I incautiously hazarded a hint of something like the truth to some scientific friends. The moment the words had left my lips I bitterly regretted having spoken, and thus given way the great secret of my life, but with a good deal of relief mixed with indignation I found my fears altogether misplaced, for my friends ridiculed me to my face, and I was regarded as a madman; and beneath a natural anger I chuckled to myself, feeling as secure amidst these blockheads as if I had confided what I knew to the desert sands.

But now, knowing so much, I resolved I would know all, and I concentrated my efforts on the task of deciphering the inscription on the Black Seal. For many years I made this puzzle the sole object of my leisure moments; for the greater portion of my time was, of course, devoted to other duties, and it was only now and then that I could snatch a week of clear research. If I were to tell the full history of this curious investigation, this statement would be wearisome in the extreme, for it would contain simply the account of long and tedious failure. By what I knew already of ancient scripts I was well equipped for the chase, as I always termed it to myself. I had correspondents amongst all the scientific men in Europe, and indeed, in the world, and I could not believe that in these days any character, however ancient and however perplexed, could long resist the search-light I should bring to bear upon it. Yet, in point of fact, it was fully fourteen years before I succeeded. With every year my professional duties increased, and my leisure became smaller. This no doubt retarded me a good deal; and yet, when I look back on those years, I am astonished at the vast scope of my investigation of the Black Seal. I made my bureau a centre, and from all the world and from all the ages I gathered transcripts of ancient writing. Nothing, I resolved, should pass me unawares, and the faintest hint should be welcomed and followed up. But as one covert after another was tried and proved empty of result, I began in the course of years to despair, and to wonder whether the Black Seal were the sole relic of some race that had vanished from the world and left no other trace of its existence—had perished, in fine, as Atlantis is said to have done, in some great cataclysm, its secrets perhaps drowned beneath the ocean or moulded into the heart of the hills. The thought chilled my warmth a little, and though I still persevered, it was no longer with the same certainty of faith. A chance came to the rescue. I was staying in a considerable town in the north of England, and took the opportunity of going over the very creditable museum that had for some time been established in the place. The curator was one of my correspondents; and, as we were looking through one of the mineral cases, my attention was struck by a specimen, a piece of black stone some four inches square, the appearance of which reminded me in a measure of the Black Seal. I took it up carelessly, and was turning it over in my hand, when I saw, to my astonishment, that the under side was inscribed. I said, quietly enough, to my friend the curator that the specimen interested me, and that I should be much obliged if he would allow me to take it with me to my hotel for a couple of days. He, of course, made no objection, and I hurried to my rooms and found that my first glance had not deceived me. There were two inscriptions; one in the regular cuneiform character, another in the character of the Black Seal, and I realized that my task was accomplished. I made an exact copy of the two inscriptions; and when I got to my London study, and had the Seal before me, I was able seriously to grapple with the great problem. The interpreting inscription on the museum specimen, though in itself curious enough, did not bear on my quest, but the transliteration made me master of the secret of the Black Seal. Conjecture, of course, had to enter into my calculations, there was here and there uncertainty about a particular ideograph, and one sign recurring again and again on the seal baffled me for many successive nights. But at last the secret stood open before me in plain English, and I read the key of the awful transmutation of the hills. The last word was hardly written, when with fingers all trembling and unsteady I tore the scrap of paper into the minutest fragments, and saw them flame and blacken in the red hollow of the fire, and then I crushed the grey films that remained into finest powder. Never since then have I written those words; never will I write the phrases which tell how man can be reduced to the slime from which he came, and be forced to put on the flesh of the reptile and the snake. There was now but one thing remaining. I knew, but I desired to see, and I was after some time able to take a house in the neighbourhood of the Grey Hills, and not far from the cottage where Mrs. Cradock and her son Jervase resided. I need not go into a full and detailed account of the apparently inexplicable events which have occurred here, where I am writing this. I knew that I should find in Jervase Cradock something of the blood of the "Little People," and I found later that he had more than once encountered his kinsmen in lonely places in that lonely land. When I was summoned one day to the garden, and found him in a seizure speaking or hissing the ghastly jargon of the Black Seal, I am afraid that exultation prevailed over pity. I heard bursting from his lips the secrets of the underworld, and the word of dread, "Ishakshar," signification of which I must be excused from giving.

But there is one incident I cannot pass over unnoticed. In the waste hollow of the night I awoke at the sound of those hissing syllables I knew so well; and on going to the wretched boy's room, I found him convulsed and foaming at the mouth, struggling on the bed as if he strove to escape the grasp of writhing demons. I took him down to my room and lit the lamp, while he lay twisting on the floor, calling on the power within his flesh to leave him. I saw his body swell and become distended as a bladder, while the face blackened before my eyes; and then at the crisis I did what was necessary according to the directions on the Seal, and putting all scruple on one side, I became a man of science, observant of what was passing. Yet the sight I had to witness was horrible, almost beyond the power of human conception and the most fearful fantasy. Something pushed out from the body there on the floor, and stretched forth, a slimy, wavering tentacle, across the room, grasped the bust upon the cupboard, and laid it down on my desk.

When it was over, and I was left to walk up and down all the rest of the night, white and shuddering, with sweat pouring from my flesh, I vainly tried to reason with myself: I said, truly enough, that I had seen nothing really supernatural, that a snail pushing out his horns and drawing them in was but an instance on a smaller scale of what I had witnessed; and yet horror broke through all such reasonings and left me shattered and loathing myself for the share I had taken in the night's work.

There is little more to be said. I am going now to the final trial and encounter; for I have determined that there shall be nothing wanting, and I shall meet the "Little People" face to face. I shall have the Black Seal and the knowledge of its secrets to help me, and if I unhappily do not return from my journey, there is no need to conjure up here a picture of the awfulness of my fate.

Pausing a little at the end of Professor Gregg's statement, Miss Lally continued her tale in the following words:—

Such was the almost incredible story that the professor had left behind him. When I had finished reading it, it was late at night, but the next morning I took Morgan with me, and we proceeded to search the Grey Hills for some trace of the lost professor. I will not weary you with a description of the savage desolation of that tract of country, a tract of utterest loneliness, of bare green hills dotted over with grey limestone boulders, worn by the ravages of time into fantastic semblances of men and beasts. Finally, after many hours of weary searching, we found what I told you—the watch and chain, the purse, and the ring—wrapped in a piece of coarse parchment. When Morgan cut the gut that bound the parcel together, and I saw the professor's property, I burst into tears, but the sight of the dreaded characters of the Black Seal repeated on the parchment froze me to silent horror, and I think I understood for the first time the awful fate that had come upon my late employer.

I have only to add that Professor Gregg's lawyer treated my account of what happened as a fairy tale, and refused even to glance at the documents I laid before him. It was he who was responsible for the statement that appeared in the public press, to the effect that Professor Gregg had been drowned, and that his body must have been swept into the open sea.

Miss Lally stopped speaking, and looked at Mr. Phillipps, with a glance of some inquiry. He, for his part, was sunken in a deep reverie of thought; and when he looked up and saw the bustle of the evening gathering in the square, men and women hurrying to partake of dinner, and crowds already besetting the music-halls, all the hum and press of actual life seemed unreal and visionary, a dream in the morning after an awakening.

"I thank you," he said at last, "for your most interesting story; interesting to me, because I feel fully convinced of its exact truth."

"Sir," said the lady, with some energy of indignation, "you grieve and offend me. Do you think I should waste my time and yours by concocting fictions on a bench in Leicester Square?"

"Pardon me, Miss Lally, you have a little misunderstood me. Before you began I knew that whatever you told would be told in good faith, but your experiences have a far higher value than that of *bona fides*. The most extraordinary circumstances in your account are in perfect harmony with the very latest scientific theories. Professor Lodge would, I am sure, value a communication from you extremely; I was charmed from the first by his daring hypothesis in explanation of the wonders of spiritualism (so called), but your narrative puts the whole matter out of the range of mere hypothesis."

"Alas! sir, all this will not help me. You forget, I have lost my brother under the most startling and dreadful circumstances. Again, I ask you, did you not see him as you came here? His black whiskers, his spectacles, his timid glance to right and left; think, do not these particulars recall his face to your memory?"

"I am sorry to say I have never seen any one of the kind," said Phillipps, who had forgotten all about the missing brother. "But let me ask you a few questions. Did you notice whether Professor Gregg—"

"Pardon me, sir, I have stayed too long. My employers will be expecting me. I thank you for your sympathy. Good-bye."

Before Mr. Phillipps had recovered from his amazement at this abrupt departure Miss Lally had disappeared from his gaze, passing into the crowd that now thronged the approaches to the Empire. He walked home in a pensive frame of mind, and drank too much tea. At ten o'clock he had made his third brew, and had sketched the outlines of a little work to be called "Protoplasmic Reversion."

Lovecraft spent two weeks with his friend Vrest Orton in the latter's rented summer home, from June 10 to June 24, 1928. The house was located in the rural woods of Guilford, Vermont. The house had been built in the early 1820s by one Samuel Akeley. The names Wilmarth, Goodenough, and Noyes were also common or well-known names in the Brattleboro area. He used them in "The Whisperer in Darkness."

Donald Burleson, whose researches supplied all the above information (see his "Humour Beneath Horror: Some Sources for 'The Dunwich Horror' and 'The Whisperer in Darkness'" in Lovecraft Studies *vol. 1, no. 2, Spring 1980), also did some digging and discovered that the article referred to in "The Whisperer in Darkness" by "The Pendrifter," in which a local columnist seconds Wilmarth's skeptical opinions, is closely based on an article ("A Weird Writer is In Our Midst," Brattleboro Daily Reformer, June 16, 1928) written by host Vrest Orton under the "Pen-Drift" column in the local paper.

The old farmhouse of Henry Akeley is clearly modelled upon the summer house rented by Orton, and thus when Wilmarth pays a visit to his correspondent Akeley, it is obviously a fictionalization of Lovecraft's own visit with Vrest Orton.

The Whisperer in Darkness

by H.P. LOVECRAFT

I

Bear in mind closely that I did not see any actual visual horror at the end. To say that a mental shock was the cause of what I inferred—that last straw which sent me racing out of the lonely Akeley farmhouse and through the wild domed hills of Vermont in a commandeered motor at night—is to ignore the plainest facts of my final experience. Notwithstanding the deep extent to which I shared the information and speculations of Henry Akeley, the things I saw and heard, and the admitted vividness of the impression produced on me by these things, I cannot prove even now whether I was right or wrong in my hideous inference. For after all, Akeley's disappearance establishes nothing. People found nothing amiss in his house despite the bullet-marks on the outside and inside. It was just as though he had walked out casually for a ramble in the hills and failed to return. There was not even a sign that a guest had been there, or that those horrible cylinders and machines had been stored in the study. That he had mortally feared the crowded green hills and endless trickle of brooks among which he had been born and reared, means nothing at all, either; for thousands are subject to just such morbid fears. Eccentricity, moreover, could easily account for his strange acts and apprehensions toward the last.

The whole matter began, so far as I am concerned, with the historic and unprecedented Vermont floods of November 3, 1927. I was then, as now, an instructor of literature at Miskatonic University in Arkham, Massachusetts, and an enthusiastic amateur student of New England folklore. Shortly after the flood, amidst the varied reports of hardship, suffering and organised relief which filled the press, there appeared certain odd stories of things found floating in some of the swollen rivers; so that many of my friends embarked on curious discussions and appealed to me to shed what light I could on the subject. I felt flattered at having my folklore study taken so seriously, and did what I could to belittle the wild, vague tales which seemed so clearly an outgrowth of old rustic superstitions. It amused me to find several persons of education who insisted that some stratum of obscure, distorted fact might underlie the rumours.

The tales thus brought to my notice came mostly through newspaper cuttings; though one yarn had an oral source and was repeated to a friend of mine in a letter from his mother in Hardwick, Vermont. The type of thing described was essentially the same in all cases, though there seemed to be three separate instances involved—one connected with the Winooski River near Montpelier, another attached to the West River in Windham County beyond Newfane, and a third centering in the Passumpsic in Caledonia County above Lyndonville. Of course many of the stray items mentioned other instances, but on analysis they all seemed to boil down to these three. In each case country folk reported seeing one or more very bizarre and disturbing objects in the surging waters that poured down from the unfrequented hills, and there was a widespread tendency to connect these sights with a primitive, half-forgotten cycle of whispered legend which old people resurrected for the occasion.

What people thought they saw were organic shapes not quite like any they had ever seen before. Naturally, there were many human bodies washed along by the streams in that tragic period; but those who described these strange shapes felt quite sure that they were not human, despite some superficial resemblances in size and general outline. Nor, said the witnesses, could they have been any kind of animal known to Vermont. They were pinkish things about five feet long; with crustaceous bodies bearing vast pairs of dorsal fins or membraneous wings and several sets of articulated limbs, and with a sort of convoluted ellipsoid, covered with multitudes of very short antennae, where a head would ordinarily be. It was really remarkable how closely the reports from different sources tended to coincide; though the wonder was lessened by the fact that the old legends, shared at one time throughout the hill country, furnished a morbidly vivid picture which might well have coloured the imaginations of all the witnesses concerned. It was my conclusion that such witnesses—in every case naive and simple backwoods folk—had glimpsed the battered and bloated bodies of human beings or farm animals in the whirling currents; and had allowed the half-remembered folklore to invest these pitiful objects with fantastic attributes.

The ancient folklore, while cloudy, evasive, and largely forgotten by the present generation, was of a highly singular character, and obviously reflected the influence of still earlier Indian tales. I knew it well, though I had never been in Vermont, through the exceedingly rare monograph of Eli Davenport, which embraces material orally obtained prior to 1839 among the oldest people of the state. This material, moreover, closely coincided with tales which I had personally heard from elderly rustics in the mountains of New Hampshire. Briefly summarised, it hinted at a hidden race of monstrous beings which lurked somewhere among the remoter hills—in the deep woods of the highest peaks, and the dark valleys where streams trickle from unknown sources. These beings were seldom glimpsed, but evidences of their presence were reported by those who had ventured farther than usual up the slopes of certain mountains or into certain deep, steepsided gorges that even the wolves shunned.

There were queer footprints or claw-prints in the mud of brook-margins and barren patches, and curious circles of stones, with the grass around them worn away, which did not seem to have been placed or entirely shaped by Nature. There were, too, certain caves of problematical depth in the sides of the hills; with mouths closed by boulders in a manner scarcely accidental, and with more than an average quota of the queer prints leading both toward and away from them—if indeed the direction of these prints could be justly estimated. And worst of all, there were the things which adventurous people had seen very rarely in the twilight of the remotest valleys and the dense perpendicular woods above the limits of normal hill-climbing.

It would have been less uncomfortable if the stray accounts of these things had not agreed so well. As it was, nearly all the rumours had several points in common; averring that the creatures were a sort of huge, light-red crab with many pairs of legs and with two great bat-like wings in the middle of the back. They sometimes walked on all their legs, and sometimes on the hindmost pair only, using the others to convey large objects of indeterminate nature. On one occasion they were spied in considerable numbers, a detachment of them wading along a shallow woodland watercourse three abreast in evidently disciplined formation. Once, a specimen was seen flying—launching itself from the top of a bald, lonely hill at night and vanishing in the sky after its great flapping wings had been silhouetted an instant against the full moon.

These things seemed content, on the whole, to let mankind alone; though they were at times held responsible for the disappearance of venturesome individuals—especially persons who built houses too close to certain valleys or too high up on certain mountains. Many localities came to be known as inadvisable to settle in, the feeling persisting long after the cause was forgotten. People would look up at some of the neighbouring mountain-precipices with a shudder, even when not recalling how many settlers had been lost, and how many farmhouses burnt to ashes, on the lower slopes of those grim, green sentinels.

But while according to the earliest legends the creatures would appear to have harmed only those trespassing on their privacy; there were later accounts of their curiosity respecting men, and of their attempts to establish secret outposts in the human world. There were tales of the queer claw-prints seen around farmhouse windows in the morning, and of occasional disappearances in regions outside the obviously haunted areas. Tales, besides, of buzzing voices in imitation of human speech which made surprising offers to lone travellers on roads and cart-paths in the deep woods, and of children frightened out of their wits by things seen or heard where the primal forest pressed close upon their dooryards. In the final layer of legends—the layer just preceding the decline of superstition and the abandonment of close contact with the dreaded places—there are shocked references to hermits and remote farmers who at some period of life appeared to have undergone a repellent mental change, and who were shunned and whispered about as mortals who had sold themselves to the strange beings. In one of the northeastern counties it seemed to be a fashion about 1800 to accuse eccentric and unpopular recluses of being allies or representatives of the abhorred things.

As to what the things were—explanations naturally varied. The common name applied to them was "those ones," or "the old ones," though other terms had a local and transient use. Perhaps the bulk of the Puritan settlers set them down bluntly as familiars of the devil, and made them a basis of awed theological speculation. Those with Celtic legendry in their heritage—mainly the Scotch-Irish element of New Hampshire, and their kindred who had settled in Vermont on Governor Wentworth's colonial grants—linked them vaguely with the malign fairies and "little people" of the bogs and raths, and protected themselves with scraps of incantation handed down through many generations. But the Indians had the most fantastic theories of all. While different tribal legends differed, there was a marked consensus of belief in certain vital particulars; it being unanimously agreed that the creatures were not native to this earth.

The Pennacook myths, which were the most consistent and picturesque, taught that the Winged Ones came from the Great Bear in the sky, and had mines in our earthly hills whence they took a kind of stone they could not get on any other world. They did not live here, said the myths, but merely maintained outposts and flew back with vast cargoes of stone to their own stars in the north. They harmed only those earth-people who got too near them or spied upon them. Animals shunned them through instinctive hatred, not because of being hunted. They could not eat the things and animals of earth, but brought their own food from the stars. It was bad to get near them, and sometimes young hunters who went into their hills never came back. It was not good, either, to listen to what they whispered at night in the forest with voices like a bee's that tried to be like the voices of men. They knew the speech of all kinds of men—Pennacooks, Hurons, men of the Five Nations—but did not seem to have any speech of their own. They talked with their heads, which changed colour in different ways to mean different things.

All the legendry, of course, white and Indian alike, died down during the nineteenth century, except for occasional atavistical flare-ups. The ways of the Vermonters became settled; and once their habitual paths and dwellings were established according to a certain fixed plan, they remembered less and less what fears and avoidances had determined that plan, and even that there had been any fears and avoidances. Most people simply knew that certain hilly regions were considered as highly unhealthy, unprofitable, and generally unlucky to live in, and that the farther one kept from them the better off one usually was. In time the ruts of custom and economic interest became so deeply cut in approved places that there was no longer any reason for going outside them, and the haunted hills were left deserted by accident rather than by design. Save during infrequent local scares, only wonder-loving grandmothers and retrospective nonagenarians ever whispered of beings dwelling in those hills; and even such whispers admitted that there was not much to fear from those things now that they were used to the presence of houses and settlements, and now that human beings let their chosen territory severely alone.

All this I had known from my reading, and from certain folk-tales picked up in New Hampshire; hence when the flood-time rumours began to appear, I could easily guess what imaginative background had evolved them. I took great pains to explain this to my friends, and was correspondingly amused when several contentious souls continued to insist on a possible element of truth in the reports. Such persons tried to point out that the early legends had a significant persistence and uniformity, and that the virtually unexplored nature of the Vermont hills made it unwise to be dogmatic about what might or might not dwell among them; nor could they be silenced by my assurance that all the myths were of a well-known pattern common to most of mankind and determined by early phases of imaginative experience which always produced the same type of delusion.

It was of no use to demonstrate to such opponents that the Vermont myths differed but little in essence from those universal legends of natural personification which filled the ancient world with fauns and dryads and satyrs, suggested the *kallikanzari* of modern Greece, and gave to wild Wales and Ireland their dark hints of strange, small, and terrible hidden races of troglodytes and burrowers. No use, either, to point out the even more startlingly similar belief of the Nepalese hill tribes in the dreaded *Mi-Go* or "Abominable Snow-Men" who lurk hideously amidst the ice and rock pinnacles of the Himalayan summits. When I brought up this evidence, my opponents turned it against me by claiming that it must imply some actual historicity for the ancient tales; that it must argue the real existence of some queer elder earth-race, driven to hiding after the advent and dominance of mankind, which might very conceivably have survived in reduced numbers to relatively recent times—or even to the present.

The more I laughed at such theories, the more these stubborn friends asseverated them; adding that even without the heritage of legend the recent reports were too clear, consistent, detailed, and sanely prosaic in manner of telling, to be completely ignored. Two or three fanatical extremists went so far as to hint at possible meanings in the ancient Indian tales which gave the hidden beings a non-terrestrial origin; citing the extravagant books of Charles Fort with their claims that voyagers from other worlds and outer space have often visited the earth. Most of my foes, however, were merely romanticists who insisted on trying to transfer to real life the fantastic lore of lurking "little people" made popular by the magnificent horror-fiction of Arthur Machen.

II

As was only natural under the circumstances, this piquant debating finally got into print in the form of letters to the *Arkham Advertiser*; some of which were copied in the press of those Vermont regions whence the flood-stories came. The *Rutland Herald* gave half a page of extracts from the letters on both sides, while the *Brattleboro Reformer* reprinted one of my long historical and mythological summaries in full, with some accompanying comments in "The Pendrifter's" thoughtful column which supported and applauded my sceptical conclusions. By the spring of 1928 I was almost a well-known figure in Vermont, notwithstanding the fact that I had never set foot in the state. Then came the challenging letters from Henry Akeley which impressed me so profoundly, and which took me for the first and last time to that fascinating realm of crowded green precipices and mut-tering forest streams.

Most of what I now know of Henry Wentworth Akeley was gathered by correspondence with his neighbours, and with his only son in Califor-nia, after my experience in his lonely farmhouse. He was, I discovered, the last representative on his home soil of a long, locally distinguished line of jurists, administrators, and gentlemen-agriculturists. In him, however, the family mentally had veered away from practical affairs to pure scholarship; so that he had been a notable student of mathematics, astronomy, biology, anthropology, and folklore at the University of Vermont. I had never previously heard of him, and he did not give many autobiographical details in his communications; but from the first, I saw he was a man of character, education, and intelligence, albeit a recluse with very little worldly sophistication.

Despite the incredible nature of what he claimed, I could not help at once taking Akeley more seriously than I had taken any of the other challengers of my views. For one thing, he was really close to the actual phenomena—visible and tangible—that he speculated so grotesquely about; and for another thing, he was amazingly willing to leave his conclusions in a tentative state like a true man of science. He had no personal preferences to advance, and was always guided by what he took to be solid evidence. Of course I began by considering him mistaken—but gave him credit for being intelligently mistaken; and at no time did I emulate some of his friends in attributing his ideas, and his fear of the lonely green hills, to insanity. I could see that there was a great deal to the man, and knew that what he reported must surely come from strange circumstances deserving investigation, however little it might have to do with the fantastic causes he assigned. Later on I received from him certain material proofs which placed the matter on a somewhat different and bewilderingly bizarre basis.

I cannot do better than transcribe in full, so far as is possible, the long letter in which Akeley introduced himself, and which formed such an important landmark in my own intellectual history. It is no longer in my possession, but my memory holds almost every word of its portentous message; and again I affirm my confidence in the sanity of the man who wrote it. Here is the text—a text which reached me in the cramped, archaic-looking scrawl of one who had obviously not mingled much with the world during his sedate, scholarly life.

> R.F.D. #2
> Vermont
> May 25, 1928.

Albert N. Wilmarth, Esq.,
118 Saltonstall St.,
Arkham, Mass.,

My dear Sir:—
    I have read with great interest the *Brattleboro Reformer*'s reprint (Apr. 23, '28) of your letter on the recent stories of strange bodies seen floating in our flooded streams last fall, and on the curious folk-lore they so well agree with. It is easy to see why an outlander would take the position you take, and even why "Pendrifter" agrees with

you. That is the attitude generally taken by educated persons both in and out of Vermont, and was my own attitude as a young man (I am now 57) before my studies, both general and in Davenport's book, led me to do some exploring in parts of the hills hereabouts not usually visited.

I was directed toward such studies by the queer old tales I used to hear from elderly farmers of the more ignorant sort, but now I wish I had let the whole matter alone. I might say, with all proper modesty, that the subject of anthropology and folklore is by no means strange to me. I took a good deal of it at college, and am familiar with most of the standard authorities such as Tylor, Lubbock, Frazer, Quatrefages, Murray, Osborn, Keith, Boule, G. Elliot Smith, and so on. It is no news to me that tales of hidden races are as old as all mankind. I have seen the reprints of letters from you, and those arguing with you, in the *Rutland Herald*, and guess I know about where your controversy stands at the present time.

What I desire to say now is, that I am afraid your adversaries are nearer right than yourself, even though all reason seems to be on your side. They are nearer right than they realise themselves—for of course they go only by theory, and cannot know what I know. If I knew as little of the matter as they, I would not feel justified in believing as they do. I would be wholly on your side.

You can see that I am having a hard time getting to the point, probably because I really dread getting to the point; but the upshot of the matter is that *I have certain evidence that monstrous things do indeed live in the woods on the high hills which nobody visits.* I have not seen any of the things floating in the rivers, as reported, *but I have seen things like them* under circumstances I dread to repeat. I have seen footprints, and of late have seen them nearer my own home (I live in the old Akeley place south of Townshend Village, on the side of Dark Mountain) than I dare tell you now. And I have overheard voices in the woods at certain points that I will not even begin to describe on paper.

At one place I heard them so much that I took a phonograph there—with a dictaphone attachment and wax blank—and I shall try to arrange to have you hear the record I got. I have run it on the machine for some of the old people up here, and one of the voices had nearly scared them paralysed by reason of its likeness to a certain voice (that buzzing voice in the woods which Davenport mentions) that their grandmothers have told about and mimicked for them. I know what most people think of a man who tells about "hearing voices"—but before you draw conclusions just listen to this record and ask some of the older backwoods people what they think of it. If you can account for it normally, very well; but there must be something behind it. *Ex nihilo nihil fit*, you know.

Now my object in writing you is not to start an argument, but to give you information which I think a man of your tastes will find deeply interesting. *This is private. Publicly I am on your side*, for certain things shew me that it does not do for people to know too much about these matters. My own studies are now wholly private, and I would not think of saying anything to attract people's attention and cause them to visit the places I have explored. It is true—terribly true—that there are *non-human creatures watching us all the time;* with spies among us gathering information. It is from a wretched man who, if he was sane (as I think he was), *was one of those spies,* that I got a large part of my clues to the matter. He later killed himself, but I have reason to think there are others now.

The things come from another planet, being able to live in interstellar space and fly through it on clumsy, powerful wings which have a way of resisting the ether but which are too poor at steering to be of much use in helping them about on earth. I will tell you about this later if you do not dismiss me at once as a madman. They come here to get metals from mines that go deep under the hills, *and I think I know where they come from.* They will not hurt us if we let them alone, but no one can say what will happen if we get too curious about them. Of course a good army of men could wipe out their mining colony. That is what they are afraid of. But if that happened, more would come from *outside*—any number of them. They could easily conquer the earth, but have not tried so far because they have not needed to. They would rather leave things as they are to save bother.

I think they mean to get rid of me because of what I have discovered. There is a great black stone with unknown hieroglyphics half worn away which I found in the woods on Round Hill, east of here; and after I took it home everything became different. If they think I suspect too much they will either kill me *or take me off the earth to where they come from.* They like to take away men of learning once in a while, to keep informed on the state of things in the human world.

This leads me to my secondary purpose in addressing you— namely, to urge you to hush up the present debate rather than give it more publicity. *People must be kept away from these hills,* and in order to effect this, their curiosity ought not to be aroused any further. Heaven knows there is peril enough anyway, with promoters and real estate men flooding Vermont with herds of summer people to overrun the wild places and cover the hills with cheap bungalows.

I shall welcome further communication with you, and shall try to send you that phonograph record and black stone (which is so worn that photographs don't shew much) by express if you are willing. I say "try" because I think those creatures have a way of tampering with things around here. There is a sullen, furtive fellow named Brown, on a farm near the village, who I think is their spy. Little by little they are trying to cut me off from our world because I know too much about their world.

They have the most amazing way of finding out what I do. You may not even get this letter. I think I shall have to leave this part of the country and go to live with my son in San Diego, Cal., if things get any worse, but it is not easy to give up the place you were born in, and where your family has lived for six generations. Also, I would hardly dare to sell this house to anybody now that the *creatures* have taken notice of it. They seem to be trying to get the black stone back and destroy the phonograph record, but I shall not let them if I can help it. My great police dogs always hold them back, for there are very few here as yet, and they are clumsy in getting about. As I have said, their wings are not much use for short flights on earth. I am on the very brink of deciphering that stone—in a very terrible way—and with your knowledge of folklore you may be able to supply missing links enough to help me. I suppose you know all about the fearful myths antedating the coming of man to the earth—the Yog-Sothoth and Cthulhu cycles—which are hinted at in the *Necronomicon*. I had access to a copy of that once, and hear that you have one in your college library under lock and key.

To conclude, Mr. Wilmarth, I think that with our respective studies we can be very useful to each other. I don't wish to put you in any peril, and suppose I ought to warn you that possession of the stone and the record won't be very safe; but I think you will find any risks worth running for the sake of knowledge. I will drive down to Newfane or Brattleboro to send whatever you authorise me to send, for the express offices there are more to be trusted. I might say that I live quite alone now, since I can't keep hired help any more. They won't stay because of the things that try to get near the house at night, and that keep the dogs barking continually. I am glad I didn't get as deep as this into the business while my wife was alive, for it would have driven her mad.

Hoping that I am not bothering you unduly, and that you will decide to get in touch with me rather than throw this letter into the wastebasket as a madman's raving, I am

Yrs. very truly,
HENRY W. AKELEY

P.S. I am making some extra prints of certain photographs taken by me, which I think will help to prove a number of the points I have touched on. The old people think they are monstrously true. I shall send you these very soon if you are interested. H.W.A.

It would be difficult to describe my sentiments upon reading this strange document for the first time. By all ordinary rules, I ought to have laughed more loudly at these extravagances than at the far milder theories which had previously moved me to mirth; yet something in the tone of the letter made me take it with paradoxical seriousness. Not that I believed for a moment in the hidden race from the stars which my correspondent spoke of; but that, after some grave preliminary doubts, I grew to feel oddly sure of his sanity and sincerity, and of his confrontation by some genuine though singular and abnormal phenomenon which he could not explain except in this imaginative way. It could not be otherwise than worthy of investigation. The man

seemed unduly excited and alarmed about something, but it was hard
to think that all cause was lacking. He was so specific and logical in
certain ways—and after all, his yarn did fit in so perplexingly well with
some of the old myths—even the wildest Indian legends.

That he had really overheard disturbing voices in the hills, and had
really found the black stone he spoke about, was wholly possible
despite the crazy inferences he had made—inferences probably suggested by the man who had claimed to be a spy of the outer beings and
had later killed himself. It was easy to deduce that this man must have
been wholly insane, but that he probably had a streak of perverse
outward logic which made the naive Akeley—already prepared for
such things by his folklore studies—believe his tale. As for the latest
developments—it appeared from his inability to keep hired help that
Akeley's humbler rustic neighbours were as convinced as he that his
house was besieged by uncanny things at night. The dogs really
barked, too.

And then the matter of that phonograph record, which I could not
but believe he had obtained in the way he said. It must mean
something; whether animal noises deceptively like human speech, or
the speech of some hidden, night-haunting human being decayed to
a state not much above that of the lower animals. From this my
thoughts went back to the black hieroglyphed stone, and to speculations upon what it might mean. Then, too, what of the photographs
which Akeley said he was about to send, and which the old people had
found so convincingly terrible?

As I re-read the cramped handwriting I felt as never before that my
credulous opponents might have more on their side than I had conceded. After all, there might be some queer and perhaps hereditarily
misshapen outcasts in those shunned hills, even though no such race
of star-born monsters as folklore claimed. And if there were, then the
presence of strange bodies in the flooded streams would not be wholly
beyond belief. Was it too presumptuous to suppose that both the old
legends and the recent reports had this much of reality behind them?
But even as I harboured these doubts I felt ashamed that so fantastic a
piece of bizarrerie as Henry Akeley's wild letter had brought them up.

In the end I answered Akeley's letter, adopting a tone of friendly
interest and soliciting further particulars. His reply came almost by
return mail; and contained, true to promise, a number of kodak views
of scenes and objects illustrating what he had to tell. Glancing at these
pictures as I took them from the envelope, I felt a curious sense of fright
and nearness to forbidden things; for in spite of the vagueness of most
of them, they had a damnably suggestive power which was intensified
by the fact of their being genuine photographs—actual optical links

with what they protrayed, and the product of an impersonal transmitting process without prejudice, fallibility, or mendacity.

The more I looked at them, the more I saw that my serious estimate of Akeley and his story had not been unjustified. Certainly, these pictures carried conclusive evidence of something in the Vermont hills which was at least vastly outside the radius of our common knowledge and belief. The worst thing of all was the footprint—a view taken where the sun shone on a mud patch somewhere in a deserted upland. This was no cheaply counterfeited thing, I could see at a glance; for the sharply defined pebbles and grass-blades in the field of vision gave a clear index of scale and left no possibility of a tricky double exposure. I have called the thing a "footprint," but "claw-print" would be a better term. Even now I can scarcely describe it save to say that it was hideously crab-like, and that there seemed to be some ambiguity about its direction. It was not a very deep or fresh print, but seemed to be about the size of an average man's foot. From a central pad, pairs of saw-toothed nippers projected in opposite directions—quite baffling as to function, if indeed the whole object were exclusively an object of locomotion.

Another photograph—evidently a time-exposure taken in deep shadow—was of the mouth of a woodland cave, with a boulder of rounded regularity choking the aperture. On the bare ground in front of it one could just discern a dense network of curious tracks, and when I studied the picture with a magnifier I felt uneasily sure that the tracks were like the one in the other view. A third picture shewed a druid-like circle of standing stones on the summit of a wild hill. Around the cryptic circle the grass was very much beaten down and worn away, though I could not detect any footprints even with the glass. The extreme remoteness of the place was apparent from the veritable sea of tenantless mountains which formed the background and stretched away toward a misty horizon.

But if the most disturbing of all the views was that of the footprint, the most curiously suggestive was that of the great black stone found in the Round Hill woods. Akeley had photographed it on what was evidently his study table, for I could see rows of books and a bust of Milton in the background. The thing, as nearly as one might guess, had faced the camera vertically with a somewhat irregularly curved surface of one by two feet; but to say anything definite about that surface, or about the general shape of the whole mass, almost defies the power of language. What outlandish geometrical principles had guided its cutting—for artificially cut it surely was—I could not even begin to guess; and never before had I seen anything which struck me as so strangely and unmistakably alien to this world. Of the hieroglyphics on the surface I could discern very few, but one or two that I did see gave me rather a shock. Of course they might be fraudulent, for others besides myself had read the monstrous and abhorred *Necronomicon* of the mad Arab Abdul Alhazred; but it nevertheless made me shiver to recognise certain ideographs which study had taught me to link with the most blood-curdling and blasphemous whispers of things that had had a kind of mad half-existence before the earth and the other inner worlds of the solar system were made.

Of the five remaining pictures, three were of swamp and hill scenes which seemed to bear traces of hidden and unwholesome tenancy. Another was of a queer mark in the ground very near Akeley's house, which he said he had photographed the morning after a night on which the dogs had barked more violently than usual. It was very blurred, and one could really draw no certain conclusions from it; but it did seem fiendishly like that other mark or claw-print photographed on the deserted upland. The final picture was of the Akeley place itself; a trim white house of two stories and attic, about a century and a quarter old, and with a well-kept lawn and stone-bordered path leading up to a tastefully carved Georgian doorway. There were several huge police dogs on the lawn, squatting near a pleasant-faced man with a close-cropped grey beard whom I took to be Akeley himself—his own photographer, one might infer from the tube-connected bulb in his right hand.

From the pictures I turned to the bulky, closely written letter itself; and for the next three hours was immersed in a gulf of unutterable horror. Where Akeley had given only outlines before, he now entered into minute details; presenting long transcripts of words overheard in the woods at night, long accounts of monstrous pinkish forms spied in thickets at twilight on the hills, and a terrible cosmic narrative derived from the application of profound and varied scholarship to the endless bygone discourses of the mad self-styled spy who had killed himself. I found myself faced with names and terms that I had heard elsewhere in the most hideous of connexions—Yuggoth, Great Cthulhu, Tsathoggua, Yog-Sothoth, R'lyeh, Nyarlathotep, Azathoth, Hastur, Yian, Leng, the Lake of Hali, Bethmoora, the Yellow Sign, L'mur-Kathulos, Bran, and the Magnum Innominandum—and was drawn back through nameless aeons and inconceivable dimensions to worlds of elder, outer entity at which the crazed author of the *Necronomicon* had only guessed in the vaguest way. I was told of the pits of primal life, and of the streams that had trickled down therefrom; and finally, of the tiny rivulet from one of those streams which had become entangled with the destinies of our own earth.

My brain whirled; and where before I had attempted to explain things away, I now began to believe in the most abnormal and incredible wonders. The array of vital evidence was damnably vast and overwhelming; and the cool, scientific attitude of Akeley—an attitude removed as far as imaginable from the demented, the fanatical, the hysterical, or even the extravagantly speculative—had a tremendous effect on my thought and judgment. By the time I laid the frightful letter aside I could understand the fears he had come to entertain, and was ready to do anything in my power to keep people away from those wild, haunted hills. Even now, when time has dulled the impression and made me half question my own experience and horrible doubts, there are things in that letter of Akeley's which I would not quote, or even form into words on paper. I am almost glad that the letter and record and photographs are gone now—and I wish, for reasons I shall soon make clear, that the new planet beyond Neptune had not been discovered.

With the reading of that letter my public debating about the Vermont horror permanently ended. Arguments from opponents remained unanswered or put off with promises, and eventually the controversy petered out into oblivion. During late May and June I was in constant correspondence with Akeley; though once in a while a letter would be lost, so that we would have to retrace our ground and perform considerable laborious copying. What we were trying to do, as a whole, was to compare notes in matters of obscure mythological scholarship and arrive at a clearer correlation of the Vermont horrors with the general body of primitive world legend.

For one thing, we virtually decided that these morbidities and the hellish Himalayan *Mi-Go* were one and the same order of incarnated nightmare. There were also absorbing zoölogical conjectures, which I would have referred to Professor Dexter in my own college but for Akeley's imperative command to tell no one of the matter before us. If I seem to disobey that command now, it is only because I think that at this stage a warning about those farther Vermont hills—and about those Himalayan peaks which bold explorers are more and more determined to ascend—is more conducive to public safety than silence would be. One specific thing we were leading up to was a deciphering of the hieroglyphics on that infamous black stone—a deciphering which might well place us in possession of secrets deeper and more dizzying than any formerly known to man.

III

Toward the end of June the phonograph record came—shipped from Brattleboro, since Akeley was unwilling to trust conditions on the branch line north of there. He had begun to feel an increased sense of espionage, aggravated by the loss of some of our letters; and said much about the insidious deeds of certain men whom he considered tools and agents of the hidden beings. Most of all he suspected the surly farmer Walter Brown, who lived alone on a rundown hillside place near the deep woods, and who was often seen loafing around corners in Brattleboro, Bellows Falls, Newfane, and South Londonderry in the most inexplicable and seemingly unmotivated way. Brown's voice, he felt convinced, was one of those he had overheard on a certain occasion in a very terrible conversation; and he had once found a footprint or claw-print near Brown's house which might possess the most ominous significance. It had been curiously near some of Brown's own footprints—footprints that faced toward it.

So the record was shipped from Brattleboro, whither Akeley drove in his Ford car along the lonely Vermont back roads. He confessed in an accompanying note that he was beginning to be afraid of those roads, and that he would not even go into Townshend for supplies now except in broad daylight. It did not pay, he reapeated again and again, to know too much unless one were very remote from those silent and problematical hills. He would be going to California pretty soon to live with his son, though it was hard to leave a place where all one's memories and ancestral feelings centred.

Before trying the record on the commercial machine which I borrowed from the college administration building I carefully went over all the explanatory matter in Akeley's various letters. This record, he had said, was obtained about 1 a.m. on the first of May, 1915, near the closed mouth of a cave where the wooded west slope of Dark Mountain rises out of Lee's Swamp. The place had always been unusually plagued with strange voices, this being the reason he had brought the phonograph, dictaphone, and blank in expectation of results. Former experience had told him that May-Eve—the hideous Sabbat-night of underground European legend—would probably be more fruitful than any other date, and he was not disappointed. It was noteworthy, though, that he never again heard voices in that particular spot.

Unlike most of the overheard forest voices, the substance of the record was quasi-ritualistic, and included one palpably human voice which Akeley had never been able to place. It was not Brown's but seemed to be that of a man of greater cultivation. The second voice, however, was the real crux of the thing—for this was the accursed *buzzing* which had no likeness to humanity despite the human words which it uttered in good English grammar and a scholarly accent.

The recording phonograph and dictaphone had not worked uniformly well, and had of course been at a great disadvantage because of the remote and muffled nature of the overheard ritual; so that the actual speech secured was very fragmentary. Akeley had given me a transcript of what he believed the spoken words to be, and I glanced through this again as I prepared the machine for action. The text was darkly mysterious rather than openly horrible, though a knowledge of its origin and manner of gathering gave it all the associative horror which any words could well possess. I will present it here in full as I remember it—and I am fairly confident that I know it correctly by heart, not only from reading the transcript, but from playing the record itself over and over again. It is not a thing which one might readily forget!

(INDISTINGUISHABLE SOUNDS)

(A CULTIVATED MALE HUMAN VOICE)

... is the Lord of the Woods, even to ... and the gifts of the men of Leng ... so from the wells of night to the gulfs of space, and from the gulfs of space to the wells of night, ever the praises of Great Cthulhu, of Tsathoggua, and of Him Who is not to be Named. Ever Their praises, and abundance to the Black Goat of the Woods. Iä! Shub-Niggurath! The Goat with a Thousand Young!

(A BUZZING IMITATION OF HUMAN SPEECH)

Iä! Shub-Niggurath! The Black Goat of the Woods with a Thousand Young!

(HUMAN VOICE)

And it has come to pass that the Lord of the Woods, being ... seven and nine, down the onyx steps ... (tri)butes to him in the Gulf, Azathoth, He of Whom Thou hast taught us marv(els) ... on the wings of night out beyond space, out beyond th ... to That whereof Yuggoth is the youngest child, rolling alone in black aether at the rim ...

(BUZZING VOICE)

... go out among men and find the ways thereof, that He in the Gulf may know. To Nyarlathotep, Mighty Messenger, must all things be told. And He shall put on the semblance of men, the waxen mask and the robe that hides, and come down from the world of Seven Suns to mock ...

(HUMAN VOICE)

. . . (Nyarl)athotep, Great Messenger, bringer of strange joy to
Yuggoth through the void, Father of the Million Favoured Ones,
Stalker among . . . .

(SPEECH CUT OFF BY END OF RECORD)

Such were the words for which I was to listen when I started the
phonograph. It was with a trace of genuine dread and reluctance that
I pressed the lever then heard the preliminary scratching of the
sapphire point, and I was glad that the first faint, fragmentary words
were in a human voice—a mellow, educated voice which seemed
vaguely Bostonian in accent, and which was certainly not that of any
native of the Vermont hills. As I listened to the tantalisingly feeble
rendering, I seemed to find the speech identical with Akeley's carefully
prepared transcript. On it chanted, in that mellow Bostonian voice
... "Iä! Shub-Niggurath! The Goat with a Thousand Young! ... "

And then I heard *the other voice*. To this hour I shudder retrospectively
when I think of how it struck me, prepared though I was by Akeley's
accounts. Those to whom I have since described the record profess to
find nothing but cheap imposture or madness in it; but *could they have
heard the accursed thing itsef*, or read the bulk of Akeley's correspondence
(especially that terrible and encyclopaedic second letter), I know they
would think differently. It is, after all, a tremendous pity that I did not
disobey Akeley and play the record for others—a tremendous pity, too,
that all of his letters were lost. To me, with my first-hand impression
of the actual sounds, and with my knowledge of the background and
surrounding circumstances, the voice was a monstrous thing. It swiftly
followed the human voice in ritualistic response, but in my imagination it was a morbid echo winging its way across unimaginable abysses
from unimaginable outer hells. It is more than two years now since I
last ran off that blasphemous waxen cylinder; but at this moment, and
at all other moments, I can still hear that feeble, fiendish buzzing as
it reached me for the first time.

"*Iä! Shub-Niggurath! The Black Goat of the Woods with a Thousand
Young!*"

But though that voice is always in my ears, I have not even yet been
able to analyse it well enough for a graphic description. It was like the
drone of some loathsome, gigantic insect ponderously shaped into the
articulate speech of an alien species, and I am perfectly certain that the
organs producing it can have no resemblance to the vocal organs of
man, or indeed to those of any of the mammalia. There were singularities in timbre, range, and overtones which placed this phenomenon
wholly outside the sphere of humanity and earth-life. Its sudden advent

that first time almost stunned me, and I heard the rest of the record through in a sort of abstracted daze. When the longer passage of buzzing came, there was a sharp intensification of that feeling of blasphemous infinity which had struck me during the shorter and earlier passage. At last the record ended abruptly, during an unusually clear speech of the human and Bostonian voice; but I sat stupidly staring long after the machine had automatically stopped.

I hardly need say that I gave that shocking record many another playing, and that I made exhaustive attempts at analysis and comment in comparing notes with Akeley. It would be both useless and disturbing to repeat here all that we concluded; but I may hint that we agreed in believing we had secured a clue to the source of some of the most repulsive primordial customs in the cryptic elder religions of mankind. It seemed plain to us, also, that there were ancient and elaborate alliances between the hidden outer creatures and certain members of the human race. How extensive these alliances were, and how their state today might compare with their state in earlier ages, we had no means of guessing; yet at best there was room for a limitless amount of horrified speculation. There seemed to be an awful, immemorial linkage in several definite stages betwixt man and nameless infinity. The blasphemies which appeared on earth, it was hinted, came from the dark planet Yuggoth, at the rim of the solar system; but this was itself merely the populous outpost of a frightful interstellar race whose ultimate source must lie far outside even the Einsteinian space-time continuum or greatest known cosmos.

Meanwhile we continued to discuss the black stone and the best way of getting it to Arkham—Akeley deeming it inadvisable to have me visit him at the scene of his nightmare studies. For some reason or other, Akeley was afraid to trust the thing to any ordinary or expected transportation route. His final idea was to take it across country to Bellows Falls and ship it on the Boston and Maine system through Keene and Winchendon and Fitchburg, even though this would necessitate his driving along somewhat lonelier and more forest-traversing hill roads than the main highway to Brattleboro. He said he had noticed a man around the express office at Brattleboro when he had sent the phonograph record, whose actions and expression had been far from reassuring. This man had seemed too anxious to talk with the clerks, and had taken the train on which the record was shipped. Akeley confessed that he had not felt strictly at ease about that record until he heard from me of its safe receipt.

About this time—the second week in July—another letter of mine went astray, as I learned through an anxious communication from Akeley. After that he told me to address him no more at Townshend, but to send all mail in care of the General Delivery at Brattleboro; whither he would make frequent trips either in his car or on the motor-coach line which had lately replaced passenger service on the lagging branch railway. I could see that he was getting more and more anxious, for he went into much detail about the increased barking of the dogs on moonless nights, and about the fresh claw-prints he sometimes found in the road and in the mud at the back of his farmyard when morning came. Once he told about a veritable army of prints drawn up in a line facing an equally thick and resolute line of dog-tracks, and sent a loathsomely disturbing kodak picture to prove it. That was after a night on which the dogs had outdone themselves in barking and howling.

On the morning of Wednesday, July 18, I received a telegram from Bellows Falls, in which Akeley said he was expressing the black stone over the B. & M. on Train No. 5508, leaving Bellows Falls at 12:15 p.m., standard time, and due at the North Station in Boston at 4:12 p.m. It ought, I calculated, to get up to Arkham at least by the next noon; and accordingly I stayed in all Thursday morning to receive it. But noon came and went without its advent, and when I telephoned down to the express office I was informed that no shipment for me had arrived. My next act, performed amidst a growing alarm, was to give a long-distance call to the express agent at the Boston North Station; and I was scarcely surprised to learn that my consignment had not appeared. Train No. 5508 had pulled in only 35 minutes late on the day before, but had contained no box addressed to me. The agent promised, however, to institute a searching inquiry; and I ended the day by sending Akeley a night-letter outlining the situation.

With commendable promptness a report came from the Boston office on the following afternoon, the agent telephoning as soon as he learned the facts. It seemed that the railway express clerk on No. 5508 had been able to recall an incident which might have much bearing on my loss—an argument with a very curious-voiced man, lean, sandy, and rustic-looking, when the train was waiting at Keene, N.H., shortly after one o'clock standard time.

The man, he said, was greatly excited about a heavy box which he claimed to expect, but which was neither on the train nor entered on the company's books. He had given the name of Stanley Adams, and had had such a queerly thick droning voice, that it made the clerk abnormally dizzy and sleepy to listen to him. The clerk could not remember quite how the conversation had ended, but recalled starting into a fuller awakeness when the train began to move. The Boston agent added that this clerk was a young man of wholly unquestioned veracity and reliability, of known antecedents and long with the company.

That evening I went to Boston to interview the clerk in person, having obtained his name and address from the office. He was a frank, prepossessing fellow, but I saw that he could add nothing to his original account. Oddly, he was scarcely sure that he could even recognise the strange inquirer again. Realising that he had no more to tell, I returned to Arkham and sat up till morning writing letters to Akeley, to the express company, and to the police department and station agent in Keene. I felt that the strange-voiced man who had so queerly affected the clerk must have a pivotal place in the ominous business, and hoped that Keene station employees and telegraph-office records might tell something about him and about how he happened to make his inquiry when and where he did.

I must admit, however, that all my investigations came to nothing. The queer-voiced man had indeed been noticed around the Keene station in the early afternoon of July 18, and one lounger seemed to couple him vaguely with a heavy box; but he was altogether unknown, and had not been seen before or since. He had not visited the telegraph office or received any message so far as could be learned, nor had any message which might justly be considered a notice of the black stone's presence on No. 5508 come through the office for anyone. Naturally Akeley joined with me in conducting these inquiries, and even made a personal trip to Keene to question the people around the station; but his attitude toward the matter was more fatalistic than mine. He seemed to find the loss of the box a portentous and menacing fulfilment of inevitable tendencies, and had no real hope at all of its recovery. He spoke of the undoubted telepathic and hypnotic powers of the hill creatures and their agents, and in one letter hinted that he did not believe the stone was on this earth any longer. For my part, I was duly enraged, for I had felt there was at least a chance of learning profound and astonishing things from the old, blurred hieroglyphs. The matter would have rankled bitterly in my mind had not Akeley's immediately subsequent letters brought up a new phase of the whole horrible hill problem which at once seized my attention.

IV

The unknown things, Akeley wrote in a script grown pitifully tremulous, had begun to close in on him with a wholly new degree of determination. The nocturnal barking of the dogs whenever the moon was dim or absent was hideous now, and there had been attempts to molest him on the lonely roads he had to traverse by day. On the second of August, while bound for the village in his car, he had found a

tree-trunk laid in his path at a point where the highway ran through
a deep patch of woods; while the savage barking of the two great dogs
he had with him told all too well of the things which must have been
lurking near. What would have happened had the dogs not been there,
he did not dare guess—but he never went out now without at least
two of his faithful and powerful pack. Other road experiences had
occurred on August 5th and 6th; a shot grazing his car on one occasion,
and the barking of the dogs telling of unholy woodland presences on
the other.

On August 15th I received a frantic letter which disturbed me
greatly, and which made me wish Akeley could put aside his lonely
reticence and call in the aid of the law. There had been frightful
happenings on the night of the 12-13th, bullets flying outside the
farmhouse, and three of the twelve great dogs being found shot dead
in the morning. There were myriads of claw-prints in the road, with
the human prints of Walter Brown among them. Akeley had started
to telephone to Brattleboro for more dogs, but the wire had gone dead
before he had a chance to say much. Later he went to Brattleboro in
his car, and learned there that linemen had found the main telephone
cable neatly cut at a point where it ran through the deserted hills north
of Newfane. But he was about to start home with four fine new dogs,
and several cases of ammunition for his big-game repeating rifle. The
letter was written at the post office in Brattleboro, and came through
to me without delay.

My attitude toward the matter was by this time quickly slipping
from a scientific to an alarmedly personal one. I was afraid for Akeley
in his remote, lonely farmhouse, and half afraid for myself because of
my now definite connexion with the strange hill problem. The thing
was *reaching out* so. Would it suck me in and engulf me? In replying
to his letter I urged him to seek help, and hinted that I might take
action myself if he did not. I spoke of visiting Vermont in person in
spite of his wishes, and of helping him explain the situation to the
proper authorities. In return, however, I received only a telegram from
Bellows Falls which read thus:

APPRECIATE YOUR POSITION BUT CAN DO NOTH-
ING. TAKE NO ACTION YOURSELF FOR IT COULD ONLY
HARM BOTH. WAIT FOR EXPLANATION.
                              HENRY AKELY

But the affair was steadily deepening. Upon my replying to the
telegram I received a shaky note from Akeley with the astonishing
news that he had not only never sent the wire, but had not received

the letter from me to which it was an obvious reply. Hasty inquiries by him at Bellows Falls had brought out that the message was deposited by a strange sandy-haired man with a curiously thick, droning voice, though more than this he could not learn. The clerk shewed him the original text as scrawled in pencil by the sender, but the handwriting was wholly unfamiliar. It was noticeable that the signature was misspelled—A-K-E-L-Y, without the second "E". Certain conjectures were inevitable, but amidst the obvious crisis he did not stop to elaborate upon them.

He spoke of the death of more dogs and the purchase of still others, and of the exchange of gunfire which had become a settled feature each moonless night. Brown's prints, and the prints of at least one or two more shod human figures, were now found regularly among the claw-prints in the road, and at the back of the farmyard. It was, Akeley admitted, a pretty bad business; and before long he would probably have to go to live with his California son whether or not he could sell the old place. But it was not easy to leave the only spot one could really think of as home. He must try to hang on a little longer; perhaps he could scare off the intruders—especially if he openly gave up all further attempts to penetrate their secrets.

Writing Akeley at once, I renewed my offers of aid, and spoke again of visiting him and helping him convince the authorities of his dire peril. In his reply he seemed less set against that plan than his past attitude would have led one to predict, but said he would like to hold off a little while longer—long enough to get his things in order and reconcile himself to the idea of leaving an almost morbidly cherished birthplace. People looked askance at his studies and speculations, and it would be better to get quietly off without setting the countryside in a turmoil and creating widespread doubts of his own sanity. He had had enough, he admitted, but he wanted to make a dignified exit if he could.

This letter reached me on the twenty-eighth of August, and I prepared and mailed as encouraging a reply as I could. Apparently the encouragement had effect, for Akeley had fewer terrors to report when he acknowledged my note. He was not very optimistic, though, and expressed the belief that it was only the full moon season which was holding the creatures off. He hoped there would not be many densely cloudy nights, and talked vaguely of boarding in Brattleboro when the moon waned. Again I wrote him encouragingly, but on September 5th there came a fresh communication which had obviously crossed my letter in the mails; and to this I could not give any such hopeful response. In view of its importance I believe I had better give it in full—as best I can do from memory of the shaky script. It ran substantially as follows:

Monday.

Dear Wilmarth—

A rather discouraging P.S. to my last. Last night was thickly cloudy—though no rain—and not a bit of moonlight got through. Things were pretty bad, and I think the end is getting near, in spite of all we have hoped. After midnight something landed on the roof of the house, and the dogs all rushed up to see what it was. I could hear them snapping and tearing around, and then one managed to get on the roof by jumping from the low ell. There was a terrible fight up there, and I heard a frightful *buzzing* which I'll never forget. And then there was a shocking smell. About the same time bullets came through the window and nearly grazed me. I think the main line of the hill creatures had got close to the house when the dogs divided because of the roof business. What was up there, I don't know yet, but I'm afraid the creatures are learning to steer better with their space wings. I put out the light and used the windows for loopholes, and raked all around the house with rifle fire aimed just high enough not to hit the dogs. That seemed to end the business, but in the morning I found great pools of blood in the yard, besides pools of a green sticky stuff that had the worst odour I have ever smelled. I climbed up on the roof and found more of the sticky stuff there. Five of the dogs were killed—I'm afraid I hit one myself by aiming too low, for he was shot in the back. Now I am setting the panes the shots broke, and am going to Brattleboro for more dogs. I guess the men at the kennels think I am crazy. Will drop another note later. Suppose I'll be ready for moving in a week or two, though it nearly kills me to think of it.

Hastily —
AKELEY

But this was not the only letter from Akeley to cross mine. On the next morning—September 6th—still another came; this time a frantic scrawl which utterly unnerved me and put me at a loss what to say or do next. Again I cannot do better than quote the text as faithfully as memory will let me.

Tuesday.

Clouds didn't break, so no moon again—and going into the wane anyhow. I'd have the house wired for electricity and put in a searchlight if I didn't know they'd cut the cables as fast as they could be mended.

I think I am going crazy. It may be that all I have ever written you is a dream or madness. It was bad enough before, but this time it is too much. *They talked to me last night*—talked in that cursed buzzing voice and told me things *that I dare not repeat to you.* I heard them plainly above the barking of the dogs, and once when they were drowned out *a human voice helped them.* Keep out of this, Wilmarth—it is worse than either you or I ever suspected. *They don't mean to let me get to California now—they want to take me off alive, or what thoretically and mentally amounts to alive*—not only to Yuggoth, but beyond that—away outside the galaxy *and possibly beyond the last curved rim of space.* I told them I wouldn't go where they wish, *or in the terrible way they propose to take me*, but I'm afraid it will be no use. My place is so far out that they may come by day as well as by night before long. Six more dogs killed, and I felt presences all along the wooded parts of the road when I drove to Brattleboro today.

It was a mistake for me to try to send you that phonograph record and black stone. Better smash the record before it's too late. Will drop you another line tomorrow if I'm still here. Wish I could arrange to get my books and things to Brattleboro and board there. I would run off without anything if I could, but something inside my mind holds me back. I can slip out to Brattleboro, where I ought to be safe, but I feel just as much a prisoner there as at the house. And I seem to know that I couldn't get much farther even if I dropped everything and tried. It is horrible—don't get mixed up in this.

Yrs—AKELEY

I did not sleep at all the night after receiving this terrible thing, and was utterly baffled as to Akeley's remaining degree of sanity. The substance of the note was wholly insane, yet the manner of expression—in view of all that had gone before—had a grimly potent quality of convincingness. I made no attempt to answer it, thinking it better to wait until Akeley might have time to reply to my latest communication. Such a reply indeed came on the following day, though the fresh material in it quite overshadowed any of the points brought up by the letter it nominally answered. Here is what I recall of the text, scrawled and blotted as it was in the course of a plainly frantic and hurried composition.

Wednesday.

W—

Yr letter came, but it's no use to discuss anything any more. I am fully resigned. Wonder that I have even enough will power left to fight them off. Can't escape even if I were willing to give up everything and run. They'll get me.

Had a letter from them yesterday—R.F.D. man brought it while I was at Brattleboro. Typed and postmarked Bellows Falls. Tells what they want to do with me—I can't repeat it. Look out for yourself, too! Smash that record. Cloudy nights keep up, and moon waning all the time. Wish I dared to get help—it might brace up my will power—but everyone who would dare to come at all would call me crazy unless there happened to be some proof. Couldn't ask people to come for no reason at all—am all out of touch with everybody and have been for years.

But I haven't told you the worst, Wilmarth. Brace up to read this, for it will give you a shock. I am telling the truth, though. It is this—*I have seen and touched one of the things, or part of one of the things.* God, man, but it's awful! It was dead, of course. One of the dogs had it, and I found it near the kennel this morning. I tried to save it in the woodshed to convince people of the whole thing, but it all evaporated in a few hours. Nothing left. You know, all those things in the rivers were seen only on the first morning after the flood. And here's the worst. I tried to photograph it for you, but when I developed the film *there wasn't anything visible except the woodshed.* What can the things have been made of? I saw it and felt it, and they all leave footprints. It was surely made of matter—but what kind of matter? The shape can't be described. It was a great crab with a lot of pyramided fleshy rings or knots of thick, ropy stuff covered with feelers where a man's head would be. That green sticky stuff is its blood or juice. And there are more of them due on earth any minute.

Walter Brown is missing—hasn't been seen loafing around any of his usual corners in the villages hereabouts. I must have got him with one of my shots, though the creatures always seem to try to take their dead and wounded away.

Got into town this afternoon without any trouble, but am afraid they're beginning to hold off because they're sure of me. Am writing this in Brattleboro P.O. This may be goodbye—if it is, write my son George Goodenough Akeley, 176 Pleasant St., San Diego, Cal., *but don't come up here.* Write the boy if you don't hear from me in a week, and watch the papers for news.

I'm going to play my last two cards now—if I have the will power left. First to try poison gas on the things (I've got the right chemicals and have fixed up masks for myself and the dogs) and then if that doesn't work, tell the sheriff. They can lock me in a madhouse if they want to—it'll be better than what the *other creatures* would do. Perhaps I can get them to pay attention to the prints around the house—they are faint, but I can find them every morning. Suppose, though, police would say I faked them somehow; for they all think I'm a queer character.

Must try to have a state policeman spend a night here and see for himself—though it would be just like the creatures to learn about it and hold off that night. They cut my wires whenever I try to telephone in the night—the linemen think it is very queer, and may testify for me if they don't go and imagine I cut them myself. I haven't tried to keep them repaired for over a week now.

I could get some of the ignorant people to testify for me about the reality of the horrors, but everybody laughs at what they say, and anyway, they have shunned my place for so long that they don't know any of the new events. You couldn't get one of those run-down farmers to come within a mile of my house for love or money. The mail-carrier hears what they say and jokes me about it—God! If I only dared tell him how real it is! I think I'll try to get him to notice the prints, but he comes in the afternoon and they're usually about gone by that time. If I kept one by setting a box or pan over it, he'd think surely it was a fake or joke.

Wish I hadn't gotten to be such a hermit, so folks don't drop around as they used to. I've never dared shew the black stone or the kodak pictures, or play that record, to anybody but the ignorant people. The others would say I faked the whole business and do nothing but laugh. But I may yet try shewing the pictures. They give those claw-prints clearly, even if the things that made them can't be photographed. What a shame nobody else saw that *thing* this morning before it went to nothing!

But I don't know as I care. After what I've been through, a madhouse is as good a place as any. The doctors can help me make up my mind to get away from this house, and that is all that will save me.

Write my son George if you don't hear soon. Goodbye, smash that record, and don't mix up in this.

                                Yrs—AKELEY

This letter frankly plunged me into the blackest of terror. I did not know what to say in answer, but scratched off some incoherent words of advice and encouragement and sent them by registered mail. I recall urging Akeley to move to Brattleboro at once, and place himself under the protection of the authorities; adding that I would come to that town with the phonograph record and help convince the courts of his sanity. It was time, too, I think I wrote, to alarm the people generally against this thing in their midst. It will be observed that at this moment of stress my own belief in all Akeley had told and claimed was virtually complete, though I did think his failure to get a picture of the dead monster was due not to any freak of Nature but to some excited slip of his own.

V

Then, apparently crossing my incoherent note and reaching me Saturday afternoon, September 8th, came that curiously different and calming letter neatly typed on a new machine; that strange letter of reassurance and invitation which must have marked so prodigious a transition in the whole nightmare drama of the lonely hills. Again I will quote from memory—seeking for special reasons to preserve as much of the flavour of the style as I can. It was postmarked Bellows Falls, and the signature as well as the body of the letter was typed—as is frequent with beginners in typing. The text, though, was marvellously accurate for a tyro's work; and I concluded that Akeley must have used a machine at some previous period—perhaps in college. To say that the letter relieved me would be only fair, yet beneath my relief lay a substratum of uneasiness. If Akeley had been sane in his terror, was he now sane in his deliverance? And the sort of "improved rapport" mentioned . . . what was it? The entire thing implied such a diametrical reversal of Akeley's previous attitude! But here is the substance of the text, carefully transcribed from a memory in which I take some pride.

Townshend, Vermont,
Thursday, Sept. 6, 1928.

My dear Wilmarth:—

It gives me great pleasure to be able to set you at rest regarding all the silly things I've been writing you. I say "silly," although by that I mean my frightened attitude rather than my descriptions of certain phenomena. Those phenomena are real and important enough; my mistake had been in establishing an anomalous attitude toward them.

I think I mentioned that my strange visitors were beginning to communicate with me, and to attempt such communication. Last night this exchange of speech became actual. In response to certain signals I admitted to the house a messenger from those outside—a fellow-human, let me hasten to say. He told me much that neither you nor I had even begun to guess, and shewed clearly how totally we had misjudged and misinterpreted the purpose of the Outer Ones in maintaining their secret colony on this planet.

It seems that the evil legends about what they have offered to men, and what they wish in connexion with the earth, are wholly the result of an ignorant misconception of allegorical speech—speech, of course, moulded by cultural backgrounds and thought-habits vastly different from anything we dream of. My own conjectures, I freely own, shot as widely past the mark as any of the guesses of illiterate farmers and savage Indians. What I had thought morbid and shameful and ignominious is in reality awesome and mind-expanding and even *glorious*—my previous estimate being merely a phase of man's eternal tendency to hate and fear and shrink from the *utterly different*.

Now I regret the harm I have inflicted upon these alien and incredible beings in the course of our nightly skirmishes. If only I had consented to talk peacefully and reasonably with them in the first

place! But they bear me no grudge, their emotions being organised
very differently from ours. It is their misfortune to have had as their
human agents in Vermont some very inferior specimens—the late
Walter Brown, for example. He prejudiced me vastly against them.
Actually, they have never knowingly harmed men, but have often
been cruelly wronged and spied upon by our species. There is a
whole secret cult of evil men (a man of your mystical erudition will
understand me when I link them with Hastur and the Yellow Sign)
devoted to the purpose of tracking them down and injuring them on
behalf of monstrous powers from other dimensions. It is against
these aggressors—not against normal humanity—that the drastic
precautions of the Outer Ones are directed. Incidentally, I learned
that many of our lost letters were stolen not by the Outer Ones but
by the emissaries of this malign cult.

        All that the Outer Ones wish of man is peace and non-molesta-
tion and an increasing intellectual rapport. This latter is absolutely
necessary now that our inventions and devices are expanding our
knowledge and motions, and making it more and more impossible
for the Outer Ones' necessary outposts to exist *secretly* on this planet.
The alien beings desire to know mankind more fully, and to have a
few of mankind's philosophic and scientific leaders know more about
them. With such an exchange of knowledge all perils will pass, and a
satisfactory *modus vivendi* be established. The very idea of any attempt
to *enslave* or *degrade* mankind is ridiculous.

        As a beginning of this improved rapport, the Outer Ones have
naturally chosen me—whose knowledge of them is already so considerable—as their primary interpreter on earth. Much was told me last
night—facts of the most stupendous and vista-opening nature—and
more will be subsequently communicated to me both orally and in
writing. I shall not be called upon to make any trip *outside* just yet,
though I shall probably *wish* to do so later on—employing special
means and transcending everything which we have hitherto been accustomed to regard as human experience. My house will be besieged
no longer. Everything has reverted to normal, and the dogs will have
no further occupation. In place of terror I have been given a rich
boon of knowledge and intellectual adventure which few other mortals have ever shared.

        The Outer Beings are perhaps the most marvellous organic
things in or beyond all space and time—members of a cosmos-wide
race of which all other life-forms are merely degenerate variants.
They are more vegetable than animal, if these terms can be applied
to the sort of matter composing them, and have a somewhat fungoid
structure; though the presence of a chlorophyll-like substance and a
very singular nutritive system differentiate them altogether from
true cormophytic fungi. Indeed, the type is composed of a form of
matter totally alien to our part of space—with electrons having a
wholly different vibration-rate. That is why the beings cannot be
photographed on the *ordinary* camera films and plates of our known
universe, even though our eyes can see them. With proper knowl-

edge, however, any good chemist could make a photographic emulsion which would record their images.

The genus is unique in its ability to traverse the heatless and airless interstellar void in full corporeal form, and some of its variants cannot do this without mechanical aid or curious surgical transpositions. Only a few species have the ether-resisting wings characteristic of the Vermont variety. Those inhabiting certain remote peaks in the Old World were brought in other ways. Their external resemblance to animal life, and to the sort of structure we understand as material, is a matter of parallel evolution rather than of close kinship. Their brain-capacity exceeds that of any other surviving life-form, although the winged types of our hill country are by no means the most highly developed. Telepathy is their usual means of discourse, though they have rudimentary vocal organs which, after a slight operation (for surgery is an incredibly expert and every-day thing among them), can roughly duplicate the speech of such types of organism as still use speech.

Their main *immediate* abode is a still undiscovered and almost lightless planet at the very edge of our solar system—beyond Neptune, and the ninth in distance from the sun. It is, as we have inferred, the object mystically hinted at as "Yuggoth" in certain ancient and forbidden writings; and it will soon be the scene of a strange focussing of thought upon our world in an effort to facilitate mental rapport. I would not be surprised if astronomers became sufficiently sensitive to these thought-currents to discover Yuggoth when the Outer Ones wish them to do so. But Yuggoth, of course, is only the stepping-stone. The main body of the beings inhabits strangely organised abysses wholly beyond the utmost reach of any human imagination. The space-time globule which we recognise as the totality of all cosmic entity is only an atom in the genuine infinity which is theirs. *And as much of this infinity as any human brain can hold is eventually to be opened up to me, as it has been to not more than fifty other men since the human race has existed.*

You will probably call this raving at first, Wilmarth, but in time you will appreciate the titanic opportunity I have stumbled upon. I want you to share as much of it as is possible, and to that end must tell you thousands of things that won't go on paper. In the past I have warned you not to come to see me. Now that all is safe, I take pleasure in rescinding that warning and inviting you.

Can't you make a trip up here before your college term opens? It would be marvellously delightful if you could. Bring along the phonograph record and all my letters to you as consultative data—we shall need them in piecing together the whole tremendous story. You might bring the kodak prints, too, since I seem to have mislaid the negatives and my own prints in all this recent excitement. But what a wealth of facts I have to add to all this groping and tentative material—*and what a stupendous device I have to supplement my additions!*

Don't hesitate—I am free from espionage now, and you will not meet anything unnatural or disturbing. Just come along and let my car meet you at the Brattleboro station—prepare to stay as long as you can, and expect many an evening of discussion of things beyond all human conjecture. Don't tell anyone about it, of course—for this matter must not get to the promiscuous public.

The train service to Brattleboro is not bad—you can get a timetable in Boston. Take the B. & M. to Greenfield, and then change for the brief remainder of the way. I suggest your taking the convenient 4:10 p.m.—standard—from Boston. This gets into Greenfield at 7:35, and at 9:19 a train leaves there which reaches Brattleboro at 10:01. That is week-days. Let me know the date and I'll have my car on hand at the station.

Pardon this typed letter, but my handwriting has grown shaky of late, as you know, and I don't feel equal to long stretches of script. I got this new Corona in Brattleboro yesterday—it seems to work very well.

Awaiting word, and hoping to see you shortly with the phonograph record and all my letters—and the kodak prints—

I am
Yours in anticipation,
HENRY W. AKELEY.

To Albert N. Wilmarth, Esq.,
Miskatonic University
Arkham, Mass.

The complexity of my emotions upon reading, re-reading, and pondering over this strange and unlooked-for letter is past adequate description. I have said that I was at once relieved and made uneasy, but this expresses only crudely the overtones of diverse and largely subconscious feelings which comprised both the relief and the uneasiness. To begin with, the thing was so antipodally at variance with the whole chain of horrors preceding it—the change of mood from stark terror to cool complacency and even exultation was so unheralded, lightning-like, and complete! I could scarcely believe that a single day could so alter the psychological perspective of one who had written that final frenzied bulletin of Wednesday, no matter what relieving disclosures that day might have brought. At certain moments a sense of conflicting unrealities made me wonder whether this whole distantly reported drama of fantastic forces were not a kind of half-illusory dream created largely within my own mind. Then I thought of the phonograph record and gave way to still greater bewilderment.

The letter seemed so unlike anything which could have been expected! As I analysed my impression, I saw that it consisted of two distinct phases. First, granting that Akeley had been sane before and was still sane, the indicated change in the situation itself was so swift and unthinkable. And secondly, the change in Akeley's own manner, attitude, and language was so vastly beyond the normal or the predictable. The man's whole personality seemed to have undergone an insidious mutation—a mutation so deep that one could scarcely reconcile his two aspects with the supposition that both represented equal sanity. Word-choice, spelling—all were subtly different. And with my academic sensitiveness to prose style, I could trace profound divergences in his commonest reactions and rhythm-responses. Certainly, the emotional cataclysm or revelation which could produce so radical an overturn must be an extreme one indeed! Yet in another way the letter seemed quite characteristic of Akeley. The same old passion for infinity—the same old scholarly inquisitiveness. I could not a moment—or more than a moment—credit the idea of spuriousness or malign substitution. Did not the invitation—the willingness to have me test the truth of the letter in person—prove its genuineness?

I did not retire Saturday night, but sat up thinking of the shadows and marvels behind the letter I had received. My mind, aching from the quick succession of monstrous conceptions it had been forced to confront during the last four months, worked upon this startling new material in a cycle of doubt and acceptance which repeated most of the steps experienced in facing the earlier wonders; till long before dawn a burning interest and curiosity had begun to replace the original storm of perplexity and uneasiness. Mad or sane, metamorphosed or merely relieved, the chances were that Akeley had actually encountered some stupendous change of perspective in his hazardous research; some change at once diminishing his danger—real or fancied—and opening dizzy new vistas of cosmic and superhuman knowledge. My own zeal for the unknown flared up to meet his, and I felt myself touched by the contagion of the morbid barrier-breaking. To shake off the maddening and wearying limitations of time and space and natural law—to be linked with the vast *outside*—to come close to the nighted and abysmal secrets of the infinite and the ultimate—surely such a thing was worth the risk of one's life, soul, and sanity! And Akeley had said there was no longer any peril—he had invited me to visit him instead of warning me away as before. I tingled at the thought of what he might now have to tell me—there was an almost paralysing fascination in the thought of sitting in that lonely and lately beleaguered farmhouse with a man who had talked with actual emissaries from outer space; sitting there with the terrible record and the pile of letters in which Akeley had summarised his earlier conclusions.

So late Sunday morning I telegraphed Akeley that I would meet him in Brattleboro on the following Wednesday—September 12th— if that date were convenient for him. In only one respect did I depart from his suggestions, and that concerned the choice of a train. Frankly, I did not feel like arriving in that haunted Vermont region late at night; so instead of accepting the train he chose I telephoned the station and devised another arrangement. By rising early and taking the 8:07 a.m. (standard) into Boston, I could catch the 9:25 for Greenfield; arriving there at 12:22 noon. This connected exactly with a train reaching Brattleboro at 1:08 p.m.—a much more comfortable hour than 10:01 for meeting Akeley and riding with him into the close-packed, secret-guarding hills.

I mentioned this choice in my telegram, and was glad to learn in the reply which came toward evening that it had met with my prospective host's endorsement. His wire ran thus:

> ARRANGEMENT SATISFACTORY. WILL MEET 1:08
> TRAIN WEDNESDAY. DON'T FORGET RECORD AND LET-
> TERS AND PRINTS. KEEP DESTINATION QUIET. EXPECT
> GREAT REVELATIONS.
>   AKELEY.

Receipt of this message in direct response to one sent to Akeley—and necessarily delivered to his house from the Townshend station either by official messenger or by a restored telephone service—removed any lingering subconscious doubts I may have had about the authorship of the perplexing letter. My relief was marked—indeed, it was greater than I could account for at the time; since all such doubts had been rather deeply buried. But I slept soundly and long that night, and was eagerly busy with preparations during the ensuing two days.

VI

On Wednesday I started as agreed, taking with me a valise full of simple necessities and scientific data, including the hideous phonograph record, the kodak prints, and the entire file of Akeley's correspondence. As requested, I had told no one where I was going; for I could see that the matter demanded utmost privacy, even allowing for its most favourable turns. The thought of actual mental contact with alien, outside entities was stupefying enough to my trained and somewhat prepared mind; and this being so, what might one think of its effect on the vast masses of uninformed laymen? I do not know whether dread or adventurous expectancy was uppermost in me as I changed trains at Boston and began the long westward run out of familiar regions into those I knew less thoroughly. Waltham—Concord—Ayer—Fitchburg—Gardner— Athol—

My train reached Greenfield seven minutes late, but the northbound connecting express had been held. Transferring in haste, I felt a curious breathlessness as the cars rumbled on through the early afternoon sunlight into territories I had always read of but had never before visited. I knew I was entering an altogether older-fashioned and more primitive New England than the mechanised, urbanised coastal and southern areas where all my life had been spent; an unspoiled, ancestral New England without the foreigners and factory-smoke, billboards and concrete roads, of the sections which modernity has touched. There would be odd survivals of that continuous native life whose deep roots make it the one authentic outgrowth of the landscape—the continuous native life which keeps alive strange ancient memories, and fertilises the soil for shadowy, marvellous, and seldom-mentioned beliefs.

Now and then I saw the blue Connecticut River gleaming in the sun, and after leaving Northfield we crossed it. Ahead loomed green and cryptical hills, and when the conductor came around I learned that I was at last in Vermont. He told me to set my watch back an hour, since the northern hill country will have no dealings with new-fangled daylight time schemes. As I did so it seemed to me that I was likewise turning the calendar back a century.

The train kept close to the river, and across in New Hampshire I could see the approaching slope of steep Wantastiquet, about which singular old legends cluster. Then streets appeared on my left, and a green island shewed in the stream on my right. People rose and filed to the door, and I followed them. The car stopped, and I alighted beneath the long train-shed of the Brattleboro station.

Looking over the line of waiting motors I hesitated a moment to see which one might turn out to be the Akeley Ford, but my identity was divined before I could take the initiative. And yet it was clearly not Akeley himself who advanced to meet me with an outstretched hand and a mellowly phrased query as to whether I was indeed Mr. Albert N. Wilmarth of Arkham. This man bore no resemblance to the bearded, grizzled Akeley of the snapshot; but was a younger and more urban person, fashionably dressed, and wearing only a small, dark moustache. His cultivated voice held an odd and almost disturbing hint of vague familiarity, though I could not definitely place it in my memory.

As I surveyed him I heard him explaining that he was a friend of my prospective host's who had come down from Townshend in his stead. Akeley, he declared, had suffered a sudden attack of some asthmatic trouble, and did not feel equal to making a trip in the outdoor air. It was not serious, however, and there was to be no change in plans regarding my visit. I could not make out just how much this

Mr. Noyes—as he announced himself—knew of Akeley's researches and discoveries, though it seemed to me that his casual manner stamped him as a comparative outsider. Remembering what a hermit Akeley had been, I was a trifle surprised at the ready availability of such a friend; but did not let my puzzlement deter me from entering the motor to which he gestured me. It was not the small ancient car I had expected from Akeley's descriptions, but a large and immaculate specimen of recent pattern—apparently Noyes's own, and bearing Massachusetts license plates with the amusing "sacred codfish" device of that year. My guide, I concluded, must be a summer transient in the Townshend region.

Noyes climbed into the car beside me and started it at once. I was glad that he did not overflow with conversation, for some peculiar atmospheric tensity made me feel disinclined to talk. The town seemed very attractive in the afternoon sunlight as we swept up an incline and turned to the right into the main street. It drowsed like the older New England cities which one remembers from boyhood, and something in the collocation of roofs and steeples and chimneys and brick walls formed contours touching deep viol-strings of ancestral emotion. I could tell that I was at the gateway of a region half-bewitched through the piling-up of unbroken time-accumulations; a region where old, strange things have had a chance to grow and linger because they have never been stirred up.

As we passed out of Brattleboro my sense of constraint and foreboding increased, for a vague quality in the hill-crowded countryside with its towering, threatening, close-pressing green and granite slopes hinted at obscure secrets and immemorial survivals which might or might not be hostile to mankind. For a time our course followed a broad, shallow river which flowed down from unknown hills in the north, and I shivered when my companion told me it was the West River. It was in this stream, I recalled from newspaper items, that one of the morbid crab-like beings had been seen floating after the floods.

Gradually the country around us grew wilder and more deserted. Archaic covered bridges lingered fearsomely out of the past in pockets of the hills, and the half-abandoned railway track paralleling the river seemed to exhale a nebulously visible air of desolation. There were awesome sweeps of vivid valley where great cliffs rose, New England's virgin granite shewing grey and austere through the verdure that scaled the crests. There were gorges where untamed streams leaped, bearing down toward the river the unimagined secrets of a thousand pathless peaks. Branching away now and then were narrow, half-concealed roads that bored their way through solid, luxuriant masses of forest among whose primal trees whole armies of elemental spirits might well lurk.

As I saw these I thought of how Akeley had been molested by unseen agencies on his drives along this very route, and did not wonder that such things could be.

The quaint, sightly village of Newfane, reached in less than an hour, was our last link with that world which man can definitely call his own by virtue of conquest and complete occupancy. After that we cast off all allegiance to immediate, tangible, and time-touched things, and entered a fantastic world of hushed unreality in which the narrow, ribbon-like road rose and fell and curved with an almost sentient and purposeful caprice amidst the tenantless green peaks and half-deserted valleys. Except for the sound of the motor, and the faint stir of the few lonely farms we passed at infrequent intervals, the only thing that reached my ears was the gurgling, insidious trickle of strange waters from numberless hidden fountains in the shadowy woods.

The nearness and intimacy of the dwarfed, domed hills now became veritably breath-taking. Their steepness and abruptness were even greater than I had imagined from hearsay, and suggested nothing in common with the prosaic objective world we know. The dense, unvisited woods on those inaccessible slopes seemed to harbour alien and incredible things, and I felt that the very outline of the hills themselves held some strange and aeon-forgotten meaning, as if they were vast hieroglyphs left by a rumoured titan race whose glories live only in rare, deep dreams. All the legends of the past, and all the stupefying imputations of Henry Akeley's letters and exhibits, welled up in my memory to heighten the atmosphere of tension and growing menace. The purpose of my visit, and the frightful abnormalities it postulated, struck me all at once with a chill sensation that nearly overbalanced my ardour for strange delvings.

My guide must have noticed my disturbed attitude; for as the road grew wilder and more irregular, and our motion slower and more jolting, his occasional pleasant comments expanded into a steadier flow of discourse. He spoke of the beauty and weirdness of the country, and revealed some acquaintance with the folklore studies of my prospective host. From his polite questions, it was obvious that he knew I had come for a scientific purpose, and that I was bringing data of some importance; but he gave no sign of appreciating the depth and awfulness of the knowledge which Akeley had finally reached.

His manner was so cheerful, normal, and urbane that his remarks ought to have calmed and reassured me; but oddly enough, I felt only the more disturbed as we bumped and veered onward into the unknown wilderness of hills and woods. At times it seemed as if he were pumping me to see what I knew of the monstrous secrets of the place, and with every fresh utterance that vague, teasing, baffling *familiarity* in his voice increased. It was not an ordinary or healthy familiarity despite the thoroughly wholesome and cultivated nature of the voice. I somehow linked it with forgotten nightmares, and felt that I might go mad if I recognised it. If any good excuse had existed, I think I would have turned back from my visit. As it was, I could not well do so—and it occurred to me that a cool, scientific conversation with Akeley himself after my arrival would help greatly to pull me together.

Besides, there was a strangely calming element of cosmic beauty in the hypnotic landscape through which we climbed and plunged fantastically. Time had lost itself in the labyrinths behind, and around us stretched only the flowering waves of faery and the recaptured loveliness of vanished centuries—the hoary groves, the untainted pastures edged with gay autumnal blossoms, and at vast intervals the small brown farmsteads nestling amidst huge trees beneath vertical precipices of fragrant brier and meadow-grass. Even the sunlight assumed a supernal glamour, as if some special atmosphere or exhalation mantled the whole region. I had seen nothing like it before save in the magic vistas that sometimes form the backgrounds of Italian primitives. Sodoma and Leonardo conceived such expanses, but only in the distance, and through the vaultings of Renaissance arcades. We were now burrowing bodily through the midst of the picture, and I seemed to find in its necromancy a thing I had innately known or inherited, and for which I had always been vainly searching.

Suddenly, after rounding an obtuse angle at the top of a sharp ascent, the car came to a standstill. On my left, across a well-kept lawn which stretched to the road and flaunted a border of white-washed stones, rose a white, two-and-a-half story house of unusual size and elegance for the region, with a congeries of contiguous or arcade-linked barns, sheds, and windmill behind and to the right. I recognised it at once from the snapshot I had received, and was not surprised to see the name of Henry Akeley on the galvanised-iron mail-box near the road. For some distance back of the house a level stretch of marshy and sparsely wooded land extended, beyond which soared a steep, thickly forested hillside ending in a jagged leafy crest. This latter, I knew, was the summit of Dark Mountain, half way up which we must have climbed already.

Alighting from the car and taking my valise, Noyes asked me to wait while he went in and notified Akeley of my advent. He himself, he added, had important business elsewhere, and could not stop for more than a moment. As he briskly walked up the path to the house I climbed out of the car myself, wishing to stretch my legs a little before settling down to a sedentary conversation. My feeling of nervousness and tension had risen to a maximum again now that I was on the actual scene of the morbid beleaguering described so hauntingly in Akeley's letters, and I honestly dreaded the coming discussions which were to link me with such alien and forbidden worlds.

Close contact with the utterly bizarre is often more terrifying than inspiring, and it did not cheer me to think that this very bit of dusty road was the place where those monstrous tracks and that foetid green ichor had been found after moonless nights of fear and death. Idly I noticed that none of Akeley's dogs seemed to be about. Had he sold them all as soon as the Outer Ones made peace with him? Try as I might, I could not have the same confidence in the depth and sincerity of that peace which appeared in Akeley's final and queerly different letter. After all, he was a man of much simplicity and with little worldly experience. Was there not, perhaps, some deep and sinister undercurrent beneath the surface of the new alliance?

Led by my thoughts, my eyes turned downward to the powdery road surface which had held such hideous testimonies. The last few days had been dry, and tracks of all sorts cluttered the rutted, irregular highway despite the unfrequented nature of the district. With a vague curiosity I began to trace the outline of some of the heterogeneous impressions, trying meanwhile to curb the flights of macabre fancy which the place and its memories suggested. There was something menacing and uncomfortable in the funereal stillness, in the muffled, subtle trickle of distant brooks, and in the crowding green peaks and black-wooded precipices that choked the narrow horizon.

And then an image shot into my consciousness which made those vague menaces and flights of fancy seem mild and insignificant indeed. I have said that I was scanning the miscellaneous prints in the road with a kind of idle curiosity—but all at once that curiosity was shockingly snuffed out by a sudden and paralysing gust of active terror. For though the dust tracks were in general confused and overlapping, and unlikely to arrest any casual gaze, my restless vision had caught certain details near the spot where the path to the house joined the highway; and had recognised beyond doubt or hope the frightful significance of those details. It was not for nothing, alas, that I had pored for hours over the kodak views of the Outer Ones' claw-prints which Akeley had sent. Too well did I know the marks of those loathsome nippers, and that hint of ambiguous direction which stamped the horrors as no creatures of this planet. No chance had been left me for merciful mistake. Here, indeed, in objective form before my own eyes, and surely made not many hours ago, were at least three marks which stood out blasphemously among the surprising plethora of blurred footprints leading to and from the Akeley farmhouse. *They were the hellish tracks of the living fungi from Yuggoth.*

I pulled myself together in time to stifle a scream. After all, what more was there than I might have expected, assuming that I had really believed Akeley's letters? He had spoken of making peace with the things. Why, then, was it strange that some of them had visited his house? But the terror was stronger than the reassurance. Could any man be expected to look unmoved for the first time upon the claw-marks of animate beings from outer depths of space? Just then I saw Noyes emerge from the door and approach with a brisk step. I must, I reflected, keep command of myself, for the chances were that this genial friend knew nothing of Akeley's profoundest and most stupendous probings into the forbidden.

Akeley, Noyes hastened to inform me, was glad and ready to see me; although his sudden attack of asthma would prevent him from being a very competent host for a day or two. These spells hit him hard when they came, and were always accompanied by a debilitating fever and general weakness. He never was good for much while they lasted—had to talk in a whisper, and was very clumsy and feeble in getting about. His feet and ankles swelled, too, so that he had to bandage them like a gouty old beef-eater. Today he was in rather bad shape, so that I would have to attend very largely to my own needs; but he was none the less eager for conversation. I would find him in the study at the left of the front hall—the room where the blinds were shut. He had to keep the sunlight out when he was ill, for his eyes were very sensitive.

As Noyes bade me adieu and rode off northward in his car I began to walk slowly toward the house. The door had been left ajar for me; but before approaching and entering I cast a searching glance around the whole place, trying to decide what had struck me as so intangibly queer about it. The barns and sheds looked trimly prosaic enough, and I noticed Akeley's battered Ford in its capacious, unguarded shelter. Then the secret of the queerness reached me. It was the total silence. Ordinarily a farm is at least moderately murmurous from its various kinds of livestock, but here all signs of life were missing. What of the hens and the hogs? The cows, of which Akeley had said he possessed several, might conceivably be out to pasture, and the dogs might possibly have been sold; but the absence of any cackling or grunting was truly singular.

I did not pause long on the path, but resolutely entered the open house door and closed it behind me. It had cost me a distinct psychological effort to do so, and now that I was shut inside I had a momentary longing for precipitate retreat. Not that the place was in the least sinister in visual suggestion; on the contrary, I thought the graceful late-colonial hallway very tasteful and wholesome, and admired the evident breeding of the man who had furnished it. What made me wish to flee was something very attenuated and indefinable. Perhaps it was a certain odd odour which I thought I noticed—though I well knew how common musty odours are in even the best of ancient farmhouses.

VII

Refusing to let these cloudy qualms overmaster me, I recalled Noyes's instructions and pushed open the six-panelled, brass-latched white door on my left. The room beyond was darkened, as I had known before; and as I entered it I noticed that the queer odour was stronger there. There likewise appeared to be some faint, half-imaginary rhythm or vibration in the air. For a moment the closed blinds allowed me to see very little, but then a kind of apologetic hacking or whispering sound drew my attention to a great easy-chair in the farther, darker corner of the room. Within its shadowy depths I saw the white blur of a man's face and hands; and in a moment I had crossed to greet the figure who had tried to speak. Dim though the light was, I perceived that this was indeed my host. I had studied the kodak picture repeatedly, and there could be no mistake about this firm, weather-beaten face with the cropped, grizzled beard.

But as I looked again my recognition was mixed with sadness and anxiety; for certainly, this face was that of a very sick man. I felt that there must be something more than asthma behind that strained, rigid, immobile expression and unwinking glassy stare; and realised how terribly the strain of his frightful experiences must have told on him. Was it not enough to break any human being—even a younger man than this intrepid delver into the forbidden? The strange and sudden relief, I feared, had come too late to save him from something like a general breakdown. There was a touch of the pitiful in the limp, lifeless way his lean hands rested in his lap. He had on a loose dressing-gown, and was swathed around the head and high around the neck with a vivid yellow scarf or hood.

And then I saw that he was trying to talk in the same hacking whisper with which he had greeted me. It was a hard whisper to catch at first, since the grey moustache concealed all movements of the lips, and something in its timbre disturbed me greatly; but by concentrating my attention I could soon make out its purport surprisingly well. The accent was by no means a rustic one, and the language was even more polished than correspondence had led me to expect.

"Mr. Wilmarth, I presume? You must pardon my not rising. I am quite ill, as Mr. Noyes must have told you; but I could not resist having you come just the same. You know what I wrote in my last letter—there is so much to tell you tomorrow when I shall feel better. I can't say how glad I am to see you in person after all our many letters. You have the file with you, of course? And the kodak prints and record? Noyes put your valise in the hall—I suppose you saw it. For tonight I fear you'll have to wait on yourself to a great extent. Your room is upstairs—the one over this—and you'll see the bathroom door open at the head of the staircase. There's a meal spread for you in the dining-room—right through this door at your right—which you can take whenever you feel like it. I'll be a better host tomorrow—but just now weakness leaves me helpless.

"Make yourself at home—you might take out the letters and pictures and record and put them on the table here before you go upstairs with your bag. It is here that we shall discuss them—you can see my phonograph on that corner stand.

"No, thanks—there's nothing you can do for me. I know these spells of old. Just come back for a little quiet visiting before night, and then go to bed when you please. I'll rest right here—perhaps sleep here all night as I often do. In the morning I'll be far better able to go into the things we must go into. You realise, of course, the utterly stupendous nature of the matter before us. To us, as to only a few men on this earth, there will be opened up gulfs of time and space and knowledge beyond anything within the conception of human science or philosophy.

"Do you know that Einstein is wrong, and that certain objects and forces *can* move with a velocity greater than that of light? With proper aid I expect to go backward and forward in time, and actually *see* and *feel* the earth of remote past and future epochs. You can't imagine the degree to which those beings have carried science. There is nothing they can't do with the mind and body of living organisms. I expect to visit other planets, and even other stars and galaxies. The first trip will be to Yuggoth, the nearest world fully peopled by the beings. It is a strange dark orb at the very rim of our solar system—unknown to earthly astronomers as yet. But I must have written you about this. At the proper time, you know, the beings there will direct thought-currents toward us and cause it to be discovered—or perhaps let one of their human allies give the scientists a hint.

"There are mighty cities on Yuggoth—great tiers of terraced towers built of black stone like the specimen I tried to send you. That came from Yuggoth. The sun shines there no brighter than a star, but the beings need no light. They have other, subtler senses, and put no windows in their great houses and temples. Light even hurts and hampers and confuses them, for it does not exist at all in the black cosmos outside time and space where they came from originally. To visit Yuggoth would drive any weak man mad—yet I am going there. The black rivers of pitch that flow under those mysterious Cyclopean bridges—things built by some elder race extinct and forgotten before the beings came to Yuggoth from the ultimate voids—ought to be enough to make any man a Dante or Poe if he can keep sane long enough to tell what he has seen.

"But remember—that dark world of fungoid gardens and window-less cities isn't really terrible. It is only to us that it would seem so. Probably this world seemed just as terrible to the beings when they first explored it in the primal age. You know they were here long before the fabulous epoch of Cthulhu was over, and remember all about sunken R'lyeh when it was above the waters. They've been inside the earth, too—there are openings which human beings know nothing of—some of them in these very Vermont hills—and great worlds of unknown life down there; blue-litten K'n-yan, red-litten Yoth, and black, lightless N'kai. It's from N'kai that frightful Tsathoggua came—you know, the amorphous, toad-like god-creature mentioned in the Pnakotic Manuscripts and the *Necronomicon* and the Commoriom myth-cycle preserved by the Atlantean high-priest Klarkash-Ton.

"But we will talk of all this later on. It must be four or five o'clock by this time. Better bring the stuff from your bag, take a bite, and then come back for a comfortable chat."

Very slowly I turned and began to obey my host; fetching my valise, extracting and depositing the desired articles, and finally ascending to the room designated as mine. With the memory of that roadside claw-print fresh in my mind, Akeley's whispered paragraphs had affected me queerly; and the hints of familiarity with this unknown world of fungous life—forbidden Yuggoth—made my flesh creep more than I cared to own. I was tremendously sorry about Akeley's illness, but had to confess that his hoarse whisper had a hateful as well as pitiful quality. If only he wouldn't *gloat* so about Yuggoth and its black secrets!

My room proved a very pleasant and well-furnished one, devoid alike of the musty odour and disturbing sense of vibration; and after leaving my valise there I descended again to greet Akeley and take the lunch he had set out for me. The dining-room was just beyond the study, and I saw that a kitchen ell extended still farther in the same direction. On the dining-table an ample array of sandwiches, cake, and cheese awaited me, and a Thermos-bottle beside a cup and saucer testified that hot coffee had not been forgotten. After a well-relished meal I poured myself a liberal cup of coffee, but found that the culinary standard had suffered a lapse in this one detail. My first spoonful revealed a faintly unpleasant acrid taste, so that I did not take more. Throughout the lunch I thought of Akeley sitting silently in the great chair in the darkened next room. Once I went in to beg him to share the repast, but he whispered that he could eat nothing as yet. Later on, just before he slept, he would take some malted milk—all he ought to have that day.

After lunch I insisted on clearing the dishes away and washing them in the kitchen sink—incidentally emptying the coffee which I had not been able to appreciate. Then returning to the darkened study I drew up a chair near my host's corner and prepared for such conversation as he might feel inclined to conduct. The letters, pictures, and record were still on the large centre-table, but for the nonce we did not have to draw upon them. Before long I forgot even the bizarre odour and curious suggestions of vibrations.

I have said that there were things in some of Akeley's letters—especially the second and most voluminous one—which I would not dare to quote or even form into words on paper. This hesitancy applies with still greater force to the things I heard whispered that evening in the darkened room among the lonely haunted hills. Of the extent of the cosmic horrors unfolded by that raucous voice I cannot even hint. He had known hideous things before, but what he had learned since making his pact with the Outside Things was almost too much for sanity to bear. Even now I absolutely refuse to believe what he implied about the constitution of ultimate infinity, the juxtaposition of dimensions, and the frightful position of our known cosmos of space and time in the unending chain of linked cosmos-atoms which makes up the immediate super-cosmos of curves, angles, and material and semi-material electronic organisation.

Never was a sane man more dangerously close to the arcana of basic entity—never was an organic brain nearer to utter annihilation in the chaos that transcends form and force and symmetry. I learned whence Cthulhu *first* came, and why half the great temporary stars of history had flared forth. I guessed—from hints which made even my informant pause timidly—the secret behind the Magellanic Clouds and globular nebulae, and the black truth veiled by the immemorial allegory of Tao. The nature of the Doels was plainly revealed, and I was told the essence (though not the source) of the Hounds of Tindalos. The legend of Yig, Father of Serpents, remained figurative no longer, and I started with loathing when told of the monstrous nuclear chaos beyond angled space which the *Necronomicon* had mercifully cloaked under the name of Azathoth. It was shocking to have the foulest nightmares of secret myth cleared up in concrete terms whose stark, morbid hatefulness exceeded the boldest hints of ancient and mediaeval mystics. Ineluctably I was led to believe that the first whisperers of these accursed tales must have had discourse with Akeley's Outer Ones, and perhaps have visited outer cosmic realms as Akeley now proposed visiting them.

I was told of the Black Stone and what it implied, and was glad that it had not reached me. My guesses about those hieroglyphics had been all too correct! And yet Akeley now seemed reconciled to the whole fiendish system he had stumbled upon; reconciled and eager to probe farther into the monstrous abyss. I wondered what beings he had talked with since his last letter to me, and whether many of them had been as human as that first emissary he had mentioned. The tension in my head grew insufferable, and I built up all sorts of wild theories about the queer, persistent odour and those insidious hints of vibration in the darkened room.

Night was falling now, and as I recalled what Akeley had written me about those earlier nights I shuddered to think there would be no moon. Nor did I like the way the farmhouse nestled in the lee of that colossal forested slope leading up to Dark Mountain's unvisited crest. With Akeley's permission I lighted a small oil lamp, turned it low, and set it on a distant bookcase beside the ghostly bust of Milton; but afterward I was sorry I had done so, for it made my host's strained, immobile face and listless hands look damnably abnormal and corpse-like. He seemed half-incapable of motion, though I saw him nod stiffly once in a while.

After what he had told, I could scarcely imagine what profounder secrets he was saving for the morrow; but at last it developed that his trip to Yuggoth and beyond—*and my own possible participation in it*—was to be the next day's topic. He must have been amused by the start of horror I gave at hearing a cosmic voyage on my part proposed, for his head wabbled violently when I shewed my fear. Subsequently he spoke very gently of how human beings might accomplish—and several times had accomplished—the seemingly impossible flight across the interstellar void. It seemed *that complete human bodies did not indeed make the trip,* but that the prodigious surgical, biological, chemical, and mechanical skill of the Outer Ones had found a way to convey human brains without their concomitant physical structure.

There was a harmless way to extract a brain, and a way to keep the organic residue alive during its absence. The bare, compact cerebral matter was then immersed in an occasionally replenished fluid within an ether-tight cylinder of a metal mined in Yuggoth, certain electrodes reaching through and connecting at will with elaborate instruments capable of duplicating the three vital faculties of sight, hearing, and speech. For the winged fungus-beings to carry the brain-cylinders intact through space was an easy matter. Then, on every planet covered by their civilisation, they would find plenty of adjustable faculty-instruments capable of being connected with the encased brains; so that after a little fitting these travelling intelligences could be given a full sensory and articulate life—albeit a bodiless and mechanical one—at each stage of their journeying through and beyond the space-time continuum. It was as simple as carrying a phonograph record about and playing it wherever a phonograph of the corresponding make exists. Of its success there could be no question. Akeley was not afraid. Had it not been brilliantly accomplished again and again?

For the first time one of the inert, wasted hands raised itself and pointed stiffly to a high shelf on the farther side of the room. There, in a neat row, stood more than a dozen cylinders of a metal I had never seen before—cylinders a foot high and somewhat less in diameter, with three curious sockets set in an isosceles triangle over the front convex surface of each. One of them was linked at two of the sockets to a pair of singular-looking machines that stood in the background. Of their purport I did not need to be told, and I shivered as with ague. Then I saw the hand point to a much nearer corner where some intricate instruments with attached cords and plugs, several of them much like the two devices on the shelf behind the cylinders, were huddled together.

"There are four kinds of instruments here, Wilmarth," whispered the voice. "Four kinds—three faculties each—makes twelve pieces in all. You see there are four different sorts of beings represented in those cylinders up there. Three humans, six fungoid beings who can't navigate space corporeally, two beings from Neptune (God! if you could see the body this type has on its own planet!), and the rest entities from the central caverns of an especially interesting dark star beyond the galaxy. In the principal outpost inside Round Hill you'll now and then find more cylinders and machines—cylinders of extra-cosmic brains with different senses from any we know—allies and explorers from the uttermost Outside—and special machines for giving them impressions and expression in the several ways suited at once to them and to the comprehensions of different types of listeners. Round Hill, like most of the beings' main outposts all through the various universes, is a very cosmopolitan place! Of course, only the more common types have been lent to me for experiment.

"Here—take the three machines I point to and set them on the table. That tall one with the two glass lenses in front—then the box with the vacuum tubes and sounding-board—and now the one with the metal disc on top. Now for the cylinder with the label 'B-67' pasted on it. Just stand in that Windsor chair to reach the shelf. Heavy? Never mind! Be sure of the number—B-67. Don't bother that fresh, shiny cylinder joined to the two testing instruments—the one with my name on it. Set B-67 on the table near where you've put the machines—and see the dial switch on all three machines is jammed over to the extreme left.

"Now connect the cord of the lens machine with the upper socket on the cylinder—there! Join the tube machine to the lower left-hand socket, and the disc apparatus to the outer socket. Now move all the dial switches on the machines over to the extreme right—first the lens one, then the disc one, and then the tube one. That's right. I might as well tell you that this is a human being—just like any of us. I'll give you a taste of some of the others tomorrow."

To this day I do not know why I obeyed those whispers so slavishly, or whether I thought Akeley was mad or sane. After what had gone before, I ought to have been prepared for anything; but this mechanical mummery seemed so like the typical vagaries of crazed inventors and scientists that it struck a chord of doubt which even the preceding discourse had not excited. What the whisperer implied was beyond all human belief—yet were not the other things still farther beyond, and less preposterous only because of their remoteness from tangible concrete proof?

As my mind reeled amidst this chaos, I became conscious of a mixed grating and whirring from all three of the machines lately linked to the cylinder—a grating and whirring which soon subsided into a virtual noiselessness. What was about to happen? Was I to hear a voice? And if so, what proof would I have that it was not some cleverly concocted radio device talked into by a concealed but closely watching speaker? Even now I am unwilling to swear just what I heard, or just what phenomenon really took place before me. But something certainly seemed to take place.

To be brief and plain, the machine with the tubes and sound-box began to speak, and with a point and intelligence which left no doubt that the speaker was actually present and observing us. The voice was loud, metallic, lifeless, and plainly mechanical in every detail of its production. It was incapable of inflection or expressiveness, but scraped and rattled on with a deadly precision and deliberation.

"Mr. Wilmarth," it said, "I hope I do not startle you. I am a human being like yourself, though my body is now resting safely under proper vitalising treatment inside Round Hill, about a mile and a half east of here. I myself am here with you—my brain is in that cylinder and I see, hear, and speak through these electronic vibrators. In a week I am going across the void as I have been many times before, and I expect to have the pleasure of Mr. Akeley's company. I wish I might have yours as well; for I know you by sight and reputation, and have kept close track of your correspondence with our friend. I am, of course, one of the men who have become allied with the outside beings visiting our planet. I met them first in the Himalayas, and have helped them in various ways. In return they have given me experiences such as few men have ever had.

"Do you realise what it means when I say I have been on thirty-seven different celestial bodies—planets, dark stars, and less definable objects—including eight outside our galaxy and two outside the curved cosmos of space and time? All this has not harmed me in the least. My brain has been removed from my body by fissions so adroit that it would be crude to call the operation surgery. The visiting beings have methods which make these extractions easy and almost normal—and one's body never ages when the brain is out of it. The brain, I may add, is virtually immortal with its mechanical faculties and a limited nourishment supplied by occasional changes in the preserving fluid.

"Altogether, I hope most heartily that you will decide to come with Mr. Akeley and me. The visitors are eager to know men of knowledge like yourself, and to shew them the great abysses that most of us have had to dream about in fanciful ignorance. It may seem strange at first to meet them, but I know you will be above minding that. I think Mr. Noyes will go along, too—the man who doubtless brought you up here in his car. He has been one of us for years—I suppose you recognised his voice as one of those on the record Mr. Akeley sent you."

At my violent start the speaker paused a moment before concluding.

"So, Mr. Wilmarth, I will leave the matter to you; merely adding that a man with your love of strangeness and folklore ought never to miss such a chance as this. There is nothing to fear. All transitions are painless, and there is much to enjoy in a wholly mechanised state of sensation. When the electrodes are disconnected, one merely drops off into a sleep of especially vivid and fantastic dreams.

"And now, if you don't mind, we might adjourn our session till tomorrow. Good night—just turn all the switches back to the left; never mind the exact order, though you might let the lens machine be last. Good night, Mr. Akeley—treat our guest well! Ready now with those switches?"

That was all. I obeyed mechanically and shut off all three switches, though dazed with doubt of everything that had occurred. My head was still reeling as I heard Akeley's whispering voice telling me that I might leave all the apparatus on the table just as it was. He did not essay any comment on what had happened, and indeed no comment could have conveyed much to my burdened faculties. I heard him telling me I could take the lamp to use in my room, and deduced that he wished to rest alone in the dark. It was surely time he rested, for his discourse of the afternoon and evening had been such as to exhaust even a vigorous man. Still dazed, I bade my host good night and went upstairs with the lamp, although I had an excellent pocket flashlight with me.

I was glad to be out of that downstairs study with the queer odour and vague suggestions of vibration, yet could not of course escape a hideous sense of dread and peril and cosmic abnormality as I thought of the place I was in and the forces I was meeting. The wild, lonely region, the black, mysteriously forested slope towering so close behind the house, the footprints in the road, the sick, motionless whisperer in the dark, the hellish cylinders and machines, and above all the invitations to strange surgery and stranger voyagings—these things, all so new and in such sudden succession, rushed in on me with a cumulative force which sapped my will and almost undermined my physical strength.

To discover that my guide Noyes was the human celebrant in that monstrous bygone Sabbat-ritual on the phonograph record was a particular shock, though I had previously sensed a dim, repellent familiarity in his voice. Another special shock came from my own attitude toward my host whenever I paused to analyse it; for as much as I had instinctively liked Akeley as revealed in his correspondence, I now found that he filled me with a distinct repulsion. His illness ought to have excited my pity; but instead, it gave me a kind of shudder. He was so rigid and inert and corpse-like—and that incessant whispering was so hateful and unhuman!

It occurred to me that this whispering was different from anything else of the kind I had ever heard; that, despite the curious motionlessness of the speaker's moustache-screened lips, it had a latent strength and carrying-power remarkable for the wheezings of an asthmatic. I had been able to understand the speaker when wholly across the room, and once or twice it had seemed to me that the faint but penetrant sounds represented not so much weakness as deliberate repression—for what reason I could not guess. From the first I had felt a disturbing quality in their timbre. Now, when I tried to weigh the matter, I thought I could trace this impression to a kind of subconscious familiarity like that which had made Noyes's voice so hazily ominous. But when or where I had encountered the thing it hinted at, was more than I could tell.

One thing was certain—I would not spend another night here. My scientific zeal had vanished amidst fear and loathing, and I felt nothing now but a wish to escape from this net of morbidity and unnatural revulsion. I knew enough now. It must indeed be true that strange cosmic linkages do exist—but such things are surely not meant for normal human beings to meddle with.

Blasphemous influences seemed to surround me and press chokingly upon my senses. Sleep, I decided, would be out of the question, so I merely extinguished the lamp and threw myself on the bed fully dressed. No doubt it was absurd, but I kept ready for some unknown emergency; gripping in my right hand the revolver I had brought along, and holding the pocket flashlight in my left. Not a sound came from below, and I could imagine how my host was sitting there with cadaverous stiffness in the dark.

Somewhere I heard a clock ticking, and was vaguely grateful for the normality of the sound. It reminded me, though, of another thing about the region which disturbed me—the total absence of animal life. There were certainly no farm beasts about, and now I realised that even the accustomed night-noises of wild living things were absent. Except for the sinister trickle of distant unseen waters, that stillness was anomalous—interplanetary—and I wondered what star-spawned, intangible blight could be hanging over the region. I recalled from old legends that dogs and other beasts had always hated the Outer Ones, and thought of what those tracks in the road might mean.

VIII

Do not ask me how long my unexpected lapse into slumber lasted, or how much of what ensued was sheer dream. If I tell you that I awakened at a certain time, and heard and saw certain things, you will merely answer that I did not wake then; and that everything was a dream until the moment when I rushed out of the house, stumbled to the shed where I had seen the old Ford, and seized that ancient vehicle for a mad, aimless race over the haunted hills which at last landed me—after hours of jolting and winding through forest-threatened labyrinths—in a village which turned out to be Townshend.

You will also, of course, discount everything else in my report; and declare that all the pictures, record-sounds, cylinder-and-machine sounds, and kindred evidences were bits of pure deception practiced on me by the missing Henry Akeley. You will even hint that he conspired with other eccentrics to carry out a silly and elaborate hoax—that he had the express shipment removed at Keene, and that he had Noyes make that terrifying wax record. It is odd, though, that Noyes has not even yet been identified; that he was unknown at any of the villages near Akeley's place, though he must have been frequently in the region. I wish I had stopped to memorise the licence-number of his car—or, perhaps it is better after all that I did not. For I, despite all you can say, and despite all I sometimes try to say to myself, know that loathsome outside influences must be lurking there in the half-unknown hills—and that those influences have spies and emissaries in the world of men. To keep as far as possible from such influences and such emissaries is all that I ask of life in the future.

When my frantic story sent a sheriff's posse out to the farmhouse, Akeley was gone without leaving a trace. His loose dressing-gown, yellow scarf, and foot-bandages lay on the study floor near his corner easy-chair, and it could not be decided whether any of his other apparel had vanished with him. The dogs and livestock were indeed missing, and there were some curious bullet-holes both on the house's exterior and on some of the walls within; but beyond this nothing unusual could be detected. No cylinders or machines, none of the evidences I had brought in my valise, no queer odour or vibration-sense, no footprints in the road, and none of the problematical things I glimpsed at the very last.

I stayed a week in Brattleboro after my escape, making inquiries among people of every kind who had known Akeley; and the results convince me that the matter is no figment of dream or delusion. Akeley's queer purchases of dogs and ammunition and chemicals, and the cutting of his telephone wires, are matters of record; while all who knew him—including his son in California—concede that his occasional remarks on strange studies had a certain consistency. Solid citizens believe he was mad, and unhesitatingly pronounce all reported evidences mere hoaxes devised with insane cunning and perhaps abetted by eccentric associates; but the lowlier country folk sustain his statements in every detail. He had shewed some of these rustics his photographs and black stone, and had played the hideous record for them; and they all said the footprints and buzzing voice were like those described in ancestral legends.

They said, too, that suspicious sights and sounds had been noticed increasingly around Akeley's house after he found the black stone, and that the place was now avoided by everybody except the mail man and other casual, tough-minded people. Dark Mountain and Round Hill were both notoriously haunted spots, and I could find no one who had ever closely explored either. Occasional disappearances of natives throughout the district's history were well attested, and these now included the semi-vagabond Walter Brown, whom Akeley's letters had mentioned. I even came upon one farmer who thought he had personally glimpsed one of the queer bodies at flood-time in the swollen West River, but his tale was too confused to be really valuable.

When I left Brattleboro I resolved never to go back to Vermont, and I feel quite certain I shall keep my resolution. Those wild hills are surely the outpost of a frightful cosmic race—as I doubt all the less since reading that a new ninth planet has been glimpsed beyond Neptune, just as those influences had said it would be glimpsed. Astronomers, with a hideous appropriateness they little suspect, have named this thing "Pluto." I feel, beyond question, that it is nothing less than nighted Yuggoth—and I shiver when I try to figure out the real reason *why* its monstrous denizens wish it to be known in this way at this especial time. I vainly try to assure myself that these daemonic creatures are not gradually leading up to some new policy hurtful to the earth and its normal inhabitants.

But I have still to tell of the ending of that terrible night in the farmhouse. As I have said, I did finally drop into a troubled doze; a doze filled with bits of dream which involved monstrous landscape-glimpses. Just what awakened me I cannot yet say, but that I did indeed awake at this given point I feel very certain. My first confused impression was of stealthily creaking floor-boards in the hall outside my door, and of a clumsy, muffled fumbling at the latch. This, however, ceased almost at once; so that my really clear impressions begin with the voices heard from the study below. There seemed to be several speakers, and I judged that they were conversationally engaged.

By the time I had listened a few seconds I was broad awake, for the nature of the voices was such as to make all thought of sleep ridiculous. The tones were curiously varied, and no one who had listened to that accursed phonograph record could harbour any doubts about the nature of at least two of them. Hideous though the idea was, I knew that I was under the same roof with nameless things from abysmal space; for those two voices were unmistakably the blasphemous buzzings which the Outside Beings used in their communication with men. The two were individually different— different in pitch, accent, and tempo—but they were both of the same damnable general kind.

A third voice was indubitably that of a mechanical utterance-machine connected with one of the detached brains in the cylinders. There was as little doubt about that as about the buzzings; for the loud, metallic, lifeless voice of the previous evening, with its inflectionless, expressionless scraping and rattling, and its impersonal precision and deliberation, had been utterly unforgettable. For a time I did not pause to question whether the intelligence behind the scraping was the identical one which had formerly talked to me; but shortly afterward I reflected that *any* brain would emit vocal sounds of the same quality if linked to the same mechanical speech-producer; the only possible differences being in language, rhythm, speed, and pronunciation. To complete the eldritch colloquy there were two actually human voices—one the crude speech of an unknown and evidently rustic man, and the other the suave Bostonian tones of my erstwhile guide Noyes.

As I tried to catch the words which the stoutly fashioned floor so bafflingly intercepted, I was also conscious of a great deal of stirring and scratching and shuffling in the room below; so that I could not escape the impression that it was full of living beings—many more than the few whose speech I could single out. The exact nature of this stirring is extremely hard to describe, for very few good bases of comparison exist. Objects seemed now and then to move across the room like conscious entities; the sound of their footfalls having something about it like a loose, hard-surfaced clattering—as of the contact of ill-coördinated surfaces of horn or hard rubber. It was, to use a more concrete but less accurate comparison, as if people with loose, splintery wooden shoes were shambling and rattling about on the polished board floor. On the nature and appearance of those responsible for the sounds, I did not care to speculate.

Before long I saw that it would be impossible to distinguish any connected discourse. Isolated words—including the names of Akeley and myself—now and then floated up, especially when uttered by the mechanical speech-producer; but their true significance was lost for want of continuous context. Today I refuse to form any definite deductions from them, and even their frightful effect on me was one of suggestion rather than of revelation. A terrible and abnormal conclave, I felt certain, was assembled below me; but for what shocking deliberations I could not tell. It was curious how this unquestioned sense of the malign and the blasphemous pervaded me despite Akeley's assurances of the Outsiders' friendliness.

With patient listening I began to distinguish clearly between voices, even though I could not grasp much of what any of the voices said. I seemed to catch certain typical emotions behind some of the speakers. One of the buzzing voices, for example, held an unmistakable note of authority; whilst the mechanical voice, notwithstanding its artificial loudness and regularity, seemed to be in a position of subordination and pleading. Noyes's tones exuded a kind of conciliatory atmosphere. The others I could make no attempt to interpret. I did not hear the familiar whisper of Akeley, but well knew that such a sound could never penetrate the solid flooring of my room.

I will try to set down some of the few disjointed words and other sounds I caught, labelling the speakers of the words as best I know how. It was from the speech-machine that I first picked up a few recognisable phrases.

(THE SPEECH-MACHINE)

" ... brought it on myself ... sent back the letters and the record ... end on it ... taken in ... seeing and hearing ... damn you ... impersonal force, after all ... fresh, shiny cylinder ... great God ... "

(FIRST BUZZING VOICE)

" ... time we stopped ... small and human ... Akeley ... brain ... saying ... "

(SECOND BUZZING VOICE)

"Nyarlathotep ... Wilmarth ... records and letters ... cheap imposture ... "

(NOYES)

" ... (an unpronounceable word or name, possibly N'gah-Kthun) ... *harmless ... peace ... couple of weeks ... theatrical ... told you that before ... "*

(FIRST BUZZING VOICE)

" ... no reason ... original plan ... effects ... Noyes can watch . . . Round Hill ... fresh cylinder ... Noyes's car ... "

(NOYES)

" ... well ... all yours ... down here ... rest ... place ... "

(SEVERAL VOICES AT ONCE IN
INDISTINGUISHABLE SPEECH)
(MANY FOOTSTEPS, INCLUDING THE PECULIAR
LOOSE STIRRING OR CLATTERING)
(A CURIOUS SORT OF FLAPPING SOUND)
(THE SOUND OF AN AUTOMOBILE
STARTING AND RECEDING)

(SILENCE)

That is the substance of what my ears brought me as I lay rigid upon that strange upstairs bed in the haunted farmhouse among the daemoniac hills—lay there fully dressed, with a revolver clenched in my right hand and a pocket flashlight gripped in my left. I became, as I have said, broad awake; but a kind of obscure paralysis nevertheless kept me inert till long after the last echoes of the sounds had died away. I heard the wooden, deliberate ticking of the ancient Connecticut clock somewhere far below, and at last made out the irregular snoring of a sleeper. Akeley must have dozed off after the strange session, and I could well believe that he needed to do so.

Just what to think or what to do was more than I could decide. After all, what *had* I heard beyond things which previous information might have led me to expect? Had I not known that the nameless Outsiders were now freely admitted to the farmhouse? No doubt Akeley had been surprised by an unexpected visit from them. Yet something in that fragmentary discourse had chilled me immeasurably, raised the most grotesque and horrible doubts, and made me wish fervently that I might wake up and prove everything a dream. I think my subconscious mind must have caught something which my consciousness has not yet recognised. But what of Akeley? Was he not my friend, and would he not have protested if any harm were meant me? The peaceful snoring below seemed to cast ridicule on all my suddenly intensified fears.

Was it possible that Akeley had been imposed upon and used as a lure to draw me into the hills with the letters and pictures and phonograph record? Did those beings mean to engulf us both in a common destruction because we had come to know too much? Again I thought of the abruptness and unnaturalness of that change in the situation which must have occurred between Akeley's penultimate and final letters. Something, my instinct told me, was terribly wrong. All was not as it seemed. That acrid coffee which I refused—had there not been an attempt by some hidden, unknown entity to drug it? I must talk to Akeley at once, and restore his sense of proportion. They had hypnotised him with their promises of cosmic revelations, but now he must listen to reason. We must get out of this before it would be too late. If he lacked the will power to make the break for liberty, I would supply it. Or if I could not persuade him to go, I could at least go myself. Surely he would let me take his Ford and leave it in a garage at Brattleboro. I had noticed it in the shed—the door being left unlocked and open now that peril was deemed past—and I believed there was a good chance of its being ready for instant use. That momentary dislike of Akeley which I had felt during and after the evening's conversation was all gone now. He was in a position much like my own, and we must stick together. Knowing his indisposed condition, I hated to wake him at this juncture, but I knew that I must. I could not stay in this place till morning as matters stood.

At last I felt able to act, and stretched myself vigorously to regain command of my muscles. Arising with a caution more impulsive than deliberate, I found and donned my hat, took my valise, and started downstairs with the flashlight's aid. In my nervousness I kept the revolver clutched in my right hand, being able to take care of both valise and flashlight with my left. Why I exerted these precautions I do not really know, since I was even then on my way to awaken the only other occupant of the house.

As I half tiptoed down the creaking stairs to the lower hall I could hear the sleeper more plainly, and noticed that he must be in the room on my left—the living-room I had not entered. On my right was the gaping blackness of the study in which I had heard the voices. Pushing open the unlatched door of the living-room I traced a path with the flashlight toward the source of the snoring, and finally turned the beams onto the sleeper's face. But in the next second, I hastily turned them away and commenced a cat-like retreat to the hall, my caution this time springing from reason as well as from instinct. For the sleeper on the couch was not Akeley at all, but my quondam guide Noyes.

Just what the real situation was, I could not guess, but common sense told me that the safest thing was to find out as much as possible before arousing anybody. Regaining the hall, I silently closed and latched the living-room door after me; thereby lessening the chances of awaking Noyes. I now cautiously entered the dark study, where I expected to find Akeley, whether asleep or awake, in the great corner chair which was evidently his favourite resting-place. As I advanced, the beams of my flashlight caught the great centre-table, revealing one of the hellish cylinders with sight and hearing machines attached, and with a speech-machine standing close by, ready to be connected at any moment. This, I reflected, must the the encased brain I had heard talking during the frightful conference; and for a second I had a perverse impulse to attach the speech-machine and see what it would say.

It must, I thought, be conscious of my presence even now; since the sight and hearing attachments could not fail to disclose the rays of my flashlight and the faint creaking of the floor beneath my feet. But in the end I did not dare meddle with the thing. I idly saw that it was the fresh, shiny cylinder with Akeley's name on it, which I had noticed on the shelf earlier in the evening and which my host had told me not to bother. Looking back at that moment, I can only regret my timidity and wish that I had boldly caused the apparatus to speak. God knows what mysteries and horrible doubts and questions of identity it might have cleared up! But then, it may be merciful that I let it alone.

From the table I turned my flashlight to the corner where I thought Akeley was, but found to my perplexity that the great easy-chair was empty of any human occupant asleep or awake. From the seat to the floor there trailed voluminously the familiar old dressing-gown, and near it on the floor lay the yellow scarf and the huge foot-bandages I had thought so odd. As I hesitated, striving to conjecture where Akeley might be, and why he had so suddenly discarded his necessary sick-room garments, I observed that the queer odour and sense of vibration were no longer in the room. What had been their cause? Curiously it occurred to me that I had noticed them only in Akeley's vicinity. They had been strongest where he sat, and wholly absent except in the room with him or just outside the doors of that room. I paused, letting the flashlight wander about the dark study and racking my brain for explanations of the turn affairs had taken.

Would to heaven I had quietly left the place before allowing that light to rest again on the vacant chair. As it turned out, I did not leave quietly; but with a muffled shriek which must have disturbed, though it did not quite awake, the sleeping sentinel across the hall. That shriek, and Noyes' still-unbroken snore, are the last sounds I ever heard in that morbidity-choked farmhouse beneath the black-wooded crest of a haunted mountain—that focus of trans-cosmic horror amidst the lonely green hills and curse-muttering brooks of a spectral rustic land.

It is a wonder that I did not drop flashlight, valise, and revolver in my wild scramble, but somehow I failed to lose any of these. I actually managed to get out of that room and that house without making any further noise, to drag myself and my belongings safely into the old Ford in the shed, and to set that archaic vehicle in motion toward some unknown point of safety in the black, moonless night. The ride that followed was a piece of delirium out of Poe or Rimbaud or the drawings of Doré, but finally I reached Townshend. That is all. If my sanity is still unshaken, I am lucky. Sometimes I fear what the years will bring, especially since that new planet Pluto has been so curiously discovered.

As I have implied, I let my flashlight return to the vacant easy-chair after its circuit of the room; then noticing for the first time the presence of certain objects in the seat, made inconspicuous by the adjacent loose folds of the empty dressing-gown. These are the objects, three in number, which the investigators did not find when they came later on. As I said at the outset, there was nothing of actual visual horror about them. The trouble was in what they led one to infer. Even now I have my moments of half-doubt—moments in which I half accept the scepticism of those who attribute my whole experience to dream and nerves and delusion.

The three things were damnably clever constructions of their kind, and were furnished with ingenious metal clamps to attach them to organic developments of which I dare not form any conjecture. I hope—devoutly hope—that they were the waxen products of a master artist, despite what my inmost fears tell me. Great God! That whisperer in darkness with its morbid odour and vibrations! Sorcerer, emissary, changeling, outsider . . . that hideous repressed buzzing ... and all the time in that fresh, shiny cylinder on the shelf ... poor devil ... "prodigious surgical, biological, chemical, and mechanical skill" ...

For the things in the chair, perfect to the last, subtle detail of microscopic resemblance—or identity—were the face and hands of Henry Wentworth Akeley.

Richard Lupoff's sequel to "The Whisperer in Darkness" makes full and ingenious use of the fact that many things deemed outrageous in Lovecraft's day are widely accepted (if no less outrageous) in our own. The idea of contact with beings from other worlds is one such. Lovecraft once wrote, in an essay on "Interplanetary Fiction," that the sheer, dumbfounding fact of standing on or contacting an alien world should by itself carry high enough voltage for the story to require no other shock.

In "The Whisperer in Darkness" any actual contact between humans and aliens, though clearly implied early on, is always presented to the reader second or third hand (a transcript of a memory of hearing a recording, seeing tracks in the road, seeming to speak with an old friend who only later turns out to be impersonated by a space alien). But Lupoff knew that today there are great numbers of people who believe they are channeling the voices of disembodied space intelligences every day. He knew that in a sequel he'd have to take this much for granted. So instead he went on to place the surprise elsewhere. And what he does is to bring Akeley's canned intelligence back into a brave new world, perhaps one as strange in its way as black-towered Yuggoth.

One thing you will notice is how Lupoff's sequel is built on a neglected possibility for interpreting Lovecraft's original tale. We usually suppose that Akeley has been forcibly supplanted before Wilmarth's arrival, that the last letters and the shadowed interview were part of a trap. We blame narrator Wilmarth for being so gullible (or rather author Lovecraft for making him so); but suppose Akeley had indeed been convinced and converted by the aliens and went with them of his own free will. A play would still have been staged for Wilmarth's benefit since the truth would simply have been too much for him to face unveiled in the circumstances. Lupoff has engaged this possibility. And with interesting results ....

Documents in the Case of Elizabeth Akeley

by RICHARD A. LUPOFF

Surveillance of the Spiritual Light Brotherhood Church of San Diego was initiated as a result of certain events of the mid and late 1970s. Great controversy had arisen over the conduct of the followers of the Guru Maharaj-ji, the International Society for Krishna Consciousness (the "Hare Krishna's"), the Church of Scientology, and the Unification Church headed by the Reverend Sun Myung Moon.

These activities were cloaked in the Constitutional shield of "freedom of religion," and the cults for the most part resisted suggestions of investigation by grand juries or other official bodies.

Even so, the tragic events concerning the People's Temple of San Francisco aroused government concern which could not be stymied. While debate raged publicly over the question of opening cult records, federal and local law enforcement agencies covertly entered the field.

It was within this context that interest was aroused concerning the operation of the Spiritual Light Brotherhood, and concerning its leader, the Radiant Mother Elizabeth Akeley.

Outwardly there was nothing secret in the operation of Mother Akeley's church. The group operated from a building located at the corner of Second Street and Ash in a neighborhood described as "genteel shabby," midway between the commercial center of San Diego and the city's tourist-oriented waterfront area.

The building occupied by the church had been erected originally by a more conventional denomination, but the vicissitudes of shifting population caused the building to be deconsecrated and sold to the Spiritual Light Brotherhood. The new owners, led by their order's founder and then-leader, the Radiant Father George Goodenough Akeley, clearly marked the building with its new identity.

The headline was changed on the church's bulletin board, and the symbol of the Spiritual Light Brotherhood, a shining tetrahedron of neon tubing, was erected atop the steeple. A worship service was held each Sunday morning, and a spiritual message service was conducted each Wednesday evening.

In later years, following the death of the Radiant Father in 1971 and the accession to leadership of the church by Elizabeth Akeley, church archives were maintained in the form of tape recordings. The Sunday services were apparently a bland amalgam of nondenominational Judeo-Christian teachings, half-baked and quarter-understood Oriental mysticism, and citations from the works of Einstein, Heisenberg, Shklovskii, and Fermi.

Surviving cassettes of the Wednesday message service are similarly innocuous. Congregants were invited to submit questions or requests for messages from deceased relatives. The Radiant Mother accepted a limited number of such requests at each service. The congregants would arrange themselves in a circle and link their fingers in the classic manner of participants in seances. Mother Akeley would enter a trance and proceed to answer the questions or deliver messages from the deceased, "as the spirits moved her."

Audioanalysis of the tapes of these seances indicates that, while the intonation and accent of the voices varied greatly, from the whines and lisps of small children to the quaverings of the superannuated, and from the softened and westernized pronunciations of native San Diegans to the harsh and barbaric tones of their New Yorker parents, the vocal apparatus was at all times that of Elizabeth Akeley. The variations were no greater than those attainable by an actress of professional training or natural brilliance.

Such, however, was not the case with a startling portion of the cassette for the session of Wednesday, June 13th, 1979. The Radiant Mother asked her congregants if anyone had a question for the spirits or if any person present wished to attempt contact with some deceased individual.

A number of questions were answered, dealing with the usual matters of marriage and divorce, reassurances of improved health, and counseling as to investments and careers.

An elderly congregant who was present stated that her husband had died the previous week, and she sought affirmation of his happiness "on the other side."

The Radiant Mother moaned. Then she muttered incoherently. All of this was as usual at the beginning of her trances. Shortly the medium's vocal quality altered. Her normally soft, rather pleasant and distinctly feminine voice dropped in register until it suggested that of a man. Simultaneously, her contemporary Californian diction turned into the twang of a rural New Englander.

While the sound quality of this tape is excellent, the medium's diction was unfortunately not so. The resulting record is necessarily fragmentary. As nearly as it has been transcribed, this is it:

"Wilmarth ... Wilmarth ... back. Have come ... Antares ... Neptune, Pluto, Yuggoth. Yes, Wilmarth. Yug—

"Are you ... If I cannot receive ... Windham County ... yes, Townshend ... round hill. Wilmarth still alive? Then who ... son, son ...

" ... ever receives ... communicate enough Akeley, 176 Pleasant ... go, California. Son, see if you can find my old friend Albert Wilmarth ... chusetts ...

"With wings. Twisted ropes for heads and blood like plant sap . ... Flying, flying, and all the while a gramophone recordi ... use apologize to Wilmarth if he's still alive, but I also have the most wonderful news, the most wonderful tales to tell him ...

" ... and its smaller satellites, well, I don't suppose anyone will believe me, of course, but not only is Yuggoth there, revolving regularly except in an orbit at right angles to the plane of the ecliptic, no wonder no one believed in it, but what I must describe to you, Albert, the planet glows with a heat and a demoniacal ruby glare that illuminates its own ... thon and Zaman, Thog and Thok, I could hardly believe my own ...

" ... goid beings who cannot ... corporeally ... Neptune ... central caverns of a dark star beyond the rim of the galaxy its ...

" ... wouldn't call her beautiful, of course ... dinary terms ... than an arachnid and a cetacean, and yet, could a spider and dolphin by some miracle establish mental communion, who knows what ... not really a name as you normally think of names, but ... Sh'ch'rrrua'a ... of Aldebaran, the eleventh, has a constellation of inhabited moons, which ... independently, or perhaps at some earlier time, traveling by means simi ...

" . . . ummate in metal canisters, will be necessary to . . . aid in obtaining . . . fair exchange, for the donors will receive a far greater boon in the form . . . ."

At this point the vocal coherence, such as it is, breaks down. The male voice with its New England twang cracks and rises in tone even as the words are replaced by undecipherable mumbles. Mother Akeley recovers from her trance state, and the seance draws quickly to a close. From the internal evidence of the contents of the tape, the Radiant Mother had no awareness of the message, or narration, delivered by the male voice speaking through her. This also is regarded, among psychic and spiritualistic circles, as quite the usual state of affairs with trance mediums.

Authorities next became aware of unusual activities through a copy of the *Vermont Unidentified Flying Object Intelligencer*, or *Vufoi*. Using a variety of the customary cover means and addresses for the purpose, such federal agencies as the FBI, NSA, Department of Defense, NASA, and National Atmospheric and Oceanographic Agency subscribe regularly to the publications of organizations like the Vermont UFO Intelligence Bureau and other self-appointed investigatory bodies.

The President of the Vermont UFO Intelligence Bureau and editor if its *Intelligencer* was identified as one Ezra Noyes. Noyes was known to reside with his parents (Ezra was nineteen years of age at the time) in the community of Dark Mountain, Windham County. Noyes customarily prepared *Vufoi* issues himself, assembling material both from outside sources and from members of the Vermont UFO Intelligence Bureau, most of whom were former high school friends now employed by local merchants or farmers, or attending Windham County Community College in Townshend.

Noyes would assemble his copy, type it onto mimeograph stencils using a portable machine set up on the kitchen table, and run off copies on a superannuated mimeograph kept beside the washer and dryer in the basement. The last two items prepared for each issue were "Vufoi Voice" and "From the Editor's Observatory," commenting in one case flippantly and in the other seriously, on the contents of the issue. "Vufoi Voice" was customarily illustrated with a crude cartoon of a man wearing an astronaut's headgear, and was signed "Cap'n Oof-oh." "From the Editor's Observatory" was illustrated with a drawing of an astronomical telescope with a tiny figure seated at the eyepiece, and was signed "Intelligencer."

It is believed that both "Cap'n Oof-oh" and "Intelligencer" were Ezra Noyes.

The issue of the *Vermont Unidentified Flying Object Intelligencer* for June, 1979, actually appeared early in August of that year. Excerpts from the two noted columns follow:

From the Editor's Observatory

Of greatest interest since our last issue—and we apologize for missing the March, April and May editions due to unavoidable circumstances—has been the large number of organic sightings here in the southern Vermont region. We cannot help draw similes to the infamous Colorado cattle mutilizations of the past year or few years, and the ill-conceived Air Farce coverup efforts *which only draw extra attention to the facts that they can't hide from us who know the Truth!"*

Local historians like Mr. Littleton at the High School remember other incidents and the Brattleboro *Reformer* and Arkham *Advertiser* and other Newspapers whose back files constitute an Official Public Record could tell the story of other incidents like this one! It is hard to reconciliate the Windham County sightings and the Colorado Cattle Mutilization Case with others such as the well-known Moth Man sightings in the Southland and especially the batwing creature sightings of as long as a half of a century ago but with a sufficient ingeniusity as is definitely not a task beyond undertaking and the U.S. Air Farce and other cover-up agencies are hear-bye placed on Official notice that such is our intention and we will not give up until success is ours and the Cover-up is blown an Sky-High as the UFO sightings themselves!

Yours until our July issue,

Intelligencer.

Vufoi Voice

Bat-wing and Moth Man indeed! Didn't I read something like that in *Detective Comics* back when Steve Englehart was writing for DC? Or was it in *Mad?* Come to think of it, when it's hard to tell the parody from the original, things are gettin' *mighty* strange.

And there gettin' mighty strange around here!

We wonder what the ole Intelligencer's been smoking in that smelly meerschaum he affects around Intelligence Bureau meetings. Could it be something illegal that he grows for himself up on the mountainside? Or is he just playing Sherlock Holmes?

We ain't impressed.

Impressionable, yep! My mom always said I was impressionable as a boy, back on the old asteroid farm in Beta Reticuli, but this is too silly for words.

Besides, she tuck me to the eye dock and he fitted us out with a pair of gen-yew-ine X-ray specs, and that not only cured us of Reticule-eye but now we can see right through such silliness as bat-winged moth men carrying silvery canisters around the skies and hillsides with 'em.

Shades of a Japanese Sci-Fi Flick! This musta been the stuntman out for lunch!

And that's where we think the old Intelligencer is this month: *Out 2 Lunch!*

Speaking of which, I haven't had mine yet this afternoon, and if I don't hurry up and have it pretty soon it'll be time for dinner and then I'll have to eat my lunch for a bedtime snack and that'll confuse the dickens out of my poor stomach! So I'm off to hit the old frigidaire (not too hard, I don't want to spoil the shiny finish on my new spaceman's gloves!), and I'll see you-all nextish!

Whoops, here's our saucer now! Bye-bye,

Cap'n Oof-oh.

Following the extraordinary spiritual message service of June 13, Mother Akeley was driven to her home at 176 Pleasant Street in National City, a residential suburb of San Diego, by her boy friend, Marc Feinman. Investigation revealed that she had met Feinman casually while sunning herself and watching the surfers ride the waves in at Black's Beach, San Diego.

Shortly thereafter, Elizabeth had been invited by a friend of approximately her own age to attend a concert given by a musical group, a member of which was a friend of Akeley's friend. Outside of her official duties as Radiant Mother of the Spiritual Light Brotherhood, Elizabeth Akeley was known to live quite a normal life for a young woman of her social and economic class.

She accompanied her friend to the concert, visited the backstage area with her, and was introduced to the musician. He in turn introduced Elizabeth to other members of the musical group, one of whom Elizabeth recognized as her casual acquaintance of Black's Beach. A further relationship developed, in which it was known that Akeley and Feinman frequently exchanged overnight visits. Elizabeth had retained the house on Pleasant Street originally constructed by her grandfather, George Goodenough Akeley, when he had emigrated to San Diego from Vermont in the early 1920s. Marc had been born and raised in the Bronx, New York, had emigrated to the West Coast following his college years and presently resided in a pleasant apartment on Upas Street near Balboa Park. From here he commuted daily to his job as a computer systems programmer in downtown San Diego, his work as a musician being more of an avocation than a profession.

On Sunday, June 17, for the morning worship service of the Spiritual Light Brotherhood, Radiant Mother Akeley devoted her sermon to the previous Wednesday's seance, an unusual practice for her. The sexton of the church, a nondescript looking Negro named Vernon Whiteside, attended the service. Noting the Radiant Mother's departure from her usual bland themes, Whiteside communicated with the federal agency which had infiltrated him into the Church for precisely this purpose. An investigation of Mother Akeley's background was then initiated.

Within a short time, agent Whiteside was in posession of a preliminary report on Elizabeth Akeley and her forebears, excerpts from which follow:

AKELEY, ELIZABETH—
HISTORY AND BACKGROUND

The Akeley family is traceable to one *Beelzebub Akeley* who traveled from Portsmouth, England, to Kingsport, Massachusetts aboard the sailing caravel *Worthy* in 1637. Beelzebub Akeley married an indentured servant girl, bought out her indenture papers and moved with her to establish the Akeley dynasty in Townshend, Windham County, Vermont in 1681. The Akeleys persisted in Windham County for more than two centuries, producing numerous clergy, academics, and other genteel professions in this period.

Abednego Mesach Akeley, subject's great-great grandfather, was the last of the Vermont Akeleys to pursue a life of the cloth. Born in 1832, Abednego was raised in the strictly puritanical traditions of the Akeleys and ordained by his father, the Reverend Samuel Shadrach Solomon Akeley upon attaining his maturity. Abednego served as assistant pastor to his father until Samuel's death in 1868, at which time he succeeded to the pulpit.

Directly following the funeral of Samuel Akeley, Abednego is known to have traveled to more southerly regions of New England, including Massachusetts and possibly Rhode Island. Upon his return to Townshend he led his flock into realms of highly questionable doctrine and actually transferred the affiliation of his church from its traditional Protestant parent-body to that of the new and suspect Starry Wisdom sect.

Controversy and scandal followed at once, and upon the death of Abednego early in 1871 at the age of 39, the remnants of his congregation moved as a body to Providence, Rhode Island. One female congregant, however, was excommunicated by unanimous vote of the other members of the congregation, and forced to remain behind in Townshend. This female was *Sarah Elizabeth Phillips*, a servant girl in the now defunct Akeley household.

Shortly following the departure of the remains of Abednego Akeley's flock from Vermont, Sarah Phillips gave birth to a son. She claimed that the child had been fathered by Abednego mere hours before his death. She named the child *Henry Wentworth Akeley*. As the Akeley clan was extinct at this point, no one challenged Sarah's right to identify her son as an Akeley, and in fact in later years she sometimes used the name Akeley herself.

Henry Akeley overcame his somewhat shadowed origins and built for himself a successful academic career, returning to Windham County in his retirement, and remaining there until the time of his mysterious disappearance and presumed demise in the year 1928.

Henry had married some years earlier, and his wife had given birth to a single child, *George Goodenough Akeley*, in the year 1901, succumbing two days later to childbed fever. Henry Akeley raised his son with the assistance of a series of nursemaids and housekeepers. At the time of Henry Akeley's retirement and his return to Townshend, George Akeley emigrated to San Diego, California, building there a modest but comfortable house at 176 Pleasant Street.

George Akeley married a local woman suspected of harboring a strain of Indian blood; the George Akeleys were the parents of a set of quadruplets born in 1930. These were the first quadruplets on record in San Diego County. There were three boys and a girl. The boys seemed, at birth, to be of relatively robust constitution, although naturally small. The girl was still smaller, and seemed extremely feeble at birth so that her survival appeared unlikely.

However, with each passing hour the boys seemed to fade while the tiny girl grew stronger. All four infants clung tenaciously to life, the boys more and more weakly and the girl more strongly, until finally the three male infants—apparently at the same hour—succumbed. The girl took nourishment with enthusiasm, grew pink and active. Her spindly limbs rounded into healthy baby arms and legs, and in due course she was carried from the hospital by her father.

In honor of a leading evangelist of the era, and of a crusader for spiritualistic causes, the girl was named *Aimee Doyle Akeley*.

Aimee traveled between San Diego and the spiritualist center of Noblesville, Indiana, with her parents. The George Akeleys spent their winters in San Diego, where George Goodenough Akeley served as Radiant Father of the Spiritual Light Brotherhood, which he had founded in a burst of religious fervor after meeting Aimee Semple McPherson, the evangelist whose name his daughter bore; each summer they would make a spiritualistic pilgrimage to Noblesville, where George Akeley became fast friends with the spiritualist leader and sometime American fascist, *William Dudley Pelley*.

Aimee Doyle Akeley married William Pelley's nephew *Hiram Wesley Pelley* in 1959. In that same year Aimee's mother died and was buried in Noblesville. Her father continued his ministry in San Diego.

In 1961, two years after her marriage to young Pelley, Aimee Doyle Akeley Pelley gave birth to a daughter who was named *Elizabeth Maude Pelley*, after two right-wing political leaders, Elizabeth Dilling of Illinois and Maude Howe of England. Elizabeth Maude Pelley was raised alternately by her parents in Indiana and her grandfather in San Diego.

In San Diego her life was relatively normal, centering on her schooling, her home, and to a lesser extent on her grandfather's church, the Spiritual Light Brotherhood. In Indiana she was exposed to a good deal of political activity of the right-wing extremist nature. Hiram Wesley Pelley had followed in his uncle's footsteps in this regard, and Aimee Doyle Akeley Pelley took her lead from her husband and his family. A number of violent scenes are reported to have transpired between young Elizabeth Pelley and the elder Pelleys.

Elizabeth Pelley returned permanently to San Diego where she took up residence with her grandfather. At this time she abandoned her mother's married name and took up the family name as her own, henceforth being known as *Elizabeth Akeley*. Upon the death of George Goodenough Akeley, Elizabeth succeeded to the title of Radiant Mother of the Spiritual Light Brotherhood and the pastorhood of the church, as well as the property on Pleasant Street and a small income from inherited securities.

Vernon Whiteside read the report carefully. Through his position as sexton of the Spiritual Light Brotherhood Church he had access, as well, to most church records, including the taped archives of Sunday worship services and Wednesday message services. He followed the Radiant Mother's report to the congregation, in which she referred heavily to the seance of June 13, by borrowing and listening carefully to the tape of the seance itself.

He also obtained a photocopy from agency headquarters of the latest issues of the *Vermont UFO Intelligencer*. These he read carefully, seeking to correlate any references in the newsletter with the Akeley family, or with any other name connected with the Akeleys or the content of the seance tape. He mulled over the Akeleys, Phillipses, Wilmarths, Noyes, and all other references. He attempted also to connect the defunct or at least seemingly defunct Starry Wisdom sect of the New England region, with the San-Diego based Spiritual Light Brotherhood.

At this time it appears also that Elizabeth Akeley began to receive additional messages outside of the Spiritual Light message services. During quiet moments she would lapse involuntarily into her trance or trancelike state. Because she was unable to recall the messages received during these episodes, she prevailed upon Marc Feinman to spend increasing amounts of time with her. During the last week of June and July of 1979 the two were nearly inseparable. They spent every night together, sometimes at Elizabeth's house in National City, sometimes at Marc's apartment on Upas Street.

It was at this time that Vernon Whiteside recommended that agency surveillance of the San Diego cult be increased by the installation of wiretaps on the church and the Pleasant Street and Upas Street residences. This recommendation was approved and recordings were obtained at all three locations. Transcripts are available in agency files. Excerpts follow:

July 25, 1979 (Incoming)

Voice #1 (Definitely identified as Marc Feinman): Hello.

Voice #2 (Tentatively identified as Mrs. Sara Feinman, Marc's mother, Bronx, New York): Marc.

Voice #1: (Pauses.) Yes, Ma.

Voice #2: Markie, are you all right?

Voice #1: Yeah, Ma.

Voice #2: Are you sure. Are you really all right?

Voice #1: Ma, I'm all right.

Voice #2: Okay, just so you're all right, Markie. And work, Markie? How's your work? Is your work all right?

Voice #1: It's all right, Ma.

Voice #2: No problems?

Voice #1: Of course problems, Ma. That's what they pay me to take care of.

Voice #2: Oh my God, Markie! What kind of problems, Markie?

Voice #1: (Pauses, sighs or inhales deeply) We're trying to integrate the 2390 remote console control routines with the sysgen status word register and every time we run it against—

Voice #2: (Interrupting) Markie, you know I don't understand that kind of—

Voice #1: (Interrupting) But you asked me—

Voice #2: (Interrupting) Marc, don't contradict your mother. Are you still with that *shicksa*? She's the one who's poisoning your mind against your poor mother. I'll bet she's with you now, isn't she, Marc?

Voice #1: (Sighs or inhales deeply) No, Ma, it's Wednesday. She's never here Wednesdays. She's at church every Wednesday. They have these services every Wedn—

Voice #2: (Interrupting) I'm sure she's a lovely girl, my Markie would never pick a girl who wasn't a lovely girl. I wish you'd kept up your music, Markie. You could have been a great pianist, like Rubenstein or even Lazar Berman that red. You still have that crazy Boxer car, Markie?

Voice #1: Yes, Ma.

Voice #2: That isn't what I called about. I don't understand, Markie, for the money that car must have cost you could have had an Oldsmobile at least, even a Buick like your father. Markie, it's your father I phoned about. Markie, you have to come home. Your father isn't well, Markie. I phoned because he isn't home now but the doctor said he's not a well man. Markie, you have to come home and talk to your father. He respects you, he listens to you, God knows why. Please, Markie. (Sound of soft crying.)

Voice #1: What's wrong with him, Ma?

Voice #2: I don't want to say it on the telephone.

July 25, 1979 (Outgoing)

Voice #3 (Definitely identified as Vernon Whiteside): Spiritual Light Brotherhood. May the divine light shine upon your path.

Voice #1: Vern, this is Marc. Is Liz still at the church? Is the service over?

Voice #3: The service ended a few minutes ago, Mr. Feinman. The Radiant Mother is resting in the sacristy.

Voice #1: That's what I wanted to know. Listen, Vern, tell Lizzy that I'm on my way, will you? I had a long phone call from my mother and I don't want Liz to worry. Tell her I'll give her a ride home from the church.

Feinman left San Diego by automobile, driving his Ferrari Boxer eastward at a top speed in the 140 MPH range, and arrived at the home of his parents in the Bronx, New York, some time during the night of July 27-28.

In the absence of Marc Feinman, Akeley took agent Whiteside increasingly into her confidence, asking him to remain in her presence day and night. He set up a temporary cot in the living room of the Pleasant Street house during this period. His instructions were to keep a portable cassette recorder handy at all times and to record anything said by Mother Akeley during spontaneous trances.

On the first Saturday of August, following a lengthy speech in the now-familiar male New England twang, Akeley asked agent Whiteside for the tape. She played it back, then made the following long-distance telephone call.

August 4, 1979 (Outgoing)

Voice #4 (Tentatively identified as Ezra Noyes): Vermont Bureau. May we help you?

Voice #5 (Definitely identified as Elizabeth Akeley): Is this Mr. Noyes?

Voice #4: Oh, I'm sorry, Dad isn't home. This is Ezra. Can I give him a—

Voice #5: (Interrupting) Oh, I wanted to speak with Ezra Noyes. The editor of the *UFO Intelligencer.*

Voice #4: Oh, yes, right. Yes, that's me. Ezra Noyes.

Voice #5: Mr.Noyes, I wonder if you could help me. I need some information about, ah, recent occurrences in or around Townshend.

Voice #4: That's funny, what did you say your name was?

Voice #5: Elizabeth Akeley.

Voice #4: I thought I knew all my subbers.

Voice #5: Oh, I'm not a subscriber, I got your name from—well, that doesn't matter. Mr. Noyes, I wonder if you could tell me if there have been any unusual UFO sightings in your region lately.

Voice #4 (Suspiciously): Unusual?

Voice #5: Well, these wouldn't be your usual run-of-the-mill flying objects. Flying saucers. I hope that phrase doesn't offend you. These would be more like flying creatures.

Voice #4: Creatures? You mean birds?

Voice #5: No. No. Intelligent creatures.

Voice #4: People, then. You mean Buck Rogers and Wilma Deering with their rocket flying belts.

Voice #5: Please don't be sarcastic, Mr. Noyes. (Pauses.) I mean intelligent, possibly humanoid but nonhuman creatures. Their configuration may vary, but some of them, at least, I believe would have large, membranous wings, probably stretched over a bony or veinous framework in the fashion of bats' or insects' wings. Also, some of them may be carrying artifacts such as polished metallic cylinders of a size capable of containing a—of containing, uh, a human—a human—brain. (Sounds of distress, possible sobbing.)

Voice #4: Miss Akeley? Are you all right, Miss Akeley?

Voice #5: I'm sorry. Yes, I'm all right.

Voice #4: I didn't mean to be so hard on you, Miss Akeley. It's just that we get
a lot of crank calls. People wanting to talk to the little green men
and that kind of thing. I had to make sure that you weren't—

Voice #5: I understand. And you *have* had—

Voice #4: I'm reluctant to say too much on the phone. Miss Akeley, do you
think you could get here? There *have* been sightings. And there are
older ones. Records in the local papers. A rash of incidents about
fifty years ago. And others farther back. There was a monograph by
an Eli Davenport over in New Hampshire back in the 1830s. I've
got a xerox of it . . . .

Shortly after her telephone conversation with Ezra Noyes, Elizabeth
Akeley appealed to Vernon Whiteside for assistance. "I don't want to
go alone," she is reported as saying to Whiteside. "Will you help me,
Vernon?"

Whiteside, maintaining his cover as the sexton of the Brotherhood,
assured Akeley. "Anything the Radiant Mother wishes, ma'am. What
would you like me to do?"

"Can you get away for a few days? I have to go to Vermont. Would
you book two tickets for us? There are church funds to cover the cost."

"Yes, ma'am." Whiteside lowered his head. "Best way would be via
Logan International in Boston, then a Vermont Lines bus to Brattleboro and Newfane."

Akeley made no comment on the sexton's surprising familiarity
with the bus service between Boston and upper New England. She was
obviously in an agitated state, Whiteside reported when he checked
in with his superiors prior to their departure from San Diego.

Two days later the Negro sexton and the Radiant Mother climbed
down from the bus at Newfane, Vermont. They were met at the town's
run-down and musty-smelling station by Ezra Noyes. Noyes was
driving his parents' 1969 Nash Ambassador station wagon and will-
ingly loaded Akeley's and Whiteside's meager baggage into the rear
cargo deck of the vehicle.

Ezra chauffeured the visitors to his parents' home. The house, a
gambrel-roofed structure of older design, was fitted for a larger family
than the two elder Noyes and their son Ezra; in fact, an elder son and
daughter had both married and departed Windham County for locales
of greater stimulation and professional opportunity, leaving two sur-
plus bedrooms in the Noyes home.

Noyes was eager to offer his own services and assistance to Akeley
and Whiteside. Elizabeth informed Ezra Noyes that she had received
instructions to meet a visitor at a specific location near the town of
Passumpsic in neighboring Windsor County. She did not explain to

Noyes the method of her receiving these instructions, but Vernon Whiteside's later report indicated that he was aware of them, the instructions having been delivered to Miss Akeley in spontaneous trance sessions, the tapes of which he had also heard.

It must again be emphasized at this point that the voice heard on the spontaneous trance tapes was, in different senses, both that of Miss Akeley and of another personage. The pitch and accent, as has been stated, were those of an elderly male speaking in a semi-archaic New England twang while the vocal apparatus itself was unquestionably that of Elizabeth Akeley, née Elizabeth Maude Pelley.

Miss Akeley's instructions were quite specific in terms of geography, although it was found odd that they referred only to landmarks and highway or road facilities known to exist in the late 1920s. Young Noyes was able to provide alternate routes for such former roadways as had been closed when superseded by more modern construction.

Before retiring, Elizabeth Akeley placed a telephone call to the home of Marc Feinman's parents in the Bronx. In this call she urged Feinman to join her in Vermont. Feinman responded that his father, at the urging of himself and his mother, had consented to undergo major surgery. Marc promised to travel to Vermont and rendezvous with Akeley at the earliest feasible time, but indicated that he felt obliged to remain with his parents until the surgery was completed and his father's recovery assured.

The following morning Elizabeth Akeley set out for Passumpsic. She was accompanied by Vernon Whiteside and traveled in the Nash Ambassador station wagon driven by Ezra Noyes.

Her instructions had contained very specific and very emphatic requirements that she keep the rendezvous alone, although others might provide transportation and wait while the meeting took place. The party who had summoned Elizabeth Akeley to the rendezvous had not, to this time, been identified, although it was believed to be the owner of the male voice and New England twang who had spoken through Elizabeth herself in her trances.

Prior to departing Windham County for Windsor County, a discussion took place between Akeley and Whiteside. Whiteside appealed to Elizabeth Akeley to permit him to accompany her to the rendezvous.

That would be impossible, Akeley stated.

Whiteside pointed out Elizabeth's danger, in view of the unknown identity of the other party. When Akeley remained adamant, Whiteside gave in and agreed to remain with Ezra Noyes during the meeting. It must be pointed out that at this time the dialogue was not cast in the format of a highly trained and responsible agent of the federal establishment, and an ordinary citizen; rather, the facade which Whiteside rightly although with difficulty maintained was that of a sexton of the Spiritual Light Brotherhood acting under the authority of and in the service of the Radiant Mother of that Church.

Whiteside did, however, succeed in convincing Akeley to wear a wireless microphone disguised as an enamel ladybug ornament on the lapel of her jacket. Akeley, of course, was garbed in ordinary street clothing at the time, reserving the ecclesiastical vestments for use during official functions of the Church.

The microphone transmitted on a frequency which was picked up by a small microcassette recorder which Whiteside was to keep with him in or near the Nash station wagon; additionally, an earphone ran from the recorder so that Whiteside was enabled to monitor the taped information in real time.

The Nash Ambassador crossed the county line from Windham to Windsor on a two-lane county highway. This had been a dirt road in the 1920s, blacktopped with federal funds administered by the Works Progress Administration under Franklin Roosevelt, and superseded by a nearby four-lane asphalt highway during the Eisenhower presidency. The blacktop received minimal maintenance; and only pressure from local members of the Vermont legislature, this brought in turn at the insistence of local residents who used the highway for access to Passumpsic, South Londonderry, and Bellows Falls, prevented the state from declaring the highway closed and striking it from official roadmaps.

Reaching the town of Passumpsic, Akeley, who had never previously traveled farther east than Indianapolis, Indiana, told Ezra to proceed 800 yards, at which point the car was to be halted. Ezra complied. At the appointed spot, Akeley left the car and opened a gate in the wooden fence fronting the highway.

Noyes pulled the wagon from the highway through the gate and found himself on a narrow track that had once been a small dirt road, long since abandoned and overgrown.

This dirt road led away from the highway and into hilly farm country, years before abandoned by the poor farmers of the region, that lay between Passumpsic and Ludlow.

Finally, having rounded an ancient dome-topped protruberance that stood betwen the station wagon and any possible visual surveillance from the blacktop highway or even the overgrown dirt road, the Nash halted, unable to continue. The vegetation hereabouts was of a peculiar nature. While most of the region consisted of thin, played-out soil whose poor fertility was barely adequate to sustain a covering of tall grasses and undersized, gnarly-trunked trees, in the small area set off by the dome-topped hill the growth was thick, lush and luxuriant.

However, there was a peculiar quality to the vegetation, a characteristic which even the most learned botanist would have been hard pressed to identify, and yet which was undeniably present. It was as if the vegetation were *too* vibrantly alive, as if it sucked greedily at the earth for nourishment and by so doing robbed the countryside for a mile or more in every direction of sustenance.

Through an incongruously luxuriant copse of leafy trees a small building could be seen, clearly a shack of many years' age and equally clearly of long abandonment. The door hung angularly from a single rusted hinge, the windows were cracked or missing altogether, and spiders had filled the empty frames with their own geometric handiwork. The paint, if ever the building had known the touch of a painter's brush, had long since flaked away and been blown to oblivion by vagrant tempests, and the bare wood beneath had been cracked by scores of winters and bleached by as many summers' suns.

Elizabeth Akeley looked once at the ramshackle structure, nodded to herself and set out slowly to walk to it. Vernon Whiteside set himself at her elbow, and Ezra Noyes set a pace just a stride behind the others, but Akeley halted at once, turned and gestured silently but decisively to the others to remain behind. She then resumed her progress through the copse.

Whiteside watched Elizabeth Akeley proceeding slowly but with apparently complete self-possession through the wooded area. She halted just outside the shack, leaned forward and slightly to one side as if peering through a cobwebbed window frame, then proceeded again. She tugged at the door, managed to drag it open with a squeal of rusted metal and protesting wood, and disappeared inside the shack.

"Are you just going to let her go like that?" Ezra Noyes demanded of Whiteside. "How do you know who's in there? What if it's a Beta Reticulan? What if it's a Moth Man? What if there's a whole bunch of aliens in there? They might have a tunnel from the shack to their saucer. The whole thing might be a front. Shouldn't we go after her?"

Whiteside shook his head. "Mother Akeley issued clear instructions, Ezra. We are to wait here." He reached inside his jacket and unobtrusively flicked on the concealed microcassette recorder. When he pulled his hand from his pocket, he brought it with the earphone. He adjusted it carefully in his ear.

"Oh, I didn't know you were deaf," Noyes said.

"Just a little," Whiteside replied.

"Well, what are we going to do?" Ezra asked him.

"I shall wait for the Radiant Mother," Whiteside told him. "There is nothing to fear. Have faith in the Spiritual Light, little brother, and your footsteps will be illuminated."

"Oh." Ezra made a sour face and climbed onto the roof of the Ambassador. He seated himself there cross-legged to watch for any evidence of activity at the shack.

Vernon Whiteside also kept watch on the shack, but chiefly he was listening to the voices transmitted by the cordless microphone concealed on Elizabeth Akeley's lapel. Excerpts from the transcript later made of these transmissions follow:

Microcassette, August 8, 1979

Voice #5 (Elizabeth Akeley): Hello? Hello? Is there—

Voice #6 (Unidentified voice; oddly metallic intonation; accent similar to male New England twang present in San Diego trance tapes): Come in, come in, don't be afraid.

Voice #5: It's so dark in here.

Voice #6: I'm sorry. Move carefully. You are perfectly safe but there is some delicate apparatus set up.

(Sounds of movement, feet shuffling, breathing, a certain vague *buzzing* sound. Creak as of a person sitting in an old wooden rocking chair.)

Voice #5: I can hardly see. Where are you?

Voice #6: The cells are very sensitive. My friends are not here. You are not Albert Wilmarth.

Voice #5: No, I don't even—

Voice #6: (Interrupting) Oh, my God! Of course not. It's been so—what year is this?

Voice #5: Nineteen seventy-nine.

Voice #6: Poor Albert. Poor Albert. He could have come along. But of course he—what did you say your name was, young woman?

Voice #5: Akeley. Elizabeth Akeley.

(Silence. Buzzing sound. A certain unsettling sound as of wings rustling, but wings larger than those of any creature known to be native to Vermont.)

Voice #6: Do not taunt me, young woman!

Voice #5: Taunt you? Taunt you?

Voice #6: Do you know who I am? Does the name Henry Wentworth Akeley mean nothing to you?

(Pause . . . buzzing . . . rustling.)

Voice #5: Yes! Yes! Oh, oh, this is incredible! This is wonderful! It means— Yes, my grandfather spoke of you. If you're really—My grandfather was George Akeley. He—we—

Voice #6: (Interrupting) Then I am your great-grandfather, Miss Akeley. I regret that I cannot offer you my hand. George Akeley was my son. Tell me, is he still alive?

Voice #5: No, he—he died. He died in 1971, eight years ago. I was a little girl, but I remember him speaking of his father in Vermont. He said you disappeared mysteriously. But he always expected to hear from you again. He even founded a church. The Spiritual Light Brotherhood. He never lost faith. I have continued his work. Waiting for word from—beyond. That's why I came when I—when I started receiving messages.

Voice #6: Thank you. Thank you, Elizabeth. Perhaps I should not have stayed away so long, but the vistas, my child, the vistas! How old did you say you were?

Voice #5: Why—why—18. Almost 19.

(Buzzing.)

Voice #6: You have followed my directions, Elizabeth? You are alone? Yes? Good. The cells are very sensitive. I can see you, even in this darkness, even if you cannot see me. Elizabeth, I have been gone from earth for half a century, yet I am no older than the day I—departed—in the year 1928. The sights I have seen, the dimensions and the galaxies I have visited! Not alone, my child. Of course not alone. Those ones who took me—ah, child! Human flesh is too weak, too fragile to travel beyond the earth.

Voice #5: But there are spacesuits. Rockets. Capsules. Oh, I suppose that was after your time. But we've visited the moon. We've sent instruments to Venus and Mars and the moons of Jupiter.

Voice #6: And what you know is what Columbus might have learned of the New World, by paddling a rowboat around the port of Cadiz! Those ones who took me, those old ones! They can fly between the worlds on great ribbed wings! They can span the very ether of space as a dragonfly flits across the surface of a pond! They are the greatest scientists, the greatest naturalists, the greatest anthropologists, the greatest explorers in the universe! Those whom they select to accompany them, if they cannot survive the ultimate vacuum of space, the old ones discard their bodies and seal their brains in metal canisters and carry them from world to world, from star to burning, glittering star!

(Buzzing, loud sound of rustling.)

Voice #5: Then—you have been to other worlds? Other planets, other physical worlds. Not other planes of spiritual existence. Our congregants believe—

Voice #6: (Interrupting) Your congregants doubtlessly believed poppycock. Yes, I have been to other worlds. I have seen all the planets in the solar system, from little, sterile Mercury to giant, distant Yuggoth.

Voice #5: Distant Yu—Yuggoth?

Voice #6: Yes, yes. I suppose those fool astronomers have yet to find it, but it is the gem and the glory of the solar system, glowing with its own ruby-red glare. It revolves in its own orbit, turned ninety degrees from the plane of the ecliptic. No wonder they've never seen it. They don't know where to look. Yet it perturbs the paths of Neptune and

Pluto. That ought to be clue enough! Yuggoth is very nearly a sun.
It possesses its own corps of worldlets, Nithon, Zaman, the mini-
ature twins Thog and Thok! And there is life there! There is the
Ghooric Zone where bloated shoggoths splash and spawn!

Voice #5: I can't—I can't believe all this! My own great-grandpa! Planets and
beasts . . . .

Voice #6: Yuggoth was merely the beginning for me. Those ones carried me
far away from the sun. I have seen the worlds that circle Arcturus
and Centaurus, Wolf and Barnard's Star and Beta Reticuli. I have
seen creatures whose physical embodiment would send a sane man
into screaming nightmares of horror that never ends—and whose
minds and souls would put to shame the proudest achievements of
Einstein and Schopenhauer, Confucius and Plato, the Enlightened
One and the Anointed One! And I have known love, child, love such
as no earth-bound mortal has ever known.

Voice #5: Lo-love, great-grandfather?

(Sound of buzzing, loud and agitated rustling of wings.)

Voice #6: You know about love, surely, Elizabeth. Doesn't your church preach
a gospel of love? In 57 years on this planet I never came across a
church that didn't claim that. And have you known love? A girl
your age, surely you've known the feeling by now.

Voice #5: Yes, great-grandfather.

Voice #6: Is it merely a physical attraction, Elizabeth? Do you believe that
souls can love? Or do you believe in such things as souls? Can *minds*
love one another?

Voice #5: All three. All three of those.

Voice #6: Good. Yes, all three. And when two beings love with their minds
and their souls, they yearn also for bodies with which to express their
love. Hence the physical manifestation of love. (Pause.) Excuse me,
child. In a way I suppose I'm nothing but an old man rambling on
about abstractions. You have a young man, have you?

Voice #5: Yes.

Voice #6: I would like to meet him. I would like very much to meet him, my
child.

Voice #5: Great-grandfather. May I tell the people about you?

Voice #6: No, Elizabeth. The time is not ripe.

Voice #5: But this is the single most important event since—since—(Pause.)
Contact with other beings, with other races, not of Earth. Proof that
there is intelligent life throughout the universe. Proof of visits between the worlds and between the galaxies.

Voice #6: All in time, child. Now I am tired. Please go now. Will you visit me
again?

Voice #5: Of course. Of course.

Elizabeth Akeley emerged from the shack, took one step and staggered.

At the far side of the copse of trees, Vernon Whiteside and Ezra Noyes watched. They saw Elizabeth. Ezra scrambled from the roof of the station wagon. Whiteside started forward, prepared to assist Mother Akeley.

But she had merely been blinded, for the moment, by the bright sunlight of a Vermont August. Whiteside and Ezra Noyes saw her returning through the glade. Once or twice she stopped and leaned against a strangely spongy tree. Each time she started again, apparently further debilitated rather than restored.

She reached the station wagon and leaned against its drab metal-work. Whiteside said, "Are you all right, Radiant Mother?"

She managed a wan smile. "Thank you, Vernon. Yes, I'm all right. Thank you."

Ezra Noyes was beside himself.

"Who was in there? What was going on? Were there really aliens in that shack? Can I go? Oh, darn it, darn it!" He pounded one fist into the palm of his other hand. "I should never have left home without my camera! Kenneth Arnold himself said that back in '47. It's the prime directive of all ufologists, and I went off without one, me of all people."

Vernon Whiteside said, "Radiant Mother, do you wish to leave now? May I visit the shack first?"

"Please, Vernon, don't. I asked him—" She drew Whiteside away from Noyes. "I asked him if I could reveal this to the world and he said, not yet."

"I monitored the tape, Reverend Mother."

"Yes."

"What does it mean, Reverend Mother?"

She passed her hand across her face, tugging soft bangs across her eyes to block out the bright sunlight. "I feel faint. Vernon. Ask Ezra to drive us back to Dark Mountain, would you?"

He helped her climb into the station wagon and signaled to Ezra. "Mother Akeley is fatigued. She must be taken back at once."

Ezra sighed and started the Ambassador's straight-six engine.

Elizabeth Akeley telephoned Marc Feinman from the Noyes house in Dark Mountain. A message had been transmitted surreptitiously by agent Whiteside in time for monitoring arrangements to be made. Neither Akeley nor Feinman was aware of the monitoring system.

Excerpts from the call follow:

August 9, 1979 (outgoing)

Voice #2 (Sara Feinman): Yes.

Voice #5 (Elizabeth Akeley): Mrs. Feinman?

Voice #2: Yes, who is this?

Voice #5: Mrs. Feinman, this is Elizabeth Akeley speaking. I'm a friend of Marc's from San Diego. Is Marc there, please?

Voice #2: I know all about Marc's friend, Elizabeth darling. Don't you know Marc's father is in the hospital? Should you be bothering Marc at such a time?

Voice #5: I'm very sorry about Mr. Feinman, Mrs. Feinman. Marc told me before he left California. Is he all right?

Voice #2: Don't ask.

(Pause.)

Voice #5: Could I speak with Marc? Please?

Voice #2: (Off-line, pickup is very faint) Marc, here, it's your little goyish priestess. Yes. On the telephone. No, she didn't say where. No, she didn't say.

Voice #1 (Marc Feinman): Lizzy? Lizzy baby, are you okay?

Voice #5: Yes, I'm okay. Is your father—

Voice #1: (Interrupting) They operated this morning. I saw him after. He's very weak, Liz. But I think he's going to make it. Lizzy, where are you? Pleasant Street?

Voice #5: Vermont.

Voice #1: What? *Vermont?*

Voice #5: I couldn't wait, Marc. You were on the road, and there was another trance. I couldn't wait till you arrived in New York. Vernon came with me. We're staying with a family in Dark Mountain. Marc, I met my great-grandfather. Yesterday. I tried to call you last night but—

Voice #1: I was at the hospital with Ma, visiting my father. We couldn't just—

Voice #5: Of course, Marc. You did the right thing. (Pause.) How soon can you get here?

Voice #1: I can't leave now. My father is still—they're not sure. (Lowering his voice.) I don't want to talk too loud. The doctor said it's going to be touch and go for at least forty-eight hours. I can't leave Ma.

Voice #5: (Sobs.) I understand, Marc. But—but—my great-grandfather . . . .

Voice #1: How old is the old coot? He must be at least ninety.

Voice #5: He was born in 1871. He's 108.

Voice #1: My God! Talk about tough old Yankee stock!

Voice #5: It isn't that, Marc! It has to do with the trance messages. Don't you understand? All of that strange material about alien beings, and other galaxies? That was no sci-fi trip—

Voice #1: I never said you were making it up, Lizzy! Your subconscious, though, I mean, you see some TV show or a movie and—

Voice #5: But that's just it, Marc! Those are real messages. Not from my subconscious. My great-grandpa was sending, oh, call them spirit messages or telepathic radiations or anything you like. He's here. He's back. Aliens took him away, they took his brain in a metal cylinder, and he's been traveling in outer space for fifty years, and now he's back here in Vermont and—

Voice #1: Okay, Lizzy, enough! Look, I'll drive up there as soon as I can get away. As soon as my father's out of danger. I can't leave my Ma now, but as soon as I can. What's this place . . . .

Late in the afternoon of August 9th Ezra Noyes rapped on the door of Elizabeth Akeley's room. She admitted him and he stood in the center of the room, nervously wondering whether it would be proper to sit in her presence. Akeley urged him to sit. The conversation which ensued was recalled by young Noyes in a deposition taken later at an agency field office. Excerpts from the deposition follow:

. . .

"Well, you see, I told her that I was really serious about UFO's and all that stuff. She didn't know much about ufology. She'd never heard about the men in black, even. So I told her all about them so she'd be on the lookout. I asked her who this Vernon Whiteside was, and she said he was the sexton of her church and completely reliable and I shouldn't worry about him.

"I showed her some copies of the *Intelligencer*, and she said she liked the mag a lot and asked if she could keep them. I said sure. Anyway, she wanted to know how long the Moth Man sightings had been going on. I told her, only about six months or so over at Townshend and around here. Then she asked me what I knew about a rash of similar sightings about fifty years ago.

"That was right up my alley. You know, I did a lot of research. I went down and read a lot of old newspaper files. They have the old papers on microfilm now; it kills your eyes to crouch over a reader all day looking at the old stuff, but it's really interesting.

"Anyway, there were some odd sightings back in the '20s, and then when they had those floods around here in November '27, there were some really strange things. They found some bodies, parts of bodies that is, carried downstream in the flood. There were some in the Winooski River over near Montpelier, and some right in the streets of Passumpsic. The town was flooded, you know.

"Strange bodies. Things like big wings. Not like moth wings, though. More like bat wings. And there seems to have been some odd goings on with Miss Akeley's great-grandfather, Henry Akeley. He was a retired prof, you know. And something about a friend of his, a guy called Al Wilmarth. But it was all hushed up.

"Well, I told Miss Akeley everything I knew and then I asked her who was in the cabin over at that dirt road near Ludlow. I think she must have got mixed up, because she said it was Henry Akeley. He disappeared in 1927 or '28. Even if he turned up, he couldn't be alive now. She said he said something to her about love, and about wanting a young man's body and a young woman's body so he could make love with some woman from outer space, he said from Aldebaran. I guess you have to be a sci-fi nut to know about Aldebaran. I'm a sci-fi nut. I don't say too much about it in UFO circles—they don't like sci-fi, they think the sci-fi crowd put down UFO's. They're scared of 'em. They want to keep it all nice and safe and imaginary, you ought to read Sanderson and Early on that some time.

"Well, how could a human and an alien make love? I guess old Akeley must have thought something like a mind-transfer, like one partner could take over the body of a member of the other partner's species, you know. Only be careful, don't try it with spiders where the female eats the male after they mate. Ha-ha-ha! Ha-ha!

"But Miss Akeley kept asking about lovemaking, you know, and I started to wonder if maybe she wasn't hinting at something, you know. I mean, there we were in this room. And it was my own parents' house and all, but it *was* a bedroom, and I didn't want her to think that she could just walk in there and, uh, well, you know.

"So I excused myself then. But she seemed upset. She kept running her hand through her hair. Pulling it down, those strips, what do women call them, bangs, over her forehead. I told her I had to get to work on the next ish of my mag, you know, and she'd have to excuse me but the last ish had been late and I was trying to get the mag back on schedule. But I told her, if she wanted a lift over to Passumpsic again, I'd be glad to give her a ride over there any time, and I'd like to meet her great-grandfather if he was living in that old shack. Then she said he wasn't exactly living in the shack, but he sort of was, sort of was there and sort of was living there. It didn't make any sense to me. So I went and started laying out the next issue of the *Intelligencer* 'cause I wanted to get it out on time for once, and show those guys that I can get a mag out on time when I get a chance.

"Anyway, Miss Akeley said her great-grandfather's girlfriend was named something like Sheera from Aldebaran. I told her that sounded like something out of a bad '50s sci-fi flick on the TV. There's a great channel in Montreal, we get it on the cable, they show sci-fi flicks every week. And that sure sounded like a sci-fi flick to me.

"Sheera from Aldebaran! Ha-ha-ha! Ha-ha!"

Marc Feinman wheeled his Ferrari up to the Noyes home. His sporty driving-cap was cocked over one ear. Suede jacket, silk shirt, gucci jeans and frye boots completed his outfit.

The front door swung in as Feinman's boot struck the bottom wooden step. Elizabeth Akeley was across the whitewashed porch and into Feinman's arms before he reached the top of the flight. Without releasing his embrace of Akeley, Feinman extended one hand to grasp that of Vernon Whiteside.

They entered the house. Ezra Noyes greeted them in the front parlor. Elizabeth and Vernon briefed Marc on the events since their arrival in Vermont. When the narrative was brought up to date, Feinman asked simply, "What do you want to do?"

Ezra started to blurt out an ambitious plan for gaining the confidence of the aliens and arranging a ride in their saucer, but Whiteside, still maintaining the role of sexton of the Spiritual Light Church, cut him off. "We will do whatever the Radiant Mother asks us to do."

All eyes turned to Akeley.

After an uncomfortable interval she said, "I was—hoping that Marc could help. It's so strange, Marc. I know that I'm the one who always believed in—in the spirit world. The beyond. What you always call the supernormal."

Feinman nodded.

"But somehow," Elizabeth went on, "this seems more like your ideas than mine. It's so—I mean, this is the kind of thing that I've always looked for, believed in. And you haven't. And now that it's true, it doesn't seem to have any spiritual meaning. It's just—something that you could explain with your logic and your computers."

Feinman rubbed his slightly blue chin with his free hand. "This great-grandpa of yours, this Henry Akeley . . . ."

He looked into her eyes.

"You say, he was talking about some kind of mating ritual?"

Liz nodded.

Feinman said, "What did he look like? Did you ever *see* your great-grandfather before? Even a picture? Maybe one that your grandfather had in San Diego?"

She shook her head. "No. At least, I don't remember ever seeing a photo at home. There might have been one. But I hardly saw anything in the shack, Marc."

Ezra Noyes was jumping up and down in his chair. "Yes, you never told us, Lizzy—Miss Akeley. What did you see? What did he look like?"

"I hardly saw anything!" Liz covered her face with her hands, dropped one to her lap, tugged nervously at her bangs with the other. "It was pitch-dark in there. Just a little faint light seeping between the cracks in the walls, through those broken windows. Those that weren't broken were so filthy, they wouldn't let light in."

"So you couldn't tell if it was really Henry Akeley."

"It was the same voice," Vernon Whiteside volunteered. "We, ah, we bugged the meeting, Mr. Feinman. The voice was the same as the one on the trance tapes from the church."

Feinman's eyes widened. "The same? But the trance tapes are in Lizzy's voice!"

Whiteside backpedaled. "No, you're right. I don't suppose they were the same vocal chords. But the timbre. And the enunciation. Everything. Same person speaking. I'd stake my reputation on it!"

Feinman stroked his chin again. "All right. Here's what I'd like to do. Lizzy, Henry Akeley said he'd see you again, right? Okay, let's surprise him a little. Suppose Whiteside and I head out there. Can you find the shack again, Vernon? Good! Okay, we'll take the Ferrari out there."

"But it's nearly dark out."

"No difference if it's so damned dark inside the shack! I've got a good five-cell torch in the emergency kit in the Ferrari."

"I ought to come along," Ezra Noyes put in. "I *do* represent the Vermont UFO Intelligence Bureau, you know!"

"Right," Feinman nodded. "And we'll need your help later. No, we'll need you, Ezra, but not right now. Whiteside and I will visit Henry Akeley—or whoever or whatever is out there claiming to be Henry Akeley. Give us a couple of hours' head start. And then, you come ahead. Lizzy, you and Ezra here."

"Can I get into the shack this time?" Ezra jumped up and paced nervously, almost danced, back and forth. "The other time, I had to wait at the car. If I can get into the shack, I can get some photos. I'll rig up a flash on my Instamatic. I want to get some shots of the inside of that cabin for the *Intelligencer*."

"Yes, sure." Feinman turned from Ezra Noyes and took Elizabeth Akeley's hand. "You don't mind, do you, Lizzy? I'm worried that your ancestor there—or whoever it is—has some kind of control over you. Those trances—what if he puts you under some kind of hypnotic influence while we're all out there together?"

"How do you know he's evil? You seem to—just assume that Henry Akeley wants to harm me."

"I don't know that at all," Feinman frowned. "I just have a nasty feeling about it. I want to get there first. I think Whiteside and I can handle things, and then you can arrive in a while. Please, Lizzy. You did call me to help. You didn't have to, you could have just gone back and never said anything to me until it was over."

Elizabeth looked very worried. "Maybe I should have."

"Well, but you didn't. Now, can we do it this way? Please?"

"All right, Marc."

Feinman turned to Vernon Whiteside. "Let's go. How long a ride is it out there?"

Whiteside paused for a moment. "Little less than an hour."

Feinman grunted. "Okay. Vernon and I will start now. We'll need about an hour, I suppose—call it two to be on the safe side. Lizzy and Ezra, if you'll follow us out to the shack in two hours, just come ahead in, we'll be there."

Ezra departed to check his camera. Vernon accompanied Marc. Shortly the Ferrari Boxer disappeared in a cloud of yellow Vermont dust, headed for Passumpsic.

As soon as they had pulled out of sight of the house, Vernon spoke. "Mr. Feinman, I've been helping Radiant Mother on this trip."

"I know that, Vernon. Lizzy mentioned it several times. I really appreciate it."

"Mr. Feinman, you know how concerned Radiant Mother is about Church archives. The way she records her sermons and the message services. Well, she was worried about her meeting with old Mr. Akeley. So I helped her to rig a wireless mike on her jacket. So we got a microcassette of the meeting."

Feinman said he knew that.

"Well, if you don't mind, I'd like to do the same again." Whiteside held the tiny microcassette recorder for Feinman to see. The Ferrari's V-12 purred throatily, loafing along the Passumpsic road in third gear.

"Sure. That's a good idea. But you needn't rig me up. I want you along. You can just mike yourself."

Vernon Whiteside considered. "Tell you what . . . ." He reached into his pocket, pulled out a pair of enamel ladybugs. "I'll mike us both. If we happen to pick up the same sounds, there'll be no harm. In fact, it'll give us a redundancy check. If we get separated—"

"I don't see why we should."

"Just in case." He pinned a ladybug to Feinman's suede jacket, attached the second bug to his own. He made a minor adjustment on the recorder.

"There." He slipped the recorder back into his pocket. "I separated the two input circuits. Now we'll record on two channels. We can mix the sound if we record the same events or keep it separate if we pick up different events. In fact, just to be on the safe side, suppose I leave the recorder here in the car when you and I go to the shack."

Feinman assented, and Whiteside peeled the sealers from a dime-sized disk of double-adhesive foam. He stuck it to the recorder and stuck the recorder to the bottom of the Ferrari's dashboard.

"You're the sexton of the Spiritual Light Church," Feinman said.

"Yes, sir."

"You know a hell of a lot about electronics."

"My sister's boy, Mr. Feinman. Bright youngster. It's his hobby."

Feinman tooled the Ferrari around the dome-topped hill and pulled to a halt where the Noyes station wagon had parked on the earlier visit. The sun was setting and the somehow too-lush glade was filled with murk.

Vernon Whiteside reached under the dashboard and flicked the microcassette recorder to automatic mode. He climbed from the car.

Feinman went to the rear of the Ferrari and extracted a long-handled electric torch. He pulled his sports cap down over his eyes and touched Whiteside's elbow. The men advanced.

The events that transpired following this entrance to the sycamore copse were captured on the microcassette recorder, and a transcript of these sounds appears later in the report.

In the meanwhile, Elizabeth Akeley and Ezra Noyes waited at the Noyes home in Dark Mountain.

Two hours to the minute, after the departure of Marc Feinman and Vernon Whiteside in Feinman's Ferrari Boxer, the Noyes station wagon, its aged suspension creaking, pulled out of the driveway.

Ezra pushed the Nash to the limit of its tired ability, chattering the while to Elizabeth. Preoccupied, she responded with low monosyllables. At the turning-point from the Passumpsic-Ludlow road onto the old farm track, she waited in the station wagon while Ezra climbed down and opened the fence gate.

The Nash's headlights picked a narrow path for the car, circling the dome-topped hill that blocked the copse of lush vegetation from sight of passers-by. The Ferrari Boxer stood silently at the edge of the copse.

Ezra lifted his camera-bag from the floor and slung it over his shoulder. Elizabeth waited in the car until Ezra walked to her side, opened the door and offered his hand.

They started through the copse. Noyes testified later that this was his first experience with the unusual growth of vegetation. He claimed that, even as he set foot beneath the overhanging branches of the first sycamore, a strange sensation passed through him. The day had been hot, and even in the hours of darkness the temperature did not drop drastically. Even so, with his entry into the copse Noyes felt an unnatural and debilitating *heat*, as if the trees were fitted to a different climate than that of northern Vermont and actually were emitting heat of their own.

He began to perspire and wiped his forehead with his hand.

Elizabeth Akeley led the way through the wooded area, retracing the steps of her previous visit to the wooden shack.

Noyes found it more and more difficult to continue. With each pace he felt drained of energy and will. Once he halted and was about to sit down for a rest, but Akeley grasped his hand and pulled him with her.

When they emerged from the copse, the dome-topped hill stood directly behind them, the run-down shack directly ahead.

Ezra and Elizabeth crossed the narrow grassy patch between the sycamore copse and the ramshackle cabin. Ezra found a space where the glass had fallen away and there was a small opening in the omnipresent cobwebs. He peered in, then lifted his camera and poked its lens through the opening. He shot a picture.

"Don't know what I got, but maybe I got something," he said.

Elizabeth Akeley pulled the door open. She stepped inside the cabin, closely followed by young Noyes.

The room, Ezra could see, was far larger than he'd estimated from the outside. Although the shack contained but a single room, that room was astonishingly deep. Its far corners were utterly lost in shadow. Nearer to him were a rocking chair, a battered over-stuffed couch and a dust-laden wooden table of the type often found in old New England homes.

Ezra later reported hearing odd sounds during those minutes. There was a strange buzzing sound. He couldn't tell whether it was organic— a sound such as a flight of hornets might have made, or such as might have been made by a single insect magnified to a shocking gigantism—or whether the sound was artificial, as if an electrical generator were running slightly out of adjustment.

The modulation of the sound was its oddest characteristic. Not only did the volume rise and fall, but the pitch, and in some odd way, the very tonal quality of the buzzing, kept changing. "It was as if something was trying to talk to me. To us. To Miss Akeley and me. I thought I could almost understand it, but not quite."

Noyes stood, all but paralyzed, until he heard Elizabeth Akeley scream. Ezra whirled from the table, whence had emanated the buzzing sounds. He saw Elizabeth standing before the rocking chair, her hands to her face, screaming.

The chair was rocking back and forth, slowly, gently. The cabin was almost pitch-black, its only illumination coming from an array of unfamiliar machinery set up on the long wooden table. Ezra could see now that a figure was seated, apparently unmoving, in the rocker. From it a voice was coming.

"Elizabeth, my darling, you have come," the voice said. "Now we shall be together. We shall know the love of the body as we have known the love of the mind and of the soul."

Strangely, Noyes later stated, although the voice in which the figure spoke was that of Marc Feinman, the accent and intonation were those of New England old-timers. Noyes testified also that his powers of observation played a strange trick on him at this moment. Although the man sitting in the chair was undoubtedly Marc Feinman—the clothing he wore, even to the sporting cap pulled low over his eyes, as if he were driving his Ferrari in a bright sun—what Ezra noticed most particularly was a tiny red-and-black smudge on Feinman's jacket. "It looked like a squashed ladybug," the youth stated later.

From somewhere in the darker corners of the cabin there came a strange rustling sound, like that of great leathery wings opening and folding again.

Noyes shot a quick series of pictures, one of the figure in the rocking chair, one of the table with the unusual mechanical equipment on it, and one of the darker corners of the cabin, hoping vaguely that he would get some results. The man in the rocking chair tilted slowly backward, slowly forward, finally saying to Ezra, "You'll never get anything from there. You'd better get over to the other end of the shack and make your pictures."

As if hypnotized, Noyes walked toward the rear of the cabin. He stated later that as he passed a certain point, it was as if he had penetrated a curtain of total darkness. He was unable to see even a little as he had previously. He tried to turn and look back at the others, but could not move. He tried to call out but could not speak. He was completely conscious but seemed to have been plunged into a state of total paralysis (except, of course, for the autonomic functions that preserve the life of the body) and of sensory deprivation.

What transpired behind him, in the front end of the cabin, he could not tell. When he recovered from his paralysis and loss of sensory inputs, it was to find himself alone at the rear of the shack. It was daylight outside and sunshine was pushing through the grimy windows and open door of the shanty. He turned around and found himself facing two figures. A third was at his side.

"Ezra!" the third figure said.

"Mr. Whiteside!" Noyes responded.

"Well, I'm glad to see that you two are all right," a voice came to them from the other end of the cabin. It was the old New England twang that Ezra had heard from the man in the rocking chair, and the speaker was, indeed, Marc Feinman. He stood, wooden-faced, his back to the doorway. Elizabeth Akeley, her features similarly expressionless, stood at his side. Feinman's sporting cap was pulled down almost to the line of his eyebrows. Akeley's bangs dangled over her forehead.

Noyes claimed later that he thought he could see signs of a fresh red scar running across Akeley's forehead beneath the bangs. He claimed also that a corner of red was visible at the edge of the visor of Feinman's cap. But of course this is unverified.

"We're going now," Feinman said in his strange New England twang. "We'll take my car. You two go home in the other."

"But—but, Radiant Mother," Whiteside began.

"Elizabeth is very tired," Feinman said nasally. "You'll have to excuse her. I'm taking her away for a while."

He started out the door, guiding Elizabeth by the elbow. She walked strangely, not so much as if she were tired, ill, or even injured. Somehow, she had the tentative, uncertain movements that are associated with an amputee first learning to maneuver prosthetic devices.

They left the cabin, walked to the Ferrari. Feinman opened the door on the passenger side and guided Akeley into the car. Then he circled the vehicle, climbed in and seated himself at the wheel. Strangely, he sat for a long time staring at the controls of the sports car, almost as if he were unfamiliar with its type.

Vernon Whiteside and Ezra Noyes followed the others from the cabin. Both were still confused from their strange experience of paralysis and sensory deprivation; both stated later that they felt only half-awake, half-hypnotized. "Else," agent Whiteside later deposed, "I'd have stopped them for sure. Warrant or no warrant, I had probable cause that something fishy was going on, and I'd've grabbed the keys out of that Ferrari, done anything it took to keep those two there. But I could hardly move, I could hardly even think.

"I *did* manage to reach into that car and grab out my machine. My microcassette recorder. Then I looked at my little bug-mike and saw that it was squashed, like somebody'd just squeezed it between his thumb and his finger, only he must have been made out of iron 'cause those bug-mikes are ruggedized. They can take a wallop with a sledge hammer and not even know it. So who squashed my little bug?

"Then Feinman finally got his car started and they pulled away. I looked at the Noyes kid and he looked at me, and we headed for his

Nash wagon and we went back to his house. Nearly cracked up half a dozen times on the way home, he drove like a drunk. When we got to his place, we both passed out for twelve hours while Feinman and Akeley were going God-knows-where in that Ferrari.

"Soon as I got myself back together I phoned in to agency field HQ and came on in."

When agent Whiteside reported to agency field HQ he turned over the microcassette which he and Feinman had made at the shack. Excerpts from the tape follow:

(Whiteside's Channel)

(All voices mixed): Yeah, this is the place all right . . . I'll—got it open, okay . . . Sheesh, it's dark in here. How'd she see anything? Well . . . (Buzzing sound.) What's that? What's that? Here, I'll shine my—what the hell? It looks like . . . Shining cylinder. No, two of 'em. Two of 'em. What the hell, some kind of futuristic espresso machines. What the hell . . . .

(Buzzing sound becomes very loud, dominates tape. Then it drops and a rustling is heard.)

Voice #3 (Vernon Whiteside): Here, lend me that thing a minute. No, I just gotta see what's over there. Okay, you stay here a minute, I gotta see what's . . . .

(Sound of walking, buzzing continues in background but fades, rustling sound increases.)

Voice #3: Jesus God! That can't be! No, no, that can't be! It's too . . . .

(Sound of thump, as if microphone were being struck and then crushed between superhard metallic surfaces. Remainder of Whiteside channel is silent.)

(Feinman's Channel)

(Early portion identical to Whiteside channel; excerpts begin following end of recording on Whiteside channel.)

Voice #1 (Marc Feinman): Vernon? Vernon? What—

Voice #6 (Henry Wentworth Akeley): He is unharmed.

Voice #1: Who's that?

Voice #6: I am Henry Wentworth Akeley.

Voice #1: Lizzy's great-grandfather.

Voice #6: Precisely. And you are Mr. Feinman?

Voice #1: Where are you, Akeley?

Voice #6: I am here.

Voice #1: Where? I don't see . . . what happened to Whiteside? Listen, what's going on here? I don't like what's going on here.

Voice #6: Please, Mr. Feinman, try to remain calm.

Voice #1: Where are you, Akeley? For the last time . . . .

Voice #6: Please, Mr. Feinman, I must ask you to calm yourself. (Rustling
    sound.) Ah, that's better. Now, Mr. Feinman, do you not see certain
    objects on the table? Good. Now, Mr. Feinman, you are an intelli-
    gent and courageous young man. I understand that your interests are
    wide and your thirst for knowledge great. I offer you a grand oppor-
    tunity. One which was offered to me half a century ago. I tried to
    decline at that time. My hand was forced. I never regretted having
    ... let us say, gone where I have gone. But I now must return to
    earthly flesh, and as my own integument is long destroyed, I have
    need of another.

Voice #1: What—where—what are you talking about? If this is some kind
    of...

   (Loud sound of rustling, sound of thumping and struggle, incoherent gasps
and gurgles, loud breathing, moans.)

   (At this point the same sound that ended the Whiteside segment of the tape
is heard. Remainder of Feinman channel is blank.)

When agent Whiteside and young Ezra Noyes woke from their
exhausted sleep, Whiteside revealed himself as a representative of the
agency. He obtained the film from young Noyes' camera. It was
promptly developed at the nearest agency facility. The film was
subsequently returned to Noyes, and the four usable photographs, in
fuzzily screened and mimeographed form, appeared in the *Vermont
UFO Intelligencer*.

   A description of the four photographs follows:

Frame 1: (Shot through window of the wooden shack) A dingy room contain-
    ing a rocking chair and a large wooden table.

Frame 2: (Shot inside room) A rocking chair. In the chair is sitting a man iden-
    tified as Marc Feinman. Feinman's sporting cap is pulled down
    covering his forehead. His eyes are barely visible and seem to have a
    glazed appearance, but this may be due to the unusual lighting con-
    ditions. A mark on his forehead seems to be visible at the edge of the
    cap, but is insufficiently distinct for verification.

Frame 3: (Shot inside room) Large wooden table holding unusual mechanical
    apparatus. There are numerous electrical devices, power units, what
    appears to be a cooling unit, photo-electric cells, items which appear
    to be microphones, and two medium-sized metallic cylinders esti-
    mated to contain sufficient space for a human brain, along with
    life-support paraphernalia.

Frame 4: (Shot inside room) This was obviously Noyes' final frame, taken as he
    headed toward the darkened rear area of the cabin. The rough
    wooden flooring before the camera is clearly visible. From it there
    seems to rise a curtain or wall of sheer blackness. This is not a black
    substance of any sort, but a curtain or mass of sheer negation. All at-
    tempts at analysis by agency photoanalysts have failed completely.

Elizabeth Akeley and Marc Feinman were located at—of all places—Niagara Falls, New York. They had booked a honeymoon cottage and were actually located by agents of the agency returning in traditional yellow slickers from a romantic cruise on the craft *Maid of the Mist.*

Asked to submit voluntarily to agency interrogation, Feinman refused. Akeley, at Feinman's prompting, simply shook her head negatively. "But I'll tell you what," Feinman said in a marked New England twang, "I'll make out a written statement for you if you'll settle for that."

Representatives of the agency considered this particularly unsatisfactory, but having no grounds for holding Feinman or Akeley and being particularly sensitive to criticism of the agency for alleged intrusion upon the religious freedoms of unorthodox cults, the representatives of the agency were constrained to accept Feinman's offer.

The deposition provided by Feinman—and co-sworn by Akeley—represented a vague and rambling narrative of no value. Its concluding paragraph follows:

> All we want is to be left alone. We love each other. We're here now and we're happy here. What came before is over. That's somebody else's concern now. Let them go. Let them see. Let them learn. Vega, Aldebaran, Ophiuchi, the Crab Nebula. Let them see. Let them learn. Someday we may wish to go back. We will have a way to summon those ones. When we summon those ones they will respond.

A final effort by representatives of the agency was made, in an additional visit to the abandoned shack by the sycamore copse off the Passumpsic-Ludlow road. A squad of agents wearing regulation black outfits was guided by Vernon Whiteside. An additional agent remained at the Noyes home to assure noninterference by Ezra Noyes.

Whiteside guided his fellow agents to the sycamore copse. Several agents remarked at the warmth and debilitating feeling they experienced as they passed through the copse. In addition, an abnormal number of small cadavers—squirrels, chipmunks, one grey fox, a skunk, and several whippoorwills—were noted, lying beneath the trees.

The shack contained an aged wooden rocking chair, a battered over-stuffed couch, and a large wooden table. Whatever might have previously stood upon the table had been removed.

There was no evidence of the so-called wall or curtain of darkness. The rear of the shack was vacant.

In the months since the incidents above reported, two additional developments have taken place, note of which is appropriate herein.

First, Marc Feinman and Elizabeth Akeley returned to San Diego in Feinman's Ferrari Boxer. There, they took up residence at the Pleasant Street location. Feinman vacated the Upas Street apartment; he returned to his work with the computer firm. Inquiries placed with his employers indicate that he appeared, upon returning, to be absent-minded and disoriented, and unexpectedly to require briefings in computer technology and programming concepts with which he had previously been thoroughly familiar.

Feinman explained this curious lapse by stating that he had experienced a head injury while vacationing in Vermont and still suffered from occasional lapses of memory. He showed a vivid but rapidly fading scar on his forehead as evidence of the injury. His work performance quickly returned to its usual high standard. "Marc's as smart as the brightest prof you ever studied under," his supervisor stated to the agency. "But that Vermont trip made some impression on him! He picked up this funny New England twang in his speech, and it just won't go away."

Elizabeth Akeley went into seclusion. Feinman announced that they had been married and that Elizabeth was, at least temporarily, abandoning her position as Radiant Mother of the Spiritual Light Church, although remaining a faithful member of the Church. In Feinman's company she regularly attends Sunday worship services, but seldom speaks.

The second item of note is of questionable relevance and significance but is included here as a matter of completing the appropriate documentation. Vermont Forestry Service officers have reported that a new variety of sycamore tree has appeared in the Windham County-Windsor County section of the state. The new sycamores are lush and extremely hardy. They seem to generate a peculiarly *warm* atmosphere and are not congenial to small forest animals. Forestry officers who have investigated report a strange sense of lassitude when standing beneath these trees, and one officer has apparently been lost while exploring a stand of the trees near the town of Passumpsic.

Forestry agents are maintaining a constant watch on the spread of the new variety of sycamores.

Here is one of Ramsey Campbell's early Cthulhu Mythos tales accepted for publication by August Derleth. Derleth accepted them, all right, but not without some mandatory revisions. The story you are about to read was originally submitted as "The Tower on Yuggoth" and was much longer. It detailed many more occult experiments by the protagonist, in that version called Edward Wingate Armitage, a name possessing something of a familiar ring! The tale was much truncated, and much the better for it, when it appeared in Campbell's collection The Inhabitant of the Lake and Less Welcome Tenants in 1964.

When Scream Press reprinted most of the same stories, adding some more recent ones, the new collection, Cold Print (1985) dropped "The Mine on Yuggoth." I reprinted both that tale and its prototype, "The Tower on Yuggoth," in Crypt of Cthulhu #43. Since then, "The Tower on Yuggoth" has appeared between book covers in Black Forbidden Things, a collection of material from Crypt of Cthulhu (now available from Borgo Press). But it seems fitting that "The Mine on Yuggoth" be made available in more accessible form as well.

In Lovecraft's tale, weren't the Plutonians miners on earth for metals they could not find on Pluto? In "The Whisperer in Darkness," yes they were. But in "Out of the Aeons," one of Lovecraft's revision tales ghost-written for Hazel Heald, he noted that the Yuggoth invaders had brought to earth certain objects fashioned of their own metal, unknown on earth. It is this which Campbell's protagonist seeks.

The Mine On Yuggoth

by RAMSEY CAMPBELL

Edward Taylor was twenty-four years old when he first became interested in the metal mined on Yuggoth.

He had led a strange life up to that point. He was born, normally enough, of Protestant parents in Brichester Central Hospital in 1899. From an early age he preferred to sit reading in his room rather than play with the neighborhood children, but such a preference is not remarkable. Most of the books he read were normal, too, though he tended to concentrate on the more unusual sections; after reading the Bible, for instance, he startled his father by asking, "How did the witch of Endor call the spirit?" Besides, as his mother remarked, surely no normal eight-year-old would read *Dracula* and *The Beetle* with such avidity as Edward.

In 1918 Taylor left school and enrolled at Brichester University. Here the stranger section of his life began; his tutors soon discovered that his academic studies frequently gave way to less orthodox practices. He led a witch-cult, centering round a stone slab in the woods off the Severnford road. The members of the cult included such people as the artist, Nevil Craughan, and the occultist, Henry Fisher; all members being subsequently exposed and expelled. Some of them gave up sorcery, but Taylor only became more interested. His parents were dead, his inheritance made work unnecessary, and he could spend all the time he wished in research.

But although he had enough normal possessions, Taylor was still not satisfied. He had borrowed the *Revelations of Glaaki* from another cultist, and had visited the British Museum twice to copy passages from the *Necronomicon*. His library included the horrible untitled Johannes Henricus Pott book which the Jena publishers rejected, and this was the book which gave him his final interest. That repulsive immortality formula which Pott wrote was more than half true, and when Taylor compared certain of the necessary ingredients with references by Alhazred, he put together a hitherto unconnected series of hints.

On Tond, Yuggoth, and occasionally on Earth, immortality has been attained by an obscure process. The brain of the immortal is transplanted from body to body at thirty-five-year intervals; this otherwise impossible operation being carried out using a *tok'l* container, in which the naked brain is placed between bodies. *Tok'l* is a metal mined exclusively on Yuggoth, but neither exists nor can be created on Earth.

"The lizard-crustaceans arrive on Earth through their towers," Alhazred tells us; not *in* their towers, Taylor noted, but through them, using the method of turning space in on itself which has been lost to men since Joiry. It was dangerous, but Taylor only had to find an outpost of the Yuggoth-spawn and pass through the barrier in the transport tower there. The danger did not lie in the journey to Yuggoth; the barrier must change the organs of bodies passing through it, or else the lizard-crustaceans could never live in their outposts on Earth, where they mine those metals not to be had on their planet. But Taylor disliked the miners; he had once seen an engraving in the *Revelations of Glaaki* and been repelled by it. It was unlike anything he had seen before; the body was not really that of a lizard, nor did its head too closely resemble that of a lobster, but those were the only comparisons he could make.

For some time Taylor could not have gone among the Yuggoth-spawn, even if he had found one of their outposts. But a page reference in the *Revelations* led him to the following in the *Necronomicon:*

> As Azathoth rules now as he did in his bivalvular shape, his name subdues all, from the incubi which haunt Tond to the servants of Y'golonac. Few can resist the power of the name Azathoth, and even the haunters of the blackest night of Yuggoth cannot battle the power of N———, *his other name.*

So Taylor's interest in travel to Yuggoth was renewed. The lizard-crustaceans were no longer dangerous, but occasionally Taylor felt twinges of unease when he thought of certain hints in the *Revelations.* There were occasional references to a pit which lay near one of the cities—a pit whose contents few lizard-crustaceans cared to view, and which was avoided during certain periods of the year by all. No description of what lay in the pit was included, but Taylor came across the words: "at those times of the year the lizard-crustaceans are glad of the lightlessness of Yuggoth." But the hints were so vague that he usually ignored them.

Unfortunately, the "other name" of Azathoth was not given in the *Necronomicon,* and by the time he needed to know it, the exposure of the cult had placed the *Revelations of Glaaki* beyond his reach. In 1924 he began a search for some person with the complete edition. By chance he met Michael Hinds, one of the former cultists, who did not have a copy but suggested a visit to a farmhouse off the Goatswood road.

"That's Daniel Norton's place," Hinds told him. "He's got the complete edition, and a lot more items of interest. He's not very bright, though—he remembers all the Tagh-Clatur angles, but he's content to live the way he does and worship rather than use his knowledge to better himself. I don't like him particularly. He's too stupid to harm you, of course, but all that knowledge going to waste annoys me."

Thus it was that Taylor called on Daniel Norton. The man lived with his two sons in an old farmhouse, where they managed to exist off a small herd of sheep and a few poultry. Norton was half-deaf and, as Hinds had mentioned, not too intelligent, so that Taylor irritated himself by speaking slowly and loudly. The other had begun to look disquieted during Taylor's speech, and remained uneasy as he answered:

"Listen, young zur, 'teant as if I haven't bin mixed up in terrible doin's. I had a friend once as would go down to the Devil's Steps, an' he swore he'd zoon have them Yuggoth ones about him, ministerin' at every word he zpoke. He thought he had words as would overcome them on the Steps. But one day they found him in't woods, and 'twas so horrible that them who carried him warn't the same ever agin. His chest an' throat was bust open, an' his face wuz all blue. Those as knew, they do zay those up the Steps grabbed him and flew off with 'im into space, where 'is lungs bust.

"Wait a minute, zur. 'Tis dangerous up them Devil's Steps. But there's zumthin' out in't woods by the Zevernford Road that could give you wot you want, maybe, and it don't hate men zo much as them from Yuggoth. You've maybe bin to it—'tis under a slab o' rock, an' the Voola ritual brings it—but did you think of askin' for what you need? 'Tis easier t' old—you don't even need Alhazred for the right words, an' it might get to them from Yuggoth fer you."

"You say they have an outpost on the Devil's Steps?" Taylor persisited.

"No, zur," the farmer replied, "that's all I'll zay till you've bin an' tried me advice."

Taylor left, dissatisfied, and some nights later visited the titan slab in the woods west of the Severnford Road. But the ritual needed more than one participant; he heard something vast stirring below his feet, but nothing more.

The next day he drove again to the farmhouse off the Goatswood road. Norton did not conceal his displeasure on opening the door, but allowed the visitor to enter. Taylor's shadow flickered across the seated farmer as he spoke. "You didn't think I'd leave you alone when it didn't awaken, did you?"

"What'd be the use if I come with you to it? If one don't raise it,
nor will two. An' anyway, maybe you like t' mess about wit' them from
Yuggoth, but I don't. They zay they carry you off to Yuggoth an' give
you t' what they're afraid of. I don't want to come near sumthin' that
might go t' them. In fact, I want t' give it all up fer good."

"Something which they're afraid of?" repeated Taylor, not remembering.

"It's in the *Revelations of Glaaki*," explained the other. "You saw
mine—"

"Yes, that's a point," Taylor interrupted. "If you're really going to
give up witchcraft, you won't be needing that book. My God, I'd
forgotten all about it! Give me that and maybe I won't ever bother you
again!"

"You can have it an'welcome," said Norton. "But you mean that?
You'll keep away an' let me stop playin' round with things from
Outside?"

"Yes, yes," Taylor assured him, took the pile of dusty volumes which
the farmer toppled into his arms, and struggled with them to the car.
He drove home and there discovered that the book contained what he
sought. It contained other relevant passages also, and he reread one
which ran:

> Beyond the Zone of the Thirteen Faveolate Colossi lies Yuggoth,
> where dwell the denizens of many extraterrestrial realms. Yuggoth's
> black streets have known the tread of malformed paws and the touch
> of misshapen appendages, and unviseagable shapes creep among its
> lightless towers. But few of the creatures of the rim-world are as feared
> as that survival of Yuggoth's youth which remains in a pit beyond one
> of the cities. This survival few have seen, but the legends of the
> crustaceans tells of a city of green pyramids which hangs over a ledge
> far down in the dark. It is said that no mind can stand the sight of what
> occurs on that ledge at certain seasons.
>
> (But nothing can battle the power of the other name of Azathoth.)

So Taylor ignored this; and two days later he drove with climbing
tools to the rock formation beyond Brichester. It stretched fully two
hundred feet up in a series of steps to a plateau; from some way off the
illusion of a giant staircase was complete, and legend had it that Satan
came from the sky to walk the earth by way of those steps. But when
Taylor parked in the road of which they formed one side, he saw how
rough they were and how easy ascent would be. He left the car, stood
staring up for a moment, and began to chip footholds.

The climb was tedious and precarious. Sometimes he slipped and
hung for a minute over nothing. Once, a hundred feet up, he glanced

down at the car, and for the rest of the climb tried to forget the speck of metal far below. Finally he hooked his hand over the edge, pulled himself up and over. Then he looked up.

In the center of the plateau stood three stone towers, joined by narrow catwalks of black metal between the roofs. They were surrounded by fungus—an alien species, a grey stem covered with twining leaves. It could not have been completely vegetable, either, for as Taylor stood up, the stems leaned in his direction and the leaves uncurled toward him.

He began to pick his way through the avenues of fungus, shrinking away when the clammy leaves stroked him, and at last hurrying into the cleared space around the central steeple. The tower was about thirty feet high, windowless and with a strangely angled doorway opening on stairs leading into blackness. However, Taylor had brought a torch, and shone it up the stairs as he entered. He did not like the way the darkness seemed to move beyond the torchlight, and would have preferred an occasional window, if only to remind him that he had not already reached Yuggoth. But the thought of the *tok'l*-bought immortality drove him on.

He had been ascending for some time when he noticed the hieroglyphics on the walls—all apparently indicating something around the bend in the passage. He turned the bend, and saw that the steps ended some feet above—not at a wall or solid barrier, but the torch-beam would not penetrate beyond. This must be where the lizard-crustaceans connected Earth with Yuggoth; and the other side was Yuggoth itself.

He threw himself at the barrier, plunged through, cried out and fell. It was as if his body had been torn into atoms and recombined; only a memory remained of something he had no conviction of undergoing. He lay for a few minutes before he was able to stand up and look about.

He was on a tower roof above a city. He directed the torch-beam downward, and realized that there was no way down the smooth wall; but, remembering the catwalks, he guessed that the building at the end of each row would afford some means of descent. This seemed the only way the crustaceans could descend, for the *Revelations* engravings had shown no method of flight. He was unnerved by the abyss below the catwalk, but could not relieve it by his torch.

There were five narrow metal walks to be traversed. Taylor did not notice their odd shape until he was on the first. It was slightly convex in section, and at intervals there protruded outward corrugated sections at an angle. He found it very difficult to change from equilibrium on the convex portions to balance on the angled stretches, and often slid to one side, but he reached the end finally, rounded the gaping blackness in the center of the roof and set out on the next walk. He had got the knack by now, and slipped less.

One thing disquieted him; the total silence of the nighted city. The clang of his footsteps broke the silence like pebbles dropped into some subterranean sea. Not even distant noises were audible, yet it seemed impossible that such a densely-populated world should be so silent. Even if, improbably, all the citizens were on Earth, surely some sound should occasionally drift from the distance. It was almost as if the inhabitants had fled some nightmare invasion of the city.

As he reached the center of the fifth catwalk, a raucous croaking rang out behind him. He tottered and slammed down on the metal, clawed and scrabbled to the last roof and looked back.

The noise came from a speaker vibrating atop a grey metal pylon. It seemed purposeless, unless it were a warning, or an announcement of his own arrival. He ignored it as a warning, not wishing to return to Earth after coming so far; and even if they realized his presence, they would flee before the name of Azathoth. He walked to the roof's edge and peered for a way down.

It consisted of an unprotected stairway which led around the outer wall of the tower, spiraling steeply to the street. He started down as the shrieking speaker quietened, and realized that the steps were set at a definitely obtuse angle to the wall, so that only their pitted surface prevented him from plunging to the street below. Ten feet down a piece of stone slid away under his foot, and had he not clutched the step above he would have toppled into the darkness. He made the remainder of the streetward journey more slowly, his heart pounding.

So he finally came to that pavement of octahedral, concave black stones. He shone the slightly-dimmed torch beam down the thorough-fare. Ebon steeples stretched away on both sides into night, and on Taylor's left was a right-angle intersection. The buildings were all set in the centers of individual ten-yard squares, through which cut paths of a blackly translucent mineral, and in which grew accurately-positioned lines of that half-animal fungi which he had seen on the plateau. As he left the tower his torch illuminated a fork in the road, at the intersection of which stood a squat black building shaped like a frustum, and he decided to take the left branch of this fork.

The metal which he sought was so brittle that it was not used for construction in the city. To gather specimens he would have to visit the actual mines, which were habitually set close to the crustaceans' settlements. But he was unsure of the city's layout. Nothing could be seen from the roofs, for his torch-beam did not reach far, nor did he know how far the settled area extended. Not even the *Revelations of Glaaki* gave maps of the cities on Yuggoth, so that his only plan was to follow some street at random. However, it was usual for such cities to be encircled by mines at quarter-mile intervals, so that once he reached the city's edge, he would be fairly near a mine. These mines mainly produced the black stone used for building, but a certain percentage of the ore was extracted from the stone and refined in factories around the mine-pits.

Five hundred yards along the left fork he noticed a change in the surroundings. While the towers still occupied one side of the street, the right side's steeples now gave way to an open space, extending along the street for fully two hundred yards and inward fifty yards, which was filled with oddly-shaped objects of semi-resilient deep-blue plastic. Despite their curious shape, he could see they were intended as seats; but he could not understand the disc-shaped attachments which rose on metal rods on each side of each seat. He had never read of such a place, and guessed that it might be the crustaceans' equivalent of a cinema. He saw that the space was littered with thin hexagonal sheets of blue metal covered with raised varicolored symbols, which he took for documents. It looked as if the space had recently been hurriedly vacated. This, coupled with that warning siren, might have hinted something to him; but he only began to continue down the street.

The open space, however, interested him. The discs might be some form of receiver, in which case the transmission might give him an idea of the direction of the mines. Perhaps the crustaceans were able to transmit mental images, for some of the legends about their outposts on Earth spoke of their using long-range hypnosis. If the discs worked on a variant of this principle, the power ought not to harm him, for since passing through the barrier he should have the metabolism of a crustacean. At any rate, he had three batteries left for his torch, and could afford to waste a little time, for he could protect himself with the feared name if any of the citizens came upon him.

He sank into the plastic of one of the deep-blue seats. He leaned back in it, placing the torch on the ground beside one of the batteries which had fallen out of a pocket. He sat up a little in the chair, and his head came between the metal discs. A deafening whine came from these, and before he could move a bright orange spark flashed from one disk to the other, passing through his brain.

Taylor leaped up, and the orange ray faded. A metallic odor came from his left pocket, where he had placed the other two batteries. He slid in his hand, and withdrew it covered with a dull grey fluid which was plainly all that remained of the batteries. The torch and one battery, which had not been in contact with his body, still stood nearby, and the bulb was still lit. But in spite of what the ray had done to the batteries, he was untouched; and he wanted very much to return to the chair, so that he turned off the torch to conserve the battery and sat back on the plastic. For that ray had the property of forming images in the mind; and in that moment between the discs Taylor had seen fleetingly a strange vision of a metal-grilled gateway, rusted and standing alone in the middle of a desert, lit by a setting green moon. What it had been he did not know, but it had an air of distinct and unknowable purpose.

The ray began to pass even before he came between the discs, and an image formed, only to fade and be replaced by another. A series of unconnected visions paraded and blurred the surrounding darkness. A snakelike being flew across a coppery sky, its head and tail hanging limply down from its midsection, where a single batwing rotated. Great cobwebbed objects rolled from noisome caverns in the center of a phosphorescent morass, their mouths opening wetly as they hastened toward where a figure screamed and struggled in the mud. A range of mountains, their peaks ice-covered, reached almost to the sky; and as he watched, a whole line of peaks exploded upward and a leprously white, faceless head rose into view.

Rather disturbed, Taylor thought defensively, "What a waste of time!" and began to stand up.

Immediately on the word "waste," a new picture formed. A close-up of one of the crustaceans appeared, and what it was doing was nauseatingly obvious, even with its unaccustomed shape. What was unusual was that it was performing this act in the garden of one of the towers, by a specimen of the ever-present fungus. When the crustacean had finished, it stood up and moved away, while Taylor received a close view of what it had left behind. As he watched in horrified fascination, the leaves of the nearby fungus bent and covered the offal; and when it rose from this position, the ground was bare at that spot. He now saw the purpose of the lines of fungi.

More important, however, he realized that he had just discovered the method of referring to the knowledge stored in this library. He must think of some key word—that was how "waste" had evoked such an unfortunate vision. Now, swallowing his nausea, Taylor thought, "mines connected with this city."

The vista which now appeared to him was an aerial view of the city. It was totally lightless, but in some way he sensed the outlines of the buildings. Then the point of view descended until he was looking down from directly above the library; and it gave him an odd vertigo to see, in the seat from which he was viewing, a figure seated. Whatever was transmitting the images began to move along the street bordering the library, traversed a straight road directly to a widening of the road, and showed him the mine-pit a few yards further on.

The transmitter, however, now seemed to be working independent of his will. Now it tracked back six hundred yards or so up the road, to a junction with a wider street at the right. Taylor realized that something important was to follow. It moved up the branching street, and he saw that the buildings ended a few yards further on; from there a rougher path stretched to the edge of a pit, much larger than the first. The transmitter moved forward, stopping at the edge of the buildings. He willed it to go closer, but it remained in that position. When he persisted, a loud noise made him start; it was only part of the transmission—not like a voice, it resembled glass surfaces vibrating together, but forming definite patterns. Perhaps it was a voice, but its message was meaningless—what did *xada-hgla soron* signify? Whatever it meant, the phrase was repeated seven times, then the image disappeared.

Baffled, he rose. He had been unable to glean any further information from the discs. The larger pit was further, but it would contain more mineral; and the buildings did not crowd so close to it, hence the danger of interruption was less likely. He decided to head for it.

When he reached the junction, he hesitated briefly, then remembering the squat black towers which had encircled the nearer mine, he turned off to the right. His shoes clanked on the black pavement and crunched on the rocks of the continuing path. The beam of the torch trembled on the crumbling rim, and then he stood on the edge of the pit. He looked down.

At first he saw nothing. Dust-motes rising from below tinted the beam a translucent green, but it showed nothing except a wavering disc of black rock on the opposite wall. The disc grew and dimmed as it descended, but dim as it was it finally outlined the ledge outcropping from the rock, and what stood upon it.

There is nothing horrible about a group of tall deserted pyramids, even when those pyramids are constructed of a pale green material which glitters and seems to move in the half-light. Something else caused Taylor to stare in fascination; the way the emerald cones were drinking in the light from his torch, while the bulb dimmed visibly. He peered downward, awaiting something which he felt must come.

The torch-bulb flickered and went out, leaving him in total darkness.

In the blackness he unscrewed the end of the torch and let the dead battery clatter far down the rock surface. Drawing the last battery from his pocket, he fumbled blindly with the pieces of metal, squinting into the darkness, and saw the torch in his hands. It was faintly limned by the glow from beneath, growing clearer as he watched. He could see the distant side of the pit now, and, noting the grating metallic sound which had begun below him, he looked down into the green light.

Something was climbing toward him up the rock face; something which slithered up from the rock ledge, glowing greenly. It was vast and covered with green surfaces which ground together, but it had a shape—and that was what made Taylor flee from the miles-deep pit, clattering down the ebon pavements, not switching on the torch until he collided with a black spire beyond the widening radius of the green light, not stopping until he reached the frustum-shaped building he remembered and the tower near it. He threw himself up the outer steps recklessly, crawled on all fours and swung from the catwalks, and reached the last roof.

He glanced across the tower roofs once, then heaved open the trapdoor and plunged down the unlit steps, through the searing barrier across the passage and clattered down into the blinding daylight, half-fell down the Devil's Steps and reached the car. Somewhere what he had glimpsed at the last was still moving—that green-radiating shape which heaved and pulsed above the steeples, toppling them and putting forth glowing arms to engulf fleeing dwarved forms...

When passers-by telephoned the Brichester police after hearing unusual sounds from a house on South Abbey Avenue, few of the documents in that house had not been destroyed by Taylor. The police called in the Mercy Hill doctors, who could only take him to the hospital. He became violent when they refused to explore the Devil's Steps, but when they tried to reassure him with promises of exploration he protested so demonstratively that he was removed to the Camside Home for the Mentally Disturbed. There he could only lie repeating feverishly:

"You fools, why don't you stop them going up the Steps? They'll be dragged into space—lungs burst—blue faces...And suppose *It* didn't destroy the city entirely—suppose *It* was intelligent? If *It* knew about the towers into other parts of space, *It* might find its way through onto the Steps—*It's* coming down the stairs through the barrier now—*It'll* push through the forest and into the town...Outside the window! *It's rising above the houses!*

Edward Taylor's case yet stirs controversy among doctors, and is a subject for exaggerated speculation in Sunday newspaper features. Of course the writers of the latter do not know all the facts; if they did their tone would certainly be different, but the doctors felt it unwise to reveal all that had happened to Taylor.

This is why the X-ray photographs taken of Taylor's body are carefully restricted to a hospital file. At first glance they would seem normal, and the layman might not notice any abnormality even upon close examination. It takes a doctor to see that the lungs, although they function perfectly, do not resemble in any respect the lungs of a human being.

J ames Wade *left us a handful of very entertaining Mythos tales. The two longest are "The Deep Ones," which appeared in the original edition of* Tales of the Cthulhu Mythos *(1969) and "Those Who Wait," an early fanzine story which saw print years after young Wade penned it in the first issue of* The Dark Brotherhood Journal. *It appears also in my anthology* The New Lovecraft Circle *(Fedogan & Bremer, 1994). Another substantial tale was "The Silence of Erika Zann," which was included in Edward Paul Berglund's anthology* The Disciples of Cthulhu *(1976).*

"A Darker Shadow Over Innsmouth" and "Planetfall on Yuggoth," both very short pieces, saw print, respectively, in The Arkham Collector #5, Summer, 1969, *and* HPL *edited by Penny and Meade Frierson in 1972.*

With the exception of the fannish "Those Who Wait," all of Wade's stories, unconnected as they may be, are based on the fundamental premise of updating the familiar Lovecraftian lore and legend and making it relevant to the fast-paced world of the 1960s and 70s. Dolphin research, drop-out drug gurus, nuclear weapons protests, the space race, acid rock: it was all there and decorated the stage for Wade's Lovecraftian ventures. This very fact, ironically, inevitably dates the stories and makes them quaint period pieces. But Wade's tales are so well written that they are still just as enjoyable, if not for their up-to-the-minute relevance, then for their nostalgic and antiquarian value.

And "Planetfall on Yuggoth" is in a sense just as much a sequel to "The Whisperer in Darkness" as Lupoff's "Documents in the Case of Elizabeth Akeley," since it jumps off from the ominous note struck at the close of Lovecraft's tale, when he bemoans the interest lately shown by scientists in the newly revealed planet which they call Pluto, but we know better as Yuggoth. In Wade's story we get to see what happens decades later when that scientific curiosity comes to fruition.

Planetfall on Yuggoth

by JAMES WADE

By the time the Pluto landing was scheduled, people were tired of planetfall stories. The first human on the moon may have taken a giant step for mankind, as he claimed; but in the half-century following, each succeeding stage in the exploration of the solar system became more boring than the last. The technology was foolproof, the risks minimal, and most of the discoveries—while epoch-making for all the sciences—were too complex and recondite to be dramatized for the man in the street, or in front of his Tri-V screen.

They even stopped giving the various expeditions fancy names, like that first Project Apollo to the moon, or Operation Ares, the Mars landing. They actually let one of the crewmen of the space craft—a radio operator named Carnovsky—name the Pluto jaunt, and he called it "Operation Yuggoth," frivolously enough, after the name for the planet used in pulp fiction by some obscure author of the last century.

Of course, the media dutifully carried the same stale old textbook research about how Pluto, the last planet to be discovered and the last to experience human visitation, was merely a tiny chunk of frozen gunk over three and a half billion miles from the Earth that took 248 earth years to circle the sun, and how if the sun was the size of a pumpkin (which it is not, so it was hard to make sense out of the comparison) Pluto would be a pea about two miles away, and how it was probably once a moon of Neptune that broke away into a very irregular orbit and thus possibly didn't qualify as a real planet at all.

The whole upshot seemed to be that here was another airless, lifeless, frozen world like all the others not on our sunward side—in which latter case they were airless, lifeless, sizzling worlds.

After the invention of the long-predicted nuclear fission drive, even such vast distances were minimized; the trip would have taken only two weeks from Earth, and from the deep space station beyond Mars it wouldn't last *that* long.

No one except scientists expressed any disappointment that remoteness did forbid live Tri-V transmission, and they'd just have to wait for the films. The fact that a brief on-the-scene radio report was scheduled to be relayed via several earthside beams even drew complaints from a few music buffs.

We had all seen pictures of the ship before (or ones just like it): a pair of huge metal globes connected by a narrow passage, never destined to touch the surface of any world—the little chemical-fuel scouts did all the real exploring.

Altogether, it was shaping up as a megabore.

The broadcast promised to be even more tedious than the build-up. Arrived in orbit over Pluto, the space craft reported no glimpse of the planet's topography, due to a cloud of frozen mist—which, however, analyzed as not too dense for the scouts to penetrate. There was a lot of delay while the first scout was prepared and launched, carrying the radioman Carnovsky who had dreamed up the Operation Yuggoth tag and five other crewmen.

Carnovsky gave a running account as the small rocket approached the surface and grounded. First he spoke of milky, churning mists hovering over the vast icefields, half-discerned under their high-power searchlights. Then, with mounting excitement, the crackling inter-planetary transmission reported a lifting and clearing of the fog. Next came a gasp of awe and that incoherent babbling which was traced in part later to garbled, half-remembered quotations from the pulp writer who had fantasized so long ago about dark Yuggoth.

Had Carnovsky gone mad? Did he somehow kill his fellow crewmen on the scout, after planting a time-bomb on the spaceship before they left it? In any event, no further transmission was ever received from either vessel after the hysterical voice from the scout abruptly broke off.

This is how the broadcast ended: "Mists are clearing—something big towering up dead ahead—is it a mountain range? No, the shapes are too regular. My God! It can't be! It's a city! Great tiers of terraced towers built of black stone—rivers of pitch that flow under cyclopean bridges, a dark world of fungoid gardens and windowless cities—an unknown world of fungous life—forbidden Yuggoth!

"Is that something moving over the ice? How is it possible in this cold? But there are many of them, heading this way. The Outer Ones, the Outer Ones! Living fungi, like great clumsy crabs with membra-nous wings and squirming knots of tentacles for heads!

"They're coming. They're getting close! I—"

That was all; except that those few on Earth—those who were not watching the variety shows on their Tri-V's but who were outside for some reason and looking at that sector of the sky where Pluto is located—experienced the startling sight of a bursting pinpoint of light

as, over three and a half billion miles away, the atomic fuel of the
spacecraft bloomed into an apocalyptic nova, writing finis to the
ill-fated expedition, and to Operation Yuggoth.

But scientists don't discourage easily. They admit that Pluto may
hold some unsurmised danger—though certainly not connected with
Carnovsky's hallucinations—and it may be best to stay away while
unmanned probes gather more data.

Now, though, they're all excited about the plan to send a manned
ship to a newly-discovered, unimaginably remote tenth planet that
hasn't even been named yet.

The new project, for some reason, has been dubbed "Operation
Shaggai."

Young August Derleth (1909-1971) sent the following story to Clark Ashton Smith, asking for criticism, but apparently only fishing for compliments, since of the former CAS had much to offer, and Derleth ignored all of it. As it stands, generations of readers have found the tale quite enjoyable, but it is nonetheless fascinating to imagine it as it might have been had Derleth incorporated the revisions Smith suggested in a letter of April 28, 1937:

...you have tried to work in too much of the Lovecraft mythology and have not assimilated it into the natural body of the story. For my taste, the tale would gain in unity and power if the interest were centered wholly about the mysterious and "unspeakable" Hastur. Cthulhu and the sea-things of Innsmouth, though designed to afford an element and interest *of conflict*, impress me rather as a source of confusion. I believe a tremendous effect of vague menacing atmosphere and eerily growing tension could be developed around Hastur, who has the advantage of being a virtually unknown demon. Also, this effect could be deepened by a more prolonged incredulity on the part of Paul Tuttle and Haddon, who should not accept the monstrous implications of the old books and the strange after-clause of Amos Tuttle's bond until the accumulation and linking of weird phenomena leaves them no possible alternative. One of the best things in the tale is the description of those interdimensional footsteps that resound beneath the menaced mansion. These could be related significantly to Hastur alone by having them seem to mount by degrees on the eastern side of the house, reverberate like strange thunder in the heavens above, and descend on the west in a regular rotation, to echo again in the subterrene depths. Eventually it would be forced upon the hearers that this rotation was *coincidental with the progress of Aldebaran and the Hyades through the heavens*; thus heralding the encroachment of Hastur from his ultrastellar lair. More could be made of the part about Amos Tuttle's corpse and its unearthly changes: the coffin could show evidence of having been violently disrupted from *within*; and the footprints in he field, though monstrous in size, could present a vaguely human conformation, like those of some legendary giant; and Tuttle's corpse, when found, would have burst open in numberless places as if through some superhuman inflation of all its tissues; showing that the unknown entity *had* occupied it but had soon found it *useless on account of the increasing corruption*. At the climax, just before the house is dynamited, a colossal figure might rise out of [it] mingling the features and members of Paul Tuttle with the transcosmic monstrosity of Hastur; and this shape, because of its *mortal* elements, could be shattered and destroyed by the explosion, compelling Hastur to recede invisibly though with soul-shaking footsteps towards the Hyades. Some fragment of the incredibly swollen and gigantic energumen might survive the explosion, to be buried hastily, with shudders and averted glances, by the finders.

The Return of Hastur

by AUGUST W. DERLETH

Actually, it began a long time ago: how long, I have not dared to guess: but so far as is concerned my own connection with the case that has ruined my practice and earned me the dubiety of the medical profession in regard to my sanity, it began with Amos Tuttle's death. That was on a night in late winter, with a south wind blowing on the edge of spring. I had been in ancient, legend-haunted Arkham that day; he had learned of my presence there from Doctor Ephraim Sprague, who attended him, and had the doctor call the Lewiston House and bring me to that gloomy estate on the Aylesbury Road near the Innsmouth Turnpike. It was not a place to which I liked to go, but the old man had paid me well to tolerate his sullenness and eccentricity, and Sprague had made it clear that he was dying: a matter of hours.

And he was. He had hardly the strength to motion Sprague from the room and talk to me, though his voice came clearly enough and with little effort.

"You know my will," he said. "Stand by it to the letter."

That will had been a bone of contention between us because of its provision that before his heir and sole surviving nephew, Paul Tuttle, could claim his estate, the house would have to be destroyed—not taken down, but destroyed, together with certain books designated by shelf number in his final instructions. His death-bed was no place to debate this wanton destruction anew; I nodded and he accepted that. Would to heaven I had obeyed without question!

"Now then," he went on, "there's a book downstairs you must take back the the library of Miskatonic University."

He gave me the title. At that time it meant little to me; but it has since come to mean more than I can say—a symbol of age-old horror, of maddening things beyond the thin veil of prosaic daily life—the Latin translation of the abhorred *Necronomicon* by the mad Arab, Abdul Alhazred.

I found the book easily enough. For the last two decades of his life Amos Tuttle had lived in increasing seclusion among books collected from all parts of the world: old, worm-eaten texts, with titles that might have frightened away a less hardened man—the sinister *De Vermis Mysteriis* of Ludvig Prinn, Comte d'Erlette's terrible *Cultes de Ghoules*, von Junzt's damnable *Unaussprechlichen Kulten*. I did not know then how rare these were, nor did I understand the priceless rarity of certain fragmentary pieces: the frightful *Book of Eibon*, the horror-fraught *Pnakotic Manuscripts*, and the dread *R'lyeh Text*; for these, I found upon an examination of his accounts after Amos Tuttle's death, he had paid a fabulous sum. But nowhere did I find so high a figure as that he had paid for the *R'lyeh Text*, which had come to him from somewhere in the dark interior of Asia; according to his files, he had paid for it no less than one hundred thousand dollars; but in addition to this, there was present in his account in regard to this yellowed manuscript a notation which puzzled me at the time, but which I was to have ominous cause to remember—after the sum above mentioned, Amos Tuttle had written in his spidery hand: *in addition to the promise.*

These facts did not come out until Paul Tuttle was in possession, but before that, several strange occurrences took place, things that should have aroused my suspicion in regard to the countryside legends of some powerful supernatural influence clinging to the old house. The first of these was of small consequence in view of the others; it was simply that upon returning the *Necronomicon* to the library of Miskatonic University at Arkham, I found myself conveyed by a tight-lipped librarian straightway to the office of the director, Doctor Llanfer, who asked me bluntly to account for the book's being in my hands. I had no hesitation in doing so, and thereby discovered that the rare volume was never permitted out of the library, that, in fact, Amos Tuttle had abstracted it on one of his rare visits, having failed in his attempts to persuade Doctor Llanfer to permit his borrowing it. And Amos had been clever enough to prepare in advance a marvelously good imitation of the book, with a binding almost flawless in its resemblance, and the actual reproduction of title and opening pages of the text reproduced from his memory; upon the occasion of his handling the mad Arab's book, he had substituted his dummy for the original and gone off with one of the two copies of this shunned work available on the North American continent, one of the five copies known to be in existence in the world.

The second of these things was a little more startling, though it bears the trappings of conventional haunted house stories. Both Paul Tuttle and I heard at odd times in the house at night, while his uncle's corpse lay there particularly, the sound of padding footsteps, but there was this strangeness about them: they were not like footsteps falling within the house at all, but like the steps of some creature in size almost beyond the conception of man walking at a great distance *underground,* so that the sound actually *vibrated* into the house from the depths of earth below. And when I have reference to steps, it is only for lack of a better word to describe the sounds, for they were not flat steps at all, but a kind of spongy, jelly-like, sloshing sound made with the force of so much weight behind them that the consequent shuddering of earth in that place was communicated to us in the way we heard it. There was nothing more than this, and presently it was gone, ceasing, coincidentally enough, in the hours of that dawn when Amos Tuttle's corpse was borne away forty-eight hours sooner than we had planned. The sounds we dismissed as settlings of the earth along the distant coast, not alone because we did not attach too great an importance to them, but because of the final thing that took place before Paul Tuttle officially took possession of the old house on Aylesbury Road.

This last thing was the most shocking of all, and of the three who knew it, only I now remain alive, Doctor Sprague being dead this day month, though he took only one look and said, "Bury him at once!" And so we did, for the change in Amos Tuttle's body was ghastly beyond conception, and especially horrible in its suggestion, and it was so because the body was *not* falling into any visible decay, but changing subtly in another way, becoming suffused with a weird iridescence, which darkened presently until it was almost ebon, and the appearance on the flesh of his puffy hands and face of minute, scale-like growth. There was likewise some change about the shape of his head; it seemed to lengthen, to take on a curious kind of fish-like look, accompanied by a faint exudation of thick fish smell from the coffin; and that these changes were not purely imaginative was shockingly substantiated when the body was subsequently found in the place where its malignant after-dweller had conveyed it, and there, at last falling into putrefaction though it was, others saw with me the terrible, suggestive changes that had taken place, though they had mercifully no knowledge of what had gone before. But at the time when Amos Tuttle lay in the old house, there was no hint of what was to come; we were quick to close the coffin and quicker still to take it to the ivy-covered Tuttle vault in Arkham cemetery.

Paul Tuttle was at that time in his late forties, but, like so many men of his generation, he had the face and figure of a youth in his twenties. Indeed, the only hint of his age lay in the faint traces of gray in the hair of his moustache and temples. He was a tall, dark-haired man, slightly overweight, with frank blue eyes which years of scholarly research had not reduced to the necessity of glasses. Nor was he ignorant of law, for he quickly made known that if I, as his uncle's executor, were not disposed to overlook the clause in his will that called for the destruction of the house on the Aylesbury Road, he would contest the will on the justifiable ground of Amos Tuttle's insanity. I pointed out to him that he stood alone against Doctor Sprague and me, but I was at the same time not blind to the fact that the unreasonableness of the request might very well defeat us; besides, I myself considered the clause in this regard amazingly wanton in the destruction it demanded, and was not prepared to fight a contest because of so minor a matter. Yet, could I have foreseen what was to come, could I have dreamed of the horror to follow, I would have carried out Amos Tuttle's last request regardless of any decision of the court. However, such foresight was not mine.

We went to see Judge Wilton, Tuttle and I, and put the matter before him. He agreed with us that the destruction of the house seemed needless, and more than once hinted at concurrence with Paul Tuttle's belief in his late uncle's madness.

"The old man's been touched for as long as I knew him," he said dryly. "And as for you, Haddon, can you get up on a stand and swear that he was absolutely sane?"

Remembering with a certain uneasiness the theft of the *Necronomicon* from Miskatonic University, I had to confess that I could not. So Paul Tuttle took possession of the estate on the Aylesbury Road, and I went back to my legal practice in Boston, not dissatisfied with the way things had gone, and yet not without a lurking uneasiness difficult to define, an insidious feeling of impending tragedy, no little fed by my memory of what we had seen in Amos Tuttle's coffin before we sealed and locked it away in the centuries-old vault in Arkham cemetery.

II

It was not for some time that I saw the gambrel roofs and Georgian balustrades of witch-cursed Arkham again, and then was there on business for a client who wished me to see to it that his property in ancient Innsmouth was protected from the Government agents and police who had taken possession of the shunned and haunted town, though it was now some months since the mysterious dynamiting of blocks of the waterfront buildings and part of the terror-hung Devil Reef in the sea beyond—a mystery which has been carefully guarded and hidden since then, though I have learned of a paper purporting to give the true facts of the Innsmouth horror, a privately published manuscript written by a Providence author. It was impossible at that time to proceed to Innsmouth because Secret Service men had closed all roads; however, I made representations to the proper persons and received an assurance that my client's property would be fully protected, since it lay well back from the waterfront; so I proceeded about other small matters in Arkham.

I went to luncheon that day in a small restaurant near Miskatonic University, and while there, heard myself accosted in a familiar voice. I looked up and saw Doctor Llanfer, the university library's director. He seemed somewhat upset, and betrayed his concern clearly in his features. I invited him to join me, but he declined; he did, however, sit down, somewhat on the chair's edge.

"Have you been out to see Paul Tuttle?" he asked abruptly.

"I thought of going this afternoon," I replied. "Is anything wrong?"

He flushed a little guiltily. "That I can't say," he answered precisely. "But there have been some nasty rumors loose in Arkham. And the *Necronomicon* is gone again."

"Good Heaven! you're surely not accusing Paul Tuttle of having taken it?" I exclaimed, half in surprise, half amused. "I could not imagine of what use it might be to him."

"Still—he has it," Doctor Llanfer persisted. "But I don't think he stole it, and should not like to be understood as saying so. It is my opinion that one of our clerks gave it to him and is now reluctant to confess the enormity of his error. Be that as it may, the book has not come back, and I fear we shall have to go after it."

"I could ask him about it," I said.

"If you would, thank you," responded Docter Llanfer, a little eagerly. "I take it you've heard nothing of the rumors that are rife here?"

I shook my head.

"Very likely they are only the outgrowth of some imaginative mind," he continued, but the air of him suggested that he was not willing or able to accept so prosaic an explanation. "It appears that passengers along the Aylesbury Road have heard strange sounds late at night, all apparently emanating from the Tuttle house."

"What sounds?" I asked, not without immediate apprehension.

"Apparently, those of footsteps; and yet, I understand no one will definitely say so, save for one young man who characterized them as *soggy* and said that they sounded as if *something big were walking in mud and water near by.*"

The strange sounds Paul Tuttle and I had heard on the night following Amos Tuttle's death had passed from my mind, but at this mention of footsteps by Doctor Llanfer, the memory of what I had heard returned in full. I fear I gave myself slightly away, for Doctor Llanfer observed my sudden interest; fortunately, he chose to interpret it as evidence that I had indeed heard something of these rumors, my statement to the contratry notwithstanding. I did not choose to correct him in this regard, and at the same time I experienced a sudden desire to hear no more; so I did not press him for further details, and presently he rose to return to his duties, and left me with my promise to ask Paul Tuttle for the missing book still sounding in my ears.

His story, however slight it was, nevertheless sounded within me a note of alarm; I could not help recalling the numerous small things that held to memory—the steps we had heard, the odd clause in Amos Tuttle's will, the awful metamorphosis in Amos Tuttle's corpse. There was already then a faint suspicion in my mind that some sinister chain of events was becoming manifest here; my natural curiosity rose, though not without a certain feeling of distaste, a conscious desire to withdraw, and the recurrence of that strange, insidious conviction of impending tragedy. But I determined to see Paul Tuttle as early as possible.

My work in Arkham consumed the afternoon, and it was not until dusk that I found myself standing before the massive oaken door of the old Tuttle house on Aylesbury Road. My rather peremptory knock was answered by Paul himself, who stood, lamp held high in hand, peering out into the growing night.

"Haddon!" he exclaimed, throwing the door wider. "Come in!"

That he was genuinely glad to see me I could not doubt, for the note of enthusiasm in his voice precluded any other supposition. The heartiness of his welcome also served to confirm me in my intention not to speak of the rumors I had heard, and to proceed about an inquiry after the *Necronomicon* at my own good time. I remembered that just prior to his uncle's death, Tuttle had been working on a philological treatise relating to the growth of the Sac Indian language, and determined to inquire about this paper as if nothing else were of moment.

"You've had supper, I suppose," said Tuttle, leading me down the hall and into the library.

I said that I had eaten in Arkham.

He put the lamp down upon a book-laden table, pushing some papers to one side as he did so. Inviting me to sit down, he resumed the seat he had evidently left to answer my knock. I saw now that he was somewhat disheveled, and that he had permitted his beard to grow. He had also taken on more weight, doubtless as a consequence of strictly enforced scholarship, with all its attendant confinement to the house and lack of physical exercise.

"How fares the Sac treatise?" I asked.

"I've put that aside," he said shortly. "I may take it up later. For the present, I've struck something far more important—just how important I cannot yet say."

I saw now that the books on the tables were not the usual scholarly tomes I had seen on his Ipswich desk, but with some faint apprehension observed that they were the books condemned by the explicit instructions of Tuttle's uncle, as a glance at the vacant spaces on the proscribed shelves clearly corroborated.

Tuttle turned to me almost eagerly and lowered his voice as if in fear of being overheard. "As a matter of fact, Haddon, it's colossal—a gigantic feat of the imagination; only for this: I'm no longer certain that it *is* imaginative, indeed, I'm not. I wondered about that clause in my uncle's will; I couldn't understand why he should want this house destroyed, and rightly surmised that the reason must lie somewhere in the pages of those books he so carefully condemned." He waved a hand at the incunabula before him. "So I examined them, and I can tell you I have discovered things of such incredible strangeness, such bizarre horror, that I hesitate sometimes to dig deeper into the mystery. Frankly, Haddon, it is the most *outré* matter I've ever come upon, and I must say it involved considerable research, quite apart from these books Uncle Amos collected."

"Indeed," I said dryly. "And I dare say you've had to do considerable travelling?"

He shook his head. "None at all, apart from one trip to Miskatonic University Library. The fact is, I found I could be served just as well by mail. You'll remember those papers of uncle's? Well, I discovered among them that Uncle Amos paid a hundred thousand for a certain bound manuscript—bound in human skin, incidentally—together with a cryptic line: *in addition to the promise.* I began to ask myself what promise Uncle Amos could have made, and to whom; whether to the man or woman who had sold him this *R'lyeh Text* or to some other. I proceeded forthwith to search out the name of the man who had sold him the book, and presently found it with his address: some Chinese priest from inner Tibet: and wrote to him. His reply reached me a week ago."

He bent away and rummaged briefly among the papers on his desk, until he found what he sought and handed it to me.

"I wrote in my uncle's name not trusting entirely in the transaction, and wrote, moreover, as if I had forgotten or had a hope to avoid the promise," he continued. "His reply is fully as cryptic as my uncle's notation."

Indeed, it was so, for the crumpled paper that was handed to me bore, in a strange, stilted script, but one line, without signature or date: *To afford a haven for Him Who is not to be Named.*

I dare say I looked up at Tuttle with my wonderment clearly mirrored in my eyes, for he smiled before he replied.

"Means nothing to you, eh? No more did it to me, when first I saw it. But not for long. In order to understand what follows, you should know at least a brief outline of the mythology—if indeed it *is* only mythology—in which this mystery is rooted. My Uncle Amos apparently knew and believed all about it, for the various notes scattered in the margins of his proscribed books bespeak a knowledge far beyond mine. Apparently the mythology springs from a common source with our own legendary Genesis, but only by a very thin resemblance; sometimes I am tempted to say that this mythology is far older than any other—certainly in its implications it goes far beyond, being cosmic and ageless, for its beings are of two natures, and two only: the Old or Ancient Ones, the Elder Gods, of *cosmic good,* and those of *cosmic evil,* bearing many names, and themselves of different groups, as if associated with the elements and yet transcending them: for there are the Water Beings, hidden in the depths; those of Air that are the primal lurkers beyond time; those of Earth, horrible animate survivals of distant eons. Incredible time ago, the Old Ones banished from the cosmic places all the Evil Ones, imprisoning them in many places; but in time these Evil Ones spawned hellish minions who set about preparing for their return to greatness. The Old Ones are nameless, but their power is and will apparently always be great enough to check that of the others.

"Now, among the Evil Ones there is apparently often conflict, as among lesser beings. The Water Beings oppose those of Air; the Fire Beings oppose Earth Beings, but nevertheless, they together hate and fear the Elder Gods and hope always to defeat them in some future time. Among my Uncle Amos's papers there are many fearsome names written in his crabbed script: *Great Cthulhu, the Lake of Hali, Tsathoggua, Yog-Sothoth, Nyarlathotep, Azathoth, Hastur the Unspeakable, Yuggoth, Aldones, Thale, Aldebaran, the Hyades, Carcosa,* and others: and it is possible to divide some of these names into vaguely suggestive classes from those notes which are explicable to me—though many present insoluble mysteries I cannot hope as yet to penetrate; and many, too, are written in a language I do not know, together with cryptic and oddly frightening symbols and signs. But through what I have learned, it is possible to know that Great Cthulhu is one of the Water Beings, even as Hastur is of the Beings that stalk the star-spaces; and it is possible to gather from vague hints in these forbidden books where some of these beings are. So I can believe that in this mythology, Great Cthulhu was banished to a place beneath the seas of Earth, while Hastur was hurled into outer space, into that *place where the black stars hang*, which is indicated as Aldebaran of the Hyades, which is the place mentioned by Chambers, even as he repeates the *Carcosa* of Bierce.

"Coming upon this communication from the priest in Tibet in the light of these things, surely one fact must come clearly forth: Haddon, surely, beyond the shadow of a doubt, He Who is not to be Named can be none other than Hastur the Unspeakable!"

The sudden cessation of his voice startled me; there was something hypnotic about his eager whisper, and something too that filled me with a conviction far beyond the power of Paul Tuttle's words. Somewhere, deep within the recesses of my mind, a chord had been struck, a mnemonic connection I could not dismiss or trace and which left me with a feeling as of limitless age, a cosmic bridge into another place and time.

"That seem logical," I said at last, cautiously.

"Logical! Haddon, it *is;* it must be!" he exclaimed.

"Granting it," I said, "what then?"

"Why, granting it," he went on quickly, "we have conceded that my Uncle Amos promised to make ready a haven in preparation for the return of Hastur from whatever region of outer space now imprisons him. Where that haven is, or what manner of place it may be, has not thus far been my concern, though I can guess, perhaps. This is not the time for guessing, and yet it would seem, from certain other evidence at hand, that there may be some permissible deductions made. The first and most important of these is of a double nature—ergo, something unforeseen prevented the return of Hastur within my uncle's lifetime, and yet some other being has made itself manifest." Here he looked at me with unusual frankness and not a little nervousness. "As for the evidence of this manifestation, I would rather not at this time go into it. Suffice it to say that I believe I have such evidence at hand. I return to my original premise, then.

"Among the few marginal notations made by my uncle, there are two or three especially remarkable ones in the *R'lyeh Text;* indeed, in the light of what is known or can justifiably be guessed, they are sinister and ominous notes."

So speaking, he opened the ancient manuscript and turned to a place quite close to the beginning of the narrative.

"Now attend me, Haddon," he said, and I rose and bent over him to look at the spidery, almost illegible script that I knew for Amos Tuttle's. "Observe the underscored line of text: *Ph'nglui mglw'nafh Cthulhu R'lyeh wgah' nagl fhtagn,* and what follows it in my uncle's unmistakable hand: *His minions preparing the way, and he no longer dreaming? (WT:2/28)* and at a more recent date, to judge by the shakiness of his hand, the single abbreviation: *Inns!* Obviously, this means nothing without a translation of the text. Failing this at the moment I first saw this note, I turned my attention to the parenthetical notation, and within a short while solved its meaning as a reference to a popular magazine, *Weird Tales,* for February, 1928. I have it here."

He opened the magazine against the meaningless text, partially concealing the lines which had begun to take on an uncanny atmosphere of eldritch age beneath my eyes, and there beneath Paul Tuttle's hand lay the first page of a story so obviously belonging to this unbelievable mythology that I could not repress a start of astonishment. The title, only partly covered by his hand, was *The Call of Cthulhu,* by H. P. Lovecraft. But Tuttle did not linger over the first page; he turned well into the heart of the story before he paused and presented to my gaze the identical unreadable line that lay beside the crabbed script of Amos Tuttle in the incredibly rare *R'lyeh Text* upon which the magazine reposed. And there, only a paragraph below, appeared what purported to be a translation of the utterly unknown language of the *Text: In his house at R'lyeh dead Cthulhu waits dreaming.*

"There you have it," resumed Tuttle with some satisfaction. "Cthulhu, too, waited for the time of his resurgence—how many eons, no one may know; but my uncle has questioned whether Cthulhu still lies dreaming, and following this, has written and doubly underscored an abbreviation which can only stand for *Innsmouth!* This, together with the ghastly things half hinted in this revealing story purporting to be only *fiction,* opens up a vista of undreamed horror, of age-old evil."

"Good Heaven!" I exclaimed involuntarily. "Surely you can't think this fantasy has come to life?"

Tuttle turned and gave me a strangely distant look. "What *I* think doesn't matter, Haddon," he replied gravely. "But there is one thing I would like very much to know—what happened at *Innsmouth?* What has happened there for decades past that people have shunned it so? Why has this once prosperous port sunk into oblivion, half its houses empty, its property practically worthless? And why was it necessary for Government men to blow up row after row of the waterfront dwellings and warehouses? Lastly, for what earthly reason did they send a submarine to torpedo the marine spaces beyond Devil Reef just out of Innsmouth?"

"I know nothing of that," I replied.

But he paid no heed; his voice rose a little, uncertain and trembling, and he said, "I can tell you, Haddon. It is even as my Uncle Amos has written: Great Cthulhu has risen again!"

For a moment I was shaken; then I said, "But it is Hastur for whom he waited."

"Precisely," agreed Tuttle in a clipped, professorial voice. "Then I should like to know who or what it is that walks in the earth in the dark hours when Fomalhaut has risen and the Hyades are in the east!"

III

With this, he abruptly changed the subject; he began to ask me questions about myself and my practice, and presently, when I rose to go, he asked me to stay the night. This I consented finally, and with some reluctance, to do, whereupon he departed at once to make a room ready for me. I took the opportunity thus afforded to examine his desk more closely for the *Necronomicon* missing from the library of Miskatonic University. It was not on his desk, but, crossing to the shelves, I found it there. I had just taken it down and was examining it to make certain of its identity, when Tuttle reëntered the room. His quick eyes darted to the book in my hands, and he half smiled.

"I wish you'd take that back to Doctor Llanfer when you go in the morning, Haddon," he said casually. "Now that I've copied the text, I have no further use for it."

"I'll do that gladly," I said, relieved that the matter could so easily be settled.

Shortly after, I retired to the room on the second floor which he had prepared for me. He accompanied me as far as the door, and there paused briefly, uncertain of speech ready for his tongue and yet not permitted to pass his lips; for he turned once or twice, bade me goodnight before he spoke what weighed upon his thoughts: "By the way—if you hear anything in the night, don't be alarmed, Haddon. Whatever it is, it's harmless—as yet."

It was not until he had gone and I was alone in my room that the significance of what he had said and the way he had said it dawned upon me. It grew upon me then that this was confirmation of the wild rumors that had penetrated Arkham, and that Tuttle spoke not entirely without fear. I undressed slowly and thoughtfully, and got into the pajamas Tuttle had laid out for me, without deviating for an instant from the preoccupation with the weird mythology of Amos Tuttle's ancient books that held my mind. Never quick to pass judgment, I was not prone to do so now; despite the apparent absurdity of the structure, it was still sufficiently well erected to merit more than a casual scrutiny. And it was clear to me that Tuttle was more than half convinced of its truth. This in itself was more than enough to give me pause, for Paul Tuttle had distinguished himself time and again for the thoroughness of his researches, and his published papers had not been challenged for even their most minor detail. As a result of facing these facts, I was prepared to admit at least that there was some basis for the mythology-structure outlined to me by Tuttle, but as to its truth or error, of course I was in no position at that time to commit myself even within the confines of my own mind; for once a man concedes or condemns a thing within his mind, it is doubly, nay triply, difficult to rid himself of his conclusion, however ill-advised it may subsequently prove to be.

Thinking thus, I got into bed, and lay there awaiting sleep. The night had deepened and darkened, though I could see through the flimsy curtain at the window that the stars were out, Andromeda high in the east, and the constellations of autumn beginning to mount the sky.

I was on the edge of sleep when I was startled awake again by a sound which had been present for some time, but which had only just then been borne in upon me with all its significance: the faintly trembling step of some gigantic creature vibrating all through the house, though the sound of it came not from within the house, but from the east, and for a confused moment I thought of something risen from the sea and walking along the shore in the wet sand.

But this illusion passed when I raised myself on one elbow and listened more intently. For a moment there was no sound whatever; then it came again, irregularly, broken—a step, a pause, two steps in fairly quick succession, an odd *sucking* noise. Disturbed, I got up and went to the open window. The night was warm, and the still air almost sultry; far to the northeast a beacon cut an arc upon the sky, and from the distant north came the faint drone of a night plane. It was already past midnight; low in the east shone red Aldebaran and the Pleiades, but I did not at that time, as I did later, connect the disturbances I heard to the appearance of the Hyades above the horizon.

The odd sounds, meanwhile, continued unabated, and it was borne in upon me presently that they were indeed approaching the house, however slow their progress. And that they came from the direction of the sea I could not doubt, for in this place there were no configurations of the earth that might have thrown any sound out of directional focus. I began to think again of those similar sounds we had heard while Amos Tuttle's body lay in the house, though I did not then remember that even as the Hyades lay now low in the east, so they were then setting in the west. If there were any difference in the manner of their approach, I was not able to ascertain it, unless it was that the present disturbances seemed somehow *closer*, but it was not a physical closeness as much as a psychic *closeness*. The conviction of this was so strong that I began to feel a growing uneasiness not untinged with fear; I began to experience a wild restlessness, a desire for company; and I went quickly to the door of my room, opened it, and stepped quietly into the hall in search of my host.

But now at once a new discovery made itself known. As long as I had been in my room, the sounds I had heard seemed unquestionably to come from the east, notwithstanding the faint, almost intangible tremors that seemed to shudder through the old house; but here in the darkness of the hall, whither I had gone without a light of any kind, I became aware that the sounds and tremblings alike emanated from *below*—not, indeed, from any place in the house, but below that—rising as if from subterranean places. My nervous tension increased, and I stood uneasily to get my bearings in the dark, when I perceived in the direction of the stairway a faint radiance mounting from below. I moved toward it at once, noiselessly, and, looking over the banister, saw that the light came from an electric candle held in Paul Tuttle's hand. He was standing in the lower hall, clad in his dressing-gown, though it was clear to me even from where I stood that he had not removed his clothes. The light that fell upon his face revealed the intensity of his attention; his head was cocked a little to one side in an attitude of listening, and he stood motionless the while I looked down upon him.

"Paul!" I called in a harsh whisper.

He looked up instantly and saw my face doubtless caught in the light from the candle in his hand. "Do you hear?" he asked.

"Yes—what in God's name is it?"

"I've heard it before,!" he said. "Come down."

I went down to the lower hall, where I stood for a moment under his penetrating and questioning gaze.

"You aren't afraid, Haddon?"

I shook my head.

"Then come with me."

He turned and led the way toward the back of the house, where he descended into the cellars below. All this time the sounds were rising in volume; it was as if they had approached closer to the house, indeed, almost as if they were directly below, and now there was obvious a definite trembling in the building, not alone of the walls and supports, but one with the shuddering and shaking of the earth all around: it was as if some deep subterranean disturbance had chosen this spot in the earth's surface to make itself manifest. But Tuttle was unmoved by this, doubtless for the reason that he had experienced it before. He went directly through the first and second cellars to a third, set somewhat lower than the others, and apparently of more recent construction, but, like the first two, built of limestone blocks set in cement.

In the center of this sub-cellar he paused and stood quietly listening. The sounds had by this time risen to such intensity that it seemed as if the house were caught in a vortex of volcanic upheaval without actually suffering the destruction of its supports; for the trembling and shuddering, the creaking and groaning of the rafters above us gave evidence of the tremendous pressure exerted within the earth beneath us, and even the stone floor of the cellar seemed alive under my bare feet. But presently these sounds appeared to recede into the background, though actually they lessened not at all, and only presented this illusion because of our growing familiarity with them and because our ears were becoming attuned to other sounds in more major keys, these, too, rising from below as from a great distance, but carrying with them an insidious hellishness in the implications that grew upon us.

For the first whistling sounds were not clear enough to justify any guess as to their origin, and it was not until I had been listening for some time that it occurred to me that the sounds breaking into the weird whistling or whimpering derived from something alive, some sentient being, for presently they resolved into uncouth and shocking mouthings, indistinct and not intelligible even when they could be clearly heard. By this time, Tuttle had put the candle down, had come to his knew, and now half lay upon the floor with his ear close to the stone.

In obedience to his motion, I did likewise, and found that the sounds from below resolved into more recognizable syllables, though no less meaningless. For the first while, I heard nothing but incoherent and apparently unconnected ululations, with which were interpolated chanting sounds, which later I put down as follows: *Iä! Iä!...Shub-Niggurath...Ugh! Cthulhu fhtagn!...Iä! Iä! Cthulhu!*

But that I was in some error in regard to at least one of these sounds, I soon learned. *Cthulhu* itself was plainly audible, despite the fury of mounting sound all around; but the word that followed now seemed somewhat longer then *fhtagn;* it was as if an extra syllable had been added, and yet I could not be certain that it had not been there all the while, for presently it came clearer, and Tuttle took from a pocket his notebook and pencil and wrote:

"They are saying *Cthulhu naflfhtagn.*"

Judging by the expression of his eyes, faintly elated, this evidently conveyed something to him, but to me it meant nothing, apart from my ability to recognize a portion of it as identical in character with the words that appeared in the abhorred *R'lyeh Text,* and subsequently again in the magazine story, where its translation would seem to have indicated that the words meant: *Cthulhu waits dreaming.* My obvious blank ignorance of this meaning apparently recalled to my host that his philological learning was far in excess of mine, for he smiled bleakly and whispered, "It can be nothing else but a negative construction."

Even then I did not at once understand that he meant to explain that the subterranean voices were not saying what I had thought, but: *Cthulhu no longer waits dreaming!* There was now no longer any question of belief, for the things that were taking place were of no human origin, and admitted of no other solution than one in some way, however remotely, related to the incredible mythology Tuttle had so recently expounded to me. And now, as if this evidence of feeling and hearing were not enough, there became manifest a strange fetid smell mingled with a nauseatingly strong odor of fish, apparently seeping up through the porous limestone.

Tuttle became aware of this almost simultaneously with my own recognition, and I was alarmed to observe in his features traces of apprehension stronger than any I had heretofore noticed. He lay for a moment quietly; then he rose stealthily, took up the candle, and crept from the room, beckoning me after him.

Only when we were once more on the upper story did he venture to speak. "They are closer than I thought," he said then, musingly.

"Is it Hastur?" I asked nervously.

But he shook his head. "It cannot be he, because the passage below leads only to the sea and is doubtless partly full of water. Therefore it can only be one of the Water Beings—those who took refuge there when the torpedoes destroyed Devil Reef beyond shunned Innsmouth—Cthulhu, or those who serve him, as the Mi-Go serve in the icy fastnesses, and the Tcho-Tcho people serve on the hidden plateaus of Asia."

Since it was impossible to sleep, we sat for a time in the library, while Tuttle spoke in a half-chanting manner of the strange things he had come upon in the old books that had been his uncle's: sat waiting for the dawn while he told of the dreaded Plateau of Leng, the Black Goat of the Woods with a Thousand Young, of Azathoth and Nyarlathotep, the Mighty Messenger who walked the star-spaces in the semblance of a man; of the horrible and diabolic Yellow Sign, the haunted and fabled towers of mysterious Carcosa; of terrible Lloigor and hated Zhar; of Ithaqua the Snow-Thing, of Chaugnar Faugn and N'gha-Kthun, of unknown Kadath and the Fungi from Yuggoth—so he talked for hours while the sounds below continued and I sat listening in a deadly, terror-fraught fear. And yet that fear was needless, for with the dawn the stars paled, and the tumult below died subtly away, fading toward the east and the ocean's deeps, and I went at last to my room, eagerly, to dress in preparation for my leave-taking.

IV

In little over a month, I was again on my way to the Tuttle estate, via Arkham, in response to an urgent card from Paul, upon which he had scrawled in a shaky hand the single word: Come! Even if he had not written, I should have considered it my duty to return to the old house on the Aylesbury Road, despite my distaste for Tuttle's soul-shaking research and the now active fear I could not help but feel. Still, I had been holding off ever since coming to the decision that I should attempt to dissuade Tuttle from further research until the morning of the day on which his card came. On that morning I found in the *Transcript* a garbled story from Arkham: I would not have noticed it at all, had it not been for the small head to take the eye: *Outrage in Arkham Cemetery,* and below: *Tuttle Vault Violated.* The story was brief, and disclosed little beyond the information already conveyed by the headings:

> It was discovered here early this morning that vandals had broken into and partly destroyed the Tuttle vault in Arkham cemetery. One wall is smashed almost beyond repair, and the coffins have been disturbed. It has been reported that the coffin of the late Amos Tuttle is missing, but confirmation cannot be had by the time this issue goes to press.

Immediately upon reading this vague bulletin, I was seized with the strongest apprehension, come upon me from I know not what source; yet I felt at once that the outrage perpetrated upon the vault was not an ordinary crime, and I could not help connecting it in my mind with the occurrences at the old Tuttle house. I had therefore resolved to go to Arkham, and thence to see Paul Tuttle, before his card arrived; his brief message alarmed me still more, if possible, and at the same time convinced me of what I feared—that some revolting connection existed between the cemetery outrage and the things that walked in the earth beneath the house on Aylesbury Road. But at the same time I became aware of a deep reluctance to leave Boston, obsessed with an intangible fear of invisible danger from an unknown source. Still, duty compelled my going, and however strongly I might shun it, go I must.

I arrived in Arkham in early afternoon and went at once to the cemetery, in my capacity as solicitor, to ascertain the extent of the damage done. A police guard had been established, but I was permitted to examine the premises as soon as my identity had been disclosed. The newspaper account, I found, had been shockingly inadequate, for the ruin of the Tuttle vault was virtually complete, its coffins exposed to the sun's warmth, some of them broken open, revealing long-dead bones. While it was true that Amos Tuttle's coffin had disappeared in the night, it had been found at midday in an open field about two miles east of Arkham, too far from the road to have been carried there; and the mystery of its being there was, if anything, deeper now than at the time the coffin had been found; for an investigation had disclosed certain deep indentations set at wide intervals in the earth, some of them as much as forty feet in diameter! It was as if some monstrous creature had walked there, though I confess that this thought occurred only within my own mind; the impressions in the earth remained a mystery upon which no light was thrown even by the wildest surmises as to their source. This may have been partly due to the more startling fact that had emerged immediately upon finding the coffin: the body of Amos Tuttle had vanished, and a search of the surrounding terrain had failed to disclose it. So much I learned from the custodian of the cemetery before I set out along the Aylesbury Road, refusing to think further about this incredible information until I had spoken with Paul Tuttle.

This time my summons at his door was not immediately answered, and I had begun to wonder with some apprehension whether something had happened to him, when I detected a faint scuffling sound beyond the door, and almost immediately heard Tuttle's muffled voice.

"Who is it?"

"Haddon," I replied, and heard what seemed to be a gasp of relief.

The door opened, and it was not until it had closed that I became aware of the nocturnal darkness of the hall, and saw that the window at the far end had been tightly shuttered, and that no light fell into the long corridor from any of the rooms opening off it. I forebore to ask the question that came to my tongue and turned instead to Tuttle. It was some time before my eyes had mastered the unnatural darkness sufficiently to make him out, and then I was conscious of a distinct feeling of shock; for Tuttle had changed from a tall, upright man in his prime to a bent, heavy man of uncouth and faintly repulsive appearance, betraying an age which actually was not his. And his first words filled me with high alarm.

"Quick now, Haddon," he said. "There's not much time."

"What is it? What's wrong, Paul?" I asked.

He disregarded this, leading the way into the library, where an electric candle burned dimly. "I've made a packet of some of my uncle's most valuable books—the *R'lyeh Text, The Book of Eibon,* the *Pnakotic*

Manuscripts—some others. These must go to the library of Miskatonic University by your hand today without fail. They are henceforth to be considered the property of the library. And here is an envelope containing certain instructions to you, in case I fail to get in touch with you either personally or by telephone—which I have had installed here since your last visit—by ten o'clock tonight. You are staying, I assume, at the Lewiston House. Now attend me closely: if I fail to telephone you to the contrary before ten o'clock tonight, you are to follow the instructions herein contained without hesitation. I advise you to act immediately, and, since you may feel them too unusual to proceed swiftly, I have already telephoned Judge Wilton and explained that I've left some strange but vital instructions with you, but that I want them carried out to the letter."

"What's happened, Paul?" I asked.

For a moment it seemed as if he would speak freely, but he only shook his head and said, "As yet I do not know all. But this much I can say: we have both, my uncle and I, made a terrible mistake. And I fear it is now too late to rectify it. You have learned of the disappearance of Uncle Amos's body?"

I nodded.

"It has since turned up."

I was astounded, since I had only just come from Arkham, and no such intelligence had been imparted to me. "Impossible!" I exclaimed. "They are still searching."

"Ah, no matter," he said oddly. "It is not there. It is here—at the foot of the garden, where it was abandoned when it was found useless."

At this, he jerked his head up suddenly, and we heard the shuffling and grunting sound that came from somewhere in the house. But in a moment it died away, and he turned again to me.

"The haven," he muttered, and gave a sickly laugh. "The tunnel was built by Uncle Amos, I am sure. But it was not the haven Hastur wanted—though it serves the minions of his half-brother, Great Cthulhu."

It was almost impossible to realize that the sun shone outside, for the murkiness of the room and the atmosphere of impending dread that hung over me combined to lend to the scene an unreality apart from the world from which I had just come, despite the horror of the violated vault. I perceived also about Tuttle an air of almost feverish expectancy coupled with a nervous haste; his eyes shone oddly and seemed more prominent than I had previously known them, his lips seemed to have coarsened and thickened, and his beard had become matted to a degree I would not have thought possible. He listened now only for a moment before he turned back to me.

"I myself need to stay for the present; I have not finished mining the place, and that must be done," he resumed erratically, but went on before the questions that rose in me could find utterance. "I've discovered that the house rests upon a natural artificial foundation, that below the place there must be not only the tunnel, but a mass of cavernous structures, and I believe that these caverns are for the most part water-filled—and perhaps inhabited," he added as a sinister afterthought. "But this, of course, is at the present time of small importance. I have no immediate fear of what is below, but what I know is to come."

Once again he paused to listen, and again vague, distant sounds came to our ears. I listened intently, hearing an ominous fumbling, as if some creature were trying a door, and strove to discover or guess at its origin. I had thought at first that the sound emanated from somewhere within the house, thought almost instinctively of the attic; for it seemed to come from above, but in a moment it was borne in upon me that the sound did not derive from any place within the house, nor yet from any portion of the house outside, but grew from some place beyond that, from *a point in space beyond the walls of the house*—a fumbling, plucking noise which was not associated in my consciousness with any recognizable material sounds, but was rather an unearthly invasion. I peered at Tuttle, and saw that his attention was also for something from outside, for his head was somewhat lifted and his eyes looked beyond the enclosing walls, bearing in them a curiously rapt expression, not without fear, nor yet without a strange air of helpless waiting.

"That is Hastur's sign," he said in a hushed voice. "When the Hyades rise and Aldebaran stalks the sky tonight, He will come. The Other will be here with His water people, those of the primal gilled races." Then he began to laugh suddenly, soundlessly, and with a sly, half-mad glance, added, "And Cthulhu and Hastur shall struggle here for the haven while Great Orion strides above the horizon, with Betelguese where the Elder Gods are, who alone can block the evil designs of these hellish spawn!"

My astonishment at his words doubtless showed in my face and in turn made him understand what shocked hesitation and doubt I felt, for abruptly his expression altered, his eyes softened, his hands clasped and unclasped nervously, and his voice became more natural.

"But perhaps this tires you, Haddon," he said. "I will say no more, for the time grows short, the evening approaches, and in a little while the night. I beg you to have no question about following the instructions I have outlined in this brief note for your eyes. I charge you to follow my directions implicitly. If it is as I fear, even that may be of no avail; if it is not, I shall reach you in time."

With that he picked up the packet of books, placed it in my hands, and led me to the door, whither I followed him without protest, for I was bewildered and not a little unmanned at the strangeness of his actions, the uncanny atmosphere of brooding horror that clung to the ancient, menace-ridden house.

At the threshold he paused briefly and touched my arm lightly. "Goodbye, Haddon," he said with friendly intensity.

Then I found myself on the stoop in the glare of the lowering sunlight so bright that I closed my eyes against it until I could again accustom myself to its brilliance, while the cheerful chortle of a late bluebird on a fence-post across the road sounded pleasantly in my ears, as if to belie the atmosphere of dark fear and eldritch horror behind.

V

I come now to that portion of my narrative upon which I am loath to embark, not alone because of the incredibility of what I must write, but because it can at best be a vague, uncertain account, replete with surmises and remarkable, if disjointed, evidence of horror-torn, eon-old evil beyond time, of primal things that lurk just outside the pale of life we know, or terrible, animate survival in the hidden places of Earth. How much of this Tuttle learned from those hellish texts he entrusted to my care for the locked shelves of Miskatonic University Library, I cannot say. Certain it is that he guessed many things he did not know until too late; of others, he gathered hints, though it is to be doubted that he fully comprehended the magnitude of the task upon which he so thoughtlessly embarked when he sought to learn why Amos Tuttle had willed the deliberate destruction of his house and books.

Following my return to Arkham's ancient streets, events succeeded events with undesirable rapidity. I deposited Tuttle's packet of books with Doctor Llanfer at the library, and made my way immediately after to Judge Wilton's house, where I was fortunate enough to find him. He was just sitting down to supper, and invited me to join him, which I did, though I had no appetite of any kind, indeed, food seeming repugnant to me. By this time all the fears and intangible doubts I had held had come to a head within me, and Wilton saw at once that I was laboring under an unusual nervous strain.

"Curious thing about the Tuttle vault, isn't it?" he ventured shrewdly, guessing at the reason for my presence in Arkham.

"Yes, but not half so curious as the circumstance of Amos Tuttle's body reposing at the foot of his garden," I replied.

"Indeed," he said without any visible sign of interest, his calmness serving to restore me in some measure to a sense of tranquility. "I dare say you've come from there and know whereof you speak."

At that, I told him as briefly as possible the story I had come to tell, omitting only a few of the more improbable details, but not entirely succeeding in dismissing his doubts, though he was far too much a gentleman to permit me to feel them. He sat for a while in thoughtful silence after I had finished, glancing once or twice at the clock, which showed the hour to be already past seven. Presently he interrupted his revery to suggest that I telephone the Lewiston House and arrange for any call for me to be transferred to Judge Wilton's home. This I did instantly, somewhat relieved that he had consented to take the problem seriously enough to devote his evening to it.

"As for the mythology," he said, directly upon my return to the room, "it *can* be dismissed as the creation of a mad mind, the Arab Abdul Alhazred. I say advisedly, it *can be,* but in the light of the things which have happened in Innsmouth I should not like to commit myself. However, we are not at present in session. The immediate concern is for Paul Tuttle himself; I propose that we examine his instructions to you forthwith."

I produced the envelope at once, and opened it. It contained but a single sheet of paper, bearing these cryptic and ominous lines:

"I have mined the house and all. Go *immediately* without delay, to the pasture gate west of the house, where in the shrubbery on the right side of the lane as you approach from Arkham, I have concealed the detonator. My Uncle Amos was right—it should have been done in the first place. If you fail me, Haddon, then before God you loose upon the countryside such a scourge as man has never known and will never see again—if indeed he survives it!"

Some inkling of the cataclysmic truth must at that moment have begun to penetrate my mind, for when Judge Wilton leaned back, looked at me quizzically, and asked, "What are you going to do?" I replied without hesitation: "I'm going to follow these instructions to the letter!"

He gazed at me for a moment without comment; then he bowed to the inevitable and settled back. "We shall wait for ten o'clock to-gether," he said gravely.

The final act of the incredible horror that had its focal point in the Tuttle house took place just a little before ten, coming upon us in the beginning in so disarmingly prosaic a manner that the full horror, when it came, was doubly shocking and profound. For at five minutes to ten, the telephone rang. Judge Wilton took it at once, and even from where I sat I could hear the agonized voice of Paul Tuttle calling my name.

"This is Haddon," I said with a calmness I did not feel. "What is it, Paul?"

"Do it now!" he cried. "Oh, God, Haddon—right away—before ... too late. Oh, God—the haven! *The haven! ... You know the place ... pasture gate. O, God, be quick! ...*" And then there happened what I shall never forget: the sudden terrible degeneration of his voice, so that it was as if it crumpled together and sank into abysmal mouthings; for the sounds that came over the wire were bestial and inhuman—shocking gibberings and crude, brutish, drooling sounds, from among which certain of them recurred again and again, and I listened in steadily mounting horror to the triumphant gibbering before it died away:

"*Iä! Iä! Hastur! Ugh! Ugh! Iä Hastur cf'ayak'vulgtmm, vugtlagln vulgtmm! Ai! Shub-Niggurath! ... Hastur—Hastur cf'tagn! Iä! Iä! Hastur! ....*"

Then abruptly all sound died away, and I turned to face Judge Wilton's terror-stricken features. And yet I did not see him, nor did I see anything in my understanding of what must be done; for abruptly, with cataclysmic effect, I understood what Tuttle had failed to know until too late. And at once I dropped the telephone; at once I ran hatless and coatless from the house into the street, with the sound of Judge Wilton frantically summoning police over the telephone fading into the night behind me. I ran with unnatural speed from the shadowed, haunted streets of witch-cursed Arkham into the October night, down the Aylesbury Road, into the lane and the pasture gate, where for one brief instant, while sirens blew behind me, I saw the Tuttle house through the orchard outlined in a hellish purple glow, beautiful but unearthly and tangibly evil.

Then I pushed down the detonator, and with a tremendous roar, the old house burst asunder and flames leaped up where the house had stood.

For a few dazed moments I stood there, aware suddenly of the arrival of police along the road south of the house, before I began to move up to join them, and so saw that the explosion had brought about what Paul Tuttle had hinted: the collapse of the subterranean caverns below the house; for the land itself was settling, slipping down, and the flames that had risen were hissing and steaming in the water gushing up from below.

Then it was that that other thing happened—the last unearthly horror that mercifully blotted out what I saw in the wreckage jutting out above the rising waters—the great protoplasmic mass risen from the center of the lake forming where the Tuttle house had been, and the thing that came crying out to us across the lawn before it turned to face that other and begin a titanic struggle for mastery interrupted only by the brilliant explosion of light that seemed to emanate from the eastern sky like a bolt of incredibly powerful lightning; a tremendous discharge of energy in the shape of light, so that for one awful moment everything was revealed—before lightning-like appendages descended from the heart of the blinding pillar of light itself, one seizing the mass in the waters, lifting it high, and casting it far out to sea, the other taking that second thing from the lawn and hurling it, a dark dwindling blot, into the sky, where it vanished among the eternal stars! And then came sudden, absolute, cosmic silence, and where, a moment before, this miracle of light had been, there was now only darkness and the line of trees against the sky, and low in the east the gleaming eye of Betelguese as Orion rose into the autumn night.

For an instant I did not know which was worse—the chaos of the previous moment, or the utter black silence of the present; but the small cries of horrified men brought it back to me, and it was borne in upon me then that they at least did not understand the secret horror, the final thing that sears and maddens, the thing that rises in the dark hours to stalk the bottomless depths of the mind. They may have heard, as I did, that thin, far, whistling sound, that maddening ululation from the deep, immeasurable gulf of cosmic space, the wailing that fell back along the wind, and the syllables that floated down the slopes of air: *Tekeli-li, tekeli-li, tekeli-li...* And certainly they saw the thing that came crying out at us from the sinking ruins behind, the distorted caricature of a human being, with its eyes sunk into invisibility in thick masses of scaly flesh, the thing that flailed its arms bonelessly at us like the appendages of an octopus, *the thing that shrieked and gibbered in Paul Tuttle's voice!*

But they could not know the secret that I alone knew, the secret Amos Tuttle might have guessed in the shadows of his dying hours, the thing Paul Tuttle was too late in learning: *that the haven sought by Hastur the Unspeakable, the haven promised Him Who is not to be Named, was not the tunnel, and not the house, but the body and soul of Amos Tuttle himself, and, failing these, the living flesh and immortal soul of him who lived in that doomed house on the Aylesbury Road!*

L in Carter (1930-1988), an omnivorous reader of fantasy, could seldom resist ringing his own changes on the themes he so loved. Here are three fragmentary experiments embellishing the mythology of Hastur, Hali, Carcosa, and the King.

The first, "Litany to Hastur," is a sequence of four sonnets from his cycle Dreams from R'lyeh. They appeared with the present title in Lin's anthology The Spawn of Cthulhu. Here Lin has assembled various of Derleth's further modifications of the Hastur character (his being served by the Byakhee, for example) which Derleth collects in no one place.

The second is the beginning of an untitled fragment labeled on the first page as "Carcosa Story about Hali." This fragment is noteworthy for the systematic attempt it makes to harmonize the different strata of the Hastur mythology: Lin has combined Bierce's sage Hali with Chambers's Carcosa and Aldones, and yet again with Derleth's Elder Gods, Hastur the Unspeakable, etc. As with most of these efforts, Lin's scribal zeal for the sport of textual harmonization tended to produce a text with much (too obviously laborious) ingenuity and little literary grace.

The third piece is an exercise of May 16, 1986, in which Lin toyed with recasting James Blish's version of "The King in Yellow" into a different verse idiom. The result is quite interesting and deserves preservation in print. Notes indicate that Lin intended simply to plug in the five bits of prose in which Cassilda tells the royal Child the history of Hastur, Alar, and Carcosa, straight from Blish's text. This seems somehow inappropriate to me, so in the interest of thoroughgoing paraphrase, I have supplied substitute verse text at the relevant points, indicated by brackets. Carter's line numbering skipped these portions, beginning again after the Blish sections. I have preserved his line numbering. Lin made no attempt to recast Chambers's original of "Cassilda's Song" either, incorporating it bodily. I have thought it better to substitute a new passage here, too.

Tatters of the King

by LIN CARTER

Litany to Hastur

XX. Black Lotus

The Coven-Master gave to me a phial
Of that dread opiate that is the key
To dream-gates opening upon a sea
Of acherontic vapours: mile on mile
Stretched ebon coasts untrod, wherefrom aspire
Pylons of rough-hewn stone climbing to skies
Alien-constellated, where arise
Grey mottled moons of cold and leprous fire.

My dream-self roamed the cosmic gulfs profound,
Past daemon-haunted Haddith, where in deeps
Of foul putrescence buried underground
The loathsome shoggoth hideously sleeps.
I saw—and screamed! And knew my doom of dooms,
Learning at last . . . where the Black Lotus blooms.

XXI. The Unspeakable

I drank the golden mead and did those things
Of which I read within the ancient book.
The wind awoke. The elms and willows shook
Before the thunder of fantastic wings.
Down from the cosmic gulfs the monster fell,
The grim, stupendous, bat-winged Byakhee,
Come from the cloudy shores of Lake Hali,
Black-furred and iron-beaked, with eyes of Hell.

When I bestrode its back, the beast unfurled
Its vast and mighty wings. Across dark seas
Of space we flew. Amid the Hyades
We reached at last that bleak and mythic world
To men forbidden and by gods abhorred,
Carcosa, where the great Hastur is Lord.

XXII. Carcosa

It was a scene that I had known before,
This barren, desolate, and drear expanse
Through which I wandered in a dream-like trance.
And there in somber splendor by the shore
Of dark Hali the nameless city stood:
Black domes and monolithic towers loom
Stark and gigantic in the midnight gloom
Like druid menhirs in a haunted wood.

These streets and walls I seem to half-recall,
Wandering blindly through the winding ways
Beneath a sky with strange black stars ablaze,
From some mad dream....or was it dream at all?
Aye, here it was I heard Cassilda sing,
Where flap the yellow tatters of The King!

XXIII. The Candidate

Down the dark street of monoliths I passed,
The shambling, faceless figure of my Guide
A voiceless thing that beckoned at my side,
And to the dreaded Gate I came at last.
Before the silent Guardian I made
The black unhallowed Sacrifice, and spoke
Names at whose sound forgotten echoes woke.
The portals gaped. I entered unafraid.

Fate, or my stars, or some accursed pride
Had brought me here. Naked, I stood alone
And took the Vow before the Elder Throne—
He laughed, and drew His tattered Mantle wide—
O do not seek to learn nor ever ask
What horror hides behind . . . *The Pallid Mask!*

Carcosa Story about Hali

I. Now, it came to pass late in the first year of the Terror that They That Reign from Betelgeuze spake in his dreams to Their Servant, the necromancer Hali, yea, even him that was called Hali the Wise; and he rose up and departed him hence from the Immemorial City and did wander for some certain time in the wilderness, beneath the twin suns and the strange moons that illume the skies of that world of Carcosa that is in the Hyades, and whereof the scribe doth write. And, in sooth, now that the grave did give up its sheeted dead, to stalk and gibber through the streets, it beseemed wise for a necromancer like Hali to make himself scarce.

II. And these things had come to pass in the days that followed hard upon the heels of the appearance of that Apparition that arose up from out of the Nothingness that was before Time and that is beyond Space, and that smote Fear into the hearts of all those that did dwell in the beshadowed ways of the Immemorial City; the which befell in the early years of the reign of that Aldones, even he that was the Last King of the Immemorial City, at least until the Coming-Thither of the King in Yellow, as had been aforetime foretold by that very Apparition of the Phantom of Truth.

III. In the fullness of time did it occur to one Elhalyn, a priest of the Elder Gods in the Immemorial City, that Hali the Wise had writ in his Testament much that foreshadowed the Curse that now smote the City of Aldones, in that he had writ of the shades and permutations of that state that "By death is wrought greater change than hath been shewn, whereas in general the spirit that removed cometh back upon occasion and is sometimes seen of those in the flesh (appearing in the form of the body it bore), yet hath it happened that the veritable body without the spirit hath walked. And it is attested of those encountering them who have lived to speak thereon that a lich so raised up hath no natural affection, nor remembrance thereof, but only hate. Also, it is known that some spirits which in life were benign become by death evil altogether."

IV. Thus writ Hali the Wise, and these words brought the priest Elhalyn to the attention of the King Aldones, for it beseemed to this priest of the Elder Gods that if this necromancer was so deeply learned in the Mysteries of Death, he might well know the cause of the curse that now plagued the very streets of the Immemorial City, where the dead walked and raved, and the living fled therefrom in fear. For it is not meet or seemly that the living and the dead shouldst commingle, since that each belongeth to a different sphere; and to these sentiments agreed, and right full-heartedly, the King, Aldones, gave as his fiat that the priest Elhalyn shouldst seek out the necromancer Hali in whatever far and fabulous bourne he now had taken as his home.

V. Now, for a time did the sage Hali wander in this wilderness, the which wast not habited by men such as he, but only by the shy and furtive Yoogs, the which be but rarely glimpsed by mortal eyes, and then but dimly and from afar; and these quaint and curious creatures, the Yoogs, be of much interest in that they perambulate about upon three legs instead of two, and in a mode and manner most novel and intriguing; and there were, as well, in these parts the loathly and abominable Nests of the Byakhee, the which were wont to roost in peaks adjacent to these regions. But of the Byakhee the Scribe writeth naught, by reason of the grisly Ways thereof, the which be not quite Wholesome to discuss.

VI. Now, the Black Lake on whose bleak shores the sage soon reared his hut or hovel was in no wise like unto the other lakes to be found upon this world of Carcosa in the Hyades; for the waters thereof were dark as death and cold as the bitter spaces between the stars, and naught that was composed of simple flesh lived or could live in the gloomy and fetid Deeps thereof. And it is said that a cold and clammy mist drifted ever above the bitter waters of the Black Lake, as a shroud clings to a moldering corpse. And this mist swayed to and fro with the wheeling of the black stars and the strange moons of Carcosa, and they in the Immemorial City knew this as the "cloud waves."

VII. And it was whispered by men that these cloud waves hid forever from the sight of men a Monstrous Thing that had fallen upon Carcosa from the stars uncounted and uncountable aeons before this time, and that this Thing yet lived albeit in a state of somnolence, from the which it woke betimes, ravening with hungers unspeakable. And the sages said that this Dweller in the Depths was of the very spawn of Azathoth and half-brother even to Dread Cthulhu, the Lord of the Great Abyss, and that the Thing in the Lake had mated with the Black Ewe with a Thousand Young, aye, even Shub-Niggurath; and upon that hellish and cloud-like Entity had begotten the Twin Abominations, even Nug and Yeb. And it was deemed unprudent to utter upon the lips of men the Name of the Thing in the Lake, wherefore was it known as The Unspeakable.

VIII. When, in the fullness of time, the priest Elhalyn had sought out the hovel wherein dwelt the necromancer, and had made converse with Hali the Wise upon that matter the which had roused all of Carcosa, and they spake of the Dead that had risen to wander abroad and to ravish the living (even the living that they themselves had loved and cherished when they had been on live), Hali mused and at length spake thusly, from the profundities of his wisdom: "Know, O Hal Elhalyn, for that there be divers sorts of death—some wherein the body remaineth, and in some it vanisheth quite away with the spirit."

IX. And sayeth yet further: "Now, this commonly occureth only in solitude (such being the will of the Elder Gods), and, none seeing the end thereof, we say the man is lost, or gone upon a long journey—which indeed he hath; but sometimes it hath happened in full sight of many, as abundant testimony sheweth. In one kind of death the spirit also dieth, and this it hath been known to do whilst yet the body wast in vigor for many years. Sometimes, as it is veritably attested, it dieth with the body, but after a season is raised up again in that place where the body dids't decay." Thus spoke the necromancer Hali to the priest Elhalyn.

X. Now, at length it came out in their converse that those of the Dead whose like had been seen to stalk and raven through the very streets of the Immemorial City were even those the which had been given over unto the Thing in the Lake in sacrifice thereunto, that it was given unto Hali the Wise to ponder greatly thereat. For such as he, that knew the many forms and shapes of death, was greatly puzzled and baffled at this manifestation of a law of the dead hitherto unbeknownst, even to a necromancer such as he.

XI. Long had Hali the Wise known of the abominable custom of binding and of hurling into the bitter depths of the Black Lake certain victims, such as were designated to feed the hunger of Him That Slept Beneath, and long had Hali the necromancer loathed and abominated this custom. And now that it was revealed unto him that those of the dead who rose to walk again the beshadowed streets of the Immemorial City were even the same as them that had been fed to the Thing in the Lake, he had great cause to think and to ponder.

XII. For well wast it known to such as Hali the Wise that the Thing that had been of old hurled into the Black Lake was even Hastur— Hastur the Unspeakable, Him Who Is Not to Be Named—Great Prince of the Old Ones, prince and rebel against the Elder Gods. Not chained in the depths of the Black Lake wast Hastur in these days, but hiding therein, wary and fearful of discovery by Those whom he hadst betrayed and fled therefrom. And very great and powerful was Hastur the Unspeakable, greater than any mere mortal man . . .

XIII. And that very night, under the blaze of black stars and beneath the leprous glimmer of strange moons, did the Elder Gods whisper in his dreams unto Their Servant, even the necromancer Hali. But whereof wast spoken the Scribe knoweth not, and therefore he writeth not. But, upon the morrow, it is said that the necromancer sought out the shale of the rocky cliffs and found thereamongst a certain grey-green stone, whose name the Scribe knoweth not; and that from this stone, with patient labor, did the necromancer cut certain signs and sigils. Five-pointed stars were these, with blunted tips, and in the very midst thereof were cutten shapes like lozenges, open at both ends, containing Shapes like unto Towers of Flame.

XIV. . . . .

The King In Yellow

A Tragedy in Verse

by LIN CARTER, after James Blish

Scene I

UOHT:	O, this unending and most dreary siege!—
	Madame my mother, is it you? Good-day.
CASSILDA:	Good-day to you, boy; and good-bye to day.
UOHT (to himself):	She is distracted; I will talk with her.
	What, all alone here on your balcony?
	Looking on Carcosa again, I fear.
CASSILDA:	No one can gaze on Carcosa, my boy,
	Before the rising of the Hyades
	Will chase away the shadows of the day.

UOHT: O, this unending and most dreary siege!—
    Madame my mother, is it you? Good-day.
CASSILDA: Good-day to you, boy; and good-bye to day.
UOHT (to himself):   She is distracted; I will talk with her.
    What, all alone here on your balcony?
    Looking on Carcosa again, I fear.
CASSILDA: No one can gaze on Carcosa, my boy,
    Before the rising of the Hyades
    Will chase away the shadows of the day.
    Nay, I but gazed across the cloudy waves   10
    Of dim Hali that drowns so many days . . .
UOHT: And we shall see it drown full many more!
    This night-mist breathes contagion vile; it crawls
    In every nook and cranny like a spy,
    Or some foul, sly assassin: come inside.
CASSILDA: Ah, no; ah, no; not now, Uoht. I fear
    Me not thy crawling mist, contagions vile,
    Nor craven spy nor skulking murtherer;
    Nor least of all am I afraid of time,
    Assassin of assassins! I have seen   20
    A lot of Hali's mist, and much of time.
UOHT: O, Hali, this interminable siege!
    Would that thy Lake would drink tall Alar down
    For once, instead of endless days.
CASSILDA: Hali
    Cannot do that, since Alar's throned on Dehme,
    And Dehme is quite another lake indeed.
UOHT: One lake is very like another lake,
    O mother mine! Black water and grey fog,
    With white bones under, where drowned sailors sleep
    In beds of oozy slime; their cold, numb flesh
    Nibbled by fish, they lie on heaps of pearls—   30
    Aye, fog and water; water, fog. Alar
    And Hastur could change sites between two dawns,
    No one would notice. O, they are the two
    Worst situated cities in the world—

CASSILDA(*ironically*):   They are the only cities in the world,
                    Thus the worst situate.
UOHT: Save Carcosa.
CASSILDA: ... What? Did you speak? Uoht,
                    I weary of these little wordy games,
                    Nor am I any longer sure at all
                    That Carcosa is really in the world: 40
                    Mayhap it slipped its mooring, bent adrift
                    Deep into Nightmare's deathly, dark domain—
                    At all events, my pretty Prince, it boots
                    Us little, all this idle talk

    (CAMILLA *enters*)

CAMILLA: O, I—
CASSILDA: Come in, Camilla; come, Camilla, hark!
                    We have not any secrets anymore,
                    For schemes and plots and plans and all device
                    Have now worn old and thin, till time hath stopped.

    (THALE *enters*)

THALE: More of your nonsense, mother mine?
CASSILDA: If so,   50
                    It likes you well to name it thus, O Thale.
                    While as for poor Cassilda, as for me,
                    Why, I am but a Queen, a pale, sad Queen,
                    And can be mocked to make your pleasure—
THALE: No!
                    I swear me that I never meant to mock
                    My fount and origin of being; no!
UOHT: Well: mockery or no, Prince Thale has struck
                    The true word truer spoke. Nonsense, I say!
                    Time does not wear away, till, old and thin,
                    It stops. For time is adamant; at least,   60
                    Its endless, weary hours weigh like lead.
                    How can time stop? 'Tis time that measures change,
                    And change will change forever; labile time!
                    To stop would time but contradict itself,
                    And how might time's self contradict—
CASSILDA (*wearily*):   Time stops.
                    There is an interval of weary pause,
                    When all the world grinds to a groaning rest,
                    And catches breath; time stops, O Uoht, stops
                    When one has heard every banality
                    Said over every banal time again.   70
                    And when has anything new happened here
                    In banal, boring, dusty, gray Hastur?
                    New words, new thoughts, new faces, forms,
                    Or aught we have not heard and seen and touched

Ten thousand, thousand times ere now? The siege,
As yourself so repeatedly observes,
Is utterly interminable. That's that.
Neither Hastur nor Alar shall prevail;
It shall be stalemate till the dull world sinks
And drowns in dust; we'll both wear down to dust—   80
Or boredom, which may drown us first in yawns.
I'm sorry for you, Uoht; I'm afraid
That all that now you do remind me of,
Is there's no future being human, now.
E'en as a babe you were a little dull.
Yes, just a little dull.

UOHT: Well, you may say
What e'er you please of me, for queenliness
Hath all its ancient privileges still.
Yet all the same not all time's in the past,
Nor all days done. There's still a future world,   90
Cassilda, still tomorrow comes, the day
Will dawn, and hours march toward night. O, Queen,
'Tis in your power to change our world so much,
Were you not weary of us all, and most
Of all things weary of yourself.

CASSILDA: Oh, my
Are we to speak of the Succession now?
As if the siege weren't boring us enough—
Nothing's more dull than dynasties.

THALE: Madame,
Must the Dynasty die only because
The Queen is bored? Only one word from you   100
And the Black Stars would rise aloft again.
Whatever your soothsaying, Mother mine,
Before their light Alar would fade and fall,
And that you know full well. 'Twould be—'twould be
An act of mercy toward the populace.

CASSILDA: Toward the what? The people? Who are they?
You care as less for them as doth Uoht;
Yes, Thale, I read your heart as 'twere a printed page.
I know your heart and I know his as well.

UOHT: Well, then, you know our hearts. What is't you know? 110
CASSILDA: The diadem means just this to you both,
It means your sister; aye, and nothing else.
There's no reward left else but her, no prize
In being King in dull Hastur! As for
Your Black Stars, well, enough of them for aye!
They shine forth nothing but the night, no more.

THALE: I hold Camilla's heart.
UOHT: You lie!

CASSILDA:	Doth he?
UOHT:	Well, ask her if you dare.
THALE:	And who would dare?

Without the diadem? Act not more bold,
Mine brother Uoht, than you care to be.   120
Or have you found the Yellow Sign, O brave?

UOHT: Silence, you fool!

CASSILDA: And drop this bickering,
You barking dogs ... and I will ask it her.

THALE: She is not ready to be asked, Madame.

CASSILDA: Not ready, say you, Thale? I say she is.
Camilla, child, come to me; now brush back
Thy pale hair from thy paler face; know
That you could have the diadem, be Queen,
And take your choice of either brother here
To be your Consort. And thus would we reach   130
The end of all our problems in Camilla.
O, how I tempt you, how I tempt you all!
Thus would the Dynasty continued be,
At least another lifetime added to
The sum of all the lifetimes gone before,
In gray and hoary old Hastur the drear.
And we'd be free of this conniving, too:
Why, it could be the very siege might end—
Well, come, Camilla, speak!

CAMILLA: O, no, no. Please!
Give not the dreaded diadem to me.   140
I will not bear its burthen on my brows,
Nor hold it heavy in my helpless hands.

CASSILDA: I understand you not: pray tell me why?

CAMILLA: O, fear, O cold gray weight of Fear upon
My falt'ring heart. Then I should be . . .
I should be sent the Yellow Sign.

CASSILDA: Perchance.
And perchance not. Perchance 'tis but a dream,
Lie, myth, illusion dire. Shall we believe
The idle runes that whisper of the thing,
Or mock them back into the realm of dreams?   150
And if 'twas sent to you, this Yellow Sign,
What then, O wan and frightened child, what then?
And would it be so very terrible,
This strange, uncanny doom of which you dream,
In dreams of dim and stealthy death that is
Not death at all, but something stranglier . . .
O speak, Camilla: say what, after all
Happens when one receives the Yellow Sign?

CAMILLA *(whispers):*   I ... It is come for some time in the night;
                     Come for by what, mother, I shall not say   160
                     But come for surely, surely.

CASSILDA: This have I heard
                     But never seen it happen. Monstrous strange!
                     To start at shadows with no substance there.
                     And yet suppose that something—someone—comes
                     To take it back. What comes, or who, and why?
                     Who comes?

CAMILLA: The Phantom of Truth, so 'tis called ...

CASSILDA: And what, pale child, is that?

CAMILLA: I ... I do not know.

CASSILDA: No more do I, or Thale, Uoht, or anyone!
                     Let us pretend, Camilla, that 'tis real;
                     This Phantom, thine, whatever it might be,   170
                     It truly is. Now, does that frighten thee?
                     But what have the Camillas of this world
                     To fear from Truth?

CAMILLA: Perhaps I've naught to fear,
                     Yet still I fear; fear never yields, you know,
                                                        to reason

CASSILDA: Well, so be it, child; and thus
                     I'll yield the diadem to one of them,
                     And end this bother in another way.
                     One remedy's as good as any else.
                     But come, and choose between them, brothers both,
                     But as unlike as night could be from day,   180
                     Or light from darkness, or most foul from fair.
                     'Twould pleasure me to see you wed in state
                     With the regalia and full circumstance;
                     For at the least, 'twould be a novelty
                     'Midst all this dreary sameness, day by day.

UOHT: A wise suggestion. Come, Camilla, choose!

THALE: Yes, choose, Camilla! Though 'tis not the least
                     Momentum of decision—

CAMILLA *(ignoring their importunement):*
                     O, Mother, there is truly something new
                     And novel in the weary streets today;   190
                     We need no nuptials to alleviate
                     The tedium of life in dull Hastur—
                     'Tis what I came to tell you, moments ere
                     The same old squabble started up again.

CASSILDA: And what is this that's new and novel, child?

CAMILLA: There is a stranger strolling in our streets.

CASSILDA: Say you in sooth? Now, by the living gods,
                     But hear you that, my princes? . . . Would 'twere true;

But, no, Camilla, Hali's creeping mists
Confuse your eye or fuddle your poor wits: 200
Each face in dreary Hastur do I know
And not one face among them that is new.
How many myriad faces do you think
There are in all this weary world, my child?
A myriad myriad, and I know them all . . . .

CAMILLA: Yes, mother, but this face is new: or new
at least to me; new in Hastur, 'tis true.

CASSILDA: No one these days goes down our dismal streets
But the hearse-driver; folks with any sense
Now hide their faces even from themselves,   210
And turn their looking-glasses 'gainst the wall
For fear of what they see—

CAMILLA: But that is it:
No one can see the stranger's foreign face
For he goes masked adown our dreary streets.

CASSILDA: What, hidden with a hood? Or veiled from view?

CAMILLA: Neither, mother. He wears another face.
A pale mask, paler than the mists, as white
As fear; a face with no expression, and
The eyes are staring, blank.

CASSILDA: Aye, this is strange;
Aye, strange and stranglier ... how doth the man   220
Explain his Pallid Mask?

CAMILLA: He speaks to none
And none so bold that they would speak to Him.

CASSILDA: Well, I shall see him; he will speak to me,
Or I will have him stretched out on the rack
Ere this dull world's an hour older. Then,
If only then, the stranger shall unmask.

UOHT (*impatiently*):   Now, mother, this is merely a conceit—

THALE: 'Tis of no import, just a trifling leaf
Upon the tree of time. Now to return:
If fair Camilla will but make her choice—   230

UOHT: Resuscitating the Succession thus—
Reviving the Imperial Dynasty—

CASSILDA(*takes diadem from lap, places firmly on brows*):
                              There will be other hours and times to come
And days unborn when we shall think on that.
Till then you have my rule and Hastur has a Queen,
And needs not any King. Camilla does
Not care to choose between her brothers twain,
Nor do I wish her so to choose. Not yet.

Send to me Naotalba now, and send   240
The stranger in the Pallid Mask.

UOHT: But see!
The sandy granules trickle down the glass!
'Tis time itself that's running out at length
For all of us. There has not been a King
In gloomy Hastur since the last Aldones—

CASSILDA: Do not recite again that tired tale.
I'll list not to that story yet again.
O, the Last King! Tell not his tale once more.
I am so weary of the lot of you:
I warn you all, goad me no more with words.   250
Hastur will have no other King again
Until the King in Yellow comes to reign!

(There is a long, shocked silence. Exit CAMILLA, *pursued by* UOHT *and*
THALE. CASSILDA *rises and goes to the parapet and leans upon the balustrade,*
exhausted and brooding on the view.)

SCENE II

CASSILDA *(sings):*
[The cloud-crests splash along the beach
And double suns drop out of reach;
Dusk creeps apace
                                        Unto Carcosa.
The night arises ghastly white,
Blackness blanched by ebon light
From stars and moons o'er
                                        Dead Carcosa.
The Hyades their voices raise
Their silken-shredded King to praise,
 But none will know in
                                        Damned Carcosa.
My soul lies mute, its cords all cut;
My wailings cease, my mouth sewn shut,
Lost as tears in Hali's deeps by
                                        Dead Carcosa.]

(Enter a CHILD *{wearing many jeweled rings and crowned with a smaller*
duplicate of the Diadem}.)

CHILD: Grandmother, grandmother, tell me a tale!
CASSILDA: I do not feel like telling stories now,
For tales aren't true and lies are lies. I have
No heart for falsehoods now. 'Tis time for truths.

CHILD *(menacing):* Grandmother?
CASSILDA: [If it must be, list then . . . .]
CHILD: That's better.

CASSILDA: [upon a day in dim-remember'd days
appeared amidst Gondwanaland's expanse
twin lakes, both nam'd by no man's voice:
One great Dehme, the other by the prophet's
Name was called. Or would be, days to come.
For age on age their surface went unscanned
by fish eye or the unborn eye of man,
Though blind fish swirl'd and dipped beneath its glass.
Worlds passed, and one day was left a city,
Dropped as if by a god's forgetful hand,
On Hali's shores, abandoned on the strand.]

({The twin suns have been slowly sinking. The Hyades come out, their image blurred by the mists.})

CHILD: That's not a story, but a history.

CASSILDA: It is the only tale I have to tell.
'Tis time for truths. If you will silent be,
I'll tell you all the rest that's in the runes.

CHILD: I'm not supposed to know what's in the runes.

CASSILDA: That doesn't matter now. But to go on:
[Upon four pillars of uniqueness was
This city built. Of these four was the first
Its birth all in one dawn. Second was this
Queer circumstance: one might not tell of it
Whether it rode upon the waves or on
The farther shore it sat, could one have seen.
The third among the wonders of the city
Was merely this: its towers seemed to pierce
The risen moon like fruit upon a spear.
Wouldst have more, or do I petrify you?]

CHILD: But I already know the tale you tell.

CASSILDA: Misfortunate prince! [By now you know too
Well how came that city to be named.
In the moment that it filled one's eye, its
true and only name rushed all unbidden
To the mind. Naught else might it ever bear.
This none doubted; no other name was broached.]

CHILD: Carcosa.

CASSILDA: Yes, even as it is today.
[And after unknown lengths of years went past,
Men journeyed from the gods know not whereof
To cast up huts rude and impertinent
Against the shadow'd waves of Hali's Lake.
Among these came forth one who would assume
A kingly crown amid his peers and win

Their dull respect, and yawn as they bow and
Genuflect. His famous name you know.]

CHILD: Was that my grandsire?

CASSILDA: It was one of them.

CHILD: 'Tis great Aldones?

CASSILDA: Yes, him, some ages back.
[He judged the place should bear the name Hastur,
Its kings henceforth his name to make their own.
He promised this: should all the sov'reigns on
His throne uphold the royal line intact,
Then poor and rude Hastur one day might match
The greatness of Empyrean Carcosa.]

CHILD: Thank you, grandmother. I have heard enough . . . .

CASSILDA: No, you have not: and on that very night
Someone, it seems, had heard his careless words—
Child, you asked a tale and now must hear it out—

CHILD: I have to leave now—

CASSILDA *(eyes closed):*   And that very night
Your ancestor, he found the Yellow Sign—

        (CHILD *runs out. Enter* NAOTALBA*)*

NAOTALBA My Queen.

CASSILDA: Good priest.

NAOTALBA   But you forgot to tell
The little prince of singularities
The fifth and final one.

CASSILDA: And you, I learn,
Are an eavesdropper, quite incurable;
Well, I am not surprised. Priests are supposed
To know all sorts of secrets, and how else
To learn such save with your ear to keyholes?

NAOTALBA: And of that final singularity?

CASSILDA: Fear not, O priest! No one were fool enough
To tell the Myst'ry of the Hyades
To a mere child.

NAOTALBA: No, but you thought of it,
My lady Queen.

CASSILDA: Why everyone imputes
Philosophy to poor Cassilda—that's   10
Another mystery! My thoughts are few
And shallow, sir; they do not run so deep.
'Tis only that the shadows of our thoughts
Commonly lengthen in the afternoon.
And dusk is—dusk.

NAOTALBA: Long thoughts long shadows cast,
At morn as well as mid of day, O Queen.

CASSILDA: And lack of news is news enough: well, priest,
                         Bury me under your banalities,
                         And join your voice to those of all my sons
                         Who have been doing nothing else this hour.   20
                         Next, you'll be prating of the Diadem,
                         Or of the Dynasty.

NAOTALBA   To tell the truth,
                         Nothing was further from my mind, O Queen.

CASSILDA: And a good place for nothing, that!

NAOTALBA: 'Tis good
                         To hear you jest, madame; but nonetheless
                         I do have other news of some import—

CASSILDA: About a stranger in a Pallid Mask?

NAOTALBA: You have already heard of him; 'tis well,
                         Then I may be as brief as brief may be.
                         I think you should not see this man—if man   30
                         Is all he is . . . .

CASSILDA (laughs):   Naught will prevent me, priest!
                         O Naotalba, think you I'd refuse
                         To face the first fresh novelty in years
                         And years, and dusty years. In truth were he
                         Some sly assassin with a thirsty knife,
                         I'd let him in to look upon his face.
                         A face I've never seen . . . would it were so!
                         I fear, cold priest, you little know your Queen.

NAOTALBA: I know you better than you know yourself.   40

CASSILDA: And naught's more certain, then, than death and … gods!
                         Banalities! I drown in a sea of them;
                         They suck me down to deeps of tedium.
                         And why should I not see this man—for man
                         Is all he is.

     (An interval of silence)
                              … a poor spy, then, I'd say,
                         To strut a mask: 'tis too conspicuous.
                         And if it came to that, what thing is there
                         Alar does not already know of us,
                         As we know all there is to know of them?
                         That's why we're in this impasse in our war.
                         Neither has aught that could the other take   50
                         By the advantage of surprise. Ah me!
                         Each of the other knows all that there is
                         To know. Aye, were one single stone to fall
                         From Alar's wall, and I not know its fall,
                         This weary war wouldst end in sheer surprise.
                         And poor Aldones' no better off than me.

The man knows me as I know him, each hair
And pinch of skin, each wrinkle, wart, and wen!
Glutted with this familiarity,
We'll die slow-stiffing in our tomb-for-two,   60
Measuring each other's hair and fingernails
in hopes of some advantage e'en in death.
Why should he send a spy? He planted three
Of them in this my womb: my bickering,
Dull brood of children . . . Naotalba, how
I wish that I could tell my husband aught
That he does not already know. He'd die
Of simple joy, and then would Alar sink
Into its lake and we, erelong, in ours!

NAOTALBA: You prize more highly novelty than I,   70
My Queen. Methinks 'it is a weakness of
Some sort or other ... But as for myself,
This creature in the Pallid Mask may be
No spy at all; I did not say for sure,
But only that 'at best' he were a spy.

CASSILDA: Well, then, sir priest, let's hear it all. At worst

NAOTALBA: The Phantom of Truth, at very worst, madame,
This thing may be, for only ghosts would go
About our tired streets in robes of white.

CASSILDA (*slowly*):   And is the moment come at last? I see.   80
Then I was wise, and wiselier than wise,
To abort the Dynasty: and that is strange.
I am not often wise, you see. Ah, well,
It well may prove perhaps that any end
At all is a good end ... if end it is.
But Naotalba ... Naotalba.

NAOTALBA: Speak.

CASSILDA: I have not found the Yellow Sign, you see.

ROBERT M. PRICE has edited *Crypt of Cthulhu* for a dozen years. His essays on Lovecraft have appeared in *Lovecraft Studies, The Lovecrafter, Cerebretron, Dagon, Etude Lovecraftienne, Mater Tenebrare,* and in *An Epicure in the Terrible* and *Twentieth Century Literary Criticism.* His horror fiction has appeared in *Nyctalops, Eldritch Tales, Etchings & Odysseys, Grue, Footsteps, Deathrealm, Weirdbook, Fantasy Book, Vollmond,* and elsewhere. He has edited *Tales of the Lovecraft Mythos* for Fedogan and Bremer, as well as *The Horror of It all* and *Black Forbidden Things* for Starmont House. His books include *H.P. Lovecraft and the Cthulhu Mythos* (Borgo Press) and *Lin Carter: A Look Behind His Imaginary Worlds* (Starmont). By day he is a theologian, New Testament scholar, editor of *The Journal of Higher Criticism,* director of The Religious Transition Project, and pastor of First Baptist Church of Montclair.